Shadow Hills

Shadow Hills

ANASTASIA HOPCUS

EGMONT
USA

NEW YORK

EGMONT

We bring stories to life

First published by Egmont USA, 2010
443 Park Avenue South, Suite 806
New York, NY 10016

1 3 5 7 9 8 6 4 2

www.egmontusa.com
www.anastasiahopcus.com

Library of Congress Cataloging-in-Publication Data
Hopcus, Anastasia.
Shadow Hills / Anastasia Hopcus.
p. cm.
Summary: Enrolling in the New England boarding school after her
sister's mysterious death, sixteen-year-old Phe Archer uncovers a secret
that could answer all her questions, but could also cost her her life.
ISBN 978-1-60684-083-2 (hardcover)
[1. Supernatural—Fiction. 2. Boarding schools—Fiction.
3. Schools—Fiction. 4. Massachusetts—Fiction.] I. Title.
PZ7.H7716Sh 2010
[Fic]—dc22
2009041168

Book design by Room39b

Printed in the United States of America

CPSIA tracking label information:
Random House Production • 1745 Broadway • New York, NY 10019

To my mother, who taught me the power of stories.

Over my lifetime, you have read hundreds of books to me,
watched thousands of hours of TV shows with me,
and you've attempted to answer the millions of questions
I've asked you. Even though you say you don't know everything,
I will always believe you do.

You are my Giles, my Lorelai, and my Keith Mars all rolled into one.
Without your unwavering support, this book wouldn't exist.

I love you with all my heart, and I can never thank you enough.

Shadow Hills

Chapter One

I had thought nothing could be worse than what they had already done to me, but I was wrong. The silent echo of nothingness filling the windowless chamber was infinitely worse. Not knowing how much time had passed, whether it was day or night. Not knowing when he would come for me.

As I sat, back pressed against the cold rock wall, I wrapped my arms around my knees, trying to conserve any warmth I still had left in my body. I was staring blankly at my bare, muddied feet when a shaft of light fell across the dirt floor. To the left of me was a small hole at the bottom of the wall. The gray stone was crumbling there, breaking into tiny pieces as fine as dust. It was disintegrating before my eyes. The hole was the size of a small fireplace now. Quickly I shimmied through it, the jagged pieces of rock ripping into my uniform like a serrated knife. And then I was free. Outside in the sunlight, staring at a gravestone. Persephone Archer.

"It isn't you," a voice said behind me, deep and melodic.

I turned and saw him. Raven black hair and eyes that seemed to shift colors—gray, blue, and pale green.

I looked at the headstone, then down at my dirty and torn clothes.

"But it is me," I whispered. He reached out, his strong hand cupping my chin.

"It doesn't have to be." His intense eyes bored into mine. "Find the branches. They will show you how your piece fits."

My gaze wandered away from him. The gravestone was changing, the letters shifting. I watched as the name was spelled out before me: Rebekah Sampson.

"You know who it is. You just have to wake up." He put his hand on my shoulder. "Phe, wake up."

"Phe, we're here." Someone was shaking me gently.

I'd been having that strange dream again. The cell, the cemetery, the gravestone—those had all been the same. Eerie, but at least they were familiar. The guy, however . . . the guy was new.

I blinked slowly, taking in my surroundings. I was reclining in a maroon vinyl seat—definitely not belonging to my dad's showy Lexus. Rubbing my eyes, I pulled myself back into reality. The towering maple trees outside the car window and the stately wrought-iron gate we drove through were beautiful but foreign.

Fresh memories bore down on me like a freight train—saying good-bye to Ariel, the awkward hug from my aunt when she met me at the baggage terminal in Boston. I was in Aunt Lisa's old Volvo in front of Devenish Preparatory School. *My new home.*

The thought twisted my insides. It had been my idea to come

here, but now that I was actually sitting in front of the building, I felt almost sick. My sister mentions a school in her diary and I decide it's my destiny to go there? The only thing I was destined for now was starting my junior year at a new school where I didn't know anyone. I already missed the palm trees, the smog, the kids selling star maps on street corners. I missed my best friend Ariel.

But my life in L.A. had become so stifling, like I was jammed in somewhere I didn't fit. I was constantly pretending—pretending I was the same person, but I wasn't. I didn't know who I was now. At least *here* no one else would know who I was either. They wouldn't know who I had been.

But I wasn't going to let myself get all emotional. The two-hour drive from Boston to Shadow Hills had been uncomfortable enough as it was. I hardly knew my aunt, which my mom blamed on her sister's dislike of L.A., but at least Lisa had come to visit; my family never went to Boston. I thanked Aunt Lisa for the ride and grabbed my backpack, grateful she'd agreed to drop me off instead of coming inside.

As I closed the car door behind me, a cool wind blew across my thighs, kicking up the hem of my skirt. I pulled my lightweight blazer tight and hurried up the gray path. If it was this cold at the beginning of September, my prospects for the rest of the year were bleak.

I looked out across the campus I was going to have to navigate alone. Most of the buildings were redbrick, with turrets and steep roofs, but there was also a simple white chapel and several newer additions.

The main building of Devenish Preparatory was a daunting structure. It was redbrick like the others, but with the double-door entrance and expansive front steps, it was statelier. And its massive clock tower presided over the campus with an imposing air.

Still, I wasn't going to be intimidated. Smoothing down the front of my skirt, I took a steadying breath and squared my shoulders. The heavy wooden doors had large wrought-iron hinges bolted onto them, like doors to an old English church. I grasped one of the handles and pulled.

As I stepped into the empty foyer of the main office, I surveyed the vaulted ceilings, marble floors, and curving grand staircase. There was a brass sign on the wall in front of me with the word ADMISSIONS and an arrow pointing to the left. I walked into the office expecting to see some ancient, possibly with a mole on her face, but I was instead greeted by the sight of a guy about my age. He was sitting in a desk chair behind the counter, scribbling on a sheet of paper and looking bored. *He is definitely not a decrepit old lady.* Even from my limited view of the side of his face, I could tell he was attractive, with dirty-blond hair and a strong jaw.

"Hi. Um, I think I'm supposed to check in." I sounded like I was getting a hotel room. "Or register, I guess," I finished awkwardly.

The boy looked up, pushing his shaggy hair out of his eyes, then broke into a big smile. There was a small chip in his left front tooth. "L.A.?"

"Huh?" My eloquence today was astounding.

"You." His clear aqua-blue eyes sparkled as he smiled again, though this time it seemed to be more like a smirk. "You're from L.A., right?"

"Is it that obvious?" I was wearing the regulation black pencil skirt and blazer with the Devenish crest embroidered on it. *How could he tell I was from L.A.?*

"Only someone from California would be shivering in sixty-eight-degree weather." He laughed. "Graham." He pointed at himself with the pen he was holding. "I'm from San Francisco. Trust me, you get used to the weather after a while. Also, about the uniform—we only have to wear them when class is in session."

"Oh." I looked down at my flat, boring Mary Janes. Old Los Angeles me wouldn't be caught dead in them.

"Don't worry about it." Graham leaned into me. "I won't rat you out." He sat back down in his chair and spun around to the file cabinet behind him. "Let me grab your file, and we can get you on your way to being a full-fledged Devenish student. It's Persephone Archer, right?"

"What are you, psychic?" I raised an eyebrow, regaining my cool.

"The head of admissions told me you were coming in today. Persephone isn't an easy name to forget." Graham was scribbling something down in the folder he'd pulled for me. I peered over the counter, trying to see what he was writing.

"I actually go by 'Phe.' I don't know if you want to put that in my file or whatever."

"Fee?" Graham wrote it down at the top of the page, misspelling it.

"Yeah, but it's spelled P-h-e," I corrected him.

"Wow, your name gets stranger by the minute. Why Phe?"

"My older sister was only two when I was born, and she couldn't say Persephone, so she called me Phe—it just kind of caught on. As for the 'P-h,' it's some weird thing my mom has. She thinks it's more eloquent than an 'F.'" I shrugged, embarrassed. "I don't know. She's crazy."

"Aren't all parents?" Graham's conspiratorial tone made me feel better.

"Okay." He tapped the papers against the desk, evening them out, before placing them back in the folder with a thin handbook. "So, this is what the administration likes to call the 'Welcome Packet.' It's got your forms to fill out, maps of the school grounds, schedules for orientation and your courses, and the *Devenish Preparatory Rules of Conduct Guide*. We're very welcoming at Devenish," Graham added sardonically. "Come on. I'll show you where your dorm is. You can fill out your paperwork later and bring it back whenever."

He stood and picked up a large ring of keys from his desk, then came around the counter and led the way out of the building. Graham locked the front door behind us.

I raised an eyebrow and nodded toward the key ring. It was so large that it looked like a prop the shifty janitor would carry in a horror movie. "Do you have the key to every door on campus?"

"Just about. Even seniors don't have the kind of access I do." Graham went down the stairs, taking them two at a time. "You should be glad you're coming here as a junior. When I started, I had to live in the freshmen dorms, where the rooms are doubles and they have these weekly meetings to discuss interacting with room-mates and 'house conduct.'" He made air quotes with his fingers.

"Too bad I missed out on that, and now I have the burden of living in a single." I shook my head.

"I actually liked having a roommate. I stuck with a double the next year and I'm gonna be in one this year, too. I want the true boarding-school experience."

"I thought that was something people tried to avoid." I raised an eyebrow.

"I always wanted a brother, and with a roommate it's like having one. Well, a brother who gets changed out every year." Graham smiled.

"So, where's your luggage?" he asked as we walked along the weathered slate path.

"All I have right now is this." I shrugged to indicate the back-pack I had slung over my shoulder. "My parents are shipping my stuff from L.A.; it should get here Monday. It was kind of a last-minute decision, my coming here."

"What are you in for?" Graham's blue eyes had a mischievous glimmer to them.

"Being a nuisance to my family," I replied lightly. "What about you?"

"Same. Plus, I think my dad was afraid I'd end up gay if I continued living with my mom and her girlfriend in San Fran." It was obvious from his tone that Graham didn't hold his father in the highest esteem.

"Girlfriend . . . Sounds like a very twenty-first-century family you've got there."

"Oh, very." Graham nodded solemnly. "What about you? Divorced parents? Homosexual scandals?"

"No. None," I said.

"Come on. There must be *some* dark shameful secret you'd like to air out to a total stranger."

I knew Graham was joking, but I tensed up anyway, gripping my backpack straps. Obviously the change in my demeanor had not gone unrecognized; the cocky smile fell from Graham's face.

"Never mind." He shook his head. "You know, I was going for irrepressible—sometimes it comes off more like asshole-ish. I should work on that."

"One to ten on the asshole scale?" I looked at Graham, sizing him up. "I'd say you're about a two."

"Thanks. Actually . . . wait. Is ten the biggest asshole or is one?"

I smiled at him knowingly.

"Okay." He nodded. "I see how it's gonna be."

We came to a stop in front of a brick building with white stone moldings around the windows. It looked even older than the main office, and some of the gray roof shingles had a slight greenish cast.

"Well, here we are. Kresky Hall." Graham opened the door for me.

To the right of the entrance was a lobby area that I guessed was the floor's common room. There was a plaid couch in front of a flat-screen TV, and along the wall was a counter with a refrigerator at one end. A vending machine was shoved in the back corner.

Graham saw me eyeing the selection of sodas, chips, and what I assumed were *very* stale sandwiches. He said, "It's not exactly a four-star restaurant, but it's better than nothing when you get hungry and the cafeteria is closed."

I nodded my tentative agreement. I would have to be really hungry to risk getting food poisoning from an old tuna-salad sandwich.

"The first room on the first floor of every residence is always the house parent's. The Kresky Hall house mistress is Angela Moore, but I saw her in the Admin Building earlier, so she's probably not here." Graham knocked twice on her door, got no response, then looked at a scrap of paper in his hand.

"Room one-sixteen. You're on the left at the end of the hall."

As we walked, he fiddled with his keys, pulling one of them off the ring. He handed it to me when we reached my door.

"So here you are. Safe and sound." Graham took a few steps back toward the entrance, then stopped and turned to me. "Hey, it's kind of quiet before everyone arrives. Do you want to do something tonight?"

It was the final Saturday of the summer. Usually I'd be going to a huge party to celebrate our last two nights of freedom before school began. But that wasn't how my life was anymore.

"We could go into town when I get off work," he went on. "I can show you around Shadow Hills—I mean, it's no L.A., but at least we could grab some non-dorm food."

"That sounds good." I felt a flutter in my stomach. It was a nice, kind of nervous feeling, exciting and somehow reassuring.

"Cool. I'm usually done around six. If you want, I can text you when I'm finishing up." We exchanged numbers, and with a little half wave Graham headed back down the hall and was gone.

I put my key in the lock and turned. The door swung open to reveal my new room. There was a bedside table against the left wall, with a twin bed next to it. A desk was on the right wall, bare except for a small metal lamp. I closed the door behind me and discovered it had been hiding a closet and narrow chest of drawers.

The gleaming white walls were almost blinding. I tried to ignore the pungent chemical odor of fresh paint. I set my backpack down on the bed and unzipped it, pulling out a green journal and a pen. I flipped past my sister's early entries to where I'd recorded my dreams. I added another hatch mark to the top of the cell/graveyard page.

New details: names on the gravestones and a strange guy. Plus, this one came at 3:33 p.m. as opposed to the usual 3:33 a.m. I hastily scribbled my notes, feeling stupid for assigning such significance to a dream. So Athena had been having the dreams, too—it didn't mean anything.

But even as I thought that, I knew it wasn't true. The time itself seemed noteworthy. Three, after all, was a mystical number: the Holy Trinity, the three jewels of Buddhism, the pyramids.

I looked at the hatch marks again. I'd had the graveyard dream for the ninth time—three times three. I could just be grasping at straws, trying to make sense of something that didn't mean anything.

Well, I knew one thing for sure, the dreams weren't going to be stopped by a change of scenery. In fact, this dream seemed more vivid than the others. I could almost hear my old shrink's "I told you so" tone of voice. You'd think for the amount of money my parents paid him, he could at least have come up with some original phrasing for his hackneyed advice. "You can't run away from your problems" had been his exact words when I brought in the brochure for Devenish Prep. The brochure that had arrived for Athena six months too late.

The sharp grief hit me like it always did when I allowed myself to think about my sister. Right after it happened, the pain had been unbearable. The enduring loneliness almost devoured me. Even after thirteen months it still felt like I had been hit in the chest with a sandbag when I walked by Athena's room. Though it looked the same, the room *felt* so different . . . hollow and torn open. It was no longer my sister's sanctuary; it had become a cavernous wound.

I opened the journal to a heavily creased page; I'd book-marked it with an envelope that had the Devenish Prep crest embossed on it. When I saw that envelope addressed to Athena after she was already gone—after the police had shown up, after I picked out a dress for her funeral, after I said good-bye at her grave—I thought I'd have a breakdown right there in front of my family's mailbox. And then I'd found her diary. . . . When I read about her dreams, so like my own, it shook me to the core.

She wrote of a recurring dream about a place she'd never been before. A place with old redbrick buildings. A place that she finally identified as a boarding school in Shadow Hills. When I had read that, everything became crystal clear to me. I wanted to feel that clarity again. I scanned to the end of the entry, to the last words my sister had written in her diary:

The nightmares are so vivid now I'm afraid to sleep. I feel my energy dragging constantly. I'm a walking zombie. I have to find a way to go to Devenish Prep; maybe there I'll be able to figure this out.

I ran my thumb over the fading navy-blue ink. There was something at Devenish. I could feel it in my bones. I didn't know what it was yet, but I was going to find out. I owed that to Athena.

It hadn't been that hard to convince my parents to send me to Devenish—in fact, they were probably happier without the reminder. My dark blond hair and green eyes, my slight build and heart-shaped face—the features I'd always been so happy to share with my amazing older sister—were now tarnished. I couldn't look into a mirror without a part of me feeling like Athena was there staring back. It was comforting, but it was also awful, like salt in a wound.

Hot tears needled at the corners of my eyes, but I pushed them down. There was no sense in crying in my dorm room. I had gotten here a day earlier than most of the students so I could "settle into a structured routine." My shrink had told my parents it would be best for me, and I was happy to have a little time to check the place out before everyone else started arriving.

But before I could go poking around, I had to change. I felt seriously conspicuous in my uniform. As I unzipped my skirt, I noticed a bright red mark just below my left hip. Drawing down my waistband, I looked to see if I had a bite or something, but there was nothing on my skin except for a small curved line that resembled a crescent moon. I rubbed my finger across the mark, wondering how I'd gotten it. Something about it gave me a weird feeling in the pit of my stomach.

Once I'd slipped on some worn-in jeans, a shrunken Clash T-shirt, and my old checkerboard Vans, I felt much better.

I was about to be on my way when I remembered that I was supposed to hang out with Graham later. I grabbed my makeup case out of my bag and went to look for the bathroom so I could freshen up.

It was easy to locate the open doorway in the center of the hall.

After I put my toothbrush back in my toiletries bag, I glanced at myself in the mirror. Apparently my hair was not going to take well to the Massachusetts humidity. It had gone from straight and sleek to wavy with uncontrollable body. I pulled it into a high ponytail, then headed back to the dorm room to get my purse and lock up.

I filled my lungs with the pristine, smog-free air as I took in the campus. The sprawling grounds were shockingly green, with rolling hills and a blue-tinged ridge of mountains in the distance. For every group of four or five buildings, there was a large open quad with flagstone paths crossing in a diamond pattern. My school in L.A. had been much smaller; this place looked more like a college than a high school. The grass was freshly cut, and without city smells getting in the way, I could actually pick up on its sharp, citrusy aroma.

There was a crescent of woods at the edge of campus, and impossibly huge trees dotted the grounds. They looked perfect for relaxing under, their thick crawling roots forming natural steps to sit on. Green ivy clung to the sides of almost all the buildings, reminding me of seaweed wrapped around my ankles in the ocean.

It really was a pretty place, with the "historical university" look, but I didn't know if I would ever get used to it. I preferred the garish pink apartment buildings of West Hollywood, the Melrose area bungalows, the birds-of-paradise at my old house in Los Feliz.

As I walked the rocky gray paths that wound in and around the school, I noticed a distinctive building up on a hill. It looked to be about a mile away. I started toward it, drawn by the imposing white stone walls and grand stature. When I got nearer, I could see the stone was marred by several decades' worth of green water-damage stains. A strange familiarity washed over me when I came to a stop in front of the building. It was tall and thick—a fortress. The parking lot next to it seemed strange and out of place, the modern ambulances and new cars in stark contrast to the old-fashioned architecture.

I wasn't surprised to see a historical plaque near the front entrance; the place looked like it was hundreds of years old.

I quickly scanned the metal script: SHADOW HILLS MEMORIAL HOSPITAL . . . BEST DIAGNOSTIC UNIT IN THE U.S. . . . ORIGINALLY AN ALMSHOUSE IN THE 1700s . . .

I noticed a discreet sign that had been placed next to the plaque. YOU ARE INVITED TO LEARN MORE ABOUT SHADOW HILLS HOSPITAL. PLEASE VISIT OUR HISTORY MUSEUM LOCATED TO THE LEFT OF THE FRONT LOBBY.

The flash of a dark shape caught my peripheral vision. My nerves clattered like cans dragged across asphalt, and I turned to see the shadow streak across the grounds and disappear behind the hospital. Without thinking, I followed it around the corner.

The building seemed to go on forever, becoming less weathered and more contemporary as I walked. After a few minutes, I reached a large courtyard. There were several dirt paths winding through patches of overgrown gardens and continuing back into a dense stand of tall trees. Instinctively, I followed the central trail leading into the woods.

There were several patients in hospital gowns milling around and talking to doctors dressed in scrubs. It made me feel a little safer just knowing there were people nearby. I could call out if I got into trouble, and as long as I stuck to the main path, I probably wouldn't get lost. I had always prided myself on having an excellent sense of direction.

Green ferns carpeted the earth beneath my feet, and the air felt cool and wet. Soon I came upon a dilapidated iron fence. The gate lay on the ground, and judging by the snaking vines that entwined it, it had fallen from its rusty hinges long ago.

My heart pounded with a strange mix of dread and excitement. *Once you cross that threshold, there's no turning back.* I didn't know where the thought had come from, but there was no way I could leave now. I wouldn't allow myself to be a coward. Cautiously, I stepped through the entrance.

The trees opened up into a circular plot of exposed land. My hands were suddenly cold as ice. Directly in front of me were the ghostly ruins of an ancient graveyard.

My breath caught in my throat, and my vision swam. This place wasn't *like* the graveyard in my dream: it *was* the graveyard in my dream.

It was filled with both upright and flat gravestones—the standing ones broken and crumbling; the ledger stones flush with the ground, overgrown by weeds and tendrils of ivy. The vertical slabs tilted toward and away from one another at different angles, the result of one side or the other sinking deeper into the earth over time. It gave the impression of a foul set of teeth: green and rotting, crooked and overcrowded, jabbing out in all directions with gaps where the ledger stones were.

I edged closer to the first row of tightly packed graves. It looked so familiar that it sent a tremor through my body. The stones that were flush with the ground were small and plain, with just a name and death year. The majority of the upright gravestones were similarly unadorned, though a few had an eerie skull with wings at the top. The markers were obviously very old—some so weathered that the engravings had been completely rubbed away, while others were obscured by the moss clinging to them.

I squatted down and ran my hand over one of the slabs that still had discernible carvings on it: ANNABELLE MARTIN, 1690–1736.

I stood back up and wound my way through the maze of stones, inspecting all the ones bearing inscriptions. GEORGE COOPER, 1704–1736. ESTHER GARRETT, 1712–1736. JOHN CATCHPOOL, 1693–1736. My hands tingled as the blood flowed through them, warm and urgent. HERBERT HICKS, 1715–1736. ELIZABETH CHURCH, 1719–1736.

A sick feeling slithered through my insides when I saw the next headstone. It held two names and sets of dates: RUTH MOORE, 1707–1736, and RACHEL MOORE, 1709–1736.

They were buried in the same plot. I checked the next row and the next; it seemed the more I looked, the more there were. Dozens of headstones with as many as three or four names on them. *Almost like the mass graves of the bubonic plague.*

Each of these people had died the same year. I surveyed the vast burial ground. *There must be at least three hundred graves.* I walked up and down the rows more slowly, looking for a death date after 1736. There were a handful from before then, but I couldn't find even one from 1737 or later. *Something had happened here—a battle or a plague.* I'd never been greatly interested in history, but I was more than a little curious about what had killed hundreds of people in the span of one year. A thought sparked in my mind. *This is exactly the kind of thing they would have information about in that hospital museum.*

"Hey. Are you okay back there?" My heart almost stopped at the sound of the dark velvety voice. *It couldn't possibly . . .*

I turned around, moving in slow motion while my thoughts raced so quickly I couldn't make sense of them.

My mouth almost dropped open when I laid eyes on him. He was about my age, well over six feet tall, and absolutely gorgeous. His strong features had a certain sweetness to them, and his unruly black hair curled into his eyes in an endearing way. And those eyes. They were light and sparkling—green and blue and gray all at once—but that wasn't why I was so stunned.

The real reason I couldn't tear my gaze away, the thing that turned my muscles to ice even as my skin burned, was the one and only thought running through my mind: *That's him. That is the guy from my dream.*

Chapter Two

I didn't feel the strap of my purse slip from my grip, but as the contents of it spilled onto the ground, I heard my cell phone skitter across one of the flat headstones.

The guy who had been staring at me in stunned silence, looking almost as surprised as I felt, immediately snapped to attention and started gathering up my things.

"Thanks," I mumbled as I knelt next to him, scooping up my stuff.

"Sorry if I startled you." His high cheekbones were stained pink. "I was standing in the courtyard, and I saw you disappear into the trees. When you didn't come back after a few minutes, I thought you might be lost."

"Not lost, just checking things out." I tried to smile at him, but my expression felt stuck. His eyes were unfathomable, pale yet vividly intense. His strong eyebrows and thick black lashes drew even more attention to the strange lightness of his eyes. I was so entranced watching them that it took me a few seconds to register that he was speaking again.

". . . and I live in town. Shadow Hills, I mean. Are you a new student at Devenish?"

"Yeah." I grabbed a magazine that was lying a few feet away and stuffed it in my bag. I was very aware of how close we were, and my body practically vibrated with an inexplicable feeling of anticipation.

"I'm Zach, by the way."

"I'm Persephone, but I go by Phe." I busied myself by returning my makeup to its travel case. Thankfully I didn't have my period right now. I was embarrassed enough as it was, but having a guy as hot as Zach handing me back my tampons would've been absolutely mortifying.

"Do you have a standing lamp in there, too?" He nodded at my purse.

"I'm sorry?" I picked up my sunglasses case, a small can of pepper spray, and a pack of tissues that had wound up behind me.

I wasn't sure why I was so immediately drawn to this guy. Of course, on the surface it made sense. He was so striking, even more attractive than Graham, but it was something else. I avoided his eyes, afraid if I looked in them again I would do something terrible and embarrassing. Like grab his face and kiss him.

"You know . . . Mary Poppins? When she's pulling all that stuff out of her bag? Those were some high-tech special effects for back then." Zach grinned at me, and a warm glow spread through my body.

"I faintly remember that. It's been a while." I grasped one end of the iPod he was holding out to me, and the screen lit up.

I frowned as the charging battery symbol came on. It was strange enough that my iPod was even working since it had died in the middle of my flight to Boston, but it was impossible for it to be charging without being plugged in. Zach followed my gaze down to our hands, then let go of the device like it had scalded him. A split second later the screen went black again.

"Zach!" A girl's voice filtered back through the trees. "What are you doing?"

"I'll be there in a second!" he called over his shoulder before turning back to me. "That's my sister; I gotta go."

"Hurry up! I've got five million errands to run before dinner, and we're already late for testing!"

"Okay, I'm coming!" Zach stood up, brushing dirt off his jeans. "It was nice meeting you, Phe."

"Yeah. You too." I watched him make his way through the trees and disappear from sight.

I looked at the iPod in my hand—it couldn't have come on. It was dead. *It must have caught the sun for a second and reflected the light, making the screen appear to glow.* Just to make sure, though, I flipped the hold switch to off and pushed the power button. The iPod came on, battery fully charged. My stomach dropped out like I was on the downswing of a roller-coaster.

If I was looking to find something weird here, I'd certainly succeeded.

I started back toward the school, my steps hurried. Something teased at my spine, a sense that I was being watched or followed. It was the same cold prickling I'd had when I first saw the graveyard.

Despite my sincere efforts not to, I couldn't help but

casually glance over my shoulder a few times. Well, maybe not a few. More like five. Or ten. I kept expecting to see Zach again. It was too surreal—this specter appearing before me, flesh and bone—I had no idea what it meant.

A beep came from my purse and I fished through my jumbled bag until I found my cell phone. I had one text message: *Ready to go. Meet you in the main parking lot.*

Graham. I had almost forgotten about my dinner plans.

When I reached the gravel parking lot, Graham was unlocking the door of a rusted-out 1970s-era Buick.

"Is this your car?" I raised an eyebrow at him.

"No. I thought I'd steal one and drive it into town. Think anyone will notice?" Graham reached across to unlock the passenger's-side door, then pushed it open. "You wouldn't know how to hotwire by any chance?"

"Very funny." I slid onto the torn vinyl seat.

The Buick had a musty scent that I found comforting, like an old movie theater or a library. After a few unsuccessful tries, Graham got the car started. The radio appeared to have been ripped out, not that you would have been able to hear it very well with the racket the engine made.

"Will you grab me my iPod? It's in the glove compartment." Graham pointed, as if I didn't know where a glove compartment was located.

I handed over the iPod. It was encased in a portable docking system with small attached speakers. Graham fiddled with it before pulling out of the parking space. I could faintly make out the song over the jet-plane-like rumbling of the car; thankfully, it wasn't some awful frat boy crap, but "Save It for Later."

"You like the English Beat?"

"Yeah. I'm guessing you do as well?" Graham asked, turning out of the parking lot.

"I'm into some of the early ska revival," I said.

"Me, too. Maybe it's a California thing."

"So where are we going to eat?" I asked after a moment.

"I was thinking about something very Shadow Hills, Massachusetts. To get you into the whole vibe of the town. Maybe McDonald's?" He cut his eyes at me.

"I'm not really much of a junk-food person."

"I was only kidding about the McDonald's. I figured we'd go to this market and deli . . . wait, you don't like junk food?" A doubtful frown was etched into Graham's brow.

"Took you a while to register that comment." I laughed.

"Well, you can imagine why. That is quite possibly the weirdest thing I have ever heard anyone say." He shook his head. "How can someone not like junk food? It's *scientifically engineered* to be addictive."

"What can I say? I guess I'm just strange." I lifted one shoulder in a half shrug. "So what weird quirks do you have?"

"Like what do you mean?"

"How'd you get the chipped tooth?"

"Surfing under the Golden Gate Bridge." He grinned proudly. "A tugboat went by, causing this huge wave that knocked me off my board. Then while I was struggling to get back on, a second shock wave sent my board straight into my face and—*voilà*. Chipped tooth." He paused. "Man, I really miss it sometimes."

"Chipping your teeth?"

"Surfing, Lombard Street . . . my mom." The longing was evident in Graham's tone.

"You know, I heard a rumor that those crazy flying contraptions can go to San Francisco," I teased.

"I have to work at the school pretty much year-round. My dad wants me to know this isn't a free ride. Which is cool. I have the Devenish office job to thank for my trusty car." Graham patted the cracked plastic dashboard as he pulled into a parking space.

I got out and, with a loud creak of defiance from the rusty hinges, closed the car door. The shops in front of us were a mix of small brick buildings and old-fashioned saltbox wood houses, but they were so close together that they looked almost like a strip mall. The buildings formed a square around a quaint town park, complete with benches, replicas of gas-style streetlamps, and a small pond. I turned back to Graham and found him holding a door open for me with an exaggeratedly patient expression on his face. The wooden sign above the door read MANSFIELD'S FAMILY MARKET AND DELI.

"Thanks." I walked inside, blinking under the fluorescent lights. As the door swooshed closed behind us, it hit a little bell that announced our arrival.

"This way." Graham took the lead, heading to the back of the small grocery store, where a butcher's counter had been transformed into a cafeteria-style food line. Graham ordered a Reuben sandwich and I got a salad. I'd barely started eating when the bell above the front door rang again.

Curious, I looked up to see who had come in and immediately dropped my fork. It was Zach, the guy I had met in the graveyard—apparently I lost my ability to grip objects whenever he appeared—but he wasn't alone. Standing by his side was a beautiful girl who looked like she was in college, or possibly a very sophisticated senior. She was statuesque and at least five eleven. I would have been painfully jealous of her if I hadn't been positive she was Zach's sister. Her bone structure and thick black hair were just like his, though she had a sharp, cold quality that was very different from his demeanor.

Zach's eyes were riveted on me, and the girl frowned as she followed his gaze over to the table where Graham and I were sitting. Spotting us, her expression turned to one of interest. As she strode toward the table with Zach behind her, I struggled to swallow a hunk of food that I had forgotten to chew.

"Hello, Graham."

Graham acknowledged the girl with a perfunctory nod.

"Who *is* your little friend here? Because anyone can see she's not Lauren." The girl curled a strand of long hair around her tapered fingers, her expression snide. "I guess it's easier to cheat when your girlfriend's off at college in Boston."

So Graham had a girlfriend? At least that solved my problem of which guy I was more into—not that Zach wasn't already winning that competition.

Graham laughed. "Sorry to cut short your stint as the morality police, but I'm not cheating on Lauren. This is Persephone Archer. She's a new student from L.A."

"Sorry, my mistake," the girl apologized, though she didn't seem a bit remorseful. "I'm Corinne, and this is my baby brother, Zach." She unwound the hair from her finger and stuck out her hand to shake mine. As I grasped it, a frozen electric current ran up my arm. Instantly, I was dizzy, my head all woozy like I stood up too fast. Quickly, I pulled my hand away. Corinne smiled; either she hadn't noticed my strange reaction to her touch, or she found it amusing.

"Los Angeles." She looked me up and down appraisingly. "Well, I guess that explains your name." Corinne's tone was light, but her eyes cut into me as if she were trying to see my insides. "So what brings you to our humble little town, Persy?" The nickname dripped with derision.

"Actually, my friends call me Phe. But you can call me Persephone." I clipped my words carefully. I had known this same girl in L.A.; actually, I'd known dozens of them. The only way to deal with them was to establish straight off that you were not someone to be messed with. "I'm here to eat dinner. Evidently this is about as close as your town comes to a gourmet restaurant," I said sweetly. "It's a very cute town, though. Quaint. Austere."

I smiled, watching the slow crack materialize in Corinne's glacial veneer.

"Well, unfortunately, we have to be going now. Zach?" She shot a stern look at her brother.

"I'll be back there in a minute," he answered gruffly before turning to me. "So I'll see you at school on Monday?"

"Yeah." In less than two days I would see him again. School had never been so exciting.

"Cool." Zach looked like he wanted to say something more, but after hesitating for a second, he turned and took off toward the grocery area of the store.

"I guess you've already met some of the townies." Graham took another bite of his sandwich. "The students from Shadow Hills are a bit . . . strange," he said around a mouthful of Reuben.

"Yeah, well, it's not like people from L.A. are known for being exceedingly conventional." I picked up my fork again, and a food-induced silence fell over the table for a few minutes.

"So you've got a girlfriend in Boston?" I asked after I had finished my salad.

"Yeah, but things are weird with us right now. Ever since she started at MIT"—Graham rubbed his temples—"I never get to see her. She doesn't visit, and when I go to Boston, she's so busy with school that I can barely get a minute of her time."

"I hear the long-distance thing is hard."

"You done?" Graham nodded at my empty plate. This was obviously a sore subject with him.

"Yeah. I'm gonna hit the restroom, and then we can take off."

"Bathrooms are back in the grocery area." Graham indicated where I should go, then put his plate on top of mine and took them over to the bus tub.

I walked along the aisles, glancing down them. As I approached the next row, I could hear faint music even though the store hadn't been playing any over the sound system. In the middle of the office supplies aisle was Zach, standing with his back to me, listening to his iPod. A familiar-sounding song came from the headphones that lay on either side of his neck, instead of in his ears. *Strange.* I stepped a little closer, trying to identify it. The violin portion was very distinctive, and it took me only a few seconds to realize the song was "Wonderlust King" by Gogol Bordello.

As I observed Zach, I noticed that several packages on the shelves were tilting out toward him, as if they were being pulled by some invisible force. On the shelf below, the spiral bound notebooks stuck an inch off the shelf farther than the notebooks beside them. *Well, that's definitely not normal.* Only the metal objects, like compasses and packages of silver tacks, seemed affected by the weird antigravity.

Zach must have felt me watching him because when he turned his head and saw me, he didn't seem all that surprised.

"Hey again." He nodded.

"I love that album."

"Huh?"

"*Super Taranta.*" I raised my eyebrows. "The album you're listening to."

"Wow. Good hearing." He frowned. "Usually I'm the only one who can hear it like this." He gestured at the earbuds hanging around his neck.

"Did they go to Boston on their last tour?" I questioned.

"I saw them a few months ago. They put on an amazing live show." My voice was getting higher and louder, like it did when I got excited. I clapped my mouth closed.

"I don't know." Zach scratched the back of his neck. "I've actually never been to a concert."

I stared at him, not sure I'd heard correctly. "You mean you've never seen Gogol Bordello live?"

He shook his head. "I mean, I've never seen *any* band live."

"Seriously?" I had been going to all-ages shows since I was in middle school, and by high school my sister and I were going to every twenty-one and up show we could talk our way into.

"Shadow Hills isn't exactly a music mecca." There was a restlessness evident in Zach's tone, but I was pretty sure it had more to do with being stuck in a small town than it did with our conversation.

"Boston's not that far. Why don't you go there?" I couldn't imagine what it would be like never to have seen a show, never to have felt that surge of adrenaline.

"Haven't had the chance." Zach shifted his weight, leaning to the side, causing all the metal objects in the aisle to pull toward him even more.

Now he was uncomfortable, and it definitely had something to do with me. I'd let my elitist-music-snob attitude rear its ugly head, probably making Zach think that I saw him as some kind of hick. When nothing could have been further from the truth. In fact, I had never been so intrigued by someone I'd just met— and I was certain I'd never seen anyone else have a physical effect on metal.

"Sorry, that was rude. It's really not any of my business."
I wanted to ask him about his seeming magnetism, but I didn't
need to come off as any nosier than I already had.

"I'll write it off as the L.A. influence." Zach flashed me a
smile. "Too much paparazzi exposure."

I laughed, accidentally letting out a snort.

"Well, that wasn't humiliating or anything," I said from
behind my hand.

"No." He was grinning widely at me now. "It was cute."

"Zach. There you are." Corinne swept past me, totally
ignoring my existence. "You haven't gotten your notebooks
yet?" She stared at him in exasperation before reaching for a
three-ring binder. The metal items swung like a pendulum away
from her. *Apparently Zach* isn't *the only one who has a physical
effect on metal.*

"What are you looking at?" she practically barked at me.

I tore my gaze from the things that now hung at an opposite
angle from the way they'd been a moment ago.

"Don't you have somewhere you need to be?"

"I was looking for the bathroom, actually," I told her coolly.

"It's at the end of the next aisle over." Corinne gave me a fake
smile.

"You're so helpful."

"Come on. We're getting out of here," she commanded as I
disappeared around the corner.

"Jesus, Corinne. Do you always have to be so rude?" Zach's
voice floated back to me, and I couldn't help but smile.

When I returned from the bathroom, they were gone.

I glanced around to make sure I was alone, then stood where Zach had been. None of the packages shifted. I held up a hand, my palm facing the notebooks. Everything remained completely immobile.

"What are you doing?" Graham was standing at the end of the aisle, watching me curiously.

"Oh. Nothing." I slapped my hand down by my side. "I thought I might buy a notebook, and I was trying to decide which one to get." I started down the row to where Graham was. "I'm ready when you are."

"But you just said you were getting a notebook." He raised his eyebrow at me.

"I said I was thinking about it," I corrected him. "And I decided not to. So we can go now."

"Whatever you say." Graham shook his head, and we headed outside to the car.

The distant mountains and towering trees loomed over the narrow road, blocking out any light from the moon as we drove.

I could see why the town was named Shadow Hills. The darkness was almost a living thing here.

"So what are you going to do tomorrow?" Graham's voice broke into my reverie.

"I'm not sure. I probably should get to know the campus so I can find my classes without carrying a map around. Maybe that way I won't stand out too much." *And hopefully I can find out about that creepy graveyard.* Going to the hospital museum was the one thing I really wanted to do.

"It would be impossible for you to blend in at Devenish, map or no map."

"Oh, yeah? And why is that, may I ask?" I hated it when someone who barely knew me tried to act like they had me all figured out.

"It's nothing bad." He threw up his hands defensively. "You're just different from most of the girls who go to school here. In a good way."

Graham seemed to sense my skepticism without looking at me.

"The students here are so *serious*." Evidently, this was not a quality that Graham valued. "Their whole lives are about doing well in their classes, getting into a top college—all so they can end up with some high-paying, boring-as-hell desk job." He shrugged. "I don't get it. It's like, you have the rest of your life to be a beleaguered disciple to the Establishment—why start now?"

I was annoyed by Graham's certainty that he had me pegged, but I had to agree.

"That's the way my dad is—constantly at his office. I don't understand why he works so hard for this money that he doesn't even seem to enjoy. . . ." Suddenly I felt very exposed.

"Exactly. Life isn't a series of steps you take to get somewhere. It's everything that happens in between. Or, you know, something like that, but more eloquent and less clichéd." Graham's laugh was easy and natural.

I could definitely see us as friends. And that was what I needed right now.

"Here we are," Graham said as he pulled into the Devenish parking lot. "Want me to walk you to your dorm?"

"Sure." The well-manicured, deserted grounds gave me a strange feeling in the pit of my stomach. It was so different from wandering around L.A. at night; there was no graffiti, no one was passed out on the park benches. Yet somehow this didn't make me feel safer.

As we walked down the sidewalk, I felt the little hairs on the back of my neck raise up and goose bumps travel across my arms. I wanted to turn around and look behind me, but I was afraid if I did Graham would think I was a crazy person.

"I'm helping with registration until one tomorrow." Graham tilted his head toward me. "Would you want to grab lunch when I get off? I could help you with your exploration of the grounds." He playfully poked me with his elbow. "Seriously, what could be more thrilling?"

"Let me think." I tapped a finger to my chin in mock contemplation. "I'm going to have to say . . . almost anything, excluding water torture and mimes."

Graham laughed, reaching in front of me to open the door to the dorm. There was a bright light coming from the first room on the right.

"Looks like Angela is waiting up for you." He knocked on the open door.

"Hey, Ms. Moore." Graham gestured to me. "This is Persephone. The new student from L.A."

"Good. I was beginning to wonder if you had made it in." Ms.

Moore—who didn't look anything like I'd expected a house mistress to look—stood up from her desk, where she had obviously been reading. She was young and fresh faced, her brown hair cut in a slightly layered bob.

"I'm not sure how this works." I fidgeted with the strap of my purse. There had never been anyone checking up on me in Los Angeles. I knew it was going to be very different here.

"That's okay." Ms. Moore smiled. "No one knows how the residency process works when they first get here. It's pretty simple: Sunday through Thursday, you need to be in your dorm by eight, and lights have to be out by ten thirty. Friday and Saturday check-in is at eleven, lights out by eleven thirty."

She picked up the clipboard that was hanging on her wall, just inside the doorway. "You sign your name here, record the time you arrived and your room number. I oversee nightly check-in and grant day or overnight excuses." Ms. Moore shrugged her shoulders. "And that's pretty much it."

She was apparently not aware that this was the longest list of rules I'd ever been given. My parents were never strict, and after Athena, they'd stopped caring altogether.

I took the clipboard she extended to me and wrote down my information before digging around in my purse for my keys. Finally, I found them and headed for my door at the end of the hall, with Graham a few steps behind me.

"Good night, Graham." Ms. Moore gave him a pointed look that stopped him in his tracks. "No boys in the dorm after eight, remember?"

"Right." Graham looked at me questioningly. "I'll see you tomorrow?"

"Yeah." I nodded. He grinned and left the way we had come in.

A noise pulled me out of my half-asleep haze what seemed like only a few minutes later. But a glance at my alarm clock told me it was 3:33 a.m. Had one of my dreams awakened me? I felt like I needed something. A drink? A snack? There was that vending machine in the common room. Tightness crept into my chest as I got out of bed. The tile beneath my feet felt cold, almost wet. I reached down and touched the floor; it was damp. Peering around my door, I stared into the dark hallway. The white tile looked black in the low light. This wasn't, in and of itself, terribly disturbing, but the reflective, rippling appearance of the floor was.

"What the hell?" I muttered. Taking a tentative step out of my room, I discovered the floor in the hall was covered in several inches of liquid. It was coming from underneath the bathroom door. *Had Ms. Moore left the water running?*

Her door was closed, and there was no light escaping from the cracks around it. I took a deep breath. What was I afraid of, an overflowing bathtub? I was trying to be calm, but the closer I got to the bathroom, the higher the water climbed. And the higher the water climbed, the more anxious I felt. The water was now over my ankles. I ignored the jittery panic building inside me and pulled swiftly on the handle. The door swung open, and an avalanche of water hit me hard in the chest. I was floating now, drowning. The water was thick and murky; my eyes stung as I opened them. I was blinking rapidly, trying to bring my blurry vision into focus, when out of the corner of my eye I saw her.

My sister. Lifeless and limp, sinking down to the bottom of the ocean. Her tiny delicate hand was wrapped around a huge ornate gold skeleton key. Its heaviness seemed to be dragging her down faster and faster.

I swam toward her with all my might, straining against the force of the water, but she was sinking too quickly for me to keep up. Her skin had taken on a bluish tinge, and her hair looked like seaweed. I tried to yell, to wake her, but all that came out of my mouth was bubbles.

Chapter Three

"Persephone! Are you okay?"

Ms. Moore was standing in front of me, wide-eyed. We were in the bathroom, but there was no water anywhere, not even a drip from the sink.

"What . . . I . . ." I shook my head, trying to rid it of the cobwebs of my dream.

"You must have been sleepwalking. I heard you scream, and I came running in. At first I thought you were awake because your eyes were open, but you were . . . unresponsive." Ms. Moore looked concerned. "Does this happen to you a lot?"

"No. I mean, I have nightmares sometimes, but I don't think I've ever sleepwalked before." I frowned, disoriented.

"Maybe it's the change in environment. These old buildings can be kind of spooky without many people around."

"Yeah, maybe." I nodded sluggishly. "I should probably get back to bed."

"Are you sure?" Ms. Moore's eyes searched mine. "Is there anyone you want me to call?"

Yes, call my parents. Tell them I'm screaming in the middle of the night. I'm sure they want to keep close tabs on my frenetic behavior.

"No, really. I'm fine." Ms. Moore's expression was still worried. "I just need to go back to sleep; I'm exhausted."

"Okay." She stood in the hall watching me, arms folded over her chest, until I disappeared into my room.

I crawled onto the thin mattress and slipped under the plain white sheets. No wonder I was sleeping worse than before; this tiny twin bed was way too hard to be comfortable, and the blankets were scratchy compared to the worn flannel sheets I had at home. My old home.

I pulled the green notebook out of the drawer on the bedside table. There was no alarm clock on the table, but I knew before I even looked at my cell that it was a little past 3:33 a.m. Quickly, I scribbled down the contents of my dream. It was new, and I wasn't sure if that was good or bad. There had been a few dreams right after Athena drowned that were similar to this one. However, they had never been so vivid, and the gold key was odd.

I really was exhausted. The nightmares always made me tired, but sleepwalking? The new experience had left me completely depleted of energy. My mind was fuzzy, and my bones were heavy as lead.

Maybe Athena was sleepwalking, too.

It might explain why she had been feeling so drained. I tried to find anything in my memory that would point to that. Bruises from bumping into furniture? Food going missing from the kitchen in the middle of the night? But before I could think of anything else, I fell into a deep dreamless sleep.

N N N

The next morning I awoke to a soft gray light streaming in the window behind my bed. The filmy white curtains would have been totally ineffective in my bedroom in California, with the floor-to-ceiling windows and bright Los Angeles sunshine, but here in dusky Shadow Hills, they were more than adequate.

As I washed up in the bathroom—which I found slightly unsettling after my dream—I checked on the strange mark I'd seen on my hip yesterday. Not only was the red half moon still there, but now there was a second one above it. While the first crescent-shaped line had been vertical and facing toward the right, this new one was horizontal and facing down. The dark pink marks were each about an inch long. I tried to ignore the creeping, itchy feeling that slipped across my skin. I had probably dug my nails into my hip during my nightmare. *No big deal.*

When I got back to my room, I noticed the screen on my phone was lit up. I'd missed a call from Ariel. I picked up my cell and hit speed dial.

We talked for a few minutes, but it was stilted and awkward. Once I was actually on the phone with her, all the things I had been planning to say sounded stupid or melodramatic.

I had wanted to tell Ariel that she was my best friend and that I didn't know how I would have made it through the last year without her. I wanted to tell her that I hated the way she had been forced to become my whole support system when my parents threw in the towel. I wanted to tell her that my leaving town had nothing to do with her, that I was different now and trying to stay the same just made me feel more out of place. But I couldn't say any of it. It was as if, by not talking about it, I thought I could pretend nothing had changed. Still, it had changed, and we both knew it. But neither of us wanted to admit it.

And Ariel's own attempts to lighten the mood only made things worse. Her story about the wild party at Josh's dad's house reminded me of Paul and the way everything had fallen apart with us. Paul and Josh were best friends. Paul had broken up with me almost a year ago, right after my fifteenth birthday. That birthday party was the most depressing celebration ever. It had only been three months since my sister's death, and I got totally smashed and lost my virginity to Paul. It was in no way the romantic earth-shattering first time I thought it would be. It was sloppy and uncomfortable, both physically and emotionally. Neither of us could remember it very clearly the next day, and I could tell Paul felt guilty—like he had taken advantage of me, even though I was the one who had initiated it, hoping it would make me feel better. Or not even better, just different. I wanted to feel anything besides loss and regret, but it only made everything worse. It was humiliating to barely be able to recall what was supposed to be such a pivotal experience in my life. And a few days later Paul dumped me. I never got a clear answer as to why, but I could tell he regretted that night almost as much as I did. He was just too much of a guy's guy to say it.

Still, it was hard for me to blame our breakup solely on the sex thing. The first few weeks after my sister's death were a dark, tangled blur, and then I became an emotional zombie. I had pushed everything away from me. My friends. My feelings. Paul. Luckily for me, Ariel had stuck it out. Unfortunately, I hadn't been able to do the same for her.

My stomach was rumbling, and it wasn't just from hunger. But eating would have to do, since I obviously wasn't going to be able to fix things with Ariel anytime soon. I grabbed the map of the campus so I could find the cafeteria and left my room. When I was halfway down the hall, Ms. Moore's door opened, and I could see the house mistress talking to someone who was still inside her room.

"Thanks again for this. I really appreciate all the extra work you've done—you're a tremendous help to those kids you tutor." Ms. Moore paused in the doorway, her back still to me. "You seem to have a knack for teaching—have you ever considered it as a career?"

"Probably not. I'm more comfortable in a lab with petri dishes than interacting with people." The unknown girl's laugh was light and sparkling. "And I've been dreaming of Harvard Medical School since kindergarten." Her voice wasn't completely recognizable, but somehow it still seemed oddly similar to—I tried to think—well, someone.

"The world's gotta have cancer researchers, too." Ms. Moore moved into the hall, and an attractive black-haired girl followed her out of the room.

Corinne. Now I knew why the voice had sounded familiar but off. The friendly, open way Corinne spoke to Ms. Moore didn't even remotely resemble the tone she took with me.

Ms. Moore locked her door, then turned around. Spotting me, she gave a little wave. "I'll see you girls later."

As soon as she was gone, Corinne turned on me. "Well, well. If it isn't Little Miss L.A." Her expression made me think of a coiled snake ready to strike. "What are *you* doing here?"

"I live here," I retorted. "Why aren't you at home in Shadow Hills?"

"I'm dropping off some papers for Ms. Moore." Corinne drew herself up to her full height, as if she didn't already tower over me. "Besides, I belong here a hell of a lot more than you do, even if I don't live in the dorms. Proximity isn't what makes a Devenish student; merit is."

"I'll be sure to keep an eye out for my badge," I replied. "It should be arriving in the mail any day now."

"I know you think you are just unbelievably cute and witty— but you're no different from the rest of the boarding students." Corinne's gaze was so intense I wanted to look away, but I had no doubt that would give her some perverse satisfaction. "You're an outsider, and that's who you belong with. We're a very tight-knit group, and we don't like people coming in and screwing everything up."

"What the hell are you talking about?" Frustration bubbled up in me. "You don't know me, and, news flash, I have absolutely *no* interest in trying to invade your snobby little group!"

"I'm not an idiot—I know Zach well enough to sense when something's going on with him. And I think that something is you." Corinne took a step closer to me, and before I could stop myself, I instinctively stepped back. "Zach doesn't belong with you, and he knows it, so don't even bother." Corinne threw her long straight hair over her shoulder—narrowly avoiding hitting me in the face with it—and stalked out of the dorm.

There wasn't time for me to think of a retort before the front door swung shut behind her.

Why in the world would Zach's sister care so much about who he dated? What could possibly be so awful about a boarder and a townie hooking up? And if Corinne thought she'd deflected my interest in Zach, she was dead wrong. If anything, it was stronger.

I stepped outside and checked my map, before heading over to the cafeteria.

After some cereal and fruit, I went to the hospital for the second time. The museum area was easy to locate, what with all the signs pointing me toward it. The first thing that caught my eye when I walked in was a large metal table behind a glass enclosure. As I got closer to the display, I could see there were heavy-duty straps on the table. Restraints. I read the small information plaque on the glass. According to it, when the hospital was still an almshouse, it had been made of wood, and the only thing left of the original structure was a crude stone basement where they had housed the mentally ill. My chest felt tight as I thought back to the cell from my dreams.

I continued to the wall that showcased pictures of the Gene Research Wing being built. Below the photos were small artifacts that had been dug up during the renovations. A drawing of the almshouse as it had looked back in the 1700s showed a plain, shingled, boxy place. There was something dark and foreboding about it. I scanned a nearby plaque. Shadow Hills was founded in 1708 by a group of people from a town in Derbyshire, England. Apparently the village had grown during the following years to include Puritan settlers from neighboring towns, and they had built the almshouse for the large number of orphans and widows who had resulted from the battles between the early settlers and the Native American population.

But these little tidbits were not what I was looking for. I moved to the next wall. And there it was:

> In 1736 an epidemic swept Shadow Hills, and the almshouse had a new responsibility: housing the sick and the dying. By 1737 almost three hundred people—roughly half of the town—had died from the mysterious disease. The cause of the epidemic was never determined, and the almshouse stood empty for years. Eventually, the structure was burned, possibly in an attempt to disinfect the area, and the almshouse was rebuilt in stone.

I moved to the next wall hanging, but the only information it offered was that the original town of Shadow Hills was where Devenish Preparatory School now stood. After the epidemic the townspeople had relocated to the area I'd been to yesterday and established a new cemetery.

Obviously, I had been right in my guess that it was an epidemic. But an epidemic of what? It was odd to me that there wasn't more information about a disease that had killed so many people.

Turning to leave, I saw a sign in the corner of the room. It was labeled ANTIQUE MEDICAL EQUIPMENT and pointed at a staircase.

I followed the flight of steps down into a long room. Three sides of the room contained old operating tables, as well as some displays of really gruesome-looking instruments. On the side nearest me was a Plexiglas shield covering a large square of stone wall. The sign beside it stated that the cutaway showed the original structure of the almshouse basement.

I moved closer, drawn to the centuries-old wall. It was built of rough stones, natural, not cut, piled on top of one another and anchored by some sort of mortar, much of it long crumbled away. It reminded me of the cell wall from my dream yesterday and I felt suddenly sick. Drops of perspiration snaked down my back despite the fact that it was cold in the basement.

Way too cold.

The stones looked different now. The plastic shield was gone, and the rocks covered the whole wall. They were exposed—slick and damp, with bits of lichen clinging to them. My stomach cramped, like fingers biting into me and twisting. It was all I could do not to double over. Sweat broke out on my forehead.

I stumbled back and drew in a deep breath, closing my eyes. When I opened them again, the Plexiglas was back over the wall. The stones were dry, without lichen. Now I was seeing things while I was wide awake. I felt even worse.

My stomach lurched, and I glanced around, suddenly desperate to get out of the basement. There was a door between the surgical displays, and I rushed through it.

I emerged into a long hallway, sterile and white, with linoleum floors. It was a relief to find something so ordinary and hospital-looking, but I still felt light-headed. Little black dots danced at the edge of my vision, and I hurried down the corridor, looking for a place to sit. Most of the doors were closed, but I found one open. The room was full of supplies. Past the shelves was a chest-high wall, forming a little inner room, and in it I could see a rolling stool.

I went in and sank down on the stool, rolling out of sight behind the wall. I wrapped my arms tightly around my chest and closed my eyes, waiting for the shivering to stop.

After a few minutes, my heart slowed to a normal pace, and my stomach unclenched. I no longer felt as if I were going to faint or throw up. I was about to stand when I heard two men arguing in the hall. Their voices quickly grew louder, as if they were walking at a fast clip toward my hideout. *I'd better wait here until they're gone.* No doubt I was someplace I wasn't supposed to be, and I didn't want to get chewed out by some pissed-off doctor.

But they didn't keep going. They stopped right outside the open door to continue their fight.

"I saw what I saw. You are violat—"

"Would you keep it down?" the other one snapped. "Come in here."

I heard the distinct click of the door swinging shut. They had closed themselves in the outer room. *Great.*

Now I was totally stuck. I scrunched down as far as I could into the corner.

"What do you think you're doing?" one of them asked heatedly. "I can't fathom why you'd endanger your position this way."

"It won't be endangered if you keep your mouth shut," the other retorted bluntly.

"So now you're saying I should lie for you?"

"Look . . . We've been friends for years, right?"

"Yeah, yeah. And Pam's practically like a sister to you. But what you're doing is foolish. You can't consort with the Banished."

Consort with the Banished? That sounded pretty biblical. My curiosity won out over my fear of discovery, and I inched up off the stool until I could see over the top of the wall. The supplies on the metal shelves in front of the wall hid me from the men's sight, but they also obscured my view of the man closest to me. The other one I could see through a gap between the boxes. He was short and compact in an athletic way, with sandy brown hair and a nondescript face. Judging from the scowl and his stance, with his arms crossed over his chest, I figured he was the one doing the lecturing.

"I know what I'm doing," the other one said.

"Yeah? What if you don't? What if they get control of you? I've heard—"

"A lot of stories, that's what you've heard. You don't know anything for a fact, just the history that's been handed down. How do we know it's true?"

"It was handed down by men like your own father. And mine.

Do you doubt them? If you let the Banished get into your head, they can twist your mind into something unrecognizable."

The man hidden from me let out a derisive snort.

Mr. Nondescript plowed on, "You're at the center of the research. You possess critical information. What if they're after that?"

"They won't get it," the other one retorted. "Give me some credit."

"It's not you I'm worried about. It's—"

"Them. I know, I know." Hidden Guy's tone of voice was beyond patronizing.

Apparently Mr. Nondescript didn't appreciate this. I saw his face get red a second before he stepped forward, out of my sight. "I'm serious here. Our whole future is at stake. You need to tell the Council about this."

The other one heaved a sigh. "Fine. I'll talk to the Council. But give me a few days, okay? I need to get all my ducks in a row." He paused, then added in more pleasant tone, "Come on, let's go grab some coffee before you leave. Talk about something else for a while."

The other man hesitated. "Okay," he finally agreed.

I crouched down again. I certainly didn't want them to spot me after the conversation I'd just heard. The door closed behind them, and I stood up slowly, cautiously peering over the wall.

What the hell was all that about?

Instead of finding answers about why Athena had wanted to come to Shadow Hills, I only had more questions.

Chapter Four

By the time I found my way out of the mazelike hospital corridors, it was after one, and Graham had texted me about meeting up for lunch. I didn't see him in the cafeteria, but I was getting hungry, so I grabbed one of the prepackaged sandwiches and a salad.

After a few minutes, Graham slid into the seat across from me and tossed his sandwich down on the table.

"Hey, sorry that took so long. I got conned into taking some new kid on a tour of the campus, and he was asking about his advisor and classes, blah, blah, blah."

"Advisor?" I questioned.

"Yeah, they're like your own little life coach." Graham's tone was ironic. "You should have been assigned one. I think I wrote it down on your classes page."

I pulled the maps and stuff out of my purse and found my schedule. Graham cocked his head so he could read it.

"It's right there." Graham pointed to the bottom of the page. "You got Sherwood; he's cool, and it looks like you have photography with him, too. They do that a lot, pair you with someone who teaches an elective you picked. I guess they figure you'll be more compatible."

"So what exactly does your advisor do?"

"They oversee your academic life." Graham took a bite of his BLT, then continued. "Keep your parents updated on how you're doing, make sure your classes are going okay . . . Don't worry about it. Advisor meetings are on Friday, so you have a whole week to get to know him in class. Plus, Sherwood's about the best advisor you can get; he's really laid back."

We ate for a moment in silence, then I said, "So I was at the hospital today, and I saw this stuff about an epidemic in Shadow Hills. I also heard something about 'the Banished.' Do you know who that is?"

"A band maybe?" Graham shrugged.

"Probably not. Some old guys were talking about them. Do they ever mention the epidemic at Devenish? Like in history class or something?"

"Not that I know of. My friend Toy loves anything related to death or horror movies, and she used to be obsessed with this graveyard behind the hospital. But I think the only information she ever found on it was a list of townspeople who died."

"Hmm." *That didn't seem particularly helpful.*

"Oh! I do remember Toy saying that she figured out that all the settlers who died had moved here from other parts of Massachusetts, but apparently the people who immigrated straight from England just got sick, then recovered. That's kind of weird, right?"

It was definitely weird, but it also didn't explain anything.

"I guess the British have a stronger constitution." I squashed down my empty sandwich wrapping.

N N N

After we were done eating, we headed back outside. Even though classes didn't start until tomorrow, there were definitely more students milling around the campus. In fact, I'd never seen so many plaid shirts and khaki pants all congregated in one place before. It was kind of freaky.

Preps weren't considered cool at my school in L.A., and these people looked like they had come from the country club for the bland.

"So what now?" Graham broke into my thoughts.

"*You're* the tour guide. Where do you think we should go?"

"Umm . . . I could show you the spot in the woods where all the secret parties are held."

"Okay." This *was something I wanted to know about.*

"Shit." Graham shook his head. "I forgot, we need a GPS. I don't have one."

"You need a GPS to find the party spot?" I stared at him incredulously.

"The woods are huge, and the students purposely make the spot insanely hard to locate so teachers won't find it." Graham shrugged. "The longitude and latitude numbers are in my wallet."

"I'm kind of a map geek—I have a Garmin handheld back at the dorm."

"Okay. To Kresky, then," he said, and led the way. "So, do you surf?" he asked as we walked.

"Sometimes. Not like you, though. I've never busted a tooth or anything," I teased.

"Are your parents going to send your board with the rest of

your stuff? 'Cause there's a great beach that's only like an hour or so away."

"I don't know if they'll think about it. I mean, I didn't mention it, and if my mom is the one packing . . ." I trailed off. The Xanax they had given my mom to calm her down after the police came had now become a daily staple.

"Forgetful?"

"Monumentally." I nodded. "Sometimes I don't think she even knows what month it is." I glanced away from Graham, afraid that if I looked into his eyes he would be able to tell how my family had fallen apart after Athena's death.

"Yeah, well. Now you're here." Graham stopped in front of the door to my dorm. "And I, for one, am happy about it."

I couldn't think of what to say; I'd never been able to express my emotions in that kind of quick, easy manner. It was something we didn't do much in my family. Luckily, it didn't seem as if Graham was waiting for a response. He just held the door open for me, and we stepped into the foyer.

Which was filled with bags. About fifteen large pieces of Louis Vuitton luggage, to be exact. Not to mention a black leather trunk big enough to fit a dead body in. *Okay, today's hospital trip had definitely put me in a morbid frame of mind.*

"How was I supposed to know that the singles here are the size of my shoe closet?" A slightly southern-accented but still commanding voice came from within the walls of luggage.

Ms. Moore was standing next to the ginormous trunk, looking like her head was about to explode. "There are dimensions for all the rooms clearly stated on both the Web site and your admissions papers," she said between gritted teeth.

I heard a bag zip shut, and the girl stood up. She was thin and toned, with a golden tan—definitely tennis team material. Her height also added to her athletic appearance; she looked to be around five feet nine, which gave her a good three inches on me.

"Well, that explains why I didn't know the measurements of the room. My personal assistant filled out all the admissions papers." The girl opened her whiskey-brown eyes in a wide, innocent manner. "I'd have never imagined that it would be so tiny."

"Well, Adriana, that doesn't change the fact that your room is the size that it is, and there is no way for me to make it bigger." Ms. Moore's smile was rigid.

"In that case, I guess we will just have to get me another room." Adriana's soft accent belied the asperity of her words.

"I'm sorry, but these are the largest singles on campus. Unless you would like me to try and place you with someone in a double."

Adriana looked at Ms. Moore as though she had completely lost her already feeble mind.

"Ms. Moore, please don't take this the wrong way, but I don't believe my father, the Virginia senator, paid a quarter of a million dollars to upgrade your athletic fields so that I can live in a *double*." She said "double" like I would say "rat-infested sewer." "Besides, I wasn't implying that *I* change rooms. I don't even know how we would arrange that with all the movers already gone."

Graham and I exchanged a look.

"Movers?" he mouthed to me.

"What I am proposing is that you find me an additional room. For my things." Adriana gestured at the bags, in case Ms. Moore was unaware of them clogging up the common room and foyer.

I could tell Ms. Moore was trying hard not to throttle this new girl. After a ten-second pause—*probably counting down to calm herself*—she took a deep breath and straightened her shoulders.

"There is a storage room on each floor. It's usually reserved for seniors in good standing, but due to your . . . special situation"— Ms. Moore's expression was pained—"you can store your bags there until we can find a more permanent solution."

Adriana considered this a moment, then nodded her approval. With her problem settled, she looked over at the entrance to the foyer, where Graham and I had been watching in rapt attention.

"Well, hello there. I'm Adriana." She gave us a glittering smile. Her perfect teeth were brighter than her white shift dress.

"This is Phe." Graham pointed at me with his thumb. "And I'm Graham."

"Sorry about all this mess." She tucked a lock of her straight golden-brown hair behind her ear. "It seems *we* weren't adequately prepared for my arrival."

Why did I get the feeling that when Adriana said "we" she really meant "the total morons who run this school"?

"Well, I'll leave you kids to get acquainted, then. Maybe you can help Adriana put her things up?" Ms. Moore was obviously in a hurry to be out of her presence. "Here's the key to the storage room." She dropped it into Adriana's waiting hand. "It's the door next to the stairwell, directly across the hall from your room."

"Perfect." Adriana practically purred as she slipped the key into her black Fendi bag.

Ms. Moore gave us a cursory nod and escaped to her room, closing the door a little harder than was probably necessary.

"What room are you in?" I had a feeling I already knew the answer, since my room was across from the stairs.

"One-fourteen," Adriana answered, confirming my thought.

"One-sixteen." I pointed at myself.

"Well, isn't that lucky?"

That, I'm not so sure about yet.

I smiled, changing the subject. "So you're from Virginia?"

"My family has houses all over, but Virginia's home base during the school year." Adriana shook her head. "Thank God I'm here now. I can almost bear the small-town thing, but the backwoods camo-crazed hunters are too much to deal with. You know what I mean?"

I shrugged. Having never been in her position, I couldn't really say.

"We better get this stuff cleared out." Graham motioned to the luggage.

After we—meaning Graham and I—had finished lugging the bags into the storage space, Adriana, who had been putting stuff away in her room, asked us to help her move the huge trunk. And by help, she of course meant do it for her.

"Just set it on the throw rug," Adriana instructed as Graham and I carried the insanely heavy trunk into the room. "Do you guys want to listen to some music?" she asked, without turning away from the iPod speaker system she was setting up.

"What do you have?" I inquired. Ariel had a saying for when I started switching out the CDs in her car changer: "All hail the music dictator." I, however, preferred to think of it as having good taste.

Athena had started me listening to bands like Bad Brains, Buzzcocks, and the Pixies when I was a kid, moving me on to The White Stripes and other more recent stuff as I got older. By the time I hit middle school, discovering new bands had become a contest between us. *If only I could tell her about all the music I'd found in the past year; she would love that.*

Adriana pulled the iPod from her purse and handed it to me. The girl had some good music—she had some pretty bad stuff, too, but it was mostly outweighed by the good.

"Arcade Fire works for me." I passed it back to Adriana.

She shot Graham a questioning look, and he held his hands up in surrender.

"Whatever you two want is fine. I'm just here as eye candy." He grinned.

A moment later the first strains of "Neighborhood #1" came on, and Adriana closed her door. I figured this was probably not allowed with a guy in the room, but she didn't seem to be much of a rules person.

Adriana walked over to the trunk and dropped into a squat. The trunk was on two-inch-high legs, and after a moment of feeling around under it, Adriana unrolled a black electrical cord from the base and plugged it into the outlet on the wall.

Turning back to us, she gave a triumphant smile, the gold flecks in her irises catching the subtle highlights in her hair.

"What is that thing?" Graham asked.

"Come over here and I'll show you." Adriana lifted the lid of the trunk. Graham and I peered inside to find an unbelievable array of . . . sweaters. Incredibly expensive, perfectly pressed, in every color of the rainbow. They were folded and placed in a black velvet-lined organizer.

Wow, talk about anticlimactic. And why the hell did the trunk weigh so much? What were these sweaters made out of, lead? Adriana *was* a senator's daughter, but I seriously doubted her clothing was bulletproof.

"Let me guess." Graham tapped his index finger against his chin, in an exaggerated thinker's pose. "It's a dehumidifier for your cashmere?"

Adriana reached into the trunk and pulled out the organizer, revealing at least twenty bottles—all filled with different liquors.

I didn't need a conduct book to know that this was *definitely* against the rules.

"It's a bottle cooler." Adriana was obviously pleased by our astonishment. "Bob Penwick Pub Gear did our family bar for next to nothing. My dad was Bob's favorite quarterback for the Washington Redskins."

Ah, an athlete and a senator—Adriana's dad was the über-American.

"And as a going-away present Dad commissioned a custom

cooler for me. It's identical to a professional one. Except, you know . . . miniature."

I looked back down at the behemoth trunk. *This was not what I called miniature.*

"How did you talk your dad into that?" My parents let me have a glass of wine now and then, but there was no way they'd ever do this.

"My dad was raised in Texas—it's more a colossal brewery than a state. He couldn't care less about underage drinking." Adriana pulled three glasses out of a box labeled FRAGILE. "How about a cocktail? I don't have ice, though."

"I'll grab some from the common-room freezer," I offered.

I pulled the door closed as quietly as I could. All I needed was for Ms. Moore to catch me drinking before school had even started. *That would be a fun phone call to my parents.*

When I returned to Adriana's room, she and Graham were sitting on the floor. I sat down across from them, reclining against the closed door.

"Thanks." Adriana dropped a few ice cubes in each glass. "What do you want?"

"Grey Goose and Sprite?" I shrugged.

She poured a hefty shot followed by a splash of Sprite then handed the cup to me. After Adriana filled her own glass she lifted it up in the air.

"A toast. To doing anything we want and never getting caught."

"That I can toast to," Graham agreed.

"It's got my vote." I clinked my glass against theirs.

"So are you both new, too?" Adriana asked.

"Been here since I was a freshman," Graham answered.

"I arrived yesterday from L.A."

"Really?" Adriana's eyes lit up. "I love, love, *love* L.A. The sun, the beaches, the boutiques—I could just *die*."

I laughed and took another sip of my drink. Adriana had put in a bit more alcohol than I was used to, but I did enjoy the way the vodka warmed my stomach.

"Yeah. I'm definitely going to miss L.A., but this place seems cool."

"Devenish has got to be better than my old school in Virginia. It was ridiculously strict." Adriana refilled my glass before I was even finished.

"You seem like you'll be able to keep the administration in check." Graham smiled. "I think Ms. Moore, for one, is going to stay out of your way."

"I have that effect on some people." Adriana reached into her purse and extracted a pack of cigarettes.

"Smoke?" She pulled three out.

I shook my head no. When I was twelve, I'd smoked five of my sister's Camels to impress her and then lost any cred I'd earned by throwing up my dinner. The taste of cigarettes and regurgitated pâté had really stuck with me.

"Graham?"

"No, thanks. Gotta keep up my surfer's lungs."

"Wow. You two are definitely from California." Adriana opened the window and took a seat on the ledge.

I smiled at her wry, deadpan tone. I was growing to like this girl. Sure, she was a prima donna, but she also seemed like fun.

"So we still have another six hours before curfew. Any plans?" A lavender cord of smoke escaped from between Adriana's lips.

"I need to go meet my new roomie. Make sure he's not some uptight chess club president." Graham glanced at his cell. "He's probably gonna get here soon, so I think I'll call it quits after this drink."

"What about you?" Adriana nodded in my direction.

"My stuff doesn't get here until Monday, so I'm free from any unpacking duties. Of course, I also don't have any fresh clothes." I glanced down at my tank top, which had magically acquired a streak of mud and some mustardlike yellow stain.

"So borrow something of mine." Adriana absentmindedly flicked her thumb against the Marlboro's filter, raining ash onto the ledge. "Then we can go into town and go shopping."

"Okay. Thanks." I smiled. "Though I don't suspect Shadow Hills has much in the way of great little boutiques."

"I'm sure we can find something." She turned to Graham. "How far is it into town?"

"I'm not sure exactly—five miles?"

"I suppose I'll have to call the limo company and get them to send my driver back." Adriana stubbed out her cigarette and sat back down next to us, leaving the window open to air out the room. "He couldn't have possibly made it all the way back to Boston yet."

"You could use my Buick," Graham offered. "I'm not sure if—"

Adriana cut him off with a laugh, laying her hand on his arm. "Sweetie. I don't do Buicks. But thanks for the offer; you're very kind." She swigged the rest of her drink as Graham and I came to the dregs of ours.

"Well, I guess I'll see you two tomorrow, then." Graham stood. "You're a wonderful host, Adriana." He gave us a wink and left.

"I'm gonna take a quick shower before we go into town," I said.

"That's fine." Adriana waved me away. "It'll probably take them that long to get the car back here."

I grabbed my towel and toiletries bag out of my room, then headed for the bathroom. There were more girls wandering the halls now, some nervous and obviously new, others in pairs gossiping about their summers.

As I waited for the water in the shower to heat up, I checked on the reddish mark on my hip again. There was now another half moon line facing to the left. Except for the small gaps between them, the three crescents formed a perfect circle. A disturbing sensation crawled up my back like hundreds of tiny spider legs. What was causing these marks? They didn't hurt, so it was unlikely that they were from an insect bite. I'd certainly never had anything like this crop up on my body in L.A.—maybe it had something to do with my being in Shadow Hills.

After I got out of the shower, I checked my jeans before putting them back on, but I couldn't find anything that could be irritating the skin on my hip.

When I walked back into Adriana's room, she was going

through her clothes—pulling stuff out of her closet, shaking her head, and shoving them back in. "What color are your eyes?" she inquired over her shoulder.

"Green." I sat down on her bed. I was curious to see her clothing collection for myself, but I didn't want to seem nosy.

"Blond hair, green eyes." Adriana tapped a French-manicured fingernail against her dainty mouth. "Now what size are you?" She seemed to be asking herself more than me. "You're petite— probably about five five . . ."

"Five six," I cut in. That inch pulled me out of the short category.

Adriana continued talking to herself as if she hadn't heard me. I was beginning to feel very much like an oversize Barbie doll. "And you're slender, but not skeletal. A four, maybe?" She turned to me.

"Are you wanting an actual answer?" I asked, in mock-surprise.

"Yes." She rolled her eyes. "You *are* going to be the one wearing it."

"I was starting to wonder," I deadpanned. "I'm anywhere from a two to a six, depending."

"Try this." Adriana held up the chosen item—a soft jersey dress in a vivid golden color.

"Are you sure that won't make my hair look brassy?" I really didn't do yellow.

"Of course not." Adriana waved this worry away. "I know what I'm doing."

The dress had kimono sleeves and was body hugging from the waist down to my knees.

"You don't look quite as good in it as I do. But you're still hot." Adriana spun me around to look in the full-length mirror hanging on the back of her door.

She was right about the mustard shade. It subtly brought out the pale golden tones in my ashy-blonde hair. However, my fair complexion needed some blush.

"So." Adriana looked down at my old Vans lying on her floor. "What are we going to do about shoes? Because those look tiny."

"Not tiny," I defended my undersize feet. "I wear a seven."

"Yeah, well, I wear a nine, and you are not wearing my dress with *those shoes*." She looked at them distastefully.

"Oh, I've got an idea!" I ignored her disparaging inflection. "Moccasins."

"I think you're a little late on that idea, honey. The Indians thought of moccasins a few hundred years ago."

"No. I mean I have some. And did you just say *Indians*?" I raised an eyebrow.

"We can't all be from California," Adriana said by way of an answer. "I mean, let's consider the name of the Washington football team my dad played on."

"Point taken." I nodded and headed next door to my room.

I grabbed the black ankle-boot moccasins out of my back-pack and slipped them on. They were simple, with one row of fringe running vertically down the side where they tied closed.

"Wow." Adriana looked at me in surprise when I came back. "That's actually really cute. Obviously not something someone like me would wear." She snorted at this notion. "But perfect for an L.A. native. Funky."

A muffled ring came from Adriana's purse, and she pulled out her iPhone. "Hello?" A pause. "We'll be out in a bit."

We walked outside to the waiting limo. It wasn't one of those embarrassingly long things, but inside it was plush, and the ride was smooth and quiet.

"This is it," I told the driver when we reached town. He pulled into a parking space and opened the back door for us.

"They might have clothes." I pointed at a store called Sarah's Boutique.

"We'll try there first, then." As we stepped inside, Adriana glanced around the dark, dingy shop with disdain. "What is all this pilgrim crap?" she muttered, luckily not loud enough for the ancient woman behind the counter to hear.

The gift shop was filled with folksy old-fashioned items. Hanging on the walls were blue and white tiles depicting ships at sea and framed squares of needlepoint with quaint sayings and intricately embroidered flowers. At the back of the narrow shop stood an antique dresser, the drawers pulled out to showcase the clothing inside.

Adriana was already picking through it, holding stuff up in disgust and putting it back. Everything was so conservative that it bordered on Amish: ankle-length, high-necked dresses; white blouses with peter pan collars; and polyester floral print jumpers. As rude as Adriana was being, I had to admit I almost gagged at the sight of the jumpers. Thankfully, the old lady was oblivious to our derision and offered us a friendly wave as we stepped back outside.

"*Hulghhh.*" Adriana shuddered. "I've seen some scary stuff in my lifetime, including my fifty-year-old uncle in stretchy bike shorts, but that"—she pointed at the offending store—"was truly horrific."

"Maybe that's a good thing." Adriana's death glare prompted me to explain my logic. "You know, get the worst over with. Nothing can be as bad as that, et cetera."

"God, I *hope* nothing else is as bad as that, or I might have a nervous breakdown."

"Let's try to avoid that, shall we?" As I linked my arm through Adriana's, I noticed my silver Tiffany's ID bracelet was missing.

Alarm rose up in me like a wave. The bracelet had originally been Athena's, and I had always thought it was beautiful. She wore it every day for a year, but then a few weeks before her accident, she'd told me that she was tired of it and I could have it if I wanted. The bracelet was engraved with the infinity symbol, and I'd worn it almost every day since. It reminded me of Athena—that a part of her was always with me.

"My bracelet must have fallen off inside. I need to find it."

"Go right ahead; I'll be out here trying to recover from the polyester attack."

As I searched through the store, I heard a strange, erratic thumping behind me. I turned. The haggard old lady was making her way over to me.

Her pace was halting, and the sound of her cane striking the floor was oddly menacing. I stood frozen to the spot, unable to look away. One of the woman's legs was shriveled and dragging behind her. Trying not to stare at it, I focused on the woman's skeletal face. When my eyes met hers, her mouth fell open, and she covered it with a weathered hand.

"Rebekah!" she breathed in awe.

"What?"

"You're Rebekah Sampson," she told me.

"No." I turned back to the dresser and started going through the next drawer more quickly. The name seemed familiar somehow and the look in the woman's eyes was inexplicably frightening to me.

"Don't you remember me? It's Sarah."

"I'm not Rebekah." My fingers hit metal, and with a sigh of relief, I pulled out my bracelet. I needed to get out of there.

"But you are the spitting image of . . ." Sarah trailed off. "I'm sorry. I must be getting confused in my old age."

But her eyes were bright and sharp as they bored into me. This had been no mistake. Her age-spot-riddled hand was wrapped so tightly around her cane that it made her thick veins press up against her paper-thin skin. It looked like blue worms were trying to wriggle their way out of her body.

"I'm sorry . . ." I took a step away from her. "I've got to go."

Sarah's intense stare burned against my back as I hurried to the front door. My throat was closing up, making it hard for me to breathe. I felt like I was choking on the scent of death. I swayed—woozy—and held on to the doorknob to steady myself. I had just remembered why the name was so familiar.

Rebekah Sampson. It had been on the gravestone in my dream.

Chapter Five

Once I was outside, my throat released, and I took a deep breath. Why had she called me by that name? *It must be some kind of coincidence.*

But I couldn't shake the feeling that Sarah knew something about me . . . maybe something I didn't even know about myself.

"Took you long enough." Adriana walked over to me. "Did you find it?"

I tried to hide my spooked expression.

"The latch is broken again. Hopefully this time I can get it fixed so that it works for longer than a few months." I held up the bracelet for her to see.

If Adriana had noticed anything weird about the way I was acting, I certainly couldn't tell.

Hanging out with someone so self-centered had its advantages.

"Where to now?" I asked.

"That place looks promising." She gestured at a door with the word *flirt* emblazoned on it.

A lime-green retro fan circulated air from its perch on the

front desk. The girl behind it had her feet propped up and was reading *ReadyMade* magazine.

"Hey," she remarked, barely lifting her eyes from the page.

Her hair was the same purple as her plastic-framed glasses, and a small silver stud next to her mouth stood in for a beauty mark.

"Rude much?" Adriana mouthed. I shrugged. It didn't seem that weird to me—who *would* be excited to be at work on a Sunday?

"Nice clothes, though." I pointed at the racks of trendy boutique labels.

"It's okay, I guess." Adriana gave me a blasé look and checked her cell phone.

It was then that I saw it: an amazing raw silk pencil skirt. This was not above-average mall clothing—this was designer.

"Aha!" I held it up, triumphant. Plucking the skirt out of my hands, Adriana checked the label, then headed straight back to the dressing rooms.

I wanted to try on that skirt. I frowned. That was why Adriana was being nonchalant about the clothes. She was using me as her truffle-hunting pig . . . *or some other metaphor that portrays me more kindly.*

"Well, you walked right into that one," I muttered.

"I'm sorry. Were you talking to me?" an attractive brunette woman asked me.

"Oh, no. I'm only chastising myself for giving away a gorgeous skirt."

"You know"—the woman leaned into me conspiratorially—"I think I have just the thing to make you feel better. I'll go get it."

A moment later she came back holding an incredible ivory silk dress. She was visibly pleased by my awed reaction. "I know it's lavish, but it would be perfect for the back-to-school dance."

"I'm sorry?"

"The first formal of the year—you're from Devenish, right?" the woman asked.

"Actually, L.A. But I'm starting school there this year."

"Another big-city transplant. My daughter Camilla and I are from New York City." The woman pointed to the girl behind the desk. They had the same heart-shaped face and dark eyes.

"We're from Brooklyn, *not* New York," the girl corrected her loudly.

"Children always know best, don't they?" The woman laughed. "It was actually Camilla who made me want to open this place. We came through town, and I noticed there wasn't much shopping."

That was putting it kindly.

"And Camilla said it was strange that they didn't have a cool boutique, what with a school full of teenage girls so near."

"Actually," Camilla smirked, "I said it was weird that there wasn't some corporate store with clothing that costs more than some people in Africa make in a year, when there's a school full of rich princesses down the street."

"Camilla..." There was a sharp note of warning in that single word. The woman turned back to me. "Obviously *not* the head of our customer service department." She rolled her eyes. "I'm Anne, by the way." She stuck out her hand.

"Persephone," I replied, shaking it. "And, just a tip, you probably shouldn't make her head of advertising either."

Anne laughed. "Do you want to try it on?" She held the dress out to me.

An hour later Adriana and I left the store with our purchases and promised to return soon.

"Is it cool if we go by that bookshop before we head back?"

"I doubt there's anything better to do in this town." Adriana shrugged.

I took this as a yes and went into the simply named Book Stop. After a few seconds of trying to appear interested in a book, Adriana turned to me.

"So . . . you and Graham?" She raised an eyebrow, a sly smile on her face.

"Me and Graham what?"

"You know . . . are you two a 'thing'?" She did little air quotes.

"No." I shook my head. "We've only known each other a day. Plus, he has some girlfriend in Boston."

Adriana, who had been strolling down the fiction aisle in front of me, suddenly stopped in her tracks.

"Hummpphff." I ran straight into her back. "What the hel—"

Adriana cut me off midsentence, laying her manicured hand on my forearm. "Don't look now, but I think *the* sexiest guy I have ever seen in my whole entire life works here."

Of course, I automatically looked up just as she had said

not to. "Oh, my God." I gazed at the tall, now-familiar form. "Him again."

Adriana's expression was so astonished I wondered if she, too, had prophetic dreams about handsome strangers. "Him who?" she breathed, apparently unable to tear her eyes away.

"His name is Zach. It seems like he's everywhere I go," I whispered, glancing around quickly, trying to spot his hateful sister lurking somewhere nearby. Luckily, she seemed to be absent.

Zach looked up, his light, sea-green eyes locking onto mine. A shiver ran through my whole body. I didn't know how, but I was certain that he had heard me—from fifty feet away. Zach pushed his shaggy black hair out of his eyes as he watched us intently.

"He is looking straight at you," Adriana hissed. "What is the deal? Do you have the *entire* hot-guy market cornered already? I mean, come on . . . leave some of the cute ones for the rest of us." She placed a hand on her hip. "Besides, if you pick up a guy while you're wearing *my* dress, he automatically reverts back to me."

"I am not picking up any guys," I said as quietly as my frustration would allow. I had to find a way to get Adriana off this subject. From the sly smile on Zach's face, it appeared he was catching every word. *What is with this guy's hearing? Is he part German shepherd?*

"Seriously, he is way too gorgeous to be with one girl. A guy like that needs to share the wealth." Adriana looked Zach up and down appreciatively. "You just know a guy that tall and well built has got a *lot* to share."

Zach's skin was turning red, and he quickly moved over to

the nonfiction side of the store. *So he could stand there and eavesdrop on us, but the second* he's *scrutinized, he runs away? Uh-uh.*

"Come on." I grabbed Adriana's hand, following him.

"What are we doing?"

"I'm introducing you." I marched us over to the end of the aisle, where Zach was pricing a biography of Nancy Reagan.

"Hi, Zach." My tone was brighter than the yellow dress I was wearing.

"Hey, Persephone." Zach rubbed the back of his neck in a show of discomfort.

"This is Adriana." I gave her a little push forward, and they awkwardly shook hands. "She's also new to Devenish this year."

"Oh. Well. That's interesting." His expression made it obvious that he wasn't interested in anything except figuring out a way to escape.

"I hear there's a school dance coming up," I commented. "What's the deal with it? Do the guys ask the girls, or is it a Sadie Hawkins, women's lib—type thing?"

"Um." Zach was gripping the pricing gun so tight that the knuckles on his hand turned white.

"Or do people arrive solo and then pair off at the end of the night to go hook up?" I continued. "'Cause that would leave Adriana and me at a real disadvantage, being that we're new and don't know anyone yet."

"I'm sure you two will do fine." Zach laid the pricing gun down on top of a stack of books and looked to his left, where the front counter was being run by a man in his mid-thirties. "If you'll excuse me for a moment, I think my dad needs my help."

I glanced over. He seemed to be in complete control of the hardly bustling store. I laid a hand on Zach's forearm to prevent him from leaving, and a jolt of electricity shot through me. My heart flipped over in my chest, and I quickly pulled my hand back.

Adriana looked from me to Zach and back again.

"I'm going outside to have a cigarette." She rolled her eyes at me before leaving.

"So y-you work here?" I almost stuttered, trying to get the words out. *That was not just a normal static electricity shock.*

"Yeah. My dad owns the place." Zach's gaze lingered on the stack of books next to him, and I noticed a barely visible twitch in one of his eyebrows.

I almost gasped when I saw what he was staring at. The plastic arm of the pricing gun he had been holding had melted so that every fingerprint, every wrinkle in Zach's palm was seared into it. Like the handle was made of molding clay instead of hard plastic.

This was all getting too weird. My iPod miraculously charging when Zach touched it. The electric shock I received from both him and Corinne. The strange effect the two of them had on metal. And now Zach's hand melting plastic like it had been set down on a hot plate.

"What the hell?" I stared at the finger indentions in the handle. "How did you do that?"

"Do what?" Zach stuck his hands in his jeans pockets.

"What do you mean, do what? You melted this pricing thingamajig." I picked it up and shook it at him.

"They look like that. It's a handgrip." He pulled the offending object from my grasp.

"So it perfectly matches *your* fingerprints? And what about metal? You were attracting it like a magnet at the grocery store the other day." I took a step closer to him.

"Um . . ." Zach tapped his foot nervously, which made him look even more adorable. "I was wearing my belt with the car-seat buckle. It must be magnetized."

"Uh-huh." I raised an eyebrow at him skeptically. "So why do I keep seeing you everywhere?"

"I don't know. Maybe you're stalking me? This *is* my father's store, you know," Zach challenged.

"Yeah, but *you're* the one who followed me into the grave-yard."

"How could I not after I saw you back there in your dirty, torn uniform? I thought you might be hurt." Zach's eyes widened, and there was a moment of dead silence. "I mean, it was weird when I saw you disappear into the trees."

"I wasn't wearing my uniform then." I tried to hide my shock. I'd been wearing a torn and dirty uniform in my dream. But Zach couldn't possibly know that . . . unless he'd had the same dream.

"I have to take these to my dad." Zach grabbed a stack of books and headed over to the front desk. I followed, hot on his heels.

"Phe?" Adriana was walking over to us, giving me a quizzical look.

"Here you go." Zach deposited the books in front of his

dad and quickly shoved the pricing gun in a drawer.

"So I guess you're done with our conversation?" I folded my arms across my chest and raised my eyebrows. I didn't want to ask about the dream straight out, at least not when there were witnesses.

"Phe? What is wrong with you?" Adriana hissed in my ear.

"Nothing, I was only asking Zach a few questions."

"And I'm pretty sure I answered them." Zach's tone was a bit louder than necessary. His dad finally looked up from the papers in front of him. He looked much younger than my father, with just the slightest hint of gray in his black hair. *He must have been college age when they had Corinne.*

"Hello." He smiled at us. It made him look even younger and more like Zach.

"Hi. I'm Persephone, and this is Adriana."

"Nice to meet you both. I'm Grant Redford." He gave us a warm smile. "I hope you're enjoying our little store."

"It's great," I assured him as the bell above the door rang, signaling a new guest.

It was a guy about our age, with dark blond hair. He wore it fairly long, about chin length, and it fell around his face in a perfect prearranged way. He stared at our little group, his eyes a bottomless gray-brown completely devoid of warmth. His expression was arrogant yet sullen, and accentuated by a pouty down-turned mouth.

"Trent." Zach's father nodded to the boy.

"Hello, Grant. Zach."

"I hope you're not intending on browsing long; we're locking up soon." Evidently, my prying questions had completely left Zach's mind. His entire attention was focused on the newcomer. His jaw twitched as he clenched his teeth. In fact, every muscle in Zach's body appeared to be tensed, ready to pounce.

"I didn't come here for a book. It's very rare I find anything in this tiny place that I want." Trent ran his hand over his hair as he inspected me. "Though every once in a while, I discover something I *must* have."

His eyes cut like a laser, as if he was gazing through my clothes, my skin, all the way to my bones and organs. My adrenaline surged. *Would it be totally insane for me to run out the front door and lock myself in the town car?*

"Get to the point, Trent," Zach practically growled.

"Zach." Mr. Redford gave him a cautionary look.

I turned to Adriana; it felt strange to be watching this interaction.

"I came to deliver a message from my father," Trent said to the older man. "He wants you to back off and leave it alone. His actions are in your best interests, and it would be wise of you to just accept the rewards happily."

"How noble of my brother to send his son to do his dirty work," Mr. Redford answered shortly. "If that's all, we do have some customers we were helping."

"Of course, Grant." Trent nodded at Mr. Redford, then held out his hand to Zach, who grasped it so firmly the tips of his fingers glowed red with blood.

All the little hairs on my arms were standing up straight, like the time I touched an electrostatic generator in science class. The two guys looked as if they were engaged in the most intense staring contest ever. Either that or a very disappointing round of arm wrestling. Finally, Trent let go, his expression amused despite his bright pink hand.

"Pretty good. But you gotta keep practicing, cuz." He winked at Zach and, after giving Adriana and me one last glance, left.

"Sorry. I forgot to introduce you." Grant smiled, trying to dispel some of the heaviness. "That's my brother's son; he's kind of . . . curt."

Zach snorted loudly at this, eliciting a glare from his father.

"That's okay." I took Adriana's arm. "We didn't realize you were closing so soon. I'll come back another time."

"Yeah, me, too," Adriana agreed, walking backward to the door.

"Well, it was nice meeting the both of you," Mr. Redford called after us as I pushed the door open.

"See you at school, Zach," Adriana said before following me out onto the sidewalk.

"What the hell?" Adriana turned to me. "Is it me, or was everyone in that store insane?"

"They were definitely acting strange." I added silently, "And you don't know the half of it."

"They weren't the only ones acting strange. What was up with your interrogation of Zach?"

"I was just letting him know you were available for the

dance. I thought he might ask you." I did my best to appear innocent.

"Probably not, after all that. Besides, I can get my own dates, thank you very much." Adriana motioned to the driver, who held open the back door for us. "I'm glad my uncle doesn't hate me that much. We have enough drama at home as it is."

"Yeah," I agreed as I slid into the car after her. "I wouldn't want to be at *that* family reunion."

"That's about the level of kindness my mom treats her sister with," Adriana snorted. "She lives in a trailer, so Mom acts likes she's the devil incarnate."

"This is *your* aunt?" She didn't sound like anyone Adriana would admit to being related to.

"Sharon's pretty much my favorite relative." Her golden-brown eyes sparkled. "She took me and my little brother to the water park when we were kids. My mom called it 'white-trash heaven.'" Suddenly the brightness in Adriana's eyes shut down. "But, you know, we hardly see her anymore—she is only my mom's half sister, after all."

The rest of the ride was quiet, and I couldn't stop thinking about Zach. There was no rational explanation for the things I'd seen him do. Hell, I couldn't even come up with anything irrational to explain it. And it seemed utterly impossible for him to have dreamed the same dream I had.

But Zach knew more about what was going on than I did. He'd been nervous when I was questioning him, but not confused. I was just going to have to find another way to get information out of him.

When we got back to Kresky Hall, I took out my bracelet and inspected it. Part of the clasp had come loose, so I squeezed it back together with my tweezers. It appeared tight enough, at least until I could find a jeweler and get it fixed. I washed up and crawled into bed with the Devenish handbook.

By the time I reached the last page, I could hardly hold my eyes open. It was barely nine, but I decided to call it an early night. I was almost asleep when my phone beeped, letting me know I had a text from my father.

The dean of admissions informed me you need a laptop. I have ordered you a MacBook that should be arriving soon, so keep an eye out. I don't want you losing it among your many boxes of clothes.

As always, my dad was about as affectionate as a parking meter. We were never close, but now we barely spoke to each other. I texted him back.

It's so nice to hear from you. The school is great so far, and I'm making friends already. Thanks for the encouragement.

I dropped my phone onto the bedside table, turned my back to it, and closed my eyes.

A very loud knocking awakened me, and I looked at my cell's clock. Six in the morning. I opened the door, rubbing my blurry eyes.

"Good morning, Phe," Ms. Moore trilled enthusiastically. I was tempted, momentarily, to stab her with the nail file lying on top of my dresser, but I was way too tired. "The deliveryman is here with your stuff, and I didn't want it left here blocking the stairway."

I peered around her out into the hall, where a burly guy stood surrounded by boxes.

"He can bring it in," I told Ms. Moore, who motioned at the man to come in.

He hauled in the boxes two at a time, and in fewer than five minutes, I was alone with my stuff. Breakfast was in less than an hour, so I didn't have time to unpack, but I felt better knowing it was here. I took a quick shower and brushed my teeth before hurrying back to my room to get dressed, almost knocking over a small Asian girl on my way.

"I'm sorry. I wasn't paying attention," I apologized.

"That's cool." She waved away my apology. The girl's black hair was cut in a short pixie style that complemented her delicate features. "Not everyone's a morning person." She squinted her dark brown eyes at me. "You're new, aren't you? I'm Toy, by the way."

"Persephone. But people just call me Phe. And, yes, I am new."

"Junior?" she asked.

I nodded.

"Cool. Well, I gotta hit the bathroom." Toy held up her toothbrush. "Maybe we'll have some classes together today. That is, after you get out of the newbie orientation."

"Yeah." I wasn't exactly looking forward to orientation. After reading the 120-page Devenish handbook, I couldn't imagine what else they could tell me.

Apparently, nothing, I thought an hour and a half later, as Headmaster Grimsby droned on and on about curfews and study halls and mandatory meals.

"And for a fun little treat tonight, we are going to have pizza and movies for the boarding students. Mr. Carr, our Student Activities Center director, is here to fill you in on the details." Mr. Grimsby gestured toward a very familiar-looking man.

It was the guy I had seen in the hospital.

I sat up straighter, my interest finally piqued. Mr. Carr was the man whom I had been able to see during the strange argument I'd overheard.

Mr. Carr gave us all a friendly wave and began his spiel: "Tonight at six we will be having pizza in the SAC instead of the cafeteria, and after that we will be showing *Beetlejuice* and *Edward Scissorhands* upstairs in the student theater. That means no mandatory dorm study, and we are also closing the library so the student aides can join us."

A few of the Senior Proctor students who were also on the stage clapped excitedly.

"Whoopie," Adriana muttered, not lifting her eyes from the text she was sending.

"I hope to see you all there." Mr. Carr finished, and with some forgettable parting words, Mr. Grimsby finally released us.

"God, that was boring," Adriana complained later as we walked over to the library.

"At least you had your iPhone," I retorted.

"So? Why didn't you bring your cell?"

I looked down, feeling slightly embarrassed. "The handbook said not to."

"Oh, but the handbook encourages drinking in the dorms?" Adriana asked snarkily. "If you did everything that thing told you to do, you'd be more boring than my teetotaling grandmother."

I followed the stream of new students through the open door into the cavernous library. Adriana took the lead in line, and since she was picking up *Pride and Prejudice*, I had to wait patiently behind her as the librarian went on and on about the genius of Jane Austen. Finally, Adriana managed to extricate herself by agreeing that the novel was the best piece of literature ever written. As soon as she was free, she ran off to find the Science Building for her first class of the day.

After the librarian handed me my textbooks, I made my way to the fiction section.

As I walked past shelves of books, I felt a warmth on the back of my neck. Turning, I found myself looking straight at Zach Redford. He was standing with Corinne about twenty feet behind me, leaning against the back wall below a huge stained-glass window. Flustered, I turned quickly into the stacks on my left.

I could hear them talking. *About me?*

"Get real," I muttered under my breath. I was just being paranoid. What could they possibly have to say about me? Unless Zach was telling Corinne about my strange interrogation the day before.

They certainly weren't using their library voices. If I moved a little closer, I could probably make out what they were saying. Curious, I walked quietly to the end of the row, staying hidden behind the shelves.

"Will you get off it?" Zach said. "I didn't even say anything about her."

"You didn't have to." Corinne's voice was also low, but more feminine. "You look like Grodin begging for a Milk-Bone every time that girl is within ten feet of you."

"What do you want me to say, Corinne? That I think she's hot? Fine. I do. That doesn't mean I'm going to do anything about it."

I tried not to smile. I was completely invading Zach's privacy; still, I couldn't make myself walk away.

"You better be damn sure you don't do anything about it. You could put us all in jeopardy, not to mention what might happen to Little Miss L.A. Sometimes I get so tired of always having to protect you."

"Protect me?" Zach repeated sarcastically. "It's more like you're trying to run my life."

Corinne sighed, and there was a moment of silence. Then she spoke again, her tone no longer scolding. "All my friends have crushes on you, gross as it is, but you always act like you have no interest. Now all of a sudden, you decide you're into some girl from California that you have absolutely nothing in common with?"

"How do you know we don't have stuff in common?" Zach countered. "She knew the band I was listening to at the grocery store—no one from Shadow Hills has even heard of Gogol Bordello."

"Oh, and that's a great thing to base a relationship on; she likes some weird, obscure band you're into." I could practically hear Corinne roll her eyes. "Trust me, that is not nearly as important as dating someone you can be honest with. This school is full of beautiful girls."

"Yeah. Beautiful, preppy, cold East Coast princesses."

"Let's see: preppy, privileged, cold—what do you want to bet that is *exactly* what she thinks of you?" Corinne snipped.

"She doesn't seem like the judgmental type."

As much as I wished that was true, I had to admit that Corinne was right. Not that I thought it about Zach, but that was basically what I assumed the whole student body here was like.

"Phe's just . . . She's different."

The way Zach said it lit me up inside.

"What makes her so different? Is it the blond hair? That tiny size-zero Hollywood figure?"

Just because I'm not an Amazon with big breasts like Corinne, she labels me as some anorexic wannabe actress.

"No. It's not only about how she looks. She's . . . I don't know, Corinne." Zach was obviously tired of talking about this. "She seems interesting and unpredictable—it sort of pulls me to her." He hesitated, then in a slightly lower, oddly charged voice, he said, "I had a dream about her."

"So?" Corinne snorted. "An adolescent boy's dreams are hardly an indication of—"

"Before I ever saw her," he interrupted. "Before we went over to the hospital the other day. I was asleep on the couch, remember, and you woke me up and told me to get ready. I was dreaming. I don't even know what I was dreaming about at first, but then suddenly I was in the old graveyard. The one behind the hospital. And she was there. She was wearing the Devenish uniform, and it was all torn and dirty. We were looking at some gravestone."

If Corinne made any response to this revelation, I didn't hear it. My blood was pounding through my veins; the sound filled my ears. I had wanted to ignore Zach's slipup in the bookstore yesterday, to pretend that he hadn't somehow seen my dream. But clearly he had.

It was bizarre enough that I was having these nightmares that sometimes mirrored my sister's. But to share a dream with a total stranger? That was *Twilight Zone* material.

With an effort, I turned my attention back to their conversation.

"It doesn't matter what we want, okay?" Corinne's voice sounded thin and strained. "Hell, I didn't *want* to lie to Antonio—to pretend I didn't care if he stayed. Do you know how much it sucked to not say good-bye when he went back to Italy? But I did what I had to do. We aren't supposed to be with outsiders. These are the rules we live by, and there's a reason for them."

"Enough with the rules, Corinne! Don't you want to be happy at least once in your life? Or is studying and eating your vegetables and pleasing the Council all the fulfillment you need?" Zach sounded kind of harsh, even to someone who disliked Corinne as much as I did.

"What do you think Mom would say if she found out about this?" I could tell from her tone that Corinne had no doubt that Zach knew what she would say.

"Listen, like I've said a million times now, I am not going to slip up. Persephone will never find out about us. She will never find out what we *are*."

I hoped this wasn't true—because I was more than a little curious.

Chapter Six

"I promise." Zach continued with an air of finality. "Come on, we have to get the archives key from the librarian, while no one else is around."

That's not ominous or anything, I thought. *I wish I knew what the hell that was all about.* A sudden wave of mental feedback hit me like a wall. I stumbled backward, feeling the hard wooden shelves dig into my spine. My ears were ringing, and my vision went black like I'd stood up too fast. *The ornate gold key from my dream.* I could see it perfectly, as if someone had pasted a picture on the inside of my eyelids. Then, as quickly as the feeling hit me, it was gone. I allowed myself to sink to the ground and leaned my head back against the bookshelf.

"Hey, Phe." A voice above my head startled me, and I looked up. "It's Toy. From the dorm?" The girl I had practically mowed down in the hallway earlier was staring at my crouched form.

"Yeah. Sorry. I guess I was spacing out again." I shook my head, trying to clear it of the lingering haze.

"You seem to do that a lot." Toy smiled. "I saw you over here, and I wasn't sure if you knew we had to be at class in five minutes."

I glanced around me; the library had almost completely cleared out.

"Oh, crap." I jumped to my feet. "I have advanced composition now."

"I can walk you if you want. I'm going to the Languages Building myself."

I nodded and followed Toy, happy to put aside all the weirdness for a while and just go to class.

After composition let out I shoved my class syllabus in my bag and went to find Graham and Adriana in the cafeteria.

"Wow. Hungry much?" Adriana raised an eyebrow at my tray as I plunked it down.

"Starving." Though I felt a little gluttonous next to Adriana with her fruit and light yogurt.

"Hey, Graham." A now-familiar voice came from behind me.

"Toy!" Graham broke into a wide smile. "Come sit with us." He motioned to the spot next to him, and Toy slid in across from me.

"So how was South Korea?" Graham asked.

"Great." Toy pulled on a short strand of hair that curled up in front of her ear. "I got to see my grandparents for the first time in almost ten years, and my big brother came with me, so that was nice."

"How is— Hey!" Graham cut himself off to yell at someone walking by our table. The guy was tall and scrawny—his narrow chest all but disappearing under his oversize T-shirt. His arms were like a scarecrow's stick limbs, all points and angles. With his scruffy light brown hair and sort of zoned-out expression, he reminded me of Shaggy from *Scooby Doo*.

"This is Brody Kincaid," Graham introduced the Shaggy look-alike. "You, of course, remember Toy, and these lovely ladies are Adriana and Phe."

"Hey." Brody gave a small half wave as he sat down. His clothes had the definite musty smell of cigarettes, but I also detected the faint hint of pot emanating from his person. Brody looked at me for a second, then screwed up his face as if he was trying to figure something out. "Are you Persephone?"

Okay. This was getting beyond *strange.*

"Yes." I eyed him warily.

"I thought so. Zach was telling me about you." Brody took a sip of the soda in his hand. "Said you were cool." The mystery of my identity solved, Brody turned back to Graham. "So, you going to the SAC tonight for that movie slash pizza party shit?"

"Yeah." Graham answered him. "It's better than dorm study."

"Well, if it's either one or the other, I guess I'm going, too," Adriana added.

"It should be fun." Toy smiled at her. "They're showing two Tim Burton films."

"Are you making an appearance?" Adriana cocked an eyebrow at me.

The picture of the gold key flashed across my mind again. They had said the library would be closed tonight; it might be the perfect time to figure out what was up with this secret archives room.

"I don't know." The faint outline of a plan was forming in my brain. "I have some homework I have to do."

By the end of the day it was glaringly obvious that I was going to have to do a *lot* of homework unless I wanted to flunk all my courses. I was practically the only one taking notes during the lectures, and what made it doubly embarrassing was that half of the students hardly paid attention. I'd also seen people in various classes scan through their books, glancing at each page then quickly moving on to the next, as if they were taking a snapshot of each one.

Finally, I was driven to ask Graham about it as we left the only class we shared, computer science. He just shrugged and said, "Townies."

"So everyone not listening is from Shadow Hills?"

"Well, probably not *everyone* who isn't listening," he conceded. "But the ones who don't pay attention and still manage to get good grades are townies. It's pretty annoying, actually. While I'm in my room studying, they spend the afternoons in the SAC playing pool."

"And they can pass these ridiculously hard classes? Are they super intelligent or what?"

"I guess."

"Doesn't that strike you as weird? A whole town of smart kids?"

"Yeah. But not everyone from Shadow Hills goes to school at Devenish. There's a public school. We must get only the high-IQ students. A lot of them are the children of doctors and researchers at the hospital, so I guess it makes sense. Plus, they must teach some kind of speed reading in elementary school."

"So the flipping through books at the speed of light deal—that *is* the way they read?"

"I guess. I'm not friends with any of them except Brody. And he doesn't do that."

"Brody's a townie?" I asked in surprise. "I thought he lived on campus."

"He does. His parents are dead. I've never really talked to him about it; he's not big on the sharing. Brody's kind of strange."

"He's not the only one."

I was glad that advanced photography was my final class. It was a combined course, covering 35 mm and digital photography, and I'd done both before. I sat down at one of the two-seater tables in the back, and at the last minute someone slid into the seat beside me. It was Zach.

"Okay, class. I am Professor Sherwood." Mr. Sherwood stood. He was tall and husky, and the way he wore his tie tucked into the vest of his three-piece suit made his round belly more noticeable. His tie with the little turtles on it, together with his jovial expression, gave him a sweet look in spite of his size.

But that didn't make it any easier to concentrate on what he was saying. I was painfully aware of Zach—the faint scent of his light sandalwood-based cologne, the heat from his body. It felt like there was an electric current running between his thigh and mine. Zach shifted in his chair, and though his knee didn't touch mine, it was almost as though his energy bumped into me. *Yeah, 'cause that's not a crazy idea or anything.* I tried to turn my focus back to Mr. Sherwood's explanation of the course.

"... then we'll change gears and do some work in the 'wet' darkroom. You should already know the basics, so you'll be allowed to develop pictures on your own."

Sitting next to Zach was making me antsy, like I'd drunk too much caffeine. I wanted to jiggle my leg, but every time I did my chair rattled. I glanced over at Zach. He was staring straight ahead, the veil of his ebony hair obscuring his eyes from me. I thought about what I'd heard in the library earlier. Not the weird stuff, but the fact that he'd said he thought I was hot. Yet now he wouldn't even look at me.

Mr. Sherwood set down his chalk and turned around to face us. "The person sitting at the table with you will be your partner for the rest of this semester."

I stole another look at Zach. He happened to glance over at me at the same time, but he turned back to the front before I had a chance to smile at him.

"I'd like you and your partner to go out into the courtyard and shoot a digital portrait experimenting with depth of field. You have until the end of class."

The awkwardness that had hung between us at our shared desk was still there when we got outside.

As everyone else started to spread out, I turned to Zach, trying for a nonchalant, matter-of-fact tone. "Why don't we start here? You can stand in front of this tree."

"Sure," he agreed quickly, probably relieved that I wasn't grilling him like yesterday.

I positioned him so that the shadows from the tree branches were falling where I wanted them. My hands tingled where they rested on Zach's shoulders, and something tugged at my mind. I was dizzy and disoriented, like I'd just stepped off a tire swing.

It seemed as if vibrations from Zach's body were intertwining with vibrations from mine. He gazed at me, his pupils huge. *He probably thinks you're insane. And maybe he's right.*

Now, concentrate on the assignment. His eye line is too low; it's going to throw shadows on his face. The steeple on the chapel would be a good focus point.

"You want me to look at the steeple on the chapel?" Zach asked before I could even open my mouth to suggest it.

"Yeah." I narrowed my eyes. "How did you know that?"

"Umm . . ." Zach looked around like he might find the correct answer to my question written on the sidewalk. "I could just feel the shadows on my face. I figured it would be good to look up."

Zach's tone was majorly lacking in conviction. Still, it was a better explanation than the alternative: that he had read my mind. That was even more impossible than all the other impossible stuff I'd thought he was doing. Well, except maybe for the dream thing. I itched to ask him what was going on, but there were people all around us. Instead, I held the camera's viewfinder up to my eye and concentrated on taking the pictures.

When it was my turn, Zach had me sit cross-legged on the ground, leaning up against the tree. As a cool breeze brushed my hair back, I closed my eyes. The light-headedness that had gripped me earlier faded into a tranquil calm. Zach was quiet and worked quickly. Before I knew it, we were back in the classroom. Mr. Sherwood went around to each table with a laptop and USB-connection cord to inspect the students' work. Since I'd picked the table in the back of the room, he got to Zach and me last.

"Very nice," he complimented me as he scrolled through the pictures on his laptop. "You have a good sense of light, and your images are crisp and clear." He handed my camera back and plugged in Zach's.

I watched as Mr. Sherwood looked over the images. The pictures Zach had taken were amazing. In one, Zach had caught me brushing a lock of hair from my face, and you could see every detail of my hand— the faint trace of blue veins, the chipped nail polish. Mr. Sherwood paused on a photo of me with my eyes closed, hair blowing out behind me from the breeze.

"Now, this is exceptional," Mr. Sherwood complimented Zach. "The way you have captured this moment, you can almost feel that wind on her face."

"Thanks." Zach said, avoiding looking in my direction.

Mr. Sherwood unplugged the camera and placed it in front of Zach and then went back up to the front of the class. As he finished his lecture, I kept thinking about Zach's pictures. They were so strange to me. I'd never thought of myself as a photogenic person. My sister had always been the one who shone in our family portraits. But in Zach's pictures, I had looked . . . beautiful.

"Phe?" Mr. Sherwood caught my eye as I was packing up my stuff to leave.

"Yeah?" I looked up.

"We have your advisor meeting on Friday, right?"

"Uh-huh."

"Great." He smiled. "Remarkable work today, by the way."

My cheeks flushed.

"Thanks, Mr. Sherwood."

As I stepped out of the building an involuntary shiver ran through me, and I whipped around to see if someone was behind me. There were several students walking by, but no one seemed to be watching me. I had almost convinced myself I was being paranoid when I heard a voice call out my name.

I turned back to find Zach's cousin from the bookstore leaning up against a tree, staring at me. "It is Persephone, right?" he asked.

"Yeah." I looked at him quizzically. He pushed himself off from the tree and strolled over to me. His movements were sinuous. "How do you know my name?" *He definitely didn't hear it from Zach's dad. There had been a distinct lack of introductions.*

"I'm in your psych class," he answered smoothly. "But we haven't formally met. I'm Trent Redford IV."

He grasped my hand in a firm shake, and again I felt the dizziness I had experienced earlier when I put my hand on Zach's shoulder. Except this time, it made my bones ache. It was like the shock I had received from Corinne, but stronger, deeper.

What we are. Zach's words floated back to me. Trent was related to them; maybe he was what they were. Maybe all the townies, with their high IQs and speed-reading skills, were "what they were." Whatever that meant.

"I usually go by Phe." I worked to keep my voice steady, but Trent was staring straight into me and gripping my hand even more tightly than before. The large ring he wore dug into my skin. This no longer felt like a handshake. He was holding me in a vise grip, one I knew I couldn't break, even if I tried.

"Phe. That's . . . cute." Trent smirked, still not letting go of my hand. "I'd like to get to know you better, Phe. At the back-to-school dance. The Saturday after next? You can be my date." It was more a command than a request.

Trent may have looked like a young Chris Pine, but he still made my insides lurch. There was something off about him, something wrong. My leg muscles were contracting, building pressure, preparing me to flee from him.

"Uh, I don't know . . ." I thought about my beautiful new dress from Flirt. I wanted to go to the dance, but not with this sadistic-seeming person. Plus, I had this irrational hope that Zach would ask me, despite all these mysterious "reasons" why we shouldn't be dating. Part of me wished he would break the rules—no matter the consequences. "I have to check with Adriana. We talked about going stag. But, you know. Together."

Trent cocked his head, looking me up and down. "If I were you, I would be careful not to bet on the wrong Redford. Some of us are much more likely to break the rules—no matter the consequences." He smiled, but it was empty; Trent was baring his teeth. "Think about my invitation. It's not a bad way to start off the year—on the arm of the most eligible bachelor in school . . . See you tomorrow, Goldilocks." Trent winked and, finally releasing my captive hand, walked away.

My hand was on fire, and the spot where his ring had made contact with my skin was bright red and splotchy. My mind whirled, and I felt as if I might faint. I walked unsteadily to the edge of the building and rounded the corner so I was sure Trent couldn't see me before I allowed myself to crumple to the ground. *How did Trent happen to say* exactly *what I'd thought?*

When I got back to the dorm, I changed out of my uniform and washed my face. I immediately felt more like myself, not as shaky and freaked out.

Whatever was up here, one thing was certain. I needed to study. This was not a school I'd be able to coast in, and if I flunked out I'd never see Zach again. But no more than an hour later, I already needed a study break. *There are probably Ivy League colleges with a less rigorous curriculum.* As I flipped through a magazine, my mind wandered back to my encounter with Trent. It was another very strange incident to add to all the other peculiar things that I had seen since I got to Shadow Hills.

I thought again of the archives room that I'd overheard Zach and Corinne discussing in the library.

Grabbing the guidebook off my desk, I thumbed through it carefully, looking for any mention of an archives room. Nothing. I went over to my dresser and pulled the welcome packet off the top. It wasn't on any of the maps either. What kind of school had a secret locked archives room? *They must have something of great value in it.* And I was willing to bet it wasn't a first edition *Moby-Dick*.

The more I thought about it, the more convinced I was that

at least some of the answers I was looking for must lie in that archives room. It was like the gold key in my dream had been pointing me to it. And tonight would be the perfect time to try to find it, while everyone was at the movie and the library was closed. Surely that was where the room was located, and luckily I knew where I could get a key to the library: Graham.

I seriously doubted that he would carry that gigantic key ring with him to the movies. *I can sneak into his dorm room and try to find it after he leaves.*

I realized that it was an insane plan, but I couldn't sit around and do nothing.

Graham had written his name and room number down when he had first given the welcome packet to me—Garrettson Hall, Room 216. *Good, that shouldn't be hard to find.* My room was 116, so if the dorms were the same, as they looked on the outside, Graham's room would be at the end of the hall on the left, like mine, only a floor higher.

A knock at my door pulled me out of my reverie.

"Yeah!" I called, sticking the map back in the folder and tossing it aside.

Adriana stuck her head in.

"You ready to go to the SAC?"

"I'm actually not feeling so good." I rubbed my stomach in a show of pain. "I think I'm going to stay here."

"What's wrong?" Adriana's expression was concerned. "Do you need me to take you to the infirmary?"

"No." I shook my head. "I'll be okay. I just have a stomachache."

"Okay. Text me if you need anything," Adriana told me before leaving.

I waited a few minutes, then followed her. The stone pathways outside were deserted. Everyone was either at the movies or studying in their rooms. There were several lights on in Garrettson, Graham's dorm, probably boarders trying to memorize their textbooks to keep up with the townies. I pushed open the front door and stuck my head in.

It was clear. I took a soft step into the lobby, one of my shoes squeaking against the tile floor. *Shit.* I slid off my Vans and dropped them into my oversize purse. Silently, I made my way along the hall, not even daring to breathe until I got to the stairs. I ran up them as noiselessly as I could, pausing for a moment outside Graham's door. *If he finds out I went into his room and stole his keys, I could lose the first friend I made at Devenish.* Was I willing to take that risk?

I thought of Trent's fiery grip on my hand. My weird dreams. My inexplicable connection to Zach. *I have to know.* I'd just make sure Graham never found out. I held my breath and turned the knob.

The door swung open. I was in. My eyes canvassed the room. *Where would Graham keep his keys?* My first two attempts at his desk and bedside table both turned up nothing. My gaze fell on the dresser. I pulled open the top drawer, and my breath caught at the loud creak it made. *Hopefully the guys on this floor are at the movie.*

There it was, a huge ring with about thirty keys on it. I

shoved it into my purse and shut the drawer, pulling Graham's door closed gently. Then I booked to the library. I had to get to the library, find the archives room, get into it, look around, and return to Garrettson to replace Graham's keys—all before the film fest ended.

Chapter Seven

My hand shook as I tried the eighth key in the library door's lock. I hadn't counted on their being labeled in some code that only Graham understood. It seemed like I had been trying different keys for at least ten minutes, and I wasn't even halfway through them. I glanced around, making sure nobody happened to be strolling along the path next to me. Finally, the eleventh key slid effortlessly into the lock. I turned it and heard a satisfying click.

I was thankful for the emergency lights they left on at night. *A lower level seems like a good place for a secret room.* I checked behind the front desk. No doors leading down to a cellar. I'd have to check the perimeter. I jogged along the wood-paneled wall, looking for some kind of opening or door. I made it all the way around. Nothing. The longer I was in here, the more likely it was that I would get caught.

I walked around the room again, more slowly this time. Maybe there was some kind of lever system, like you pulled on a certain book and it revealed a hidden entrance behind a panel somewhere. There was no way I could try every book in the library, though—I would be here forever. If I were going to be clever and hide a key or lever, where would I put it?

I was about to just start pulling on any book with the word "secret" in the title when a loud crash reverberated through the library. Instantly, I broke out in a cold sweat and my chest tightened. The sound had come from across the library.

I held my breath in apprehension as I crept over to the back wall. The noise had come from directly across the room, but I felt safer sticking to the shadows, in case there was someone else in here.

The bookcases lorded over me, tall and forbidding, as I continued down the opposite wall. In front of the darkest section of shelves, lying on the floor as if they had fallen there, was a pile of books. Either somebody was in here hiding, or the books had moved of their own accord. Neither option was comforting. I glanced up at the scientific journal section in front of me.

There were only six bookcases in the whole library that were facing out like this, perpendicular to all the others, and for some reason this one seemed stranger than the rest. I inspected the bookcase. It stuck out farther from the wall, like its shelves were deeper. That in itself was weird, and add to it the subject matter . . . I had never seen this kind of book in any school library before. *What high schooler in their right mind checks out scientific journals?* There was a large empty space on one of the higher shelves. I picked the books up and placed them there. Every one of them hung an inch off the shelf. It was as if something wouldn't let them go in all the way. I pulled the books back out and set them on the floor.

My bracelet knocked against the shelf as I felt along the back of the bookcase. I held my breath. Maybe this was some kind of trap, and I was going to pull back a bleeding stump. But nothing bit off my hand; all I felt was wood. Then my fingers hit a cold circle of metal. It was a very large lock. I looked at Graham's key ring. There was no way that *any* of these would fit it. *Shit!*

I ran back to the front counter in a half crouch just in case there was someone around. Zach had said they had to get the key from the librarian, which meant she must have one. Possibly the only one. I hoped she kept it here instead of taking it home with her. I slid open the top drawer of the desk. Paper clips, rubber bands, and loose Tic Tacs. No keys. I tried the side drawer. *Aha.* A large metal lockbox was hidden under some file folders. I pulled it out and set it on the counter to study it. It needed a pass code like my dad's law briefcase, the kind you typed in on a keypad.

What would a fifty-year-old librarian have as her code? At least it was in letters. If I'd had to break a numerical code, I would be totally screwed. I thought back to the woman's endless speech to Adriana. I typed in "Jane Austen." Nope. I tried "Pride and Prejudice." Uh-uh. *I've got it!* "Darcy." *Seriously? It's not "Darcy"?* I had to stick with my theme or I would be here until morning. I thought for a moment, then tried "MrDarcy." With a little mechanical pop, the lock released. *Oh, thank God for predictable people.*

There, nestled in the black velvet lining of the box, was an ornate gold skeleton key. Exactly like the one from my dream.

The key was weighty and large, almost as long as my palm. My hand shook as I carried it back to the lock I had discovered. I turned it to the left and heard a soft click before the whole book-case moved closer to me. My heart was beating in my throat; I could hardly draw a breath. I grasped the right edge of the book-case and pulled. It opened slowly, and only with great effort.

This was the archives room. It was real. I stepped into the small space but left the bookcase/door standing open. Several shelves of books lined the left wall, and to the right were three tall file cabinets. The back wall held two locked glass cases filled with old-fashioned books, and in the middle of the room stood a sturdy wood desk.

The drawers of the file cabinets were labeled with letters, starting with *A–B* and ending with *W–Z*. I tried each drawer on the three towers; all of them were locked. I continued to the glass case on the left. Some of the books in it looked old and worn, but some were newer and marked by subject. Two in particular caught my eye: *Characteristics and Evolution of the Epidemic* and *Shadow Hills: An In-Depth History*.

I tried to slide the glass door open, but the lock held firm. I let out a sigh. I'd gotten in, but still I couldn't get any actual information.

Or maybe I could. The shelves on the left side of the room were accessible. However, the books there seemed strangely ordinary. They were all fairly new, and nothing about them sug-gested that they were particular to the town of Shadow Hills.

I grabbed an old receipt and a pen out of my purse so I could write down some of the titles. Maybe there was a theme here, something that would be apparent if I looked up the books. I scribbled down several of the most interesting ones: *The Body Electric: Electromagnetism and the Foundation of Life; Distant Mental Influence; Quantum Speed Reading.*

On the top shelf were a number of spiral-bound books. I took one down. The cover read *Identification of a Novel Mutation Associated with Gravell's Dementia.* I had no clue what that meant, but I glanced through it anyway. I couldn't understand enough of the terminology to even guess at what they were discussing.

As I continued to browse through the books one caught my eye—Derbyshire, England. According to the hospital plaque, that was where the first settlers of Shadow Hills were from. I turned to the title page: *Study of the CCR5 Gene Mutation Delta 32 of Individuals in Eyam, Derbyshire, England.*

Thumbing through the pages, there were several mentions of bacterium and organisms, and I saw the phrase "DNA inheritance" often. As I scanned the book I noticed several mentions of "the delta 32 mutation" and "Shadow Hills genotype," but there was no explanation of what they were. Halfway through the book was a chart that looked fairly readable, titled "Eyam."

The next page was identical, but its heading read "Shadow Hills." Toward the bottom of the chart, the name "Redford" jumped out at me. Zach's family. A few lines above that, it said "Kincaid." Wasn't that Brody's name?

I turned the page and found what looked like a genealogy chart, with lines going from one box to another. But the way the boxes were divided up with letters in them reminded me of the Punnett squares from biology. At the bottom of the page a legend gave the meaning of the different letters: the big *S* stood for the "Shadow Hills Mutation."

I closed the book and set it back on the shelf. I was beginning to understand, I thought, or, at least, have a glimmer of understanding. The people of Shadow Hills carried some kind of gene mutation that they seemed to have inherited from their ancestors in Eyam, England. From what Graham had told me, the people who didn't die from the epidemic two hundred years ago were the settlers from Derbyshire. So the mutation probably had to do with their surviving the epidemic.

There'd be plenty of time to dwell on this later. I needed to finish before the movies let out, or I'd be in big trouble.

Turning, I moved back over to the glass cases that held about twenty identical leather books. The first was labeled THE COUNCIL: 1800–1810, and the last one on the bottom shelf read THE COUNCIL: 2000–2010. *The books covered about two hundred years, starting not long after the epidemic. These I needed to see.* The bookcase had a separate lock on each of the shelves' sliding-glass doors. I started at the top, where the 1800s books were— it wouldn't budge. I tried the next one down, then the next, and so on, until finally I felt one give. *It was unlocked.*

I grabbed the first book off the shelf and flipped quickly through it. The pages looked like my dad's court documents, and every once in a while there would be a mention of the Brevis Vita Alliance. I pulled out the next book, labeled THE COUNCIL:

1970–1980. One of the later entries caught my eye, and I stopped flipping. This page was different—for one thing, I could actually read it.

Articles of Banishment

Therefore, Be It Resolved,

That for numerous and serious violations against the Brevis Vita Canon of Ethics, the following persons shall be required to remove themselves and their possessions, after a fair and just recompense for all properties abandoned from the environs of the township of Shadow Hills, Massachusetts:

Robert Henry Cowper, age 44
Emily Rutherford Cowper, age 42
Derek William Cowper, age 19
Gregory Douglas Rutherford, age 39
Sherry Milton Rutherford, age 39
Jennifer Elizabeth Rutherford, age 17
Stephen Alexander Rutherford, age 14
Alan Benjamin Nicholson, age 35
Melissa Sanders Nicholson, age 34
Leslie Anne Nicholson, age 13
Christina Rose Nicholson, age 11
Marilyn Cowper Gates, age 39
Damon Gates, age 17

The list went on for about twenty more names, but I stopped reading.

Banished? People were actually being banished in the 1970s? And banished from what? I presumed it must be from this Brevis Vita Alliance, or maybe it was the Council. But what had these people done that was awful enough to warrant banishment? Were these the same people that Mr. Carr and the other man had been arguing about when I'd overheard them in the hospital? For all I knew, they routinely kicked people out of . . . whatever it was they were kicking them out of.

I turned back to the first few pages, hoping maybe the Canon of Ethics was in the beginning of all the books. *No such luck. Most likely it was in one from the 1800s, probably when it was first established.*

I checked my cell's clock. It was a little past eight thirty. *Two movies and pizza? That had to take at least three and a half hours.* Which meant I should have until nine thirty. I turned around and pulled the chair out from the desk so I could open the top drawer. I sifted through it, looking for a key to the file cabinets, but instead I found a set of flash cards and two folders rubber-banded together.

Flash cards? Curious, I picked them up and turned them over. On top was a blue star. I went to the next. It showed a red ball. I went through them rapidly, finding drawings of different shapes in assorted colors. Pretty simplistic flash cards for a gang of high IQs. But there was something familiar looking about them . . .

I remembered a TV show I had seen where they were investigating psychics—they had used cards like this to test people with ESP abilities. *Okaaay . . . Cue the* Twilight Zone *theme now.*

I straightened the cards and returned them to the drawer, then pulled out the folders and removed the rubber band connecting them, setting them side by side on the desk. There was a note paper-clipped to each folder. I tried to decipher the scrawl of the memo that had been attached to the bottom file.

> *Ms. Grier,*
> *These are the last of the folders for this month's*
> *evaluation. Sorry for the delay; these two boys*
> *were hard to pin down. Trent Redford is displaying*
> *some disturbing warning signs. His psychological*
> *test results show his attitude toward both ethics*
> *and power to be a little troubling. His folder needs*
> *to be sent to the board for special consideration*
> *and, possibly, more extensive testing.*
>
> *Sincerely,*
> *Valerie Kramer*

Ms. Kramer? My psychology teacher was doing some kind of weird, secret testing thing? I pulled the note off the folder that had been on top. It was labeled Brody Kincaid.

> *Ms. Grier,*
> *I'm afraid Brody is again exhibiting some of the same*
> *antisocial signs that were first seen after his father's*

death when he was four. He failed to show up for testing appointments multiple times over this summer, and even after he came, Brody was uncooperative. He is emotionally detached, distrustful of authority figures, and obstructive to any attempt to connect with him. Without proper guidance, I worry that Brody's attitude could revert to being as grim as it was after his mother's death two years ago. I think he would greatly benefit from revisiting his therapy sessions. Group counseling with Brody and his legal guardians might also be prudent. While he seems fond of Mr. Carr, I sense there is some tension with Mrs. Carr. Please take this advisement under consideration.

Sincerely,
Valerie Kramer

Even though Graham had already told me that Brody was an orphan, I still felt an overwhelming sense of sadness reading about how Brody's parents' deaths had affected him. I knew how awful it was to lose someone important in your life, and I wouldn't wish it on anyone, but I couldn't even imagine what it would be like to have no family whatsoever.

I opened Brody's file, hoping for some kind of record of what had happened to his parents, but there were only three pages, all dated August 29 of this year. They were meaningless to me, a bunch of numbers with one letter from *A—D* next to them, like answers to a multiple-choice test. I looked back at the file cabinets. *What do you want to bet Brody's permanent file with his whole history is in there?*

I renewed my search for keys, dropping into a squat so I could look in the side drawers.

"Hello, Goldilocks."

My hand tightened around the drawer handle instinctively, my knuckles going white.

Trent was standing on the other side of the desk. His folder was still lying there, out in the open, with the note on top. *He knows I read it.* I forced myself to loosen my grip on the handle, and then I stood up slowly. My feet felt embedded in the floor, like concrete had been poured all around them.

"Looks like you've been doing some snooping." Trent smiled, picking up the paper clip and the advisory note that had been on his file.

I watched Trent warily. After reading Ms. Kramer's note, I was even more uneasy around him than before. He stuck the slip of paper into the front pocket of his jeans, then slid the other note back under the paper clip on Brody's folder. Trent placed the rubber band back around the two folders, Brody's on top, his on bottom. Except now there was no note on Trent's folder.

I took a deep breath. I had to say something, but what? *I decided to break into your secret society's hidden crypt to dig up answers you don't want me to find?* Honesty was probably not the best policy at this point in time.

"I'm trying to cheat on a test," I blurted out. Being turned in to the campus security had to be better than being turned over to "the Council."

"A test?" Trent was so not buying this load of crap.

"For psychology on Monday." At least Trent was in that class with me and we were actually having a test.

"So why aren't you in Ms. Kramer's office, then?" Trent raised an eyebrow.

"I, um, overheard some students talking about a secret psychology office in the library where Ms. Kramer kept her tests and stuff. . . ." I trailed off lamely.

"Um-hmm." Trent pursed his lips, regarding me as if he found me mildly amusing. "And who were these students you heard saying this?"

"I didn't actually see them. I was sort of eavesdropping." That part was mostly true.

"Okay." Trent's cold eyes glittered. "I'll pretend to believe this story of yours for now. And tomorrow after school, when we go to the café at the SAC, you'll have had some time to construct a slightly more plausible alibi."

"The café at the SAC? For, like, a date?" My voice came out all squeaky.

"Yes, a date. Unless you would rather I talk to some of your friends." Trent cocked his head to the side as if he was thinking, his long hair falling across one eye. "Doesn't that Graham guy work in the school office? Maybe he could tell me where you got the library key."

I felt like I couldn't breathe. Trent knew he had me with this.

"Sure." I tried to muster up the brightest smile I could. "Sounds great. But I can't do it tomorrow afternoon."

"Fine. We'll make it Wednesday after school." Clearly he wasn't going to be easily dissuaded.

"All right," I agreed. "I'll meet you Wednesday."

"Wonderful." The self-satisfaction in Trent's voice made me want to rip out his perfectly disheveled hair. "Now, we should get this place back in order, don't you think?"

I nodded silently. Trent put the folders into the drawer and followed me out of the room. He removed the gold key from the bookcase after he pushed it closed. He obviously knew where the key was kept because he headed straight to the front desk and dropped it in the box, then put it back in the drawer. A minute later, I was locking the library door with my stolen keys. I was afraid Trent would try to walk me to my dorm, and I had to get back to Graham's room pronto. I was trying to think of an excuse to get rid of Trent when I heard a man say his name.

"Dad?" Trent spun around. "What are you doing on campus so late?" He instantly sounded less arrogant and more like a child.

I looked at my phone: 9:28. People would be leaving the SAC any minute now. I had to get out of here.

"I could ask you the same thing." Trent's father seemed menacing, standing in the shadows outside the light from a nearby lamp. "Mom said you were here late studying, though it looks to me like the library is closed." His tone was suspicious, which was a little hypocritical, given that he was here skulking around in the dark. "I was getting off work, so I thought I'd offer you a ride home." I couldn't see his dad's eyes in the dim light, but as he turned them on me, I had a feeling they were the same dark, cold color of Trent's. "Of course, if you're busy with your friend, I can certainly understand why you might be reluctant to leave."

I grasped this chance at escape.

"Actually, I have to go back to my dorm to study. I guess Trent and I were both under the same misconception that the library would be open. We just bumped into each other. But nice meeting you." I trotted off before his dad could get a chance to realize he hadn't actually met me. For all I knew, he worked here at Devenish, and I didn't need any more witnesses to where I was tonight.

Once I was out of their sight I ran as fast as I could back to Garrettson. I didn't even bother to take off my shoes when I reached the tile lobby. I closed my eyes tightly as I crossed in front of their housemaster's door. *The old peek-a-boo trick—if I can't see you, you can't see me.* It must have worked. When I opened my eyes again, the hall was still clear. I ran up the stairs, taking them two at a time, and burst through Graham's door.

"Holy shit!" A boy was sitting on the other bed in Graham's room, and at my entrance he jumped to his feet. "What the hell are you doing in here?"

Chapter Eight

I stared back at the guy in almost equal astonishment. *Crap, why hadn't I remembered that Graham had a roommate?*

"Umm . . ." I knew I had maybe five minutes before Graham returned and found me in his room with his stolen ring of keys in my pocket. "I think Graham's mom is sick. Some woman called me and left a hysterical message; I can hardly understand it. Do you know where he is?"

"No. I'm not his keeper." The boy was obviously annoyed.

"His mom could be dying! You should check the bathroom. He might be in there!" I tried not to exclaim *too* loudly; the last thing I needed was for the housemaster to discover me.

"Why would Graham be in the bathroom?"

It was like this guy was trying *to stall me.*

"Because he had chili for lunch. Just go find him."

Finally, he got up and left. I opened the drawer and put the keys back where I'd found them.

"He's not in there." Graham's diabolical roommate had come back before I could leave. "Do you want me to call him?"

"Oh, no. The woman called back and it turns out it was my

mom, not his. And she, um, won the lottery," I improvised. "She was just really excited." A familiar voice was floating up from the sidewalk. I walked over and looked out the window. Graham was home.

How could I avoid running into him now? Could I possibly go out the window? I peered at the lush green lawn below. There *was* a pipe next to the window that I could hold on to. And characters were always going down trellises in movies. Hell, I used to climb my gym's rock wall all the time in L.A. This wouldn't be that different, right?

"Actually . . ." I pushed open the window. "I have a huge crush on Graham, and it would be so embarrassing if he found out I came by. He would probably think I was stalking him or something."

The roommate raised his eyebrows.

"Which I'm totally not. I just got confused, but now I'm not, so maybe we could keep this between you and me. I'd really appreciate it."

"I wouldn't even know what to tell him if he asked." The roommate shook his head.

"Well, then, I'm going to be leaving now." I slung a leg out of Graham's window, ignoring the vertigo that seized me when I looked down.

"You're going out the window?" the roommate asked, appalled.

"I'm on the rock-climbing team." *I was pretty sure Devenish had an indoor rock-climbing wall at the Athletics Center.* "Gotta get all the practice I can, you know." I swung the other leg out and held on to the ledge while my feet searched to find the pipe next to the window. I made contact. "Thanks again," I added before dropping out of sight.

Crap, crap, crap, I chanted to myself as I slowly made my way down the metal pole, bracing my feet against the brick wall. *Maybe I really should take rock climbing here,* I pondered. *It might be a good skill to have if I'm going to be breaking into places all the time.* Finally, I felt soft earth under my feet, and I collapsed onto the ground. A guy who was walking by gave me a strange look as I dusted myself off and ran back to Kresky Hall.

As soon as I got to my room, I changed into my pj's, turned off my light, and slid into bed. The safest thing, I figured, was to pretend I was asleep if Adriana or Toy came by to see how I was feeling. But there was no way I could actually *go* to sleep; I'd probably be up all night going over the things I had found at the library and worrying about whether Graham's roommate would describe me and my bizarre visit.

But, in fact, I fell asleep almost as soon as I closed my eyes and slept straight through the night. The next morning I jotted a few dream fragments down in the green journal, but they were just remnants of old dreams. I read over the entry to see if any of it seemed important, but after deciding it wasn't, I closed the journal and started my morning routine. I was dreading going to breakfast. I couldn't imagine Graham's roommate not telling him about the insane girl who crashed into his room, spouting a wild story, and exited through the window. I certainly would have.

But apparently his roommate was less of a gossip than I was—or perhaps Graham was so cute that the guy just assumed teenage girls invading his dorm room was a regular occurrence—because at breakfast, Graham was the same as always. He asked only if I was feeling better. Though my sickness had been imaginary, my guilt over stealing from and lying to a friend set my stomach churning.

I found it hard to concentrate in my classes. They were different than Monday's classes, and I soon learned that in French they were way ahead of where I was in my old school. Math was more boring than usual, and I couldn't keep myself from daydreaming as the teacher droned on. My thoughts kept returning to the library and what I had and hadn't found out there. I wasn't sure I was any better off now. I couldn't see how the information I had found related to Athena or why she had wanted to come to Devenish.

Later that afternoon, I walked over to the Athletics Center for my first day of swim club. I used to swim almost every day in L.A., and I was looking forward to getting back to it, but I was a little bummed because we didn't have photography on Tuesdays. Which meant I hadn't seen Zach at all.

My swim club teacher turned out to be Mr. Carr, the SAC director whom the headmaster had introduced at orientation— and one of the men I'd overheard in the hospital. I barely suppressed a groan. He definitely had a "rules" guy vibe and was probably the kind of hard-ass coach who would push us to be competitive swimmers whether we wanted to or not. But, as it turned out, Mr. Carr was nothing like that. He was helpful but didn't seem obsessed with improving our swim times or anything.

It felt good to be in the water again—even if it was a pool and not the ocean. The more I swam, the more everything melted away, and soon the muscles in my neck and shoulders started to unknot themselves.

When class was over, Mr. Carr stopped me as I headed toward the locker room. "I'm impressed, Miss Archer. Excellent technique." He smiled, and his friendly brown eyes crinkled up at the corners. "And you swim like you enjoy it. That's important."

"Well, I'm from southern California; I've been swimming all my life."

"Don't suppose you'd consider moving to the swim team," he suggested, the little twinkle in his eyes telling me that he had already figured out how I would probably respond.

"Sorry. I'm not really a 'team person.'" He was so amiable I kind of hated to turn him down.

"Yeah. Well, had to ask. See you next class." He walked off, and I went on to the showers.

As I massaged shampoo into my scalp I watched the soapy water run down my hair, dripping onto my hip. The three red half moons there had interlocked with a new pinkish outline.

It's just a birthmark, I tried to tell myself. *Yeah. Right.* An intricate red pattern that grew daily and looked like an ancient symbol was some kind of late-onset strawberry birthmark? There was something happening to me. I was changing—physically *changing.* I didn't know why. And I couldn't stop it.

All the other girls were gone by the time I got out of my longer-than-necessary shower. It was freezing in the locker room, so I dressed quickly, fastening Athena's bracelet back on my wrist as I walked out to the pool area.

Some of the other swimmers were logging individual practice time, but they must have been on teams because I didn't recognize anyone from swim club. I glanced across to the diving pool and stopped, my eyes on the figure climbing the ladder to the diving board.

It was Zach Redford.

I stood for a moment, watching, as he reached the top of the ladder and walked the length of the board. His lean, toned body was slick with water, his dark hair wet. He paused at the end of the board, positioning his toes, before drawing a slow breath as he raised his arms. With a powerful bunching of his muscles, he jumped, jackknifing into a perfect dive. He broke the water with barely a ripple, and in a few strokes he was at the side of the pool, climbing out, the water sluicing over him.

I realized that I was staring. I cast a quick glance around. Hopefully my mouth hadn't been hanging open. Turning, I walked out of the Athletics Center.

As I left the building, a cold breeze wound its way through my wet hair. Shivering, I picked up my pace. I needed to get back to the dorm. While I didn't have firm plans, as I had told Trent I did, Toy had said that she would drop by this afternoon to set up my Devenish computer network—that was provided, of course, that the laptop my dad had promised me had arrived.

When I got back to the dorm, I found a note taped to my door:

A package was delivered for you. It's in my room.
—Ms. Moore

I gave my dad a quick call to say thank you, but as usual he was in court helping some rich person get richer. Mom said she would relay my thanks, but she sounded so spaced out that I kind of doubted that Dad would get my message.

I shook off the gloom that came with trying to talk to my parents and went down the hall to Ms. Moore's. I ripped the UPS box open before I even made it back to my room. A new MacBook. I set the laptop on my desk before pulling open the desk drawer that held my iPod.

I took care of the most important thing first: installing my music onto the computer. Firewalls and Office programs could wait. I turned the Pixies up as loud as I dared with Ms. Moore down the hall. *Doolittle* vibrated through the computer's speakers as I pulled my things out of the moving boxes. It took me a minute to hear the knocking over my music.

I pulled open the door to find Toy standing there.

"Did you get your laptop in yet?" She adjusted the black messenger bag slung over her shoulder.

"Yep. Come in." I turned down my music so we wouldn't have to shout over it. Toy settled herself at the desk.

"It'll only take me a minute. I'm the fastest tech they have." Toy smiled. "If they counted the number of computers set up instead of the hours worked, I would be golden. Well, except for the fact that I don't get paid."

"Isn't that some kind of child labor law violation?" I joked, lying down on my bed.

"Not when you're part of an after-school computer club that volunteers to do it. We're all geek-tastic," she laughed. "Though I have to say, I think I've even managed to freak out some tech-connect guys with the breadth of my knowledge. My mind borders on the morbid."

Maybe Toy would know some stuff that could help me. I sat up. "Hey, I wanted to talk to you about something. . . ."

"Yeah?"

"I stumbled onto that old cemetery behind the hospital when I was exploring. Graham said you had checked into it."

Toy eyes lit up. "Yeah. It's what got me interested in that strange epidemic they had here in the 1700s."

"What was so strange about it?" I prodded.

Toy pulled her knees up to her chest, wrapping her arms around them. "Well, only the original settlers recovered from the disease; all the people who weren't from Derbyshire, England, died."

"How'd you figure that out?"

"I went to the museum in town—"

"There's a museum in Shadow Hills?" *Wow, I could rule out a career as a detective.*

"Just a little one right off the square. They have the list of original settlers, and then later tax rolls. All I had to do was compare the names."

"Are a lot of those names still here?" I asked. "I mean, are the townies descended from those people who survived the epidemic?"

"I'm not sure. Well, the Redfords are; I remember noticing their name. And the Blackwells . . . and the Westfields." Toy frowned. "Yeah . . ." She shrugged. "I guess a lot of the students from town *do* have the same last names as the original settlers. I hadn't thought about that, but it's kind of unusual, isn't it?"

"It would be where I come from, but in L.A. everybody is from somewhere else." I paused. "Did you find out anything about what caused the epidemic?"

Toy turned back to the computer. "No. I'm assuming it was influenza or something like that. If it had been smallpox or the bubonic plague, they would have recognized it."

"I wonder why the people from Derbyshire survived and the others didn't."

"Superior immune systems, maybe?" Toy offered.

"Do you think it might have been genetic?" I thought of the charts I'd seen in the archives room. "Like they had a mutation that made them able to fight off the disease?"

"I know there are mutations that make people more prone to a certain disease—like the breast cancer gene—I guess it's possible one could make you able to withstand a disease."

"So if they stayed here and had kids with other survivors, the gene would probably become more dominant," I theorized. "And their immune systems, or whatever, would get even stronger."

"Seems likely." After a minute, Toy sat back in the chair. "Okay. I'm all done here."

"Thanks." I followed Toy toward the door.

At the doorway, she turned back to me, frowning. "But you know . . . the thing is, if the Derbyshire people had a gene mutation, I don't think that it made them healthier than other people. When I was looking up info on the epidemic, I went to the cemetery in town, the newer one. And what was really weird about it was that all the death dates weren't that long after the birth dates. Even the recent graves. Hardly anybody in Shadow Hills lives past the age of forty."

As I closed the door behind Toy all I could picture was Zach lying cold and waxen in a wooden box. Dead long before he should be.

I sat down at the computer. Brevis Vita Alliance—the organization I'd found mentioned in the archives room—had been on my mind all day. It looked like Latin to me, and though I hadn't taken Latin, I'd absorbed enough of it through vocabulary lessons that I was pretty sure that the word "vita" meant life. "Brevis" I wasn't so sure of, but based on the sound of it, I had an icy suspicion about what it meant, too.

I clicked on a translations site and typed in "brevis vita," changing it from Latin to English. I had been hoping I was wrong, but there it was right in front of me. The meaning of "brevis vita." Short life.

I sat back in my chair, losing interest in looking up anything else. If I was right, then the Derbyshire settlers and their descendants survived the epidemic because of a gene mutation and that gene mutation produced some extraordinary talents in the people of Shadow Hills. But it was looking as though the descendants were paying a high price for it.

N N N

I spent most of Wednesday afternoon dreading my impending meeting with Trent. In psych class he watched me with a fascination that severely creeped me out. As annoying as it had become to see the townies read their textbooks at the speed of light, I wished Trent would join in with them. At least then he couldn't stare at me. After I finally escaped psychology, the rest of the school day seemed to fly by instead of dragging on like it had for the first two days. Swimming let out far too soon, and since the diving team didn't practice on Wednesdays, I couldn't postpone my fate by hanging around to gaze at Zach.

I decided not to change before heading over to the SAC. While I didn't want to be the über-dork who wore her school uniform outside of class, I also didn't want to make my meeting with Trent look any more like a date than it already did.

When I wandered into the SAC about five minutes late, Trent was already at the coffee counter waiting for his drink. *Ordering without your date, that's gentlemanly.*

"Hey, Goldilocks, sorry I didn't wait for you, but it's not something I'm accustomed to doing." His mouth curved into a smile, but his eyes were flat.

"Don't worry about it."

I ordered a nonfat latte and a bran muffin from the girl behind the counter. She had curly blonde hair and was dressed in way too much pink, including a pink watch with pink rhinestones around the dial. She was gazing at Trent with a dreamy expression that made me want to gag.

"Do you want to sit outside?" I asked. I didn't think I would be able to eat with this girl making googly eyes at Trent. *Didn't she see the sleaze that practically dripped from him?*

"Okay," Trent agreed, casting a glance at the girl. "I hate it when they do that," he added as the door closed behind us. "Just stare like I'm royalty."

"Who?" *Did the girls at Devenish really think Trent was that hot?*

"Scholarship kids," Trent answered, sitting down at one of the small patio tables. Reluctantly, I took the seat across from him. "They think they can fool us with their fake Rolexes and Coach knockoffs, but I can spot them a mile away."

I was having coffee with the devil incarnate. *Lovely.*

"I was thinking about what happened in the library—" I began.

"Were you able to concoct a better excuse?" Trent interrupted me.

"Nope." I shook my head. "I'm sticking with my original story."

"That's too bad." Trent took a sip of his coffee. "I figured you were more creative than that."

"Guess not. Anyway, it occurred to me that you snuck into the library, too. Granted, I did the 'breaking,' but there is no doubt you participated in the 'entering.' And I figure that the headmaster might be rather interested in that little memo you stole, as well. As for Graham . . ." I arched one eyebrow at him. "Who do you really think he's going to believe when you tell him this wild tale about his keys? You or me?"

Trent's eyes darkened until they were almost black. My heart beat loudly in my ears.

"It seems we have ourselves what they call a Mexican stand-off."

"How PC of you."

"Please. Don't go all California on me, Goldilocks."

I gazed steadily back at him.

Quickly, Trent shifted gears, leaning back in his chair and folding his hands over his torso. "Go ahead and ask me."

"Ask you what?"

"You obviously want to know something, or else you wouldn't have been sneaking around the library Monday night. So ask. It's possible I'll even tell you the truth." A self-assured smile spread across Trent's face.

I took a sip of my coffee, giving myself a moment to think. I had considered questioning Trent about my theories. But I was pretty sure that any answer I got from him would be unreliable at best—especially given the fact that he was *offering* to give me information. I decided to stick with my story and ask some innocent questions.

"What is that hidden room for? It's hard to imagine they would go through that much trouble to hide a psychologist's office."

"It was originally a bomb shelter. They're scattered all over campus, but most of them have been vacant since the Cold War ended. The one in the library they turned into an archives room. The books in there are priceless. Which is why they keep the room on a need-to-know basis."

It actually sounded plausible, and if I trusted Trent the tiniest bit, or if I hadn't found the notes about the "testing," I might have believed him. But I didn't.

"What's the Council?"

"A bunch of imperious tyrants who are under the misconception that they can control anyone they want."

Before I could ask him to elaborate on just who and what they wanted to control, Trent went on. "But now that I've answered your questions, I think it's only fair you answer one of mine." Trent raised an eyebrow, as though he thought I had some idea what he was talking about.

"Which question would that be?"

"I faintly remember requesting the pleasure of your company at the back-to-school dance."

"Oh, that." I wasn't going to let this guy blackmail me into another date. He wouldn't tell anyone about the library when he risked incriminating himself. Trent was definitely the self-preservation type. "You know, I think I'm going solo to this one. I'm still getting to know people, and it will give me more of an opportunity to be social."

"Let me get this straight." Trent's eyes bored into me. "You are turning *me* down?"

"I'm not turning you down, exactly; I'm just not accepting your offer."

His eyes were darker than coal again, and I could see the muscles of his jaw moving as he gritted his teeth.

"That's what I get for trying to be charitable." Trent's smile was as warm as dry ice. "I really should thank you. Now I can take someone who is worthy of being on my arm." His knuckles were white where he was grasping the sides of the little metal table in front of me. He leaned in so close to me I could feel his hot breath on my face, smell the pungent coffee scent of it.

"If you *ever* mention a word to anyone about that note on my file, there will be hell to pay." He stood up, pushing back his chair violently. As the metal legs scraped across the concrete, sparks shot out from where Trent's hands still gripped the table. "You get me, Goldilocks?"

My mouth became parched. I nodded silently.

"Good." Trent strode angrily toward the parking lot, triggering the alarms on several cars as he passed by. Climbing into a black Maserati, he slammed the door and roared off, leaving the cacophony of competing car alarms behind.

Chapter Nine

It had probably not been a great idea to piss off a guy who could shoot sparks from his fingertips. But it was too late to change it, and anyway, I was sure I wouldn't act any differently even if I had a chance to do it over. I wasn't big on letting people bully me.

I stood up and tossed my half-drunk coffee in the trash. The ID bracelet on my wrist caught the sun, glinting as if to remind me what I was doing all this for. I smoothed my finger over the engraved infinity symbol. I couldn't see how Athena had anything to do with the townies or their strange powers. It felt like I was getting nowhere, like I was failing her. I hadn't come any closer to finding out why she had wanted to come to Devenish. But frankly, right now I was getting tired of all the weirdness. Maybe I'd go hang out with Adriana for a little while and do something girly, like paint my toenails. Though what I really needed to do was devote my evening to studying if I hoped to keep a decent GPA.

When I got back to the dorm, I changed into a pair of faded black jeans and a black T-shirt. The outfit was fairly drab—which suited my mood—but I added my red flats for a pop of color. Then I went next door to Adriana's and found her deep in the study of a new *Elle* magazine. That looked like more fun than painting my toenails, so we spent the next hour inspecting the clothes and trashing the styles we didn't like.

When I returned to my room later that evening, I changed into my pj's for my study session. As I pulled on my pajama pants, I couldn't help but notice that the mark on my hip had grown. Again. Already. This was getting too creepy. The symbol was now outlined by a perfect ring. The whole thing seemed too symmetrical to be a rash, but I couldn't imagine what else it could be. *Maybe I ought to go to the infirmary tomorrow and have them look at it.*

But I didn't want to. I hated doctors with their needles and throat swabs. And I had the distinct feeling that this thing wasn't really a medical condition. I decided to ignore it for now; I was determined to actually get some studying done tonight.

I got my French book out first. It was what I was worst at, so it seemed best to get it over with. An hour was as much as I could take of that, though, so I traded it out with the psych book. When I wasn't being scrutinized by my old shrink, and now Trent, psychology was actually really interesting. It was also easier to learn when I wasn't having to scramble to try to take notes at the speed of light.

By the time ten-thirty lights out rolled around, I'd read the first five chapters of my psychology textbook—more than our teacher had assigned us for the whole week.

This didn't help me much the next day since we didn't have psych on Thursday, and I felt even more behind in my classes than I had before. By the time I made it to swimming, I was itching to get in the pool and work off my nervous energy and pent-up frustration.

I felt more awake and alive with each lap. Soon my muscles were pulsating with energy. Mr. Carr gave us the option of doing some racing at the end of class, just for fun, and I came out with the best times. After swim club was over, I was so buzzed from exercise endorphins that I decided to practice longer. Most of the other students staying late were actually on teams and kept to themselves. It was kind of nice to be around other people without having to make conversation.

The rhythm of the laps, the continuous low hum of the underwater lights, the burning in my legs—all of it lulled me into an almost hypnotic state.

When I finally climbed out, there was no one left in the room except for Zach, who was working on his high dive. He gave me a wave when he saw me, and I sat and watched him for a few minutes while I drank from my water bottle. Zach's form was perfect, and though he was large—at least six foot four and leanly muscled—he was very graceful. There was no doubt in my mind that he was Devenish's lead diver. If I hadn't been so tired from all my laps, I might have stayed to see if I could spot any imperfections in Zach's style. Any tiny detail out of place. It didn't seem possible for a person to be so flawless at something.

But I had the feeling that I would pass out from exhaustion soon. I headed to the women's locker room. It was empty and so quiet that it reminded me of the stone silence of a mortuary.

I stood under the hot rush of water, letting my mind drift. I thought about Zach—his wavy hair, how it curled up when it was wet, the black tendrils falling over his forehead and almost obscuring his thick, dark eyebrows . . . his strong powerful body and the intense control with which he moved it. It was strange how connected to him I felt, even though we'd spoken only a few times. For the past year, I hadn't been interested in anyone—and now I found myself daydreaming about Zach constantly. Was I just finally coming out of my emotional deep freeze, or was there really something between us?

As I washed out my shampoo, I looked down at the spot below my left hip. The mark had been growing so quickly I was scared that in the next day or two I was going to discover that my entire torso was covered in an elaborate red pattern. Like waking up after a drunken night out with Angelina Jolie and her tattoo artist. The mark wasn't nearly that large, but its newest transformation was almost as alarming.

In the middle of the symbol there was a small circle. At the center of that inner ring was a wheel-like shape with six spokes that reminded me of the curved kind of throwing star. I didn't know why, but I was positive that the mark was now complete.

For a second I felt like I was going to faint. I decided to forgo the conditioner. I was so tired that I could barely keep my eyes open—not a good state to be in when trapped in a tiny room made of hard tile and glass. I figured getting out into the cooler air might help, but as I pulled my uniform from my locker and put it back on, I could tell the haziness in my head was getting worse instead of better. *Was I sick? Maybe I had a fever.*

"Persephone . . ."

I whipped around, almost losing my balance. *Had someone just whispered my name?*

But there was no one there. I was completely alone.

I made myself concentrate on the task at hand. Getting dressed was taking way too much effort—all I could think about was how nice it would feel to rest awhile. Once I got my uniform back on, I sat down on the bench that ran in between the rows of lockers. I started pulling on my shoes, but even that little bit of effort was too much—all I wanted to do was to go to sleep.

"So sleep," a genderless voice echoed through my mind, and fighting my better judgment, I reclined on the bench.

Soft muted sounds swirled around my head. I could tell I was on the edge between waking and dreaming. There was a roaring in my mind, and I drifted further down into the darkness.

Then I was awake again, no longer in the locker room. I was on my small dorm mattress under the soft glow of a moonlit sky. Whipping around on my bed, I looked for the plain wood headboard, but instead I found a gravestone. It was as tall and wide as the twin bed, and it read REBEKAH SAMPSON. I was outside in the hospital graveyard. I closed my eyes in the hopes that when I opened them, I would be safe and sound back in the locker room. This, however, was not the case. When I opened my eyes, I was still in the graveyard—but I was no longer alone. My sister stood at the foot of the bed. Her blonde hair was wet, her skin blue and peeling, her eyes covered in a thick white film.

"Athena?" I whispered. She looked right through me.

"She cannot hear you." Another woman appeared at the end of my bed. She wore a plain cotton nightgown, and her incredibly long blonde hair was braided into one thick plait running down her back. "She is too new. She doesn't know how to communicate yet."

"Who are you?" I asked. The woman's features were strong and attractive, and her resemblance to Athena was unsettling. I stared at the silver pendant that lay against her chest. It was the same symbol that was now on my hip.

"Who *are* you?" I asked again, more insistently.

"You would not know me. You have not been made ready," she answered. "I am here to warn you. I feel it is the least I can offer after everything I have done."

"What did you do? Why am I here?" I felt the hysteria rising up in me, tasting like bile on the back of my throat.

"This is your place. The birth of your spirit, the land of your death. Trust your instincts, but do not let your guard down."

The bed began shaking, and I looked over the edge to find the earth cracking, splitting open.

My sister and the other woman were gone when I looked up again, and I knew I had to escape the graveyard. I rolled off the bed and dropped down to the ground. The earth started quaking again, this time more violently, and I crawled as fast as I could, glancing behind myself every few seconds to make sure no one was following me. Then I was falling. Farther and farther down I went, landing hard at the bottom of a grave.

I clawed desperately at the soft dirt walls surrounding me, trying to get out. Dirt flew into my face, burning my eyes and nostrils.

I tasted the thick, acrid, ancient flavor of the ground. Smelled the vinegary tang of death . . . moldy, putrid decay . . . other things I had never known had a scent. The moist, stomach-turning odor of earthworms. My lungs filled with it until I was coughing, choking. Even so, I kept digging, trying to find a root, anything to grab onto. If I could just get a firm grasp on something, I could pull myself up out of this mess I had fallen straight into. But I was making no progress, no difference. *I'm going to die here.*

And then my frantically pawing fingers touched something solid. I grasped and pulled with all my might. Slowly it came free of the earth. The thing was thin and cylindrical and brown. *Was I holding an ancient bone?* Filled with revulsion, I almost dropped it, but then I realized that it was made of wood. A cane. My hand trembled as I turned it right side up so that the wooden knob on the end was facing me. I knew what was on it before I looked. Carved into the top of the cane was the same circular mark I had on my hip.

A banging noise was coming from somewhere, and I could hear a voice as well, but it was distant and tinny, like I was listening to it through a can on a string. I tried to open my eyelids, but they felt like they were made out of lead.

"Are you dressed?" It was Zach.

"Yeah . . . ," I answered sluggishly.

"I'm coming in," he warned. I smelled the comforting woodsy scent of Zach as he pulled me up off the floor. I was like a rag doll in his arms.

"Persephone? Phe?" He swept a lock of hair back from my face and my skin tingled where he had touched me. *"Phe."* He was more insistent now. "Phe. Look at me." I opened my eyes finally, and Zach's face swam into view. "Are you okay?"

"Kinda groggy."

"What happened?" He watched me with concern.

"I don't know." I shook my head and a ripple of nausea hit me. *Not a good idea.* "I was showering . . . and maybe I was dehydrated or something. I started feeling really tired so I lay down on the bench for a second and I must have fallen asleep. Then I guess I rolled off onto the floor."

"You decided to take a nap on the locker-room bench?" Zach looked at me like I was crazy.

"Yeah," I answered. "Um, I'm feeling better now." I shot a pointed look at Zach, who was still holding me. Not that I really wanted him to let me go, but it was hard to think with my body pressed against his.

"Oh . . . Yeah." Zach set my feet down on the floor but held my shoulders for a second to see if I was steady enough to stand on my own. Apparently I passed the test. He released me and stepped back a pace.

"We should get you to the infirmary." Zach's expression was unyielding. "Passing out isn't normal."

None of this was normal. The dreams had been bad enough, but now I was having . . . visions.

"I'm all right now," I hastened to assure him. "Really."

He looked doubtful.

"I don't have a headache or anything." I felt my own forehead. "No fever. I feel perfectly fine."

Well, that wasn't quite true. I was completely freaking out. But I knew who I had to talk to, the only person who could tell me what the mark was. Sarah. The strange old woman I had met on Sunday. She had called me by the name that had been on a gravestone in two of my dreams now, and there was no doubt in my mind that the cane I had pulled from that wall of dirt was identical to hers. I hadn't seen the carved symbol on it before, but my instincts told me that it was there.

"Is there a bus that goes into town?" I asked.

It took Zach a second to register my abrupt change in topic.

"Yeah." He looked at me quizzically. "There's one that leaves right after athletics, but that was about forty-five minutes ago."

"Shit," I muttered as I chewed on my thumbnail.

"I'm taking Corinne's car over to our dad's shop to pick up a book," Zach said. "I was actually about to leave when I heard the thump in here." He glanced over at the bench I had fallen off, and I fought down the blush that was rising up my neck.

"Are you coming back to the school later?" I asked hopefully.

"Yeah. I've got to pick up Corinne when she gets out of . . ." Zach frowned in contemplation. "I don't know—whichever one of the after-school clubs she has on Thursdays."

"She's into the extracurricular activities, I guess?"

"All of them except the social ones." Zach smirked. "I can get you back here in an hour if you want to ride into town with me."

"That would be perfect." I bit my bottom lip, trying to pin

down the wide smile that wanted to spread across my whole face.

Zach had changed into his regular clothes while I'd been having my weird episode, and he was gorgeous in his plain white T-shirt and dark-washed jeans. The ordinariness of the outfit emphasized just how un-ordinary Zach was, with his striking bone structure, his hypnotic eyes, and his commanding stature.

As we walked out to the car, I noticed that everything was more still and yet somehow more alive than ever before. The crunching of fallen leaves beneath my feet sounded clearer, louder. The brilliant green of the grass was heightened. The rays of light falling on my skin were brighter, but somehow softer. Now that I was with Zach, the terror that had gripped me in the locker room was rapidly fading. But I needed to know what that dream had meant. I had to talk to Sarah.

"This is it." Zach rubbed the back of his neck as we approached the black Jaguar. I had noticed him rubbing his neck like that before when he was nervous. It was like Zach didn't want to draw attention to himself with anything as showy as Corinne's car.

He unlocked my door and opened it before going around to the driver's side. *That's definitely a first,* I thought to myself as he started the engine. Zach had this old-school gentlemanly quality that I'd never encountered before. If any other guy did that kind of thing, it would be stupid or fake, but with Zach it seemed natural.

It occurred to me that this would be the perfect time to ask him about the stuff that I'd found out in the library. I'd been wanting to run some of my theories by him, but it was hardly the kind of thing we could discuss in photography class.

The car started up with a rich purr, and the radio came on at the same time. I couldn't help but laugh as Vanessa Carlton's voice came blasting out of the speakers.

"Interesting music choice," I teased.

"It's my sister's CD. Thankfully, she lets me borrow it on occasion." Zach gave me a sly grin to let me know he was kidding, then ejected the CD and put in a Les Savy Fav disc.

"Pretty sophisticated taste for a small-town boy," I said flirtatiously. Inside, I was working to keep my cool. He was beyond gorgeous, but not in a studied way like Trent. And even if Zach didn't seem to know how hot he was, I certainly had noticed.

"Well, we small-town folks do what we can to find out about new bands. But it's hard when all the radio stations in Shadow Hills only play Frank Sinatra and Billie Holiday."

"Point taken," I laughed.

"So how are you enjoying our tiny backward village?" Zach asked.

"It's okay," I allowed. "Once they get those outhouses put up, we'll really be living the life."

"Indoor plumbing's just a bit too advanced for us, I guess."

We joked back and forth, making small talk—that was a lot more fun than small talk is ever supposed to be—until Zach pulled the car into a space in front of the Book Stop. I still hadn't asked him anything that I'd meant to, but the conversation had been flowing so well that I hadn't wanted to interrupt it. *I'll be more focused on the way back.*

"I'm only going to be a few minutes," Zach said as we got out of the car. "Where do you want me to meet you?"

"I'm going over there." I pointed at the sign for Sarah's Boutique.

"Okay. See you in a bit."

As I started toward the store, the cold fear I had felt in my dream gripped me again. I steeled myself and entered the dimly lit shop. Sarah looked up.

"I've been waiting for you to come again." Her eyes were sharp and bright, peering out of her worn face.

"You have?"

Why was some old lady waiting for me, a total stranger, to show up? Why was she acting like she knew me?

"How could you possibly know I would be back?" I demanded.

"It was foretold to me long ago," she answered sagely.

"What do you think this is? The second coming of Christ?" I couldn't control the rising tenor of my voice. "I'm just a girl from the boarding school."

Sarah took a deep breath, then stood up from her chair. Walking haltingly on her cane, she made her way around the front desk to where I stood. Every grain of wood in her cane—every bend and knot—was exactly as I had seen it in my dream, but her hand was covering the top. Still, I knew what symbol was underneath.

"If you are just some girl . . ." She blinked at me and cocked her head to the side, reminding me of a crow. "If you haven't experienced anything unusual . . . why are you back here? Looking for answers?"

I opened my mouth, then closed it again. Now that I was here, I didn't know what to say. I was operating on the idea that my dreams were somehow prophetic. Were they really? There was only one way to find out.

I unzipped the side zipper on my skirt. I felt horribly strange and embarrassed. Exposed. Sarah's hand flew to her mouth as the mark on my hip came into full view. Quickly, I yanked the zipper back up.

"What is it?" I tried to keep my words steady, but my whole body was shaking.

"You are the one." She made her way back to her chair and sank into it. Her smile was wobbly, her eyes shiny and wet. Sarah laid her walking stick across the desk, and gingerly I picked it up. It was made out of a single piece of wood and carved into the top was the symbol. My symbol.

An image flashed in my mind: the pendant necklace and the woman who'd worn it in my dream.

"Who is Rebekah Sampson?" I asked Sarah.

"She was a very dear friend of mine. She was the one who told me that someday you would come."

"Can I speak to her?" I set the cane back down on the desk like a peace offering to Sarah. I wanted so badly to talk to this woman, the one who might have the answers I was searching for. Answers to questions I didn't even know how to ask.

"She has been gone for a very long time now." Sarah slid open a drawer on the desk and pulled out a heavy book. She placed it in my hands. "But she wanted you to have this."

I wondered if this was why Athena had been drawn to Devenish Prep. Maybe she was the one this woman was expecting. Maybe it wasn't me at all.

The ancient book had a wraparound cover that looked like a large leather envelope with a tie closure. The brown leather was thick and mottled with age. I traced my finger over the emblem that had been carved into the cover. It was the same mark I had on my body. Excitement began to rise in me. Could the answers to my questions all be in this old book?

"Rebekah always told me it was meant to be with you." Sarah nodded at the book. "You belong to it, and it to you."

"The symbol?" I let my unfinished question hang in the air.

"It is Hekate's Wheel."

"Hekate's Wheel." I repeated her words under my breath. It felt as if they'd rolled off my tongue many times before. "But I don't understand. What does it mean? Why did you say that I was 'the one'? The one for what? And why—"

Sarah held up her hand, smiling kindly. "I'm sorry. It's not my place. You must be patient. It will all be revealed to you eventually."

"But—" I began in frustration.

The sound of the front door swinging open startled me, and the shaft of outside light that now fell across the room was blinding. I shifted the large book to one arm so I could shade my eyes with the other hand.

"Hey." Zach was looking in, smiling at me expectantly. "You ready?"

"Yeah." It was obvious that I wasn't going to get anything else out of Sarah. But at least I had the book. I shoved it into my backpack and started toward the door, then turned back. "Thanks."

She gave me a nod, and I walked out of the store.

"Did you get what you needed?" Zach asked.

"Yeah. I think so," I assured him with a smile.

"Do you mind if we make another stop before we go back to Devenish? My dad wanted me to check on my grandfather."

"Sure."

Zach drove past the square and turned onto a road I hadn't noticed before. We passed several large, dignified houses on expansive plots of land before turning onto a tree-lined drive. Though Zach drove slowly over the loose gravel road, the ride was still rather bumpy. Once it jostled me so much that my shoulder came into contact with Zach's. It felt very intimate, even through our clothes, and I turned to look out my window so he wouldn't see me blush.

The building at the end of the drive had a circular central hub with three wings coming off it, and though it was in the same dark brick as much of the rest of Shadow Hills, it reminded me strongly of the nursing homes I'd seen in Los Angeles. As Zach pulled into the unpaved parking area on the right, I glanced at the sign next to the front entrance. OAKHAVEN ADVANCED CARE FACILITY.

How old was Zach's grandfather, anyway? His dad had looked pretty young to me—certainly younger than mine. I would have figured that Zach's grandfather would be in his early sixties—not exactly "advanced care facility" age.

Zach got out of the car, then stopped and looked at me. I'd already grabbed my purse, getting ready to go in with him, when it dawned on me that maybe he was expecting me to wait here.

"You don't have to come in if you don't want." Zach echoed my concerns.

"I don't mind." I was stuck awkwardly standing with one foot out of the car. "I mean . . . unless you don't want me to."

"I didn't mean that." He smiled.

We were halfway to the entrance when the front door of the building opened and two men and a woman emerged. Zach stiffened beside me. Curiously, I glanced from him to the group outside the nursing home.

One of the men looked over. Upon seeing us he hesitated, then said something to his companions. The woman nodded and slipped her hand through the second man's arm, leading him away toward the cars on the far side of the lot.

The man who was now coming over to us seemed strangely familiar.

"Zach. Good to see you."

"Hello." Zach's tone was just short of rude, which made me wonder even more who this was.

He looked to me to be in his thirties. An elegant gray suit draped perfectly over his trim frame. With dark blond hair and refined features, he was handsome in an uninteresting sort of way. He shook Zach's hand briskly, then turned to me.

"And who is this lovely young lady?" I could tell from his smile that he thought he was charming, but there was something calculating in his gaze. Maybe it was Zach's attitude toward him influencing me, but I already had a feeling that I wouldn't like this guy.

"Aren't you going to introduce us, Zach?"

"Phe, this is my uncle, Trent Redford III," Zach said with some reluctance. "Uncle Tripp, this is Persephone Archer; she's a student at Devenish."

Oh. When Trent and I had locked up the library after our little break in, this was the man who had come up to us. What if he said something about that now, in front of Zach? At the very least, it would sound like I had some interest in the cousin Zach obviously hated. I crossed my fingers that it had been dark enough that he wouldn't recognize me on sight. And hopefully Trent hadn't told his dad my name after I'd bolted.

"That uniform makes it pretty easy to identify you kids." He smiled as he said it, but that didn't make my worries recede. So he hadn't given me away yet, that didn't mean he wouldn't in a minute.

I fiddled with the zipper on the front pocket of my purse.

"It's a pleasure to meet you, Persephone." He reached out his hand, and I shook it as quickly as possible. The shock was so strong that I cringed in pain even though I'd been sure it was coming. I recovered quickly, though, pasting on a tight smile.

"Nice to meet you, too, Mr. Redford." I went back to playing with the zipper. Open, then closed, and back again.

"Please, call me Tripp," he told me.

"Okay." I let go of the zipper pull, realizing the repetitive noise I was making with my purse was probably annoying as hell. I clasped my hands in front of my skirt.

"As beautiful as you are, I'm sure that my son Trent has introduced himself."

"Yes, I know Trent." I forced myself to smile again. Maybe Tripp really didn't have a clue who I was.

"That's wonderful to hear." Tripp acted as if I'd said I adored Trent. He turned once more to Zach. "Coming to visit your grandfather? I think you'll find him in excellent spirits today."

"Really?" Zach's tone was doubtful.

"Good days and bad days, you know," Tripp added, somewhat cryptically.

"Yeah. Well, we should go in." Zach glanced at the hefty black watch he wore. "I've got to get back to Devenish soon so I can pick up Corinne on time."

"You'd better get to it." Tripp raised his eyebrows. "These Redford women can be quite the spitfires when they're irritated."

"Say hello to your parents for me. And Corinne, too, of course."

"Sure," Zach said in a clipped tone. "You ready?" He looked sideways at me, and I nodded.

I wondered if he realized how stony he looked walking away from his uncle without a backward glance. *What was up with this family?*

"Sorry about that. I'm sure you didn't bargain on having to see my whole family when I offered you a ride into town."

"It's okay." I was itching to ask him why the Redford men seemed so distant, even antagonistic, but I couldn't think of any remotely polite way of doing so.

"Uncle Tripp's not as bad as Trent," Zach went on. "I guess that's not saying much, though."

Zach started to speak again, then stopped and finally said, "Has Trent— I mean, have you hung out with him any?"

I shrugged. "Once or twice. I don't think we have much in common."

"So you're not like into . . ." He let the question hang there unfinished.

"Not at all," I answered emphatically.

Zach nodded, looking pleased. A delicious warmth filled me. While jealousy isn't exactly an admirable trait, I couldn't deny that I was happy that Zach didn't want me interested in Trent.

When we stepped inside the elegant lobby, the receptionist greeted Zach by name and directed us toward the rear of the building. "Mr. Redford's in the garden."

"Thanks." Zach led the way to the French doors.

A man shuffled past us, with a nurse at his side. His arms and head shuddered erratically. Outside on the patio, a woman sat in a wheelchair, a sheet bound around her and the chair to keep her upright. She was facing a beautiful rosebush, but she stared past it vacantly, her mouth working as though she was talking. I had volunteered at an advanced care facility for the community service requirement at my old school, and all of it was pretty normal behavior.

What was odd, though, was the fact that none of the patients here were white haired or wrinkled. In fact, just looking at them, I would have been surprised if they were sixty years old.

One woman looked up at me and smiled brilliantly. An instant later, her expression changed to one of confusion, and she sank back against her chair, her fingers picking at the crocheted throw across her lap. I did my best to hide my astonishment. None of these people looked anywhere near as old as my father's parents, who lived in Palm Springs and spent the majority of their lives out on the golf course.

A man with salt-and-pepper hair sat in a wheelchair beside the fountain, basking in the sun, his eyes closed. Even seated, it was obvious that he was a tall man with shoulders that were still broad. I suspected that this was Zach's grandfather, and the resemblance was more striking when he opened his eyes and smiled at us. His eyes were not the same color as Zach's—no one's were—but his smile was much the same.

"Zachary," he said warmly, reaching out to him.

"Hello, Granddad." Zach grinned and took his hand. "You look good. How are you feeling?"

"I'm great. Sit down, sit down." He looked up at me, and his smile faltered. "I—I'm sorry. Have we met? I don't remember your name."

"It's okay, Granddad, you don't know Phe. She's new here."

"Ah." He nodded, but his expression had lost a little of its glow, and I felt bad that I had inadvertently spoiled his mood. "It's nice to see you, Phe. Grant should date more; I told him. Always got his nose in a book, that one." He smiled at Zach.

"I'm Zach, Granddad," Zach told him gently.

"Of course you are, who else would you be? How's school? Must feel nice being a junior, only one more year and you'll have the run of the place."

Zach and his grandfather talked for a while, including me in their conversation when they could. For the most part, Mr. Redford was lucid and spoke eloquently, but now and then he seemed a bit vague, like he had forgotten what he was saying. His left hand, which lay in his lap, had a slight tremor. My chest ached, watching Zach's grandfather. This had to be so hard on their whole family. But at this moment Zach seem elated, and he lingered even after they'd finished covering all the usual topics. I had a feeling this was a very good day for his grandfather.

I wondered what was wrong with him. With all of them. They were too young to be so feeble. And, if Toy was right, these were the lucky ones. The other residents of Shadow Hills had passed away before they reached this age.

I was more determined than ever to find out what was going on in this town.

A few minutes later, after we pulled out of the parking lot of Oakhaven, I turned to Zach and asked in a casual tone, "So . . . what's a Brevis Vita?"

Chapter Ten

"What?" Zach whipped around to look at me, his hand jerked on the steering wheel, and the car swerved into the opposite lane. Hastily, he pulled it back. "Sorry. I—um, what did you say?"

"Smooth cover," I told him sarcastically. "I said, what is a Brevis Vita?"

"I don't know. *Where* did you hear that?"

"I overheard some students say it." I wasn't about to tell him about breaking into the library. I was majorly into Zach, but it seemed a little too soon to start confessing my illegal activities.

"Who said it?"

"I couldn't see them, I just heard them talking. That's not the point."

"I don't know what the point is," he said, watching the road so intently you'd have thought he was afraid it might vanish around the next curve. "How should I know about Brevis Vita?"

"Because you're one of them?" I countered.

"Phe . . . this is crazy. I don't know what you think, but—"

"Okay. I'll tell you what I think. I think that you have some kind of strange energy deal that makes you able to attract metal objects and recharge my iPod with your bare hands."

"Some people naturally have more of an electromagnetic charge in their bodies than others," Zach said evasively. "Some people can't even wear watches because of it."

"And do these same people melt plastic with their fingers?"

He shot me a frustrated look. "I told you—"

"Nothing," I supplied. "Or, at least, nothing that was true. Look, I know that you dreamed the same dream about the graveyard that I did. You as good as admitted it that day at the store."

Zach's fingers curled tightly around the steering wheel.

"And I know that it isn't only you who can do strange things," I pressed on. "Corinne and Trent practically give me electroshock therapy when they shake my hand. Trent also has a little habit of setting off the alarms on cars merely by walking by them, and—oh, yeah—he shoots sparks out of his fingers!"

"He what?" Zach turned to look at me. "In front of you?"

I nodded. "Yes. He grabbed hold of the table outside the SAC, and sparks went flying."

"What a jackass." Zach returned his attention to the road. "Why'd he do it? What happened?"

"He might have been kind of mad," I admitted. "I'd just told him I would rather go to the dance alone than go with him."

Zach let out a short burst of laughter. "I'd like to have seen that." He contemplated this idea for a moment, his lips curved up in a little smile. Then his expression became serious again. "I guess it's a family thing. We have too much electricity in our bodies or something."

"Too much electricity in your bodies? Is that the scientific term for it?"

Zach stayed focused on the road.

"Look," I continued, "I know it's not only your family; it's all the townies. I know about the epidemic. I know that only the settlers from Derbyshire, England, survived it. And you and your family—and several other families—are descended from those same survivors. What I haven't figured out yet is exactly how your ancestors survived the epidemic. But my best guess is it was because they had some kind of gene mutation." Of course, I'd only come up with that theory after seeing all the charts in the secret archives room, but Zach didn't need to know that.

"Phe . . ." Zach let out a groan. "Where do you get this stuff?"

"Once I figured out about the epidemic and the gene mutation, it all started falling into place. How you townies are so smart and can read a book in two minutes flat. How you guys have this crazy electric energy thing happening. Oh, and there's the fact that you have better hearing than a beagle." Zach opened his mouth, but I kept barreling forward. I wasn't going to let him start arguing his point before I'd made mine. "I started thinking—could it be the result of a gene mutation? And what if, over the course of the last two hundred fifty years, marrying other people with the same mutation, these traits got stronger and stronger, until now you townies have developed these superpowers? Like mind reading and walking through people's dreams."

"I don't have superpowers!" Zach exclaimed. "You're being ridiculous."

"I'm being ridiculous?" My voice rose involuntarily. "What about Corinne with her not-so-veiled threats, trying to make me stay away from you? What sister cares that much who her brother dates?" The moment the word passed my lips I wished I could take it back. *Can you say "getting ahead of yourself"?* Sharing a class and a car ride did *not* count as dating. I willed my cheeks not to catch fire. I couldn't let myself be thrown off by some stupid slipup. "What the hell is going on in this town? And don't lie to me—I'm not going to stop looking because you give me some lame excuse."

"I wish you *would* stop, Phe. I think I can trust you, but what if I'm just letting my feelings get in the way? It seems like all logic leaves my head when you're around. It's not smart. For me or you."

"I'm okay with that." I leaned closer to Zach. I watched his Adam's apple move beneath his skin as he swallowed.

"Well, I'm not okay with it," he said, not making eye contact with me. "The people in Shadow Hills aren't easily intimidated, and they've been hiding this stuff for hundreds of years. There are people here who believe we're one nosy person away from being made into government lab rats." Zach shook his head. "I don't know how far some of them would go to protect themselves and their families. We have to be closed off; it's the only way to make sure we stay safe."

"Do you really think I would call the FBI down on you?" I crossed my arms over my chest, waiting for an answer.

"You never can know with people."

"Maybe not, but you *can* trust me. You were right about that." Zach's eyes met mine; the emotions behind them were so intense I had to look away.

"How can I trust you when you obviously don't trust me? When you think I'm some kind of mutated freak?" Zach demanded. "You wouldn't even believe me if I told you the truth—hell, you probably think I'm not human."

"How can you say that?" I stared at him. "Do you think I would get in the car with someone I thought was dangerous? Do you really think I would be asking you all this if I thought you were some subhuman serial killer? God, how stupid do you think I am?"

"I don't think you're stupid." The muscles of Zach's jaw were working under his skin. He let off the accelerator, and the car slowed. "I think you're . . . I don't know what I think. You're different from anyone I've ever met before. You seem incapable of being fake, of being anything other than what you are. You're so free, so authentically . . . you."

I wondered how he could see me so clearly when I felt like I was struggling every day to hold on to some scrap of my own identity.

"It's like you're not afraid of anything." His voice was low, almost a whisper.

"Trust me, that isn't true." Sometimes I was surprised at how well my shell hid me. I felt sure everyone could see right through it to my soft squishy insides. "I'm just not afraid of *you*. I don't believe you could ever hurt me."

"I wish you were right about that." Zach gritted his teeth even harder. "But it's not really me that I'm worried about. *I* don't have to hurt you for you to be in danger. I put you in danger the moment I tell you about us. It's not just my secret. I give away everyone—hundreds of people—if I tell you. And if they find out you know—if you told anyone else . . ." The threat hung there unspoken.

My need to know what was going on—my need to know Zach—overshadowed all of his warnings. Besides, I couldn't actually imagine anyone here locking me up or killing me. These people were highly developed intellectuals, not cavemen.

"So does this mean you're going to tell me?"

"I don't know. Part of me wants nothing more than to walk away from this, to not have to deal with these complications—all the what-ifs—even if that means never speaking to you again."

My stomach clenched. The idea of never speaking to Zach again panicked me. It was irrational, but I couldn't help it. Every second I spent around him made me want to be with him more.

"But there's another part of me, a bigger part than I would like to admit, that can't stop thinking about you." He raked a hand through his hair, but kept his eyes on the road, avoiding my gaze. "I've imagined what it would be like to tell you. To be reckless for once in my meticulously planned life." Zach turned right at the next road and then pulled onto a narrow dirt lane. "And as much as I hate it, that part of me seems to be winning."

He stopped in front of a closed gate and turned off the engine.

"Last chance, Phe—you say the word, and I'll drive you back to school and we can both pretend this day never even happened."

That was the last thing in the world I wanted.

"Tell me," I said simply.

With a curt nod Zach got out of the car. I followed him, and we walked over to the low stone wall that came out from the gate.

"Where are we going?" I asked. "What is this place?"

"I don't know." He shrugged. "The turnoff to somebody's property. I don't want to talk about this in Corinne's car. It's another reminder of how I'm not supposed to be doing this." He paused, then went on, "Listen, I'm serious when I say this is very secret. I'd be in deep shit if anyone knew I told you."

"With the Council, you mean?"

His eyebrows shot up. "And you think *I* have the ability to read minds?"

"Well, do you?"

He sighed. "I wouldn't call it that, but, yeah, sort of."

No wonder he knew me so well; he probably had more insight into my psyche than I did. *And he's still here.* He hadn't decided I was shallow or dumb or emotionally screwed up beyond repair. He liked me—enough that he was breaking rules he'd followed his entire life. Another thought occurred to me. How many times had I imagined what it would be like to kiss Zach? To feel his strong arms around me, his fingers entwined in my hair? God, this was mortifying. *Shit! I'm doing it again!*

"So what would you call it instead of mind reading?" I asked casually, hoping I could somehow cover up all the feelings building like a tornado inside of me.

"I don't call it anything. In fact, I try to do it as little as possible; it's not always good to know how people really feel about you."

I couldn't see anyone thinking something bad about Zach—except maybe Trent.

"But I guess if I had to give it a name," Zach went on, "I'd call it *patchworking*."

"Patchworking?" I raised an eyebrow.

"It's like I get thrown this jumbled mess, and I have to piece it together. I can't direct it or control it; sometimes I can't even make sense of it. I'll get flashes of images but never the whole picture," Zach explained. "Often, I'll just see a flicker of a color or a symbol that stands for a certain feeling. At most I'll get a visual of a memory, but completely out of context. It's not an audio thing at all—I can't hear what you're thinking."

I relaxed a little.

"Besides, I can only do it when I make physical contact with someone," Zach added.

So that's why Trent wouldn't let go of my hand the other day; he was listening in on—or watching, whatever—my thoughts.

"What about the dream thing?"

"I don't know. I've never had that happen before. Really," he added at my look of skepticism. "I couldn't believe it when I saw you in the cemetery that day. That's why I followed you. I thought you just resembled the girl in my dream. But there you were; you *were* the girl."

I remembered the expression on his face that afternoon. He

had looked as amazed as I'd felt. "Okay, I'll buy that. But what about the rest of it?"

"Well, you're on the right track with the gene-mutation thing. But you don't quite have it. First off, our ancestors didn't come from all over Derbyshire, though that's what the Council wants outsiders to believe. They were from the village of Eyam."

Eyam . . . I thought back to the chart I had seen in the library.

"And they had this mutation known as Delta 32," Zach continued. "That's why the Council isn't too specific with our history. The descendants of Eyam are kind of a big deal in the scientific community, and the last thing we need is a bunch of lab coats coming in, wanting to test our DNA."

"But if they already know about the mutation, why would they care if you have it, too?"

"We don't have Delta 32." Zach ran a hand over his face. "I guess I need to give you some background. You know about the bubonic plague, right?"

I nodded.

"Well, it hit Eyam in 1665, and, knowing how badly it spread, they quarantined themselves."

"But wouldn't that be like a death sentence for everyone in the town?" I couldn't imagine doing that. I didn't like being near someone with a cold.

"It would have been, but if people fled, they risked spreading it to the whole area. So they cut themselves off, burying their own dead and living on food that other villages left for them at the edge of town. And even though the plague went on for a year, at the end of it, almost half of the villagers were still alive."

"The mutation protected them," I filled in.

"It seems so, based on the DNA tests they've done of descendants still living in Eyam. The mutation was probably a reaction to some earlier pathogen, and when the plague hit, the people with Delta 32 were immune."

"Is that why they survived the epidemic in Shadow Hills, too?"

"Most likely, but somewhere along the line, the mutation must have changed, because none of the townies have Delta 32 now. Our mutation is different; it carries some very strange side effects."

"Magical side effects?" I teased.

"Not magical, just extremely abnormal." Zach grinned.

"So how does it all work? What makes you like you are?"

"If I knew all the answers, we wouldn't need the genetic research wing of the hospital." I could almost see Zach switch into scientific mode. It reminded me of the way my dad got all authoritative when conversation turned to anything legal. "Apparently we have more myelin than other people, and that allows information to travel between parts of our brain more quickly. We also have more acetylcholine, which is a neurotransmitter that aids in memory."

"So your brain processes everything at the speed of light and you never forget anything," I translated.

"Pretty much. And it also gives us an advantage, hearing-wise."

"Wow, life really isn't fair."

He shrugged. "There are some trade-offs that aren't so good.

BVs do have a stronger electromagnetic field than most people."

"No shit." I smirked. "I can't see how you don't attract more attention going around shocking people all the time."

"We don't shock people all the time," Zach said. "It rarely happens, in fact, and when it does, it's usually nothing more than the amount of static charge you would get pulling a blanket out of a dryer."

I stared at him incredulously. "So why does it hurt me more than the time my hair dryer short-circuited on me? Am I insanely sensitive?"

"I don't really think that's it. Your energy is totally unlike other people's—it's one of the things that's so different about you. It's very strong, but not in an electrical way. Your—I don't know what to call it—life force? Aura? Any word I can think of sounds stupid and New Age-y." Zach scrunched his eyebrows together.

"It's okay, I'm kind of used to it. My mom's a recovering hippie."

"Okay then, I'm going with life force, because it's very pushy. Force seems appropriate."

"How is my energy pushy?" I almost laughed, but Zach's serious expression stopped me.

"Most people's energy is tightly contracted inside them; it only really shows up when provoked, and ours always bests it. But yours is widespread, a shield that's constantly surrounding you, three feet on every side. And it's as strong as ours. Maybe even stronger. When you shake hands with us, it's like . . . well, I guess the best analogy is when you try to put two magnets of the same pole together."

"They pop apart." I didn't like the idea of my energy pushing Zach away. Especially when I felt just the opposite, like I was being pulled to him.

"Not exactly." Zach exhaled. "Let's see if this explains it any better. Imagine you are a car battery, and I'm a car battery. When we touch, it's like the jumper cable connecting us and we both get . . . charged." Somehow it all sounded much more sensual than it should have.

"Your energy is impossible to ignore," he went on. "It's exhilarating for one of us to stand in your . . . space, or whatever. Corinne's noticed it, too, and I have no doubt Trent thrives on the push and pull he gets off of you." Zach's expression went dark.

I thought of the way I always felt sitting next to Zach in photography. "Do you feel like you've had too much caffeine when we're near?"

"Caffeine, alcohol, it's probably like some drugs, too, but I wouldn't know," Zach said. "I have this storm raging in me, yet I'm incredibly centered at the same time. That probably sounds crazy."

"No, it doesn't," I assured him. "I feel it, too."

He looked down at me, and it was as if everything had paused except for us. The birds that had been twittering at the coming nightfall were silent, and the air seemed to be completely still. I wanted to kiss him so badly, to pull him as close to me as possible. But I was terrified. I had never felt this strongly about anyone, not even Paul. What if I somehow ruined everything? What if our energies really couldn't coexist?

"So, uh . . . what other things does your energy effect? I mean, what does it do besides shock the crap out of me?" The words came tumbling out of me, breaking the moment, leaving me both relieved and disappointed.

"Umm . . ." Zach blinked several times like he had awoken to sunlight streaming onto his face. "Well, it transmits our emotions. That's why when we get upset it can disrupt car alarms, TVs, radios." He scratched the back of his neck, breaking eye contact with me. "Or, you know, sometimes it starts small fires," he finished in a rush.

"Like Drew Barrymore in that old Stephen King movie?"

"No." He looked at me as though I was being absurd. "We can't do it by staring at something. We have to touch it."

"Oh, well, that's reassuring," I commented sarcastically.

"Most of us learn to control it as we get older, but sometimes when we get frustrated, we . . ."

"Melt pricing guns?" I offered.

He gave me a glinting look from under his eyelashes, and a rueful smile curved his lips. "Yeah, melt pricing guns. But that only happens when certain very pushy girls start following you around asking a lot of questions and trying to bait you into inviting somebody to a dance."

I laughed. "You deserved it for eavesdropping on Adriana and me."

"And you made me pay for it, too."

I put a hand on my hip in a challenging pose. "As if it would have been that awful to take out an attractive, confident girl."

"Confident?" Zach gave me a look. "That girl is a man-eater. A designer-clad piranha."

"Hey." I frowned at him. "You're talking about my closest friend at Devenish."

"I'm not saying I don't like Adriana; I actually find her pretty amusing. And I can see how she would be the yin to your yang or whatever." He laughed. "But romantically? *She*'s not my type."

Did that slight emphasis on "she" mean that I *was* his type?

He shifted and glanced back toward the car, and I knew that he was ready to end this conversation. I hesitated. I didn't want to ask him my last question; I knew it would be painful for him. But I couldn't stop here. I had to know the rest of it.

"There's another bad trade-off, isn't there?" I asked softly. "Brevis Vita . . . what it means. Short life."

"Yeah." He nodded, not looking at me. "We don't . . . well, we don't get old. It's like the mutation speeds us up—makes us sharper, smarter, but we burn out quickly. It's almost as if we're missing the circuit breaker in our minds. And the researchers can't figure out why we're that way. That's what really spurred all the gene research. They keep trying to find a way to stop it, but so far they haven't. BVs die young." Zach stared at the hard-packed dirt. "And if you don't die, your mind turns on you. Dementia. Nerve ailments. Advanced psychosis. New medicines are helping us to drag it out a little longer now, but I don't really know what's worse. Dying when you're forty or living like my granddad."

I thought of the people I'd seen in the nursing home—how awful it must be for them, to go from being geniuses to being unable to put their thoughts together, sitting in their wheelchairs, shaking and weak.

"That's terrible," I murmured. "I'm sorry."

"I shouldn't have taken you there," Zach said. "It was stupid."

"No. No, I'm glad you did." I looked up into his face. His taking me there had meant something. I knew he trusted me. That single decision, to expose that part of his life, showed he trusted me even more clearly than his confession about the BVs. I really was connected to him now.

He smiled a little, and his hand slid around mine. There wasn't any shock this time, only warmth. Holding hands, we walked to the car.

When we got back to Devenish, it was almost time for dinner. Afterward I went back to my room and locked the door behind me. Getting out the book Sarah gave me, I settled onto the bed. I untied the leather straps on the book's cover and opened it. The pages were thick, yellowed with age, and gilded along the edges. I flipped through the pages in alarm; it was in a different language with a completely different alphabet! I let out a groan of frustration. Sarah had given me a book written in what I could only guess was Greek, and I had *thanked her*. What was the matter with the woman? Now I was right back where I started.

Well, not quite. I knew the name of the mark on my hip. I went over to the computer and typed Hekate's Wheel into Google. And there it was.

Hekate's Wheel

Just looking at it set the little hairs on the back of my neck standing on end.

I read the paragraph below the picture, "This mazelike symbol represents the labyrinth of knowledge. It also represents Hekate's affinity with the number three." *Maybe this explains why my dreams always come to me at 3:33.*

"Her power is triplicate, giving her control over both nature—heaven, earth, and the underworld—and the life cycle—birth, life, and death."

I clicked on a link for the page titled "The FAQs About Hekate."

As I read the section on her origin, I saw that there was some confusion, but the prevailing theory was that she was a Titan who preceded the Olympic gods. And according to this, her realm of powers was vast:

"Hekate is the goddess of witchcraft and spirits, and she is considered to be a dark goddess. It is also said the she sends demons that cause nightmares."

Goose bumps rose on my arms.

I read on, "Hekate could be kind, and she often helped people move from life to the underworld *as she did with Persephone.*"

I jumped up from my chair and started pacing.

Naturally, I'd heard the myth of Persephone. She'd been kidnapped by Hades, god of the underworld; and her mother, Demeter, had blighted the earth so no plants would grow. Eventually, Persephone was allowed to return for all but a few months out of the year. And during the months when Persephone was in the underworld, everything would die again, and that was how winter was explained. But I didn't remember Hekate having anything to do with it.

I returned to the computer and typed in a search for Hekate and Persephone together. A lot of the information was dense and confusing, but as I made my way through it, I came upon something very interesting.

Hekate had helped Demeter by guiding Persephone from the underworld back to earth, lighting the way with her trademark torch. After this, Hekate was the protector of Persephone.

Ever since Athena's death, I had felt as though I was searching for something even though I didn't know what it was. Could it be that I'd been led to Devenish by Hekate? Was I being guided? My dreams always seemed to be trying to tell me something. And I couldn't deny that what I'd read about Hekate resonated with me. I picked up the strange book I'd tossed aside and ran my fingers over the leather cover.

They offered courses in Greek at Devenish; maybe the Greek teacher could tell me what the book said. Luckily, tomorrow was

Friday, which meant we had shorter classes and no electives, to give us time for our advisor meetings and extra study. I had my first advisor meeting with Mr. Sherwood, but after that I could drop by the Language Department.

As I slipped the book under my mattress, I noticed something was missing from my wrist—Athena's ID bracelet.

I panicked. I began to dig through my purse, then dumped its contents out and checked the zippered pockets. They all turned up empty.

I checked the desk drawer, but there was nothing but my iPod.

Okay. Think. So much had happened today. I was pretty sure I'd put on the bracelet this morning. I always did. Swimming—of course. I took it off for swim class and put it in my purse. But I couldn't remember if I had put it back on after I dressed. It had all been so confusing, with that vision and Zach rushing in to help me. I could have dropped it when I was feeling faint, or it could have fallen out of my purse. I wouldn't have noticed it. The odds were it was lying at the bottom of my locker or on the floor of the gym.

I took a deep breath and tried to calm down. There was no reason to work myself into hysterics over nothing. I knew where it probably was. I could just check the next day and find out. But no matter how hard I tried to put it out of my mind, I couldn't shake the fear that I had lost Athena's bracelet forever.

Chapter Eleven

When I woke up the next morning I went to the Athletics Center to look for my bracelet, but it was closed until three for maintenance. I figured if I was going to be forced to wait, I might as well get something done, so when I left Mr. Sherwood's office after my advisor meeting, I cut across the campus to the Language Building.

I checked the directory and headed up to the third floor. The very last classroom had a plaque beside it stating: PAMELA CARR, LATIN AND GREEK.

I peeked through the narrow window in the door. The room was empty except for a small woman seated at the teacher's desk, red pen in hand, skimming through papers. *So this is Mr. Carr's wife*, I thought. She was dressed in a plain gray suit, and with her wire-rimmed glasses and mousy brown hair, she was the very image of a teacher of dead languages.

Tentatively, I knocked on the door, and Mrs. Carr glanced up. She gazed blankly at me for a moment, then waved me in.

"Yes? May I help you?" she asked when I stepped inside the room.

"Hi. I'm Persephone Archer. I'm a junior here. And I have this book someone gave me. I think it's in Greek, but I wasn't sure. I was hoping maybe you could look at it and tell me?"

She raised her eyebrows a little but nodded, reaching out her hand for the book. I pulled off my backpack and dug out the book, handing it to her.

"My," she said softly. "It's quite large." She set it down on the desk and studied it. "And quite old. Where did you say you got it?"

"It was a gift." I wasn't going to tell a complete stranger about my insane interaction with Sarah. "My, um, aunt sent it to me."

"Well . . ." Mrs. Carr opened the book and frowned. "I'm not sure how much help I can be. About the only thing I can tell you is that this is not written in Greek."

"Oh."

"Many of the letters are Greek, but there are some other symbols as well. And the words they form are not any words I recognize. It's not a language I've ever seen." She flipped through a few more pages, pausing at a drawing of a circle surrounded by various little figures. Taking off her reading glasses, she leaned in closely, her nose inches from the page. "Most unusual. You realize that it's handwritten, don't you? Not printed?"

"No. I didn't really look at it that closely." In my disgust at discovering I couldn't read it, I had slammed the book shut without examining it. I peered over her shoulder. It did appear to be a person's printing. It was too uneven, the lines not entirely straight, the ink fluctuating in color.

"And your aunt didn't send any explanation?"

"No. She just said she thought I'd get a kick out of it. She's, um, a little odd."

Mrs. Carr continued to gaze at the book, tapping her fingernails lightly on her desk. "It almost looks . . . well, I don't know, of course, but I am tempted to say that it seems like a made-up language."

I stared at her blankly for a moment, then said, "You mean—a code of some kind?"

She nodded. "I couldn't swear to it, of course. But, yes, it looks rather like a code."

I thanked Mrs. Carr for her time, exiting with the mysterious book in hand. *Great. A lot of good that did.* Breaking some predictable code on a locked box was one thing, but breaking a code written in ancient letters and symbols that mystified even a professor of dead languages? I couldn't imagine how I would ever do that.

It was past three, so I hurried over to the Athletics Center to look for my bracelet. After I checked my locker and the counter where I'd set my toiletries bag, I crouched down to search the floor. Nothing. I asked Mr. Carr if anyone had turned it in. No one had, but he pulled out the lost-and-found box for me to look through anyway. When I saw that it wasn't there, he wrote down a description of the bracelet and my name and cell number just in case it turned up. But it didn't look good.

How could I have been so careless with something of my sister's? I wanted to yell at someone, but the only person to blame was me. The bracelet and the dream journal were the two things I had here at Devenish that had belonged to Athena, and I had the sickening feeling that one of them was now gone forever.

The fact that it was Friday was the only thing that made the whole frustrating day bearable. I was done with my first week of classes. I could hang out with my friends, maybe go to the SAC, take Graham's cocky attitude down a notch by dominating the pool table. Pretend I was a normal girl at a normal school, at least for one evening.

After our group left the SAC that night at ten p.m.—Graham with his tail between his legs, and rightly so, since I'd whipped him in pool five times straight—Adriana and I went back to her dorm room to hang out. Our discussion ran the gossip gamut, with topics ranging from the hottest guys at school—Adriana's vote: Trent and Graham; my vote: Zach and Graham—to the absolute worst-dressed boarding students. (It didn't seem fair to include the townies, since we rarely saw them in anything but their uniforms.) We both agreed that the blonde girl with the pink fixation who worked at the SAC took that honor. Without even realizing it, we managed to stay up half the night talking.

Which was why the next morning Adriana and I were the last ones to make it to breakfast. As I settled in with my plate of pancakes, I saw that Brody was sitting with us.

Brody's eyes were massively red today. I wasn't sure if it was sleepiness or just part of the half-stoned state he seemed to perpetually operate under. It was weird that he and Zach were such good friends. Zach was über-responsible, and Brody had this kind of reckless air about him. Then again, I didn't really know Brody that well.

One thing I was positive of, though, was that he had developed a massive crush on Adriana. He watched her in rapt attention constantly.

"Okay." Adriana clapped her hands together, getting everyone else's attention. "I wasn't sure what you guys wanted to do tonight, but since it's Saturday, I was thinking—"

"Thinking, Adriana?" Graham looked concerned. "You better be careful; you don't want to strain yourself."

"That's funny." Adriana cocked her head to one side. "Especially coming from the guy who got a C on his first physics quiz."

Graham rolled his eyes. "What kind of teacher gives a quiz the first week of school?"

"You know, if you need some tutoring, I could probably carve out a little time for you," Adriana continued. "I did tie for the highest score in the class."

She ducked as Graham threw his napkin at her head.

"So, back to what I was saying," Adriana started again. "I think we should do something fun tonight."

"What are you proposing?" Toy asked.

"I was contemplating the revolutionary idea of a party. What do you guys think?" Adriana asked. "Blow off a little steam?"

"I'm in." The idea certainly appealed to me after the roller-coaster week I'd had. "Although it might be harder with the dorm full now."

"We could have it at the woods spot," Graham offered. "Are you in?" he asked Toy.

"Yeah." She smiled shyly. "What time?"

"How about midnight? Give the dorm heads thirty minutes to go to sleep after lights out?" Adriana offered.

"I'll be there," Brody said. As if that had ever been in question—I had a clear picture in my mind of Brody leaning up against a tree, smoking a joint and being vaguely antisocial. *But there was always the possibility he'd bring Zach.* The thought started my pulse racing.

"Course since it's after hours, probably only boarding students will come," Brody added, bringing my heartbeat back down to a normal pace.

"We don't want everyone and their badly dressed mom there anyway." Adriana picked some invisible lint off her pristine ivory silk blouse.

"As long as you're there, it doesn't matter who else comes," Brody said slyly.

"Not gonna happen, Brody." She stood up with her tray.

"We'll just have to wait and see." He leaned back and cocked an eyebrow at her.

Adriana rolled her eyes, then turned to me. "You going over to the library to study?"

"I can't seem to find any way around it."

"You guys wanna meet up later tonight?" Toy asked before we left the table.

"Sure. Meet at the hedge outside my window?" I grabbed my tray.

"Cool." Toy grinned. "See you at midnight."

N N N

At 11:55 that night, I'd put on my black hoodie and was grabbing my GPS when a sharp rap at my window made me jump.

Toy was standing outside. She gave me a little wave.

"Hey," I whispered after I unlatched the window. "I didn't know you were here already—how long have you been outside?"

"Not long. Don't worry about it."

I swung my leg over the sill. As I dropped down to the soft earth below, I managed to catch the elbow of my hoodie on a branch. After I disentangled myself, I pulled my window closed and followed Toy out of the hedges and around the corner of the building.

"Okay, here are the coordinates." She handed a little slip of paper to me, and I noticed that Toy, like me, was dressed all in black.

I punched the coordinates into my GPS, and it started whirring and making little beeping sounds. I hadn't realized how loud the thing was until now. I pressed my palm against the small speaker, trying to muffle it, but it was too late. I froze, listening to the footsteps behind us, crunching in the fallen leaves. It was probably a teacher. *Being expelled the first week of school will look great on my transcripts.*

"Hey, kids," Adriana said casually as she rounded the corner, carrying a large duffel bag. "Why so freaked out?"

"I thought you were a teacher," I said as quietly as I could, holding my hand to my pounding heart.

"Not that I'd even be able to see you two in your stealthy

robber clothes." Adriana nodded to the black hoodie that hid my blonde hair. "Are we cat burglars now? Or is this just your night-time camo?"

Adriana had, of course, dressed with no regard for the event at hand. Her bright blue silk minidress was not exactly low pro-file. But then again, I wouldn't expect anything less from her.

"There's nothing wrong with wearing something practical," I defended Toy and myself.

"Hey, my shoes are very practical," Adriana insisted.

If you could call suede boots with a wedge heel practical.

"At least they don't have four-inch heels," Toy commented.

"Precisely." Adriana smiled triumphantly. "Now let's get going." As we headed where the GPS was pointing us, I couldn't help but notice the loud clanging of bottles in Adriana's bag.

"I'm guessing that's the booze." I pointed at the cacopho-nous bag.

"Yeah. I didn't want to throw it out my window and break any of the bottles. So I left through the front."

"You carried that bag right past Ms. Moore's door?" I asked.

"You're really not worried about getting caught, are you?" Toy added.

"I don't get caught," Adriana replied coolly.

But even she fell silent as we walked across the deserted campus toward the woods. The expansive open grounds sur-rounding Devenish didn't make it a great place for sneaking out. It was at least ten yards to the nearest tree large enough to hide behind.

Suddenly, I felt a slimy crawling in the pit of my stomach—we weren't alone. I glanced over in time to see a shadowy figure slip into the woods.

My blood turned to ice, and I stopped in my tracks.

"Did you guys see that?" Sharp needles of fear pricked my skin, and I broke out in a cold sweat.

"See what?" Adriana asked, turning in a large circle to look around us. Her mystified expression and the noisy rattle of bottles would have been comical if I hadn't been so petrified.

"It was probably a shadow of a tree branch or something." Toy shrugged.

"But it moved!" I whispered. I was totally freaked out, but I still didn't want to wake up any of the on-campus teachers.

"It could have been the wind." A gust of cool air blew back Adriana's hair as if to illustrate her point.

"Okay," I relented. "But let's hurry up and get to the party spot."

Once we were surrounded by the thick cover of the trees, Toy turned on a little flashlight. It should've been comforting to see where I was going, but it just made me more apprehensive. The tiny beam of light illuminated only the ground directly in front of us, which didn't do much beyond keeping us from stepping in a hole and twisting an ankle. It didn't stop the inky darkness from creeping in all around, and it didn't warn me before an errant tree branch brushed against my neck like cold, sharp fingers.

The path we followed seemed scarcely traveled, though Toy assured us that students had been using it for decades. We continued along, stepping over fallen logs wrapped in the emerald velvet of moss and crossing shallow creeks that were littered with boulders. The sound of the water normally would've been relaxing, but every unexpected noise sent my heart jittering around in my chest.

After almost twenty minutes, we finally arrived at the secluded clearing. I hadn't realized how tense I had become, until I saw the other boarders milling around and I felt my muscles relax.

"You guys made it." Graham got up from where he was sitting, talking to Brody and some other guys I didn't know. He grabbed the duffel of booze from Adriana's hand.

Setting it down, he opened a cooler full of ice next to him and handed us each a Devenish cafeteria cup. After Adriana mixed me a Grey Goose and Sprite, I walked around the small area, checking it out. Students had obviously been dragging rocks and tree trunks over here for years, and now there was a circle of seating around the perimeter of the clearing. There was more than enough room for the fifteen or so people who had shown up tonight, and it was so far from the school that I wasn't worried about the noise reaching back to the dorms.

I looked around for someone to talk to. Adriana was griping to Toy about some problem with her computer, and Graham was chatting with some red-headed jock-type guy.

That was it. Three friends. All occupied. At least in L.A., I'd had acquaintances for when Ariel was busy. I felt a sharp tug of homesickness, mixed with another kind of longing.

I wish Zach was here. I didn't want to be obsessing over a guy I wasn't even dating, but I couldn't help it. I kept picturing the way he'd looked the other day, when it had felt almost like he was going to kiss me.

"Phe!" Graham was walking toward me, his friend a few paces behind him.

"This is George." Graham nodded his head at the jock guy. "He said he wanted to meet the hot new girl from California."

Heat rose from my cheeks all the way up to my hairline.

"Have you seen her around anywhere?" Graham made a show of searching the woods.

"Shut up, dude," George said, punching him in the arm. Judging from the size of George's biceps, I had to imagine it didn't feel spectacular.

"Oh, I see how it is." Graham rubbed his injured shoulder. "I do a good deed. Introduce you to some chicks. And what do I get in return?"

"I believe it was punched," I chimed in. "I'm Phe, by the way."

"Nice to meet you, Phe. Like this moron said, I'm George." He ran a hand over his bright auburn hair. "My sister and I just moved here from Greenwich, Connecticut. Luckily, we met Graham in the quad, and he told us about this little soirée."

"Hey, Howdy Doody! I see Sybil coming!" a random guy yelled at George.

"Howdy Doody, my favorite unimaginative nickname." He grinned. "If you'll excuse me, it seems my sister is here."

"Yeah, sure." I smiled back. "And for the record, I like red hair."

"Thanks. I keep waiting for my parents to get divorced and remarried so I can be an honest-to-God red-headed stepchild."

"I'll keep my fingers crossed for you."

He laughed, then made his way over to an attractive girl with strawberry-blonde hair. *So this was Sybil.* I had spotted her leaving orientation on Monday. Her porcelain doll features and striking height were memorable. Sybil was even taller than Corinne and willowy thin in her black Chanel dress. Obviously Sybil, like Adriana, thought beauty was more important than being warm.

A nasty little knot of envy burned inside me. I wondered if Zach had met this girl who could be a model. Curious to see her closer up, I walked over to where she and Adriana were having a staring contest.

"Looks like a catfight is brewing," Graham whispered as he came up next to me.

George checked out Adriana, then whistled. "The girls never dressed like this in the woods back home."

"Please, George." Sybil rolled her eyes. "You make us sound as if we're from *Virginia*." She might as well have said "seventh circle of hell," from her tone.

Wow, this girl was good. I didn't dare make eye contact with Adriana, but I could see her clenching her fist in my peripheral vision.

"It's okay." Sybil laughed. "We're not." She gave Adriana the once-over. "I just love your boots."

"Thanks," Adriana said through her teeth.

"Marc by Marc Jacobs, right? I think it's great that they started that little secondary line." Sybil shrugged one shoulder. "Not everyone can afford his real designs."

I saw the flash of anger in Adriana's eyes, and I grabbed her elbow before she could say anything.

"Okay, time to go." Graham took her other arm, and we pulled her back over to where Brody stood. Toy trailed behind us, her brows knitted together, as if she didn't know what had just happened.

"That new girl reminds me of someone." Brody squinted at Sybil.

"Nicole Kidman?" I suggested.

"More like Satan." Adriana refilled her drink almost entirely with vodka. "And I *do* own real Marc Jacobs." She pointed her cup accusatorially at Brody. "These are my casual shoes."

"*Okaaay.*" He held his hands up in surrender. "Did I say something about her shoes that I don't remember?" Brody asked me out of the side of his mouth.

"She practically called me poor white trash," Adriana went on.

"No, she didn't." I shook my head. This was obviously a sore spot for Adriana. The way she'd talked about her aunt gave me the feeling that her mom's embarrassment over their family background had been instilled in Adriana, too.

"Did you totally miss the whole *Virginia* comment?" She glared at the group of guys who had focused their attention on Sybil.

"I bet she doesn't even know you're from Virginia," I soothed.

"You'd be surprised. My dad's political ads center around the all-American family portraits." Adriana snorted derisively. "'Cause nothing says I love my kids more than dumping them at boarding schools." She threw back the rest of her drink, which was basically an enormous shot. If she were Ariel, this would be when I'd drag her home.

"I brought dominos." Brody pulled a small travel pack out of the back pocket of his baggy jeans. "Anyone want to play?"

"I guess I could do that." Adriana shrugged.

"Looks like Brody distracted the bull," Graham whispered as we followed them over to the edge of the clearing. Two logs had been placed on either side of a large flat rock, forming a make-shift table. Graham had snagged one of the many camping lanterns that were illuminating the area, and he set it on a stump next to us so we could see more clearly. Once everyone had settled in and drawn their dominos, Adriana inspected our "table."

"Here, give me that." She motioned at Toy's drink, which was now mostly ice. Adriana added a large helping of vodka. "No one should be walking around with an empty cup at one of my parties."

"I guess it's a good thing we're at your party then." Brody pulled out a pack of Camels and lit one. Smoke curled up into his brown eyes, making them crinkle. Gripping the cigarette between his teeth, he reached back into his hoodie's pocket and extracted a flask.

"Jesus Christ. How much crap do you have on you right now?" Adriana held out her hand. "And don't you know it's impolite not to ask anyone else if they want a smoke?"

"Sorry, Emily Post. I'll have to write that one down in my etiquette notebook." He deposited a cigarette in Adriana's waiting palm.

I raised an eyebrow as she crossed her legs toward Brody. Anyone who'd ever read a magazine knew this was body language for "I'm into you." Brody must have felt my gaze because he tore his eyes away from Adriana's thighs and trained his stare on his dominoes.

An hour later, we were still playing.

"Twenty-five!" Toy slapped down her last domino and beamed as Graham marked her points on our impromptu scoreboard by placing five sticks under one of the columns drawn in the dirt.

"See, I told you we shouldn't have let her play. Computer people are way too good at math." Graham bumped her with his shoulder and grinned.

Toy giggled. She was looking a bit bleary-eyed. Which wasn't surprising, what with her tiny size and Adriana's heavy-handed pours. Her giggles quickly turned into hiccups.

"Hey, I gotta go to the bathroom," Toy said in between hiccups. "But there's no bathroom here."

"I'll go with you." I stood and offered her my hand. "We'll just head into the woods a bit." With my help, Toy got to her feet, albeit unsteadily. "I know going behind a tree isn't glamorous, but it's pretty much the only option right now."

We found a secluded spot out of sight, and I stood lookout for Toy.

"Sorry." She hiccupped again as she zipped her jeans back up, leaning against her chosen tree for support. "I don't drink very much, and it always gives me the hiccups."

"Here, hold your nose and bend over at the waist," I instructed. "Now, breathe in through your mouth while I count to twenty. Breathe in the whole time, okay?"

"Okay." Toy's muffled voice floated back up to me. I started counting slowly, and by the time I reached twenty, her hiccups were gone.

"Thanks." She stood, swaying a little.

"No problem." I smiled. "You might want to slow down, though." Toy's cheeks were bright red, and her normally perfect pixie cut was disheveled.

"I didn't mean to get so drunk. When I'm nervous I drink more and . . ." Toy looked to the right and the left, as if she was checking to make sure we were still alone. "I've had this huge crush on Graham since last year, and sometimes I get nervous when he's around. I know I shouldn't; we're just friends. And he's got this genius older girlfriend at MIT. I'm being totally stupid." Toy hung her head.

I wasn't sure if she was sad or just tired of holding up her head.

"It's not stupid. He likes you, I can tell." Toy was into all the guy things Graham was into—but it seemed like there was more between them than that. "Plus, I don't think he's very happy with his girlfriend," I continued. "I wouldn't be surprised if they broke up soon. Not that I'm saying you *should* wait around for him. But if no one else catches your eye . . ." I shrugged.

"So you don't think it's totally hopeless?" Toy stepped carefully over a tree root as she followed me back to the clearing.

"No. I really don't."

"Thanks." She yawned widely as we sat back down. "I feel kinda tired."

"You want to go back to the dorm?" I was starting to get bored anyway, sitting in the woods watching other people flirt when Zach was nowhere around.

"Yeah." Toy tried to stand, coming back down hard on the tree stump.

"Okay, here we go." I put my arm around Toy, supporting her as she got to her feet again.

"I'm gonna walk her back," I said. Adriana and Brody were still playing dominos, but Graham was watching the two of us.

"I'll come with you guys." He handed his cup to Brody. "Here, finish this for me, okay?"

"Sure." Brody set the cup next to his other drink.

"See you at breakfast tomorrow?" Adriana asked as I picked up Toy's messenger bag and slung it over my shoulder.

"Of course." I gave a little wave to her and Brody as we tromped back into the woods, Graham holding the beeping GPS unit.

After only a few minutes of walking, I felt Toy getting heavier on my arm.

"I think she's falling asleep," I murmured to Graham. Toy was tiny—almost half a foot shorter than me—but even so, I was about to collapse under her dead weight.

"Got it." Graham swooped her up in his arms like a parent

carrying his kid out of a late-night movie. "I've never seen her this wasted," he whispered.

I wanted to tell Graham to wake up. He clearly cared about Toy, but if he kept screwing around, hanging on to this other relationship he seemed unhappy with—well, it couldn't be long before some more perceptive guy saw the hotness lurking under Toy's geeky demeanor. But I knew she would kill me tomorrow if I spilled about her crush. *Maybe I can do some recon instead.*

"So how's the girlfriend? I haven't heard you mention her in a while." *Or ever,* I added silently.

"I don't know actually." Graham's voice was sour. "She thought we should take a few weeks off from talking. You know, until she gets settled into the school year. Whatever the hell that means."

"Seriously? Why do you put up with that?" I frowned. "You could find a way better girl here."

"Hey, you've never met her, okay? You don't know anything about how great she is," he snapped.

"You're right; I don't." I lowered my voice, hoping he'd follow suit. We were pretty close to the dorms now. "It just doesn't seem logical to stay with a girl, no matter how amazing she may be"—I headed off his interruption—"if your relationship and communication is basically nonexistent."

"I know," he conceded. "But we met when I was just a clueless freshman and she was this gorgeous senior who could recite pi to the three hundredth decimal."

"Hot," I teased.

"It was. And so were we. Now I'm lucky if I get a lukewarm e-mail from her. Whatever. It's all high-school crap. It's not even worth talking about." Graham's expression was hard as we neared the lights outside Kresky.

"It's really none of my business. Sorry." I'd obviously *way* overstepped my new-friend bounds.

After a second Graham made eye contact with me.

"It's okay." He shrugged. "I know you're trying to look out for me. It's kinda sweet, in an annoying sort of way."

"You are so unlike most guys." I shook my head.

"I know. I'm pretty much the most amazing guy ever." Graham grinned.

Toy's room was easy to find, her window being the only one with a sticker that read: THE INTERNET—ALL THE PIRACY, NONE OF THE SCURVY. I pushed open the window and climbed through, then gestured to Graham. He hoisted Toy up and halfway into the room, and I hooked my arms through hers. I staggered back under her weight, and we came crashing down onto the bed. Graham, of course, was cracking up outside the window.

"Ha-ha." I rolled Toy off me and got to my feet. I draped the light blanket on the end of her bed over her, then turned back to the window.

Graham was still standing outside, his arm braced on the sill.

"What are you doing?" I whispered. "Somebody might see you. Go away."

"Do you think she's going to be okay?" He leaned farther into the window, ignoring my instructions. "I don't want to get her in trouble, but maybe we should take her to the infirmary, just to be sure."

God, Graham was so infuriatingly blind about his feelings for Toy!

I resisted the urge to shake him. "I was watching earlier, and she only had two drinks—granted, Adriana made them, so it's probably more like three, but still . . . She'll be fine." I looked down at Toy, who was snoring loudly now. She definitely wasn't having any trouble breathing.

"Tilt her on her side," Graham instructed. "Just in case she has to puke."

I was glad Toy wasn't awake to hear this; she would be mortified. I turned her over and put the trash can next to her head.

"Listen, I'll get my blanket and sleep on her floor tonight." *Out of vomit range,* I thought to myself. "I'll make sure nothing happens to her."

"Thanks, Phe." Graham, looking relieved, headed back to his dorm.

As I settled into my makeshift bed on the hard floor, I cursed myself for not thinking to bring a blow-up air mattress to Devenish. But despite my less than five-star accommodations, I fell asleep the moment I closed my eyes.

Chapter Twelve

"I think you might be even more beautiful up close." Zach's face was centimeters from mine, searching my features, taking in all of my imperfections. "I love the hint of copper in your eyes, radiating out like the sun, turning your pupils into an eclipse." He ran his thumb down my cheekbone. "The different striations of color, how every band of green is its own unique shade. A shard of a broken Heineken bottle, a blade of grass, moss on a rusty can."

"Romantic . . ." I laughed.

His hand moved back up, and he followed the curve of my left eyebrow. "I love this little scar next to your eye."

"Got it in a knife fight." I dropped my mock tough-guy voice. "Actually, I got scratched by a kitten when I was little. Apparently he didn't like me using his tail as a rope for tug-of-war."

Zach grinned, his gaze never leaving my face. I studied the darker blue circle that defined the edge of his pale blue-gray eyes. The tea-green starburst around his pupils. I brushed a stray lock of wavy black hair away from his face and let my fingertips trail lightly over his strong jaw. I wanted to memorize every angle, every plane, of his gorgeous face.

Having Zach lying in my dorm room with me, his huge hand completely surrounding mine, made my heart race, my blood pound, my every nerve ending sizzle. My lips tingled, and it was all I could do not to press them against his perfect mouth.

Suddenly, Zach looked startled, confused. Like he had no idea where he was.

"I didn't mean to . . ." His eyes scanned my room as if looking for some kind of clue. "I don't know how I could have done it. I mean, I can't do it." The low rumble of his coarse baritone vibrated through me.

"What can't you do? What are you talking about?" The uncertainty in his voice made me anxious.

Before he could answer, another person came into the room.

"Oh, I'm sorry. Am I ruining something?" Corinne's icy gray-green eyes, so much like Zach's, were flashing. "Were you two lovebirds having a moment?" Sarcasm dripped from her tongue like poison.

"Corinne, did you do this?" Zach demanded vehemently.

"Do what?" I practically shouted, forgetting that I should try not to wake Ms. Moore. "What the hell is going on?"

Corinne ignored my little outburst. "No, I didn't *do this,* Zach. You did. Evidently, when it comes to something you care about, you're much more skilled."

"Did you— Is this—" My thoughts flitted away before I could find them.

"Don't worry your pretty little head, L.A. We're leaving." Corinne gave Zach a piercing look, and they were gone.

I awoke from my dream with a jolt that sat me up straight,

my back rigid. Toy was still snoring away on her bed. I wasn't sure where her clock was, but it was like a magnet pulling my gaze. There it was in bright green digital numbers: 3:33 a.m. Hekate's time.

The worst thing about a new dream was having to record it before I could go back to sleep. The waking "visions" really stuck with me, every detail standing out starkly. But the dreams faded if I didn't write them down right away. With a small grunt of annoyance, I got up and padded down the hall to my room. Truthfully, I couldn't imagine forgetting that dream. Especially not Corinne's whole "when it comes to something you care about, you are much more skilled" comment. *Did Zach enter my dream on purpose?*

I pulled the green notebook out of the drawer on my bedside table and quickly jotted everything down. Then I turned around and went back to Toy's.

When I woke up the next morning, Toy wasn't in her bed, but there was a note taped to the inside of her door.

> *Phe,*
> *Thanks for being my guardian angel last night.*
> *Hope I wasn't too horribly annoying.*
> *See you at breakfast!*
> *—Toy*

I looked around the small dorm room. I hadn't noticed the night before because it had been too dark, but Toy seemed to be quite a collector. She had two bookshelves filled with tons of graphic novels and a huge vinyl toy collection. I recognized the Frank Kozik toys since my ex-boyfriend Paul had also been a fan. But the thing that really interested me was her crate of records. I'd heard Graham mention that her older brother was a DJ in New York, and from the looks of this collection, Toy was following in his footsteps. I flipped through the albums and saw they were mostly indie hip-hop and grime. I recognized M.I.A., Lady Sovereign, Dizzee Rascal, and The Cool Kids, but I would have to get Toy to play me some of the more underground records. I'd never heard a lot of the stuff she had, and I was always hungry for new music.

I'd never had a friend like Toy before, but I had a feeling that was just going to make things more interesting. I grabbed my pillow and blanket and headed back to my room.

Flipping open my laptop, I went to iTunes and turned on TheDeathSet. After my not-so-restful night I needed some crazy-energetic music to feel completely awake. I raked my brush through my snarled, unruly waves—*thanks, Massachusetts humidity*—then slipped on my shower sandals and grabbed my toiletries bag and towel.

I was conditioning my hair and humming to myself when the person in the shower next to my stall let out an exasperated groan.

"Phe. *Pleeease stop that*," Adriana whined.

"How could you tell it was me?" I asked the tile wall in puzzlement.

"I don't know," Adriana's voice floated back to me. "Maybe because you are humming the same song that was blaring in your room earlier. In case you forgot, we do share one very thin wall."

I washed the conditioner out, then turned off the water. Wrapping the towel around myself, I stepped out of the shower. Adriana was standing there, one hand on her bathrobed hip.

"Sorry. Geez." I rolled my eyes and walked over to the sinks to brush my teeth.

"It's fine," Adriana relented grumpily. "I just have a bit of a brain-splitting headache this morning."

No surprise there.

"So how was the party after we left?" I asked.

She tilted her head to one side, thinking, then said in a faintly surprised tone, "Actually, it was fun. Brody's kind of cool." Adriana's smile was enough to make me wonder if she had a crush. "I don't know that many guys who can drink me under the table, but he was sure keeping pace last night. Plus, I didn't hate kicking his ass at dominoes."

Breakfast hours would have been long over by the time we were dressed if it had been a weekday, but luckily for Adriana and me, the cafeteria served brunch until the middle of the afternoon on Sunday. After we finished eating, Adriana went to tennis practice, and I took a stroll around the campus, trying to decide what to do with my day. I wasn't going to study until this evening, and I wanted to relax. It was a beautiful day, with just a nip of coolness in the air.

I was getting used to the softer sunshine in Shadow Hills, and I found I kind of liked it. In L.A. the sidewalks were blinding by midafternoon, but the gray slate walkways that led past the teachers' cottages were pretty, the rocks faintly sparkling in the light.

I started walking in the direction of the hospital. The book had been useless, but I was still determined to find out what was going on with the dreams Athena had and the ones I was experiencing now. Maybe there was a reason I was so drawn to the graveyard. There could be something there that would help me. At worst, I'd get a little exercise.

I hiked up the hill to the hospital and curved around toward the cemetery, then walked through the trees and stopped. The eerie aura of the place still caught me a little off guard.

I gave myself a shake. Following the rows, I carefully inspected the headstones. I wasn't sure what I was looking for. It seemed unlikely that I'd find an ancient decoder ring for my book.

As I went farther and farther back, the plots became more crowded. They had been running out of space. Images of disease-ravaged men, women, and children lying all packed together in the old almshouse flashed through my mind. I could smell the sour note of death, like wilting roses. I tried to focus on the moss-covered stones in front of me, but it was hard with my imagination running rampant.

"Oww!" My right foot came crashing into a rock. "Shit!"

I sat down on the ground, applying pressure to my big toe as it throbbed fiercely. My flats were about as protective as a pair of socks. The rock I had walked into was masked by a matted tangle of green vines. I crawled a little closer. It appeared to be a well-hidden gravestone. *It's so far away, though.* The back row of graves was about fifteen feet from here. The headstone was strangely tucked under a large tree, the roots of which grew up on both sides of the stone, encircling it in a shielding way. Pushing the crawling vines to one side, I looked down at the inscription.

Lichen almost obscured the crude engraving, but I was able to make it out. This was Rebekah Sampson's grave. Air whooshed out of my lungs as if I'd been punched in the stomach. I felt light-headed and nauseated. The edges of my vision went dark, like a storm cloud rolling in, obscuring my mind.

My arms crumpled, and a second later my head hit the tightly packed earth.

I was in an unfamiliar room, lit only by the sunshine leaking in around the heavy drapes that covered the windows. My eyes swept across the large glass-doored bookcases filled with leather-bound books. This looked like some old guy's home office. In the middle of the room sat an imposing mahogany desk with two leather tub chairs in front of it and a traditional wing-back one behind it. I walked around the desk and sank into the buttery-soft armchair.

The air in the office was soft and thick, like I was submerged in invisible quicksand. I reached out and opened a drawer, my arm moving in slow motion. The drawer was full of files, and I flipped through them until I saw one labeled BVA BANISHMENT DOCUMENTS. *Like the Articles of Banishment I found in the secret archives room.*

Curiously, I lifted out the set of papers. The first page was the same as the one I'd already seen: a list of people who had been banished from Shadow Hills. But the page behind it was the Brevis Vita Canon of Ethics, and stapled to it were notes on what rules each of the Banished had violated. I scanned the rest of the pages, attempting to concentrate. Something was wrenching my mind away, tearing at my thoughts. I gritted my teeth and tried harder to read, but my eyesight was swimming. All I could make out was a picture of a man with dark brown hair and a full beard. His face was gaunt, bony like a skeleton, and his eyes were the blackest eyes I had ever seen. Their darkness wasn't a color; it was harshness and hatred, the very soullessness of evil. Those eyes filled me with terror and revulsion even as they pulled me in. Like I was falling into a pit, an endless well of despair.

And a moment later I was back. Lying in the graveyard, looking up into the branches of a tree, my head and foot both pulsing with pain. I was flat on my back six feet above Rebekah Sampson's coffin.

I sat up, trying to clear my head. Had I actually been led here? I'd literally stumbled over Rebekah Sampson's grave—could the stuff I'd read about Hekate guiding people be true?

As usual, I wasn't sure what I was supposed to learn from this vision. I'd never seen that room before, and the insanely creepy-looking guy wasn't familiar either. And what was it about these Banished people? This was the third reference I'd found to them, but they hadn't lived in Shadow Hills for more than forty years. Was I supposed to do something about the

Banished? The only thing I felt capable of doing right now was freaking out.

It seemed impossible that Rebekah Sampson could be buried here. I had gotten the impression from Sarah that Rebekah Sampson was away somewhere, not dead. I wished I could remember exactly what Sarah had said about her. Was it that she hadn't been here for a while? That she was gone? Maybe I had interpreted her words wrong; perhaps she'd used some euphemism, like the way my grandmother would say a person had "passed" instead of died.

I was pretty sure, though, that Sarah had said that she'd known Rebekah Sampson. And while Sarah was obviously extremely old—much older looking, I realized as I thought about it, than any of the people I'd seen in the Shadow Hills nursing home—surely someone she knew would have died in the last half of the twentieth century, at least. So what was Rebekah Sampson's grave doing in this ancient cemetery? All the other graves in the place were from 1736 and earlier.

I crept closer to the rough gravestone, leaning in to examine it carefully. I traced my fingers over the letters of her name. Like many of the other markers in this graveyard, the carving did not look professionally done. Some letters were deeper than others, some uneven. The engraving in the bottom right-hand corner had been all but obscured by the moss.

I picked up a twig from nearby and scratched gently at the growth. I couldn't make out the month or date, but the year was legible: 1735.

I sat back with a thump: *1735*? That was before the epidemic struck Shadow Hills. Sarah had been given a book meant for me by someone who had died more than 250 years ago?

On the weekend, the buses ran into town every two hours, presumably so that the students would have a chance to spend some time off campus. I checked my cell; I had twenty minutes before the next bus left. I managed to make it home, grab my purse, sign out at Ms. Moore's door, and run over to the Admin Building just in time to catch it.

During the ride over, I tried to organize my thoughts, but by the time I got off at the square, I had so many questions and frustrations bubbling up inside of me that I felt like a shook-up soda bottle. I marched up the block to Sarah's Boutique, pulling the door open with a force that threatened to knock the bell off its perch.

Sarah, behind the counter as usual, glanced up, startled by my entrance. I was struck again by the realization of how much older she looked than any of the people in this town. She was dried and gnarled, with wrinkles upon wrinkles, and her hair was perfectly white. Was she not a native of Shadow Hills? Had her ancestors not been among the survivors of the epidemic? Or was she an anomaly, a BV who had managed to outlive all the others?

"How can I help you, dear?" she asked. Either Sarah didn't sense the anger rising off my body like steam, or she was pretending not to notice.

"You could start by telling me the truth. Like who is Rebekah Sampson? Why did you tell me that she gave you that book? Why am I having these dreams—these visions?" I spit out my questions rapid fire, not really caring if she could keep up.

"I told you the truth. I gave you Rebekah's book to help you on your path."

I snorted. "You gave me a book I couldn't read! It's not even written in a foreign language. It's written in code!"

"I cannot read it. But you will be able to understand it," she replied. "When the time is right."

I rolled my eyes. "Okay, *Yoda*. You could have at least told me. I lugged that stupid thing over to the Greek teacher, thinking it was something she could translate."

Sarah just nodded.

"Do you understand what's going on?" I asked her, irritated. "I keep having these dreams, and I don't know why. I don't know what they mean. I've dreamed of Rebekah's grave. Only sometimes it's my grave. Sometimes my sister is there, and I feel like I need to do something for her. And then this other woman appears. And she looks a lot like my sister, only she isn't."

Sarah continued to nod, as if what I was saying made some kind of sense. She smiled a little tremulously, and I would have sworn that there was the glimmer of tears in her eyes. "That is Rebekah. She comes to help you."

"I wish she'd be a little clearer about it." My voice was sharp with bitterness.

"It is hard for us to understand their ways. But you must

trust. You must open yourself to her guidance. That is how you will find your destiny. You are a daughter of Hekate, just as Rebekah was. Your power is already immense, maybe even greater than Rebekah's. But understanding it, learning to control it, takes longer."

"What does that mean—a daughter of Hekate? You're talking about a mythological figure."

"I am talking about the Goddess. The queen of the underworld."

"I know, I know." I held up a hand to halt a recital of all the names I had read the other night. "But it doesn't make any sense. How do you know I'm one of these daughters? How do you know I'm supposed to have this book? And what in the world am I supposed to do with it?"

"I know because Rebekah told me."

I stared at her. After a moment, I said carefully, "You mean you see her in dreams, too?"

"Now and then I have done so," Sarah said, smiling that odd little smile again. "Especially in the beginning, not long after she died. But she told me before that, too. When she was still alive."

I stared at her. "But she died over two hundred and fifty years ago."

"Yes, I know."

"But that's not possible." I wasn't sure who was crazier—Sarah, for what she seemed to be suggesting, or me, for trying to get answers from this woman who thought she'd been alive for almost three centuries.

"It shouldn't be possible, should it?" Sarah's smile was watery and thin. "Sometimes I wish it wasn't. But here I stay, slowly aging, falling apart piece by piece, but never dying."

"I . . . I need to sit down." My head was spinning.

Sarah motioned to her chair, offering it to me. I may have been shook up, but I wasn't stealing a seat from someone with a bum leg who claimed to be more than 250 years old.

"Okay. Let's say I choose to believe you." It was getting to the point where I couldn't just assume someone was lying because things didn't make sense, not when I was having visions and growing mystical symbols on my body. "How did this happen? Why are you still alive?"

"Back in 1735, Rebekah sensed the darkness coming to Shadow Hills. She told me to leave, to take her daughters with me and keep them safe. So my husband and I moved to Boston with the girls. But not before Rebekah protected me."

"How?" I wasn't sure any answer could convince me.

"It was simple, really; she laid a hand on my head and stated, 'Be ye forever and always protected.' And except for the polio in my leg and the occasional cold, nothing has harmed me since." Sarah's sadness was thickly worn behind her eyes.

"That's it? Why couldn't she protect herself, too? Why didn't she leave?" *Why would Rebekah have stayed here to die?*

"She knew she was sick already, before I left. Besides, she could not leave. People hunted witches back then, and they regarded Rebekah, with her power and her visions, as in league with Satan."

"The basement." My stomach knotted. I thought of my dream, of the dread that had rolled through me when I looked at the old stone walls of the hospital basement. "That cell."

Sarah nodded.

"She was locked in with the insane. But that was later; at first the almshouse staff worked her like a dog just like they did to everyone unfortunate enough to end up there. I was the only one who seemed to feel sympathy for the poor girl. Her family had been killed during the Indian wars." Sarah shook her head slowly. "She was an orphan when she came to our town looking for someplace that would take her in. Years later, when the director of the almshouse had her committed to the basement, I tried to help her escape. I worked there, had a key to her cell. But we were caught, and I was stripped of my duties."

We sat silently for a while as I attempted to sort through what I had just heard. Was it real? Part of it? All of it? It sounded insane, but it felt true to me.

A thought popped into my head. "Do you know if I'm related to Rebekah?"

"You are, my dear." Sarah reached across the desk and patted my hand. "Not closely, of course, but you are one of her descendants."

"How do you know?"

"I kept track of her descendants—all the daughters of Hekate." Sarah smiled. "She told me about you, the girl who would have powers that rivaled her own. All the daughters have had the dreams, but the power was wildly different from girl to girl."

"So my sister was like this, too?" My heart thudded loudly in my ears.

"Yes, but it is unlikely she understood the dreams. You are the only one since Rebekah who bears the mark. Are you sixteen years old?"

"Almost."

"That is when it appeared on Rebakah, too. You are truly Hekate's daughter."

I wondered if Athena had gotten the mark, too. My suspicion was that she hadn't, since I had never seen it when we went swimming.

"I still don't understand what Hekate has to do with anything." I sighed. "What are we, Greek witches or something?"

"All I know is that Rebekah said her power was ancient, passed down through generations. She said it predated the pagans by many centuries." Sarah smiled again. "But I am not privy to the knowledge of Hekate. That is what the book is for."

"But I can't read the stupid book!" I knew she was only trying to help me, but the holes in her knowledge were beyond frustrating.

"Someday you will be able to. Don't ever doubt that."

Graham was already in the cafeteria when I came in for lunch the next day. Brody sat next to him like usual, but today Zach was sitting on the other side of Brody. Zach looked up, and our eyes met. I blushed and made a beeline for the food.

It was the first time I had seen Zach since my dream about him, and just that one look had put me back there, lying in bed with him. My lips tingled like they were slicked with menthol, and I pressed my fingers to them. Maybe if I applied pressure, the way I did when my eye twitched, it would stop. No such luck.

After I got my food, I stalled at the salad bar as long as I could—laboring over my choice of salad dressings—but I knew I had to sit down eventually. The longer I avoided it, the stranger it would look.

Toy was at the table now, too, talking animatedly to Graham. As I sat down next to Adriana, I caught the tail end of something Toy was saying about a game night Mr. Carr had planned.

I stole a glance at Zach, and my stomach flipped over. I felt sure that if he looked into my eyes, he would know every-thing I was thinking. He would know about my dream from the other night. He had said that he had to touch a person to sense thoughts, but mine were so vivid that it wouldn't have surprised me if they leaped straight across the lunch table and into his mind.

Strangely, after a moment I realized he was hardly looking at me. My heart skipped a beat. *Maybe it actually had been* Zach *in my dream.*

He had dreamed the same dream I'd had about the grave-yard. What if he'd shared this one, too? My face flooded with fire, and I looked down at my food. And there was the strange comment Corinne had made, as if he'd come into my dream on purpose.

"So, Adriana, are you going to go to the SAC on Wednesday for game night?" Brody asked hopefully.

"Probably." Adriana sighed. "I doubt anything better will be going on."

"Awesome." Brody rubbed his hands together excitedly. The lukewarm tone of Adriana's acceptance was obviously lost on him. "What about you, Zach? You down?"

Zach looked over at me. "Yeah, I think so," he finally answered. "Are you going, Phe?"

The way he said my name made me feel warm inside, and I couldn't keep from looking up at him. Gazing into his eyes, I was almost certain that he knew about my dream. But the heat creeping through me now had little to do with embarrassment.

"Sure," I agreed. "It sounds like fun."

Unfortunately for me, game night proved to be more tragic than fun. Early Wednesday evening, I was at the SAC and feeling more than a little regretful about my decision to attend. There had been a large turnout since those who had opted to do it didn't have to participate in the—usually mandatory—two-hour dorm study.

Almost a hundred students had shown up, which made it necessary that we be broken into groups. Randomly. Everyone had given their student IDs to Mr. Carr, and he'd put them in ten different piles. Which was how I came to be on the same team as

Corinne, and playing *against* Zach. At Pictionary. A game I was truly dreadful at.

Corinne had suggested that I be the first person to draw for our team, and while I'd protested extensively, she had sweetly insisted. Now here I was: standing in front of a blank whiteboard and staring at a Pictionary card, trying to figure out how in the hell I could possibly draw "self-service" without resorting to some kind of highly inappropriate representation. I was fairly certain that would be frowned upon at a school-sponsored game night.

"At least draw something!" Corinne watched time diminish from our hourglass. It appeared she hadn't fully thought through the consequences of humiliating me.

I sketched a misshapen gas pump.

"Hair dryer!" The pink-clad Bouncy Blonde Barista from the SAC had also ended up on my team. And as luck would have it, she was excited not only by Trent—Pictionary seemed to do it for her, too. She'd even shouted out answers when the other team was drawing. Thankfully, none of her answers were right; if they had been, I was pretty sure Corinne would have made the rest of the game a living hell for her.

"Gas pump!" one of my teammates yelled. I did the "go on" gesture with my hand.

"Gas prices!" Corinne called. I drew a stick figure next to the pump.

"Gas station attendant!"

On top of the stick figure I drew the circle with a diagonal line across it that stood for no.

"Bad gas attendant!" Bouncy Blonde exclaimed.

"What are you—mentally deficient?" Corinne snapped at the girl. "Do you actually think they would print that on a card?"

"Time!" a guy on the other team called as the last grain of sand drained into the bottom of the hourglass.

"It was 'self-service,'" I said, putting down the dry-erase marker.

"Good job, L.A.," Corinne clapped slowly as I sat back down. "I guess the stereotypes about dumb blondes really do apply."

"Shut up, Corinne." Zach's tone was uncharacteristically harsh.

"Hey! We are *not* all dumb!" Bouncy Blonde piped up.

"Oh, come on!" Corinne threw her hands up in exasperation. "Like anything you've ever said has even bordered on intelligent. How you got into this school is a mystery to me." She eyed the girl's outfit with disdain. "And I don't know if you're aware of this, but you look like you're wearing cotton candy."

"Pink looks good on me," Bouncy Blonde said, her voice shaky.

"Whatever you say." Corinne rolled her eyes.

Okay, now I felt really bad about making fun of Bouncy Blonde's clothes with Adriana the other night. Just because I hated all the matchy-matchy pinkness didn't mean she deserved to be ridiculed.

"George." Zach handed the marker to the red-headed guy I'd met at the party in the woods. "You're next."

"Okay." George crouched down to draw a card. "Wow." He looked over at me. "It's not as bad as 'self-service.' But this edition is definitely not for beginners." George stood and walked over to the board.

I glanced at Corinne, who'd picked up the timer and flipped it before he'd finished studying his card.

George started sketching something resembling a koala bear.

"Anteater!" a guy I didn't know yelled.

"Groundhog!" a girl with tightly curled red hair called out.

George shook his head and moved on to a new part of the board, where he drew a stick figure with a huge round belly.

"Pregnant!" The red-headed girl's foot was jiggling excitedly.

George gave an almost imperceptible nod.

"No gesturing!" Corinne practically screamed.

I hadn't heard her objecting when I was gesturing to our team. Corinne was the absolute worst kind of person to play a game with: competitive and controlling, with a hair-trigger temper.

"Baby animal? Calf?" Zach offered.

George drew a circle in the belly with a fetus inside.

"Womb!" the red-headed girl cried.

George drew a bat next to it. Their time was almost up.

"Wombat!" a girl yelled excitedly.

Oh, shit. It was Bouncy Blonde.

"Yes!" George cried. "We get to roll again!"

"Screw that!" Corinne yelled. "She isn't even on your team!"

"Doesn't matter," George countered. "She guessed correctly."

"What is wrong with you, you moronic, wannabe Barbie doll?!" Corinne turned on the blonde. "You can guess 'wombat,' but you can't think of something simple like 'self-service'?"

"It's not like you thought of it, Corinne," I pointed out.

"You really should mind your own business," she warned me. "For once it's not you I have a problem with."

"Give it a rest, Corinne," Zach said.

"If this mentally deficient spaz hadn't opened her mouth, we wouldn't be losing right now!" Apparently Corinne felt this twisted logic exempted her from having to show the smallest amount of compassion.

Tears of embarrassment rolled down Bouncy Blonde's cheeks, and she jumped up and ran to the bathroom.

"Kerry! Hold on a second!" The red-headed girl from Zach's team hopped up and hurried after her.

I stood up as well. Finally, I had the vertical advantage on Corinne.

"I don't know what your problem is—if this is some kind of tough-girl act to try to scare people into respecting you, or if you really are this big of a bitch"—my tone was venomous—"but right now I don't care." Corinne made a noise as if she was going to protest, but I barreled on. "Because I would rather be at dorm study than remain on a team with someone as nasty and spiteful as you."

I picked up my purse and turned to go.

"Phe, wait." Zach stood up. I paused, looking at him. "You don't have to go back to the dorms. I'm sure we can find something else to do."

"Okay." I smiled.

"You can't leave, Zach," Corinne said through gritted teeth.

He walked right past her. "Watch me."

Chapter Thirteen

"I'm sorry about my sister." Zach sat across from me at one of the two-person tables on the small deck outside the SAC—the same place where Trent had done his little fireworks show. We were allegedly playing twenty-one. Mostly we were fidgeting with the cards and talking.

"I don't know what the deal is," he went on. "Recently she's been worse than usual. Maybe her mountain of AP classes are getting to her."

"Don't people mostly take electives their last year?"

"Yeah. But Corinne's not most people. She's got a full college-level course load and is the head of every committee here." Zach let out a gruff laugh. "Well, except for the ones that are elected by classmates."

"It's amazing she isn't more popular," I snarked.

"Well, there are several girls who follow her around, hoping her power in the school will rub off on them. But I doubt they've ever had a normal conversation with her; Corinne can't seem to talk without debating or lecturing. But at least she does have a few people who want to be around her, even if they are more lackeys than friends."

"I'm sure the fact that her brother is hot helps her out a little in that department." The statement popped out of my mouth, unbidden.

"Yeah. Because senior girls are just dying to date juniors."

I decided not to point out that Zach was no ordinary junior.

"Only one of Corinne's friends could be accused of flirting, and I'm pretty sure it's solely because she's in theater and she wants me to do publicity photos for her," he continued.

"The photographs you take in class *are* amazing."

"I don't know if you can really say that since we haven't developed the photos yet. And your judgment could be clouded by the fact that you're my subject. Maybe you just like looking at yourself." Zach grinned, and I pretended to glare at him. "I mean, it would be hard to take a bad picture of you."

I felt the blush creep all the way up to my hairline.

"Time for a change of subject?" Zach raised his eyebrows at me, and I nodded gratefully. "So what about your family? Do you have any heinously awful siblings?"

Usually I would have said no. Technically, it was the truth, I had become an only child the night my sister died. But it felt different now. I wanted to say something about Athena. I wanted to tell Zach.

"My older sister was definitely my parents' favorite, though they would never admit it." I chewed on my thumbnail. "Athena was the best. She made perfect grades without ever studying, partied with celebrities' kids, knew about every clothing and music trend before MTV had caught on to them."

I thought of her empty bedroom, her abandoned record

collection I couldn't bring myself to listen to. Zach must have seen the tears welling up in my eyes because he placed his hand over mine. It was warm, and it made my nerves tingle.

"What's wrong?" Zach asked.

"Athena died about a year ago."

"I'm so sorry." Zach sat back, pulling his hand away from mine. Instantly, I missed it. "I shouldn't have brought it up. You don't need to tell me what happened."

"No," I stated. "I want to. I never talk about her, and I hardly allow myself to think about her." I dug my nails into my palm, trying not to cry. "I'm afraid if I continue like this, I'm going to forget her completely."

"Okay," Zach said cautiously. "If you want to."

"I do." I smiled to show him I wasn't going to have a nervous breakdown or anything. "About two years ago Athena started dating this asshole named Jason. I never liked him," I added, as if this wasn't already obvious. "She stopped hanging out with everyone except for Jason and his friends. I didn't know any of them. They went to his old school."

I paused. I didn't want to expose all of Athena's secrets, or mine for that matter. I decided to keep quiet about the dreams and how moody they had made her. At the time I even thought maybe she was doing coke, but she denied it. Still, I didn't completely believe her, until I found her diary and realized the nightmares she'd been having were mostly to blame.

"After Athena and Jason had been together for six months, she caught him cheating on her," I went on.

Zach stared at me intently, listening but not interrupting.

"She broke up with him, but he kept begging her to forgive him, and in the end she did. I argued with her for weeks, but she wouldn't listen to me." I shook my head.

"Not long after they got back together, there was this big party out on some girl's yacht, and Athena wanted to keep an eye on Jason. Which is obviously the sign of a great relationship."

I looked down at the table. Zach took my hand again, and after a second I was able to go on.

"Athena asked me to go with her. She'd dropped all her friends, and she wanted someone to talk to at the party." I bit the inside of my cheek, trying not to cry. "I told her that if she didn't like not having friends, she should dump Jason and get her real life back."

My eyes stung with unshed tears.

"No one was there with her, and it was hours before they realized she was missing. That she had fallen overboard." A hot tear rolled down my cheek. "If I had just gone with her, I might have been able to get to her in time. I was always a stronger swimmer than Athena." I wiped the tear away. "It was the only thing I was better at."

Zach came around the table and pulled me out of my chair. I pressed my face against his broad chest, and he wrapped his arms around me. He smelled comforting, like grapefruit and leather.

"It shouldn't have been like that," I whispered, knowing that he could still hear my voice, faint as it was. "She should have died an old lady with her friends and family gathered around her. She shouldn't have been alone." I started crying again, and Zach held me even tighter. "She lived her life with people who loved her, and she died with that piece-of-shit boyfriend and a bunch of strangers." My voice broke, and I let Zach support me as I collapsed into him, sobbing like I hadn't since the night the cops had showed up at our house and ripped my life to shreds.

That night had changed everything. It had changed me. My face, so similar to Athena's, was just another reminder of what my parents had lost. Like the wisp of smoke hanging in the air after a candle is snuffed out.

"I feel like I'm irreparably broken. Like there is this piece of me that's just . . . missing. And I know that no matter what I do, I can't get it back. She's gone forever." I wasn't sure whom I was talking about anymore, myself or Athena.

Zach continued to hold me, stroking my hair as the heaviness lifted from my chest and my sobs slowly subsided. I felt calmer, and my breathing was becoming more regular. Zach pulled back and looked into my eyes.

"You okay?" He searched me over as if my scars were physical instead of emotional.

"I think so." I nodded.

"Are you sure?"

Strangely, I was. The fear and hurt were no longer pushing in, threatening to suffocate me. "Yeah." I wiped the tears from my face. "Let's do something, okay? Something fun."

"You ready for some twenty-one?" Zach checked his cell. "We have an hour."

"Sounds good." I settled into the metal chair, feeling lighter.

"Oh, tricky. Fourteen." He raised an eyebrow at me. "You wanna hit?" His flirtatious smile made my heart beat faster. I wasn't sure what I should do. Fourteen wasn't enough to win, but I could easily go over with a number that high. It was risky to go for it, but my only other option was to not even try. I had never felt more sure of a bet.

"Hit me." I smiled. There was no going back now.

I woke up the next morning with a grin plastered on my face. Zach and I had stayed in our own little world the rest of the night, and he'd asked me if I wanted to develop my pictures with him this evening. Which, since Mr. Sherwood had told us we could do it solo, meant that Zach *wanted* to spend time with me in a small, dimly lit room.

I was overcome with the urge to call Ariel and tell her my good news, but she didn't even know who Zach was. Besides, I really didn't want to relive the awkward phone call we'd had when I first got to Devenish. Instead, I rolled over and picked up my phone from the bedside table so I could send her a quick text just to say hi.

After I got out of bed, I put on Wolf Parade and turned it up until it vibrated my computer speakers.

"Someone is happy this morning," Adriana observed as I bopped into the bathroom. I couldn't stop smiling, even as I brushed my teeth.

"You and Zach looked pretty cozy last night," Adriana added. I hadn't even noticed she was at the SAC. "So what's going on with you two?" she prodded as I put my toothbrush back in my toiletries bag.

"I don't know." I tried to suppress my grin, but it was next to impossible. "We were just hanging out."

"Uh-huh." Adriana was not convinced, but apparently she had better things to talk about. "Did you see Sybil last night?"

"Nope." I started putting on my makeup.

"She was totally throwing herself at Trent."

I hated that Adriana was interested in Trent. He wasn't a good guy, but I'd learned the hard way with Athena that trying to convince someone not to date a creep had the opposite effect. "Sybil might as well have said, 'I'll have sex with you if you ask me to the dance.' It was so obvious she would," Adriana continued.

"So did he?"

"What?" Adriana squinted into the mirror as she plucked her eyebrows.

"Trent. Did he ask Sybil to the dance?"

"Oh. Maybe." Adriana shrugged. "I heard her shrieking like a hyena in heat at one point, so either she was doing really well at Taboo or he asked her."

I laughed. Adriana had a way of totally tuning out anything that didn't interest her anymore.

"I'll see you at breakfast," I told her before heading back to my room to finish getting ready. After I was dressed, I threw my cell into my purse, and I felt a pang as I thought of Athena's ID bracelet.

N N N

When I walked into the cafeteria a few minutes later, I spotted Graham and Toy already seated at our table. I grabbed a bowl of fruit and some yogurt and headed over to sit down with them.

"Hey, guys. What's up?" I slid in next to Brody, who had arrived while I was getting my food.

"We were just talking about our complete and utter lack of dates for the dance," Toy informed me.

"Though I think Adriana is on the verge of asking me," Brody announced proudly.

"You also believe pot enhances cognitive skills," Graham retorted. "It doesn't mean you are in any way correct."

"Yeah." I frowned. "I hate to break it to you, Brody, but even if Adriana's into you, she would never ask a guy to a dance. It's not in her nature."

"I can't ask her, though," Brody retorted. "What if it's too soon, and I destroy all the groundwork I've laid?"

"I've got an idea," Graham offered. "How about we all go as a group? We've already established that none of us have dates, and this way we don't have to go alone."

"I'm in," Brody readily agreed.

"Sounds good to me," Toy answered. All three of them turned to look at me. Sure, I didn't have a date, but there were still two and a half days before the dance; someone could ask me. *Someone tall, dark, and handsome, with hypnotic eyes.*

"What's the deal, Phe? You already have a date, or would you just rather go alone than be seen with us?" Graham asked.

"Sorry, I was spacing out." I couldn't turn down my friends because of a vain hope. "Of course I'll do the group thing."

"Score." Brody did his stoner-guy head nod.

"Good morning." Adriana walked up and sat down across from me.

"Hey, Adriana." Brody smiled euphorically at her.

"Hi, Brody." She rolled her eyes.

"We were discussing the idea of all of us going to the dance together. As a group. You into it?" I figured it would sound less like a setup coming from me than it would if one of the guys suggested it.

"I guess. It doesn't seem like I have much of a choice at this point." Adriana brooded. "Who decides to have a school dance only two weeks into the year, anyway? Do they really expect us to have met someone in that amount of time?"

"It's possible." The optimistic mood I had been in all morning reared its ugly head.

"Maybe for you, Miss Everyone-in-a-Five-Mile-Radius-Falls-in-Love-with-Me-Instantly," Adriana groused.

"Oh, come on." I shook my head. "That is so not true."

"Yeah," Brody agreed quickly. "I have absolutely zero interest in Phe. She's like vanilla yogurt or tapioca pudding. She's unflavored oatmeal."

"Why, thank you, Brody." I smiled sweetly.

"Fine. I'll go with you guys," Adriana relented. "But only because I have no better options."

"What a gracious acceptance speech." Graham smirked.

As everyone else talked about the dance, I let my mind wander. Tonight it was going to be just Zach and me in the darkroom, and I was almost as anxious as I was excited.

The entire afternoon I alternated between untethered optimism and an assurance that Zach was interested in me to paralyzing fear that I had totally misread the situation. By the time photography rolled around, I was a hopeless tangle of nerves.

I sank into my chair, disappointed to find Zach wasn't already in class. But he got there just as the late bell rang—and the instant his eyes met mine I knew any worrying had been unnecessary.

Mr. Sherwood, who today wore a tie with little elephants on it, had us go to the darkrooms to develop our film. Unfortunately, we did it solo, and I didn't get a chance to be with Zach. But at least I had one good set of negatives when class was over.

"I have a long diving practice today," Zach told me as we walked toward the Athletics Center. "How about we meet at your dorm around seven?"

"Do you think we can be done before dorm study starts at eight?"

"You can get a pass to work on campus for a class," Zach said. "We'll have until ten."

I was so excited I felt like I was going to burst out of my skin.

"I'll get a pass from Ms. Moore when I'm done with swimming." I tried to sound calm.

"See you then." His voice was low and rough—beyond sexy. Three hours never seemed so long.

N N N

Zach broke into a slow grin as I stepped out of Kresky Hall that night. "You're stunning."

"Thanks." I blushed. I was only wearing a green tank top and jeans, but he was staring at me like . . . I couldn't even think of a word to describe it.

Zach had also changed out of his uniform, and he looked amazing. He was wearing dark jeans that clung to him perfectly, and a navy blue tee that emphasized the pale intensity of his eyes. His hair curled softly over the snap collar of his charcoal wool motorcycle jacket.

"So how was diving?" I asked as we walked down the flagstone path.

"It was diving." Zach shrugged.

"You don't sound terribly enthusiastic about it," I said.

"It's fine. I'm just not into it like you are swimming."

I looked up at him in surprise.

"What do you mean? I'm not on the team or anything."

"Exactly. You do it because you want to. Your face is always all lit up when you get out of the pool. You look blissfully happy."

"I love it . . . the weightlessness, the sensation of the water running over my skin. It's so peaceful . . . I don't get why some people don't like swimming. And I certainly can't see why you'd do it if you didn't like it."

"People do things they don't want to do all the time. Because it will make their parents happy, or because it looks good on their transcripts." Zach's eyes held mine captive. "People even try to deny the strongest feelings they've ever felt, because they don't want to let other people down."

His gaze made my pulse race, but I tried to ignore it. "But you're so good at diving. How can you not love doing it?"

"I used to love it, but there's so much pressure now that it kind of takes the fun out of it. I wish I could have just one thing that wasn't for anyone but myself, you know?"

"Yeah. I know what you mean." And I did. It was as if all the things I learned about Zach were already there, tucked away in my subconscious. Like I had known him forever.

"Ever since I was a kid, it was drilled into me that no outsider would ever understand. That if I let anyone near me it would end in disaster. I'm sick of that—living my whole life as if the only thing that matters is this town and its rules." Zach looked down at me, and my heart stopped, like it was waiting for him to finish before it could go on beating. "I can't do it anymore. I won't."

"Are you . . . ?" I began, but I didn't know how to finish the question.

"I'm gonna let the herd fend for itself for a while." Zach grinned and walked into the Arts Building. "I'd like to see what kind of trouble I can get into, making my own decisions."

He opened the door to the darkroom and flicked the amber safelight on.

"Do you want to go first?" Zach asked politely, holding the door open for me.

"Sure," I accepted. I wanted to jump up and down and clap, but I contained myself. If Zach meant what I thought he did, I was one very happy girl. I smiled over at Zach, and he smiled back, his face bathed in red. I placed the negative in the enlarger and slid the photographic paper under it; then I flicked the enlarger on and exposed the paper.

"I'm glad you made it back to your dorm okay last night—I mean, Shadow Hills isn't crime infested, but I worry about you," Zach said.

"Hopefully they'll station several guards around the premises for when the dance lets out on Saturday," I teased.

"About the dance." Zach pushed a lock of wavy hair back behind his ear. "I was wondering . . ."

The timer went off, cutting Zach's sentence short.

I cursed internally as I picked up the paper with the tongs, letting the excess liquid drain off before placing it in the stop bath tray. After an agonizingly slow thirty seconds, I was able to take the print back out. I set the timer for five minutes and dropped the paper into the fixer.

"Sorry about that." I turned to Zach. "What were you saying?"

"It's not important."

"No, really. I want to know," I urged him.

"I thought if you didn't already have plans, you might like to go to the dance. With me."

The group thing didn't count as actual plans, did it? I hated to ditch my friends for a guy, but it wasn't like I was *needed* there. In fact, without me, it would be two couples. Much more conducive to dancing.

"That sounds great," I answered. I'd figure out how to break the friend plans later.

"Cool."

Zach looked down at me, and I studied the way the red light threw shadows on his face. The room suddenly seemed very still and quiet, and I wondered if Zach could hear the loud thumping of my heart.

The sound of the timer broke the silence, and I placed the print in the wash. When it was done, I squeegeed off the excess liquid, then repeated the process on four of the other photos.

"Why don't you put those in the drying cabinet, and we can go get some coffee while we wait?" Zach suggested. "I can't do my prints until yours are finished anyway."

This sounded like a perfect plan to me.

"Okay," I agreed.

As we stepped back onto the sidewalk, I heard a cell ringing. My first instinct was to search my purse, but its weight was conspicuously absent from my shoulder. "I forgot my bag in the darkroom."

"Do you want me to get it for you?" Zach pulled the ringing phone out of his pocket and checked the caller ID.

"It's Corinne." He sighed in annoyance. "I better answer, or she'll keep calling."

"Why don't you talk to her, and I'll get my stuff?" I said. "Be back in a second."

"Okay." Zach flipped open the phone as I stepped back into the building.

I hadn't noticed how dim the lighting in the corridor was earlier, but now that I was alone it was eerie. I hurried to the darkroom and pulled open the door. My purse was on the far counter. I took two steps toward it when the red safelight blinked, then went out.

I froze. It was utterly dark—no windows, no light seeping in around the door. My heart thudded against my ribs. I felt my way toward the door, bumping my hip bone on the corner of the metal worktable. I was going to have a bruise tomorrow, but at least now I had an idea of where I was. Sweeping my hand back and forth in front of me, I crept slowly forward. In the total blackness, the tiny room suddenly seemed enormous.

Finally, my hand hit the edge of another counter. Gratefully, I gripped it and moved up close, sliding down the counter until it ended. I reached out, groping for the light switch. I turned on the ceiling light, and it flickered and sputtered in crazy bursts of brightness. The loud humming and popping sounds it was making were not helping my nerves, but at least I was able to see the door. I reached for the doorknob.

Something crashed at the far end of the hall, and I jumped, all my nerves sizzling. It was the heavy outside door, I realized. Just Zach coming back to see what was taking me so long. But that didn't make sense. I had left Zach standing outside the front door. This sound had come from someone slamming through the back exit.

I went still. A door opened at the end of the hall, then closed. Another door opened. Someone was walking down the hallway, looking into every room.

Stop the paranoia. So someone else had come into the building. It was a public place.

I forced myself to reach for the doorknob again. Cracking open the door, I peered out. The lights in the hall were flickering wildly, too, creating a strobelike effect. I eased open the door and, taking a deep breath, stepped out into the hall. I turned my head toward the far end of the corridor, and at that moment, a dark figure emerged from one of the rooms.

"Zach?" My voice was small and strangled. I could barely get the words past my closed-up throat. It felt like I was choking.

The shadowy form took a step toward me, and every light in the building went out.

I was plunged into complete darkness.

Chapter Fourteen

As my eyes adjusted to the blackness I realized there was dim light coming in the windows on the entrance doors. The dark figure stalked toward me. *This definitely isn't Zach.* Terror bubbled up inside my chest as the slow, deliberate footsteps echoed in the empty corridor. My body flooded with adrenaline, the liquid fear pumping through my veins. I whirled and ran toward the entrance.

Zach was right outside the front doors. I could see his silhouette through the small windows. As I got closer I could tell he had his back to the entrance. *I have to get his attention.* But I had a feeling the heavy metal double doors hindered sound. Then again, Zach did have the extraordinary BV hearing.

That's when I saw them, bright white against the charcoal gray of his jacket. Two ear buds lying on either side of his neck. *Great.* Zach's love of music was less than endearing right now.

"Zach!" I had to try, just in case, but as I suspected, he remained motionless. He couldn't hear me. *If only I could get closer . . .*

I was less than six feet away from the door when the dark

figure tore past me. He whirled to face me, blocking the entrance. Instinctively, I took a step back. Suddenly, I was aware of a sickly sweet vanilla aroma. It was emanating from the menacing figure. I was already nauseous with fright, and the odor made me want to gag. The man tilted his head to the side, inspecting me, like I had seen Ariel's dog do once when it encountered a frog—right before it squished it. The shadowy silhouette was waiting, calculating, before making the next move. *I can run around him. Even if I can't reach the door, I might be able to make enough noise to alert Zach.* Just as I thought this, the figure put his shoulder to the side of the soda machine that stood next to the entrance. With one swift push, he tipped it over, and it came crashing down in front of the doors, blocking my escape.

I spun around to run to the back exit, but again the shadow was already in my path. His eyes glittered in the darkness. I darted across the hall to the classroom opposite me. Any of the darkrooms would be a trap; none of them had windows. But the classrooms did, and I could lock the door and crawl out a window to get away.

I grabbed the doorknob and twisted. It was locked. *Shit!* I wasted precious seconds rattling the knob, then turned and ran back to the front entrance.

"Zach!" My heartbeat pounded in my ears.

The figure behind me stopped, and I seized the chance to scramble up onto the overturned soda machine. I pushed as hard as I could on the doors but it did no good. They opened the other way. I beat on the doors, yelling Zach's name.

Zach whipped around, startled. He immediately recognized the terror in my eyes.

"Phe! What's going on?" The doors rattled as he pushed futilely. I looked behind me. The shadow was still standing in the middle of the hallway, poised and unmoving. *Waiting to see if Zach can manage to get the door open.* If Zach couldn't, he would know that he had me trapped.

Zach pushed against the blocked doors, straining with the effort. They didn't budge.

"Phe, stand back!" he yelled, his eyes fierce.

I hopped off the soda machine, moving as far to the side as I could, and pressed my back against the wall, wishing I could shrink into it.

Zach shoved with all his strength. The door didn't move an inch. He pulled back, then ran at it like somebody in a movie, slamming into it with his full weight. The sound reverberated through the building, like a crack of thunder, but still the doors didn't move. The soda machine was too heavy.

"Shit!" Zach slammed his palms against the doors.

The figure started toward me again, slow and deliberate.

"Zach?!" My voice rose.

"Phe, get back!" Zach's voice was sharp. "You need to be farther away from the door!"

I forced myself to edge down the hall toward the intruder. I wished I'd grabbed my purse earlier so that I'd at least have my pepper spray.

I waited, expecting Zach to batter in the doors with something, or maybe break one of the windows. But Zach stood completely still. Even from this distance, I could see the intense concentration in his eyes. He held up his hand, palm pointed at the doors. I stared. Down the hallway, the sound of the intruder's footsteps halted, and I suspected that he was watching Zach, too.

The air around me felt strange, the hairs on my arms rising, like I was standing too close to a TV set. My skin prickled with goose bumps.

The soda machine flew away from the entrance and righted itself all in one swift movement—landing back in its original spot on the wall with a loud clatter. I jumped at the sound. *What the hell . . . ?*

The guy in the hallway turned and ran as Zach finally burst through the front doors. The intruder slammed out the back, and the lights flickered, then came on.

Zach pulled me close, wrapping one arm around my torso, the other arm enfolding me, protecting my neck and face. I nuzzled against his warm chest, the feel of his hand on my head calming me. I could hear his pulse hammering faster and harder than anyone's heart should beat. He pulled away, holding my shoulders, inspecting me.

"Are you all right? Did he do anything to you?"

"No. I think he was afraid of you. As soon as you did . . ." Suddenly, I was shaking all over. "What did you do?"

"Are you sure you're not hurt?" Zach ignored my question, brushing my hair away from my face, searching for bruises or bumps.

"I'm fine, I promise. Just freaked out." I looked up into his worried face. "What the hell is going on?"

"I don't know." Zach glared down the corridor at the back door.

I knew he was thinking about going after the guy, and I grabbed his arm. "Please don't. I don't want to be by myself."

Zach enveloped me in his arms again. "I won't leave you." He held me, his pulse gradually slowing. I relaxed, letting him support my weight as I tried to pull my scattered thoughts together. "What happened?" Zach asked after a moment.

I described it with as much detail as I could recall through my fear-addled memory. "He was so fast and strong. He was behind me, and then all of a sudden, he was at the front door, and he turned over the vending machine!" My voice was rising, and I forced myself to take a slow breath.

I leaned my head against Zach's chest, and his steady heartbeat soothed me. We walked back to the darkroom, and I sat down on one of the stools with Zach across from me, still holding my hand.

"Who could that have been?"

Zach shook his head. "I have no idea."

"How could anyone move that fast? Or turn over a soda machine?"

"I've heard of people tipping over soda machines. They may weigh a ton, but they're top heavy."

"Okay, but what about the lights?" My mind was racing, full of suspicion. "Why did the lights suddenly go out when he appeared? Why did they flicker like crazy first?" I looked straight into Zach's eyes.

His eyebrows went up as he caught my implication. "You think it was a BV?"

"Who else do you know who can manipulate electricity like that?"

"I don't know. But it couldn't have been one of us," he protested. "Why would a BV want to hurt you?"

I hesitated. "Maybe they don't want to hurt me. Maybe they're trying to scare me off because they don't like me."

"No offense, but most of the BVs don't know who you are, much less know you well enough to decide they dislike you."

That stung a little, but I had much bigger things to worry about than being popular.

"Really, who would hate you enough to go to the trouble of setting this whole thing up?" Zach asked.

"I can think of two people right off the top of my head. And you're related to both of them."

Zach considered this for a moment. "Trent's an ass, and he might do something because he resents you, but he's not a very big guy. And his upper-body strength is pathetic. I can't see him being able to topple a several-hundred-pound machine under any circumstances."

I mulled this idea over for a second. I'd barely been able to see the outline of the figure, but it did seem a bit bigger than Trent. Corinne was a different story, however. She was tall—and not willowy tall, but Amazon tall. Based on her build and personality, I figured she was also fast and strong.

And that strong vanilla scent . . . It seemed unlikely for a guy to be wearing such a syrupy cologne.

"Do you think it's possible that it was Corinne? That she was playing a prank on me?" I hastened to add. I didn't want to piss Zach off, but she did seem to be the most likely suspect.

"Corinne was on the phone with me just minutes before I heard you yelling. Besides, she may like to intimidate people, but she would never chase someone down and corner them." Zach's tone was more than a little defensive. "Especially not you—she knows I . . . she knows that I care about you."

I didn't want to tell him, but that was exactly why I thought it might have been her. The fact that Corinne didn't want me around Zach was no secret, and I wasn't sure how far she would go to keep us apart.

"We should tell someone," Zach said. "The police or the administration."

"What would we tell them? I can't describe the person; it was too dark. And he didn't actually *do* anything." I couldn't imagine the police would be much help.

"I guess I'll hold off for now." Zach frowned.

"So I think you have some explaining to do." I crossed my arms and put on a stern look, but my tone was teasing. I did it partly to change the subject, but also because I wanted to know how the hell Zach had moved the soda machine.

He gave me a puzzled look.

"You know," I prodded. "The whole 'shoving a several-hundred-pound object just by looking at it' thing? You never told me about that particular ability."

"Oh." My question seemed to throw Zach off balance.

"Yeah, well, I've always been able to do telekinesis stuff. When I was a kid, I'd move things without consciously meaning to. As I got older and gained more control, I stopped doing it. It made me feel like a freak." He ran his thumbnail along the metal counter.

"I wasn't actually sure I could still do the telekinesis," he continued. "And I definitely didn't know if I could move something that heavy. But when I saw you trapped behind those doors"—Zach's jaw worked under his skin—"the look of fear on your face . . . I've never felt more anger in my life. Nothing else mattered except getting you safe. I think I could move a bus if I needed to get to you."

"Zach . . ." I reached out and laid my hand over his. I didn't know what I wanted to say. Emotions were bubbling up in me in a way that I couldn't express.

He glanced up, and the look in his eyes took my breath away. "Everything's so different with you. I feel things . . . do things I've never done. Never thought I could do."

"Like that dream the other night?" I wanted desperately to know if my suspicions were right.

"Then you *did* dream it, too." He let out a sharp breath. "I thought you had, the way you wouldn't look at me at lunch on Monday."

"Well, you're the first person I've ever had invade my dreams. I'm still trying to adjust to it."

"I swear I've never done it before, not until you came here," he assured me. "I didn't know I could."

"I don't understand. How is it even possible?"

"It has to do with the Akashic field." Zach paused. "Do you know what that is?"

I shook my head no. Zach immediately went into science mode like he had when he first explained the BVs. The look on his face was so serious—it was insanely cute.

"It's a strong electromagnetic field in the earth's atmosphere. Supposedly information passes—in these patterns like radio waves—from a person out into this field. BVs who've worked at advancing their abilities say that they can tap into the Akashic field and get into the subconscious minds of people who are sleeping." He shrugged. "At least that's the theory."

It made about as much sense to me as quantum physics.

"I know. It's hard to understand," Zach agreed.

"So if you'd never done it before, how'd you know what to do? Why did you do it with me?" I realized too late how that sentence sounded. "I mean, um . . . ," I floundered.

"I didn't try to do it. It just happened. I was thinking about you when I went to sleep."

The image of Zach lying in bed sent a shiver through my body.

"And all of sudden, there I was in your dream. I asked Corinne about it the next day, and she said you're very accessible when you dream; your subconscious is wide open."

And now I was severely creeped out.

"So Corinne was really there in my dream with you?" I asked, my voice rising.

"She was apparently tailing me in my dream, and she followed when I went into yours."

Great. That's not mortifying at all.

"Don't be embarrassed," Zach responded to my unspoken thought. "She's the one who shouldn't have been there. That was between me and you."

I slipped off the stool, not looking at Zach. "Do you want to do your pictures? Mine are probably dry." It seemed ridiculous to talk about class projects after all that had happened, but they were still due.

"That's okay. I'll do mine tomorrow. Why don't you grab yours, and we can go over to the SAC—if you want."

"I want to," I assured him. Truthfully, it didn't matter anymore if I was doomed to get hurt, or if Zach and I were fundamentally incompatible. At this point I couldn't stop myself from falling for him.

I went to the dryer and began to pull my prints from it. As I set the first photo in my folder, I noticed that there was a faint ring of light around Zach, like a body-wide halo. I frowned. I looked at the next photograph, then the next. They were all the same. When I had first done darkroom work, I'd had some problems with overexposure, but it never looked like this.

"Uh, Zach . . ."

"What?" He turned, and I held up the pictures.

"Oh." He sighed. "Yeah . . . well." He shrugged. "It's the electric-field thing."

"So you always look like Our Lady of Guadalupe in photos?" I turned, laying the pictures out on the cabinet side by side.

"No. It doesn't normally show up. I can sort of meditate

to bring my body's energy down." He paused, then added, "It's you."

"Me? What does that mean?"

He came over and pointed at the prints I had lined up on the cabinet. I was very aware of how close he was to me. "If you look at them, you can see that it gets brighter in every picture."

It was true. "Okay. But why?"

"Because I have trouble controlling it."

I gazed up at him, suddenly breathless.

"The longer I'm around you, the less I can control myself," Zach whispered, his face just inches from mine. He ran a hand under my hair, his fingers lightly skimming over the back of my neck. A tremor ran through me at his touch, and for a moment I forgot how to breathe. Zach brushed his thumb across my cheek and I shivered again; this time I had no doubt he had seen it. Zach's eyes darkened. Every second was excruciatingly long, yet I didn't want it to end.

He bent his head to mine, and every thought I had evaporated. His lips were velvet. I pressed myself against him, wanting more. His mouth opened slightly, and a fire burned through me, urgent and new.

It felt like I was spinning dizzily, like if Zach's hands weren't in my hair and on my waist, I would collapse to the ground. I melted into his body, and he lifted me off my feet as though I weighed nothing. The energy poured off us in waves. When he set me back down, my head was swimming, but in a wonderful way.

"We've only got fifteen minutes until curfew." Zach brushed

my mussed hair back into place. "Want me to walk you back to your dorm?"

What I wanted was for Zach to be kissing me again; I wanted him never to stop. But that obviously wasn't an option.

"Okay." I could barely get out the word, my brain was so jumbled.

He interlaced his fingers with mine as we walked down the hall to the door. All my senses were heightened; even the night air on my face felt like silk. Nothing was ordinary anymore. The feel of Zach's palm, his fingers shifting with every step we took, his skin softly rubbing against mine. It was more intimate than I would have ever thought holding hands could be.

Kresky Hall was far too close, and my heart sank a little as it came into view. I didn't want this to end. I wanted to stay with Zach through the night, just to be close to him, to feel his chest rise and fall with every breath.

"I know." Zach stopped walking and turned to me. "I wish I didn't have to leave."

My steps became awkward, the movements jerky and out of sync.

"I thought you couldn't read my thoughts all the time." I stopped walking and crossed my arms over my chest, consequently pulling my hand from his.

"I can't—your emotions are just so strong right now." Zach took my face in his hands.

"But you don't have to be embarrassed." He placed a soft kiss on my lips, and they tingled as blood surged to them. Zach's breath quickened, and I could feel the warmth of it against my cheek. At that feather-light touch, everything inside me responded, and I pulled him closer. I wanted to bind our bodies together so we could never be apart.

When we finally made it back to Kresky Hall, I was five minutes late for check-in. But Ms. Moore's stern expression couldn't wipe the smile from my face.

I remained in a state of euphoria all day Friday. Since Friday was our short day, I didn't see Zach at lunch or photography, but I couldn't stop thinking about him.

Kissing Zach had been incredible. I wasn't sure if it was because of all the extra energy flowing between us or if this was the way everybody felt when they were falling in love. Either way, it was amazing. I couldn't imagine ever kissing anyone else again. As I left the library that afternoon, I was still reliving every second of our evening together.

"Hmmpf." I'd been so involved in my own daydreams that I had blindly walked straight into someone.

"Better watch where you're going, Goldilocks."

Trent.

"You wouldn't want to get yourself hurt, now, would you?"

"Sorry," I mumbled as I brushed past him. He reached out lightning fast and grabbed my wrist.

"You're not sorry yet." Trent's tight grip burned my skin. "But you will be."

I tried to wrench my arm away, but he was much stronger than me. "Let me go," I said through gritted teeth.

"What?" Trent gave me an innocent expression. "It's okay for Zach to touch you, but I can't?"

"Exactly," I spat the word out, hoping I looked pissed instead of scared. "Now, I told you to let me go."

"You can tell me anything you want, Goldilocks." Trent's tone was menacing. "But I'm the one with the control. You should think long and hard before doing something I won't like."

"Excuse me?" I stared. Did this guy seriously think he could tell me what to do?

"I guess you changed your mind about going to the dance alone." Trent went on, then deliberately looked me up and down. "It's too bad you chose Zach; he won't even know what to do with you."

Revulsion and disgust flooded through my body, nauseating me.

"How'd he hook you, anyway? Did he give you that whole sensitive loner-guy act?" Trent asked mockingly. "Or are you just too scared to go out with a real man?"

I wanted to bend over in pain, the way my stomach was churning, but I wouldn't allow him the pleasure of seeing me squirm.

"Answer me!" He squeezed my wrist so tight it was cutting off the circulation to my hand.

"Why would I want to be with scum like you when I can be with Zach?"

"Zach's not as perfect as you think." Trent's eyes narrowed. "He's no different than—"

A flash of movement caught him off guard, and suddenly Zach was between us.

"I don't care what your problem with me is, but you leave her out of it." Zach's formidable stature dwarfed Trent, and he let go of my wrist.

"You afraid of what I might tell her?" Trent taunted, but I noticed he took a step back.

"Everyone knows you're full of shit." Zach was clenching his fist tightly by his side. "But if you ever touch Persephone again, I will end you."

"You're willing to beat down your own flesh and blood over some slut from Los Angeles?" A vile smile spread across Trent's face, as if something had just occurred to him. I felt sicker at the sight of it. "She's dirtier than the streets of the city she comes from. Fifteen years old, and she's not even a virgin."

Chapter Fifteen

The second the words were out of Trent's mouth, Zach's fist slammed into his cheek. I jumped back as a spray of blood flew from Trent's face.

I couldn't believe this was happening. To have private facts of my life thrown in my face—to have this be the way Zach found out—was unbearable. Bile rose in my throat; I tasted its bitterness on the back of my tongue, but I forced it back down.

"Don't you ever talk about her again," Zach hissed. "If you so much as say her name . . ." He let the unspoken threat hang in the air.

"Screw you." Trent spit blood onto the grass, giving me one last hate-filled glare before walking away.

"Are you okay?" Zach turned to me.

I nodded, unable to speak.

I felt violated—stripped of all my power, my dignity. Trent had been pulling memories out of my head. Intimate memories. *What did Zach think of me now?* The way Trent had said it was so awful. If I had told Zach myself, at least I could have explained the circumstances. *You can still tell him it was only that one time.* I pulled back and stared up into Zach's eyes.

"About what Trent . . ."

"I know it's not true," Zach said before I could finish.

Unwelcome tears welled up inside me.

"Actually . . . it is." I kicked at the ground with the toe of my black flats, not wanting to see his face.

"No. It's not." Zach tilted my chin up so I was looking at him. "Just because you slept with someone—which really isn't my business—it doesn't change how I feel about you," he finished firmly.

"But it was a mistake. It was after my sister died, and I was all screwed up. . . ." Everything in me was burning. Rage toward Trent. Embarrassment and regret. The emotions I'd pushed down bubbled to the surface.

Even now, I could feel the intense loneliness that had driven me to sleep with Paul. I'd longed to be close to someone, to have that connection. But it had been drunken and meaningless. I remembered how empty I was the next morning.

"You don't have to explain yourself to me." Zach stroked my hair, pushing it back from my face. His expression hardened a little then, and I wondered if he felt the remnants of that night inside of me. If he could feel how humiliated I'd been when Paul broke up with me—ashamed that I'd been stupid enough to think he was the right guy.

"I have to say it's a good thing I'll never meet the guy; he wouldn't stand much of a chance if we came toe-to-toe." Zach ran his thumb down my cheek. "No one is ever going to treat you badly again—not while I'm around."

The fierceness in Zach's eyes was enough to make me believe him.

Before I could respond, he bent down and kissed me, pushing all other thoughts out of my mind.

As I walked into the dormitory, I met Adriana coming out of the hall bathroom.

"My, my. What have we been up to, Ms. Phe?" She arched her eyebrow suggestively.

I touched two fingers to my reddened lips. Zach and I must have been kissing in the courtyard for at least a half hour. I took a deep breath. I had been dreading the moment when I would have to back out of our plans, but now seemed as a good a time as any to break the news.

"I got asked to the dance, so I'm not going to be able to do the group date." The words tumbled out of my mouth, and I waited for the outburst I felt sure was coming.

"Okay," Adriana replied, shrugging one shoulder.

"I thought you were going to be mad."

"Why would I be mad at you for having a date?" Adriana laughed. "I'd dump Chace Crawford if Zach asked me out. You are going with Zach, right?"

I smiled, not saying anything.

"Okay. Gossip time, my room, ten minutes," she ordered.

"I'll get Toy," I supplied.

The three of us spent the rest of Friday evening talking and going through Adriana's clothes to pick out a dress and accessories for Toy.

By lights out we'd agreed to meet around six the next day to get ready for the dance.

At seven on Saturday night, we were sitting in Adriana's room doing manis and pedis. Toy giggled as I painted her toenails gunmetal gray. "That tickles," she squealed, her foot jerking in my hand.

"If you don't hold still, the whole top of your foot is going to look like a postmodern Impressionist art piece," I warned.

"Primping is more entertaining than I imagined." She steeled her leg.

"Have you ever had any female friends, Toy?" Adriana asked without sarcasm. In fact, she looked almost concerned.

Toy scrunched up her face. "I guess not." She shrugged. "I pretty much hung out with my brother and his friends in New York, and ever since I came to Devenish, I've been friends with Graham and the guys who are in TechConnect."

"Well, that all changes this year," Adriana declared. "You now officially have girlfriends—we'll do a lot of fun things that guys don't do."

"Like what?" Toy asked.

"Dance parties to cheesy eighties music. All-night *Sex and the City* marathons. Talking about cute guys for hours on end." Adriana ticked the things off on her fingers.

"I can definitely see the appeal in that last one," Toy admitted. "I've always wanted to have a friend who could teach me how to *not* be one of the guys."

"A few tips from me and you'll have those geeks eating out of your hand. No offense," Adriana added.

"None taken," Toy assured her. "Most of the guys I like are geeks. Except for Graham." She blushed.

An hour later, everyone was dressed, but Adriana was still doing Toy's makeup. Adriana had put on Santigold—according to her she couldn't do makeup without a sound track—and she was clicking her black satin heels together in time with the beat.

I ran a hand over my dress, wondering what Zach would say when he saw me in it. The sleeveless ivory shift had a relaxed A-line shape and a high circular neckline with deeply cutaway shoulders. It perfectly showcased my collarbone—a great look for someone like me who had no cleavage to speak of. Since the dress was rather subdued, I had decided to wear my red suede pumps with the outrageously large bow on the back of each heel.

"It's time for me to go meet Zach," I declared as the clock clicked over to eight. I'd been watching it in rapt attention, anticipating this moment. I stood up from Adriana's bed. "You two both look awesome," I added.

"Just wait until you see the finished product," Adriana told me as I walked out of the room. "Toy is going to leave Graham speechless."

"I have no doubt." I grinned, shutting the door behind me.

As I walked down the hall, my heels clacked against the floor, echoing the rapid beating of my heart. I couldn't wait to see Zach. By the time I stepped outside, I was what could only be described as giddy. Zach, who was walking up the path toward me, stopped short.

"Wow," he breathed. *Just the reaction I was hoping for.*

Chapter Sixteen

"You look unbelievable." Zach shook his head in awe. "Are you sure you're not supposed to be meeting someone else out here? Like Tom Cruise?"

"How old do you think I am?" I laughed. "That guy is ancient, not to mention married."

"Sorry, I don't know the names of any of the young hot guys." Zach grinned.

He was flawless in his slim-fitting black suit.

He held his arm out for me, and we linked elbows. I felt so elegant and grown-up: dressed to the nines and walking across this beautiful expanse of campus with the most amazing guy I had ever met.

"So, Persephone Archer—are you liking Devenish?" Zach asked.

"It's perfect," I answered him truthfully. He stopped midstep and pulled me to him. I felt warm and slightly light-headed, the way I always felt when he touched me.

"*You* are perfect," he replied, leaning down to kiss me.

By the time we made it to the ballroom on the second

floor of the SAC, Adriana and Toy were already there. They had probably swept right past while Zach and I were kissing, and I had been so lost in it that I hadn't noticed.

Toy looked sexy in a nonconformist way. The gray racer-back dress she'd borrowed from Adriana was cut short and extremely tight, but on Toy's tiny frame it was loosely fitted and hit her just below the knees. The blue heels I'd given her were even more striking since she normally wore flats. Adriana's red backless Valentino gown was the most gorgeous one in the room. "So where's Brody?" Zach asked Adriana.

"I don't know—playing video games with Graham?" She rolled her eyes. "They were supposed to meet us here five minutes ago."

"There they are." Toy gave a little excited hop.

The guys were standing in the entrance; Graham was cute in his tux, and even Brody looked nice. His hair was clean and shiny and not hanging in his eyes. The suit jacket also helped him out by camouflaging how skinny he was.

Graham was scanning the crowd on the opposite side of the room, but Brody's eyes immediately searched out Adriana. He elbowed Graham and pointed to us. As they walked over, I could see the expression on Graham's face change to one of stunned amazement. He must have just spotted Toy.

"Oh, my God," he said when he reached us. "You look . . . I mean . . ." Graham shook his head at Toy. "I don't think I've ever seen you in a dress before." The way he was staring, it probably would have sounded more appropriate for him to say, "I've never seen *you* before."

"You look great," Graham added quickly.

"Thanks." She beamed so brightly you could probably see her from space.

"I'm going to grab something to drink," Graham announced. "Do you want anything?" He looked straight at Toy.

"Sure. I'll come with you."

As they made their way over to the refreshment table, Adriana propped her hand on her hip and stared at Brody expectantly. "Well?" She opened her eyes wide. "Aren't you going to give me some kind of compliment?"

"You are, hands down, the hottest girl here," Brody replied.

"I know *that*." Adriana rolled her eyes. "I was hoping for something a little more specific. Something about my dress, perhaps."

"Umm." Brody tapped his foot, thinking. "Your dress is really sexy?"

"I guess that's probably the best I'm going to get out of you." She sighed.

The decorations for the dance were minimal, consisting of a few small tables near the refreshment center. In addition to sodas and punch there was a platter of little sandwiches, and an arrangement of mums that served as a centerpiece. Mrs. Carr was behind the punch bowl—probably stationed there to guard it against would-be spikers. She was staring stonily out across the room while Mr. Carr, beside her, seemed to be carrying on an intense, though rather one-sided, low-voiced argument.

The DJ's table was in the corner, and the Rihanna song he was playing was not inspiring anyone to dance. Everyone was either milling around or standing in little clumps, talking. Of course the lack of dancing could also be attributed to the presence of several teachers and other adults who stood around the perimeter of the room, looking very chaperone-y. I wasn't sure who the other adults were, but since I didn't recognize them, I assumed that they were probably parents of some of the townies.

Sure enough, Zach's uncle Tripp was standing over by the exit to the balconies. *That would suck,* I thought, *to have your parents watching you and your friends.* I had the sudden panicked thought that maybe Zach's parents were there, and I did another scan of the room. I relaxed when I saw no sign of Grant Redford.

Bouncy blonde Kerry and the red-headed girl from the Pictionary game were by the entrance of the ballroom, giggling about some guy who had come in sporting a tuxedo T-shirt. I was pleased to see Kerry was wearing her standard bubblegum pink. The color was still beyond awful, but after Corinne had torn her down at the SAC, I figured she'd never be seen in it again. I was glad she had more backbone than I'd given her credit for.

Just then, Corinne strolled in, wearing a simple emerald green column that hugged her statuesque curves. She was flanked on either side by nondescript girls who would have been interchangeable if they hadn't been wearing different dresses. Zach took my hand firmly. Corinne's pale eyes narrowed when they landed on us, and she stalked off to the back of the room.

"Your sis is real friendly," Adriana told Zach.

"Yeah, she takes a while to warm up to people," he conceded. "I'm going to go talk to her for a sec." Zach squeezed my hand. "If that's okay?" he asked me softly.

"Sure." I smiled. If I wanted to be with Zach, I had to accept the fact that he came with some family baggage. It wasn't like I was angst-free.

As Zach walked away, Adriana gave Brody a pointed look.

"What did I do?" Brody crossed his arms over his chest defensively.

"It's more what you're *not* doing." Adriana shooed him away. "Go get me a drink or something."

"As you wish, princess." Brody bent at the waist in an exaggerated bow. But, of course, he loped off a second later.

"Thank God." Adriana exhaled loudly. "If anyone thinks I actually came here with Brody as my date, I am going to be mortified."

"Brody's not that bad." I smiled.

Zach was already making his way back over to us, stepping around the few couples who had taken to the dance floor. Two of the dancers were Toy and Graham. I pressed my lips together, trying not to laugh at Graham's joyful but comically bad water-sprinkler move. Luckily, Toy had fared better in the dance skills department.

"Sorry about that." Zach slipped his hand back into mine.

"That's okay." I gave him a soft kiss on the lips.

"Oh, barf." Adriana rolled her eyes. "I guess if my only choices are hanging out with you lovebirds or dancing with that epileptic out there, I'm going to have to go with the public humiliation." Brody had apparently decided that, instead of getting drinks, he was going to get down. He and Graham seemed to be having a can-opener/Roger Rabbit contest. I shook my head in awe. It took real skill to be that bad.

"I sure know how to clear a room, huh?" Zach asked after Adriana walked onto the dance floor. "Do your friends hate me for some reason I don't know about?"

"No," I laughed. "They all really like you. We're probably giving off some kind of couple vibe that's—" I stopped mid-sentence. *Were we actually a couple?* It was probably way too soon to say that.

"There is nothing I would like more than to be coupled with you." Zach pulled me to him, burrowing his hands in my hair. His face was warm against my cheek. "You look so gorgeous tonight." Zach's breath tickled at my ear, sending shivers all through me. "I don't know if I can resist you."

"So don't." I could barely get the words out; it felt as if desire was filling me up, pushing the air out of my lungs, taking over every inch of my body. Then Zach kissed me so passionately I was afraid a chaperone was going to come over and separate us.

"Umm," I murmured, when he released me a little. "I have a feeling I am in dire need of a makeup reapplication after that."

"You don't need any such thing." He kissed me again, and the heat in the pit of my stomach spread through me like wildfire.

"Hmm-humph." A woman with a bland bob haircut stood next to us, her lips pursed and eyebrows raised. I could feel a lecture about "being a lady" coming on. I certainly didn't want to spend the rest of the night with this woman following my every move.

"Excuse me." I gave Zach a quick peck on the cheek. "I have

to use the restroom." I made a beeline for the hall, praying the lady wouldn't decide the toilet was a perfect place to discuss my raging hormones.

I should have been praying for something else entirely. As I stepped out of the bathroom stall a few minutes later, my eyes fell on emerald green satin shoes.

Great. I knew this night was going too smoothly. I steeled myself before looking up. Unlike some extremely tall girls, Corinne was not the least bit bothered by her stature—besides standing ramrod straight, she was also wearing four-inch heels. Which made her about the same height as Zach. But while he tried to minimize the distance between us by stooping down a little, Corinne was more than happy to lord her vertical advantage over me.

"Listen." Corinne's pale eyes bored into mine. "I know that you wormed all this information about us out of Zach. He's always been naïve and trusting, but apparently 'young love' has completely turned his brain to mush."

"Zach knows he can trust me," I replied, keeping my voice even. "I would never reveal anything he said."

"Yeah, right. Till you get bored with him or need something to gossip about."

I braced myself, staring back into her eyes with all the fierceness I could muster. "I told him I wouldn't tell anyone, and I won't. I keep my word."

"You better." Corinne leaned in closer. I could almost hear the electricity snapping between us. "Because any one of us can get into your mind, but Zach and Trent are amateurs compared to me. And if you ever, *ever* tell anyone anything about us, I will visit you in your dreams, and the next day you won't remember a thing he told you. I will wipe you clean."

"Okay." I tried not to sound shaken. "Now you've delivered your warning." I stepped around Corinne and went to the sink to wash my hands.

I had hoped that would signal an end to our conversation, but Corinne drew a long breath and let it out, then followed me to the sink. She had schooled her face into something resembling calm.

"I know you think I'm the devil incarnate," she told me. "And you have absolutely no reason to believe what I say to you, but I am going to say it anyway. At least that way, when something horrific happens, I can rest easy, knowing I did everything in my power to prevent it."

She paused as I dried my hands. Obviously she wanted my full attention. Finally, I turned to face her, hand on my hip, and she continued. "You need to end things with Zach. Find some other guy at this school, one who's more like you."

"I don't care about that." I stared back at her defiantly.

"You may not care now, but you will. Sooner than you know. And by then, it may be too late. Who knows what could happen if Zach—" Corinne stopped herself and drew in a steadying breath. Her pale eyes were glossy. If I had thought she was capable of genuine emotion, I would have been convinced she was tearing up.

"I would never hurt Zach," I said vehemently. "I care about him very much. If you'd taken the time to get to know me instead of doing everything in your power to frighten me away, you might realize that." I was fighting tears myself, and I wasn't quite sure why. "And I'm not breaking up with him, no matter what you say to me. If you really loved him, you would want him to be happy, even if it was with me."

"I *do* want him to be happy, but more than that, I want him to be reasonable. I want him to do what he has to, to protect himself and us." Corinne let out an exasperated breath. "But I won't do anything about what he's already told you—unless you force me to take desperate measures. Whatever you may think of me, I don't relish the idea of picking apart someone else's mind. So I really do hope you care about him enough to keep quiet. Even after you two are apart."

Her words, the idea of not being with Zach, tore through my heart.

"Because you won't last—you can't. The human body isn't meant to be bombarded with so much energy; it kills *us,* and little by little it will kill you. You and Zach may not want to believe it, but it's true."

"I'm stronger than that," I protested, hoping I was right. "My energy . . . it . . . Zach and I are stronger together, not weaker."

"I can't explain your energy. I've never encountered it before." Corinne gritted her teeth. "But I do know what history has taught us; we *can't* be with outsiders. If you weren't so incredibly pigheaded, you would see that I'm trying to protect you."

"Why would you try to protect me?" My words echoed off

the tile walls of the restroom. "You're probably the one who tried to attack me in the Arts Building!"

"That soda machine crap? Zach already gave me the third degree *and* checked with our parents to make sure I was really at home that night. It wasn't me—must've been someone else you pissed off." Corinne snorted. "Besides, why would I chase you down a hallway? That's totally ridiculous."

"Maybe because you hate my guts?" I suggested.

"I don't hate you. I just know this will end badly." Corinne's voice was steady, sure. "If you break up with him now, it'll be easier on all of us. You will save yourself and my family a lot of heartache."

"Oh, so you're pretending to have a heart now?" I spat nastily. "Because as far as I can tell, the only thing residing in your chest is a cold hard block of ice."

"I am trying to save you, you ungrateful idiot!"

"Don't do me any favors." I swept past her, letting the bathroom door swing shut in her face. I was practically shaking, I was so angry—or afraid; I wasn't positive which it was. Maybe a bit of both.

I spotted Zach and Brody over by the DJ table talking to the guy running the music. Zach burst out with his thick, deep laugh. I wanted desperately to be near him, to feel his reassuring presence wash over me. I wanted to ask him if Corinne could really erase my memories. I suspected that it was true, and the idea horrified me—that everything that had happened the last couple of weeks, my whole relationship with Zach, could be gone from my mind one day, just like that. But I knew if I asked him, he would be furious with Corinne and the whole evening would be ruined. And that was exactly what Corinne wanted.

I couldn't go over there right now. I glanced around the room and saw George, but he was talking to a group of guys I didn't know. Then I spotted Adriana leaning against the wall behind the table that the administration had given the parent-friendly title of "refreshment center." She was observing the party revelers with detachment. There was at least one person who was self-involved enough not to notice I was upset.

"How's it going?" I asked after grabbing a bottle of water.

"It's whatever." Adriana shrugged. "Why do you think he wanted to go to the dance with her?"

She was eyeing Trent and Sybil, who were standing at the entrance of the room. Trent seemed bored as he watched Sybil talk animatedly to some sophomore who had been following her around since the beginning of the week. *Sybil's building her army of lackeys, one insecure girl at a time.*

"If the story you told me about game night is any indication, he invited her because he thinks it will get him laid," I answered.

"But he's so hot. I bet there are tons of girls willing to sleep with him. Girls who aren't related to Satan." Adriana pointed at Sybil's shoes. "Notice how she doesn't ever wear peep toes? It's to hide her cloven hooves."

We strolled past the refreshment table, where Mrs. Carr was dipping out punch, no disgruntled husband in sight. She gave us a mechanical smile as we went to join Brody and Zach.

"Hey, you guys!" Toy came bounding over, a sweaty Graham right behind her. "Why aren't you dancing?"

"There should be some kind of protective barrier set up around Graham and Brody when they're dancing. That is a majorly hazardous danger zone," Adriana informed her. "I was afraid I was going to lose an eye."

"I'll have you know I took the all-preschool dance trophy," Graham said proudly.

"Wow. Impressive," Toy teased.

"Shush, you." He chucked her lightly under the chin, and she practically glowed with happiness. Watching Toy and Graham, I was glad I had encouraged her to go after him. They would make a perfect couple. *Not that they'll ever be able to compete with Zach and me.* I looked up at Zach, and he planted a kiss on my forehead.

"Jesus. Get a room already." Adriana nudged me. "I'm going to have to go back to that perilous dance floor before I enter insulin shock."

As always, Brody followed close behind her.

Toy and Graham exchanged a look. "Yeah. We're going to go dance some more, too."

"I guess we scared everyone off again, huh?" Zach laughed.

"I don't mind," I assured him.

"I just want to tell you, in case I forget later, that I had a wonderful time tonight." Zach smiled.

I laid my head against his arm and let out a little sigh of contentment.

"Happy?" Zach asked with a wide grin.

"Very," I assured him. *Or at least I had been.* Now Corinne was walking toward us.

"I need to talk to my brother. In private."

"I'm kind of busy here," Zach told her through gritted teeth.

"I'm sure Phe won't mind. I'll return you good as new."

Somehow I doubted that. Corinne was determined to ruin our night—our whole relationship, in fact—and since I hadn't folded, she was now trying to break Zach.

"It's fine. I'm not going anywhere." I arched an eyebrow at Corinne to make sure she got my double meaning.

"Thanks, L.A., I knew you'd understand." She gave me a nasty little smile.

"I'll be right back," Zach said before following Corinne out onto the balcony.

I tapped my heel as I waited. Who knew what she was out there saying. I just had to trust that Zach would take it with a grain of salt. Or arsenic, in Corinne's case.

My small evening bag started vibrating, and I extracted my ringing cell phone from it. I didn't recognize the number.

"Hello?" I answered curiously.

"Persephone." The voice sounded just like my swim teacher's. "It's Mr. Carr."

Probably because it was my swim teacher. I glanced at the punch table where he had been earlier. Only Mrs. Carr was there now.

"Where are you?" I did a complete 360.

"I'm at the pond behind the SAC." His voice sounded strange, almost panicked. "Can you get away for a second? Come meet me here? By yourself?"

I glanced out at the balcony. Corinne was still chewing Zach out.

"I guess," I agreed hesitantly. This didn't feel right. And not in a "I think my teacher is hitting on me" way. It felt wrong in a "something bad is going to happen" sense.

"It's important. I have something to tell you. Something you really need to know." Mr. Carr was trying to hold his voice steady, but I could hear the desperation creeping in around the edges.

"Okay." This wasn't a good idea, but as usual my impulse control was less than stellar. "I'll be there in a minute."

"Thanks, Persephone." He let out a sigh of relief, and I hung up the phone.

I felt weird leaving without saying something to Zach. If he came back in and found me gone, he would be extremely worried. But I couldn't believe that Mr. Carr was going to hurt me, and he had said to come alone. *I'll just have to get back before Corinne's done bitching.* That meant I had at least ten minutes.

A dense fog had descended on the campus while we had been in the SAC, and now I could barely see two feet in front of my face. I felt my way around the corner of the building.

The adrenaline pumping through my veins was telling me to run, but I knew that was a bad idea. I couldn't tell where I was going—what if I twisted my ankle like some idiotic girl in a horror movie? That was a sure way to end up dead. I forged on through the eerie white vapor, praying that I would see Mr. Carr. Because if he wasn't here, then this was some kind of trap. And I had walked right into it.

Fear was spreading through my chest like thick creeping ivy—I was halfway to the pond, and the fog had grown even denser. It was rising off the water like smoke from dry ice, obscuring everything. I couldn't even see the huge willow tree that stood next to the pond. Why had I come out here? I was completely defenseless. And Zach didn't know where I was. What if someone grabbed me from behind and slit my throat? I felt something damp touch the back of my neck and I started running blindly.

All of a sudden, my legs were knocked out from under me and I was falling, the mist cold on my skin. I hit the ground with a thud. A flash of silver glinted at me from the grass. Athena's ID bracelet. I wrapped my fist around it tightly.

Only then did I notice what was lying beside the bracelet. A human hand. My entire body quaked as I followed the outline of the body up to the face. I was staring into the unseeing eyes of Mr. Carr. They were terrifying in their emptiness. There was no soul behind them. These were the eyes of a shell. Mr. Carr was gone.

I couldn't fully comprehend the horror of what I was seeing. *I was just on the phone with him.* He had been alive, and now he was dead. A corpse with a raw red handprint burned into either side of his head.

There was a roaring in my ears. What if his killer was still here? What if I was next? I whipped my head around and saw a figure running at me through the fog. My heart stopped momentarily, and I couldn't breathe, my lungs constricted by the steel trap my rib cage had become. There was nothing left for me to do—he was too near; there was no chance for escape. I closed my eyes tightly, hoping to shut out the searing pain I knew was coming.

Chapter Seventeen

"Phe! Phe, are you okay?"

Zach was gently shaking me. I blinked my heavy eyelids, dazed and disoriented. I was lying in the cold wet grass a few feet away from Mr. Carr's body.

"I thought you were the person who . . . I thought you were . . ." I clutched the bracelet in my hand so tightly that the sharp metal corners dug into my skin. "I must have fainted."

"You were just lying here when I ran up. I could barely see you through all the fog." Zach took my outstretched hand and hoisted me off the ground. Kissing the top of my head, he murmured into my hair, "You scared the shit out of me."

At this, I started crying. Zach was here and I was safe, but Mr. Carr wasn't. Mr. Carr would never be anything ever again.

Teachers and various parents were hurrying past us, screaming at one another about CPR and ambulances.

"What happened?" A girl I didn't know came running up, looking panicked. A teacher stopped her with one arm.

"We think Mr. Carr had a heart attack," the teacher told her. "Please go wait inside the SAC with the other kids, and we'll tell you what happened when we know more."

Heart attack? I felt my mind getting fuzzy again. I could hear the commotion all around as Zach picked me up, cradling me in his arms. Then it blended into an unintelligible din, and I slipped into unconsciousness. When I awoke, I was lying on a couch with my head in Zach's lap.

"Hey." He gave me a small sad smile.

"Mr. Carr?" Maybe it had been one of my dreams. A terrible nightmare.

"He's gone. The coroner took him away."

"He's really dead?" The tears in my throat were choking me. I sat up. "Was he . . . did somebody . . . ?" I couldn't quite bring myself to say the word *murder.*

"No," Zach reassured me.

"Phe. You're awake." Ms. Moore broke off from the group of teachers and parents next to us. "How are you feeling?"

"Awful. Out of it." That barely touched on all the emotions swirling through me.

"I am so sorry you had to find him like that." Ms. Moore's eyes were shiny with unshed tears.

"Thanks." I was trying not to cry myself. The entire school was crammed into the downstairs of the SAC, and I didn't want to break down in front of them.

"I'll give you some time." Ms. Moore patted me on the shoulder, then walked back over to the other adults.

Zach watched the group intently.

"What are they talking about?" I had no doubt he was using his superhearing to his advantage.

"They're trying to decide how much to tell us right now. They want to wait for the hospital's test results before they make an official statement, but several of them think it was an aneurysm." Zach closed his eyes in concentration. I could barely pick out the low buzz of their voices in this crowd of noise.

"Apparently he'd been complaining of headaches for a few days. They're saying maybe a blood vessel in his brain . . ." Zach saw the look on my face and trailed off. "I'm sorry."

"It's okay." It wasn't the description of the aneurysm that was getting to me. I just I didn't want to go through all this again. I was tired of death.

"Listen up, everyone." Mr. Potterson clapped his hands together. "We aren't going to find out anything concrete tonight, so we have come to the decision that everyone should go back to their dorms and get some sleep. We will hold a meeting as soon as we know what happened to Mr. Carr."

"Was he murdered?" a male voice called out from the middle of the crowd.

Several students echoed the sentiment.

"Are we safe?" a girl yelled.

"I can assure you that you are all safe. Mr. Carr's death was a natural one." Mr. Potterson's booming voice drowned out the others. "The paramedics think it was a heart attack. But as I said before, we won't know anything for sure until they have had time to run some tests. Now, I am going to have all the houses break up into groups, so please go stand by your respective dorm heads. Day students whose parents are here may leave with them. The rest of the day students, remain with me. I will walk you out to your cars when the boarding students have cleared out."

The teachers lined up at the front of the SAC.

"I wish I could come with you." Zach tucked a lock of hair behind my ear and kissed my forehead. "I'll see you tomorrow, though."

I nodded silently. I was afraid if I spoke, I would start crying. I felt like a raw nerve. I wanted Zach to stay with me now more than ever. I wanted to fall asleep next to him, curled in the shelter of his arms. He squeezed my hand one last time before I went over to stand with Ms. Moore's group. Adriana was at my side the moment we stepped out of the SAC, and she walked right next to me, silent as a ghost, all the way back to the dorm. Even when we reached our rooms, she only gave me a little sad wave before going in.

I closed my door behind me and locked it. As soon as I was alone, my shaky legs gave out on me, and I sank to the floor. I let a tear roll down my cheek.

The teachers had said his death was natural, but I had seen Mr. Carr's body. The red handprints seared into his head. That was anything but natural. I opened my purse, shaking its contents onto the floor. The silver ID bracelet was still there. Why did Mr. Carr have it? Had he found it in the Athletics Center? Maybe he'd just come across it recently. That made sense.

But what didn't make any sense was the way he had spoken to me, his voice rushed and shaky. *Urgent.* What could have been so important about my lost bracelet? And why would he have felt that he needed to talk to me about it outside and alone?

I ran my thumb along the engraved infinity symbol, like it was a genie's lamp that could provide me with answers. What was Mr. Carr going to tell me? Had someone killed him to keep it secret?

Everything had finally felt right in my life, and now it had been ripped apart again. In a surge of anger I threw the bracelet across the room. It bounced off the bedside table and fell harmlessly to the floor. I took my heels off and threw them, too, not caring that they were my favorites.

The loud thump the shoes made as they hit the wood table was satisfying. But it didn't get rid of the fright that permeated me, like a deep, cold ache in my bones. It wasn't just the red handprints on Mr. Carr's body that scared me. It was death. I had felt it when Athena died, too.

I stood up and pulled off my dress, catching a glimpse of myself in the mirror. I looked exactly how I felt: small, vulnerable, tortured. It was like I had curled into myself. Then I noticed something else in the mirror.

The mark.

Had my Hekate's Wheel protected me tonight? If I had gotten there a few minutes sooner, would I be dead, too?

This idea sent a sickening shiver through my body. I turned away from my reflection and put my pajamas on. But even with the mark covered up, it still weighed on me. I could pretend it wasn't there, but I knew it was.

The night Athena died, it had been unbearable in our house. When the police showed up at our door, my mom broke down immediately, sobbing and wailing in my dad's arms. But I didn't scream or cry. I was mute. I just sat in my room for hours, staring blankly at the walls my sister had helped me paint dark teal.

I could hardly sleep that first week, so I started pretending that Athena was over at her friend's house and she'd be home in the morning. After a while, I'd pretend she was on a backpacking trip. The one she was supposed to take after graduation.

I spent months pretending, trying to fool myself. But when the letter from Devenish came, I had no one to give it to, no forwarding address. I finally had to admit Athena was really gone. Gone forever. And I couldn't do anything to change it. There wasn't anyone to blame, not really. It was an accident, a horrible, stupid accident that could never be made right.

But Mr. Carr . . . that hadn't been an accident, and no matter what the teachers said, his death wasn't natural. There was someone to blame. I just didn't know who yet. Mr. Carr's death couldn't be undone; it could never be made right. But maybe he could have justice. Somehow.

Chapter Eighteen

After a fitful night's sleep I spent most of Sunday in bed, drifting in and out of consciousness. I awoke to the sound of my cell phone ringing late in the afternoon.

"Hello?" I rubbed my eyes, forgetting to look at the caller ID before answering.

"Persephone?" It was Zach. "Is this a bad time? You sound tired."

"No, it's fine. I was just getting up from a nap." I tried to shake the fog from my head. "What's going on?"

"I came over to campus to talk to Brody. See how he's handling everything, but it's like trying to have a conversation with a brick wall. Anyway, I thought if you wanted, I could come by. Corinne gave me her car for the day."

"That sounds good." A massive understatement considering that the only thing I wanted to do today was see Zach.

"Okay. How's five minutes from now?"

My room looked like a tornado had hit it, thanks to my pre-dance rummagings, and I looked even worse.

"Can we make it thirty?" Mascara was smeared under

my eyes, my breath was gross, and my long hair was tangled. I needed to do some major freshening up.

Exactly thirty minutes later I heard a knock at my door. I was dressed, but I had just started cleaning up my room. I let out a little grunt of frustration and shoved the remainder of my stuff into the closet. Zach was far too prompt. Not that I was actually going to complain about his being here.

"Hey." I held the door open, and as Zach came in he glanced over at my bed. My mind immediately went back to my dream— our dream—when we had been lying there together.

It hit me that this was the first time he'd been in my room. In real life, at least. I didn't think the dream visit quite counted. I looked at the plain white walls, my bare dresser, and suddenly wished I had made my dorm room more personal—put up some pictures or something. It was like no one lived in here.

"How are you doing?" Zach tucked a damp tendril of hair behind my ear. The surge of energy I always felt at his touch flooded my nervous system, spreading throughout my body.

"I'm better now that you're here."

Zach pulled me into a tight hug that smelled of Ivory soap, pine trees, and freshly cut grass. All things warm and comforting. I pressed my head against his chest and breathed in his scent.

"I'm so sorry about last night." His deep, faintly rough voice reverberated through his chest and into mine.

"I'm glad you were there. That you're here now. I've been

so scared I could hardly sleep," I admitted, my voice muffled by Zach's soft black T-shirt.

"You don't need to be scared." He stroked my hair. "I won't let anything hurt you."

I knew without a doubt that Zach believed what he was saying, but the pit of my stomach was icy. Something was telling me that my dreams, my mark, meant even more than I had once thought. I had a destiny. And I wasn't sure I would ever truly be safe again.

Zach placed a sweet, comforting kiss on the top of my head, and the deep freeze in my stomach melted away. I leaned back to look up into his face. Zach's hands on the small of my back were getting warmer, scorching me right through my clothes. I slid my arms around his neck, my eyes closing naturally as our lips met.

When Zach kissed me, I could hear the roaring of the ocean in my ears; I could feel the blood coursing through my veins; I could taste the metallic energy our bodies created when they were pressed together. We kissed more and more deeply, urgently. I caught his bottom lip between my own lips, taking in the softness of it. I had never had this feeling before. It was stronger than a want; it was a burning need. It was hunger.

"You're amazing," Zach whispered hoarsely. "Thank you . . . for telling me how you feel." He ran a hot fingertip down the side of my face. "Everyone's always covering up the messy parts." He sighed, then released me and took a step back. I felt coldness creep into my chest, where his body had been touching mine.

"Especially Brody. I doubt he'll ever say how he really feels about what happened to Mr. Carr."

"It's got to be hard for him," I offered. "First his parents die, then his guardian."

"How did you know about that?" Zach squinted.

"Graham told me," I answered.

"Oh." An emotion flitted across Zach's face so quickly that I wasn't sure if it had even been there. Maybe I had imagined it. How could Zach possibly be jealous of a guy like Graham?

"Sometimes I forget you have this whole life after school lets out." Zach ran a hand through his hair, making it more gorgeously rumpled than it had been before. "Brody said something about some of the boarders having a party last weekend, but I guess I don't really think of you as one of them. Stupid, right?" He laughed.

"It's not stupid." I *wished* my life could be nothing but Zach. When he wasn't around, it felt like a little piece of me was missing, too. But I couldn't say that. I wasn't willing to take that risk yet. "I know it's got to be weird for the day students. I mean, we all live together, eat breakfast and dinner in our little groups. There's no way the townies wouldn't feel kind of different— especially since . . ."

"Since most of us townies are different," Zach finished for me. I thought of the BVs electrical complexities, the way they could melt things with their bare hands. The image of Mr. Carr's body filled my mind. The marks burned into his flesh.

"Zach . . . what if Mr. Carr didn't die of a heart attack or a brain aneurysm?"

"What?" He looked at me, puzzled.

"Did you see him? When you got to me, did you look at Mr. Carr's face? Did you see those handprints?"

His frown deepened. "Yeah."

"Doesn't that seem weird to you?" I pressed. "An aneurysm wouldn't put red handprints on either side of your head. But somebody with a great deal of electricity in his body, with the ability to—"

"You think he was murdered by a BV?" Zach shook his head in disbelief.

"What else can I think? Who else could have made those marks on his temples? And there's another thing—I wasn't there by accident. Mr. Carr called me on my cell phone right before he died."

"What?"

"While you were talking to Corinne, I got a call from Mr. Carr. He *asked* me to meet him there. He sounded odd . . . scared, maybe."

"But why did he want you to meet him?"

"He wanted to tell me something. I don't know what."

"What did he say?" Zach crossed his arms over his chest.

"I don't remember exactly." My voice tightened in frustration. "He said it was urgent or important or something like that."

"That's weird." A harsh line was etched between Zach's eyebrows.

"It was. I mean, I hardly knew him. But what's even stranger is that when I found him, he had my bracelet in his hand."

"Your bracelet? The one you asked me about last week?"

"Yeah. I thought I might have left it in the gym, but Mr. Carr couldn't find it."

"Well, he must have. And that's why he called you—he wanted to give it back."

"No, there must have been something more. Why arrange a secret meeting to give me back my bracelet? He could have just handed it to me at the dance."

"I don't know." Zach shrugged. "Maybe people do strange things before they have an aneurysm."

I looked at him skeptically.

"They do with brain tumors," he pointed out. "Sometimes their personalities change or they imagine things. Maybe it's the same way with aneurysms. Some of the teachers said Mr. Carr had complained about headaches."

"That still doesn't explain the handprints."

"Look, let's say he had a really bad headache. So he put his hands up to his head." Zach demonstrated, placing his hands on his temples.

I nodded. I'd done the same thing lots of times, as though I could somehow squeeze my headache into submission.

"Only, because he's a BV he's got this extra electricity, and what if, with this excruciating pain, he couldn't control the surge of heat, and he accidentally burned himself?"

"I guess it's possible," I conceded. Having seen the plastic Zach melted when I was harassing him in the bookstore, I was aware of the tremendous heat a BV could produce unintentionally.

"I know you're upset about Mr. Carr, but I really don't think you should worry about all this. BVs know how to control themselves. They don't just fly off the handle and kill people."

Zach stayed until he got a phone call from his mom asking him to run by the grocery store before dinner.

Now, hours later, my mind returned to what Zach had said. Did Mr. Carr really make those scorching handprints himself? I knew it was better than the alternative, but it still left me feeling deflated. If Mr. Carr hadn't been killed, there was no mystery to solve, nothing I could do to help. It just was what it was. Like it had been with Athena.

Later that night I could hear the voices around me: not actual words, but the murmur of hushed discussion. My head felt heavy, and my arms were like lead. I strained inwardly, trying to shift one of my legs or wiggle a toe. Anything that would force my body to pull out of this half-asleep, half-awake state. I might as well have been attempting to break free of a full body cast. Panic rose in my chest. No matter how hard I tried, I couldn't open my eyes. I felt like a coma victim in some horror movie. One of those scenes where you can hear them screaming inside their head because they can't escape the prison their body has become. Then, suddenly, a wave of calm swept over me. A hand was stroking my face.

Zach.

I knew who it was, even through the confusion swirling in my mind. I would know that touch even if I *was* in a coma. The prickling energy from his fingers was awakening every nerve in my body. Finally, I was able to kick my foot then, a few seconds later, open my eyes. Zach was sitting on the couch in the SAC, cradling my head in his lap.

"Welcome back," he whispered in his deep, throaty tone.

"What happened?" My voice was raw and hoarse.

"Mr. Carr is dead," Zach said grimly.

A cold hand gripped my lungs. I could hardly draw a breath in around it.

Zach's irises darkened quickly. His voice rumbled out of his throat, harsh and unforgiving. *"All because of you."*

I jerked awake in my bed. My heart was pounding so hard I could see it through the thin camisole I was sleeping in. It was trying to escape from my chest. I put a hand to it and concentrated on slowing down my frenetic breathing. *It was just a dream.*

Well, not all of it. Mr. Carr had died.

My throat burned as I inhaled through my mouth. I needed a glass of water. I threw my legs over the side of the bed, but before I could stand up, I felt something wet drip on my head and roll down the side of my face. *Great. Now my ceiling is leaking.* But that didn't make sense. I was on the first floor of the dorm building—which meant I was under some other girl's room, not a bathroom. I felt another drip and looked up in annoyance.

Mr. Carr's dead eyes stared down at me. His lifeless body was suspended on the ceiling right over my head, spread-eagle, like someone strapped to one of those spinning wheels at a carnival. I screamed, but no sound came out; Mr. Carr's gaping mouth mirrored my own.

"Help me." His lips did not move, but I heard his grating whisper. "You've got to help me."

As I watched in horror, blood began pooling in his eyes until they were brimming with the red liquid, then the blood rained down, splattering across my face.

Chapter Nineteen

I flew awake. For an instant, I was still frozen in terror. Then I pinched myself to make sure my waking up was for real this time. The red mark on my arm told me it was. I was drenched in sweat, my head was throbbing, and my eyelids felt like they were made of sandpaper.

I squinted against the dim sunlight falling onto my bed. The alarm clock read 10:30. I'd already missed breakfast. Not that my queasy stomach was going to let me eat very much.

Stepping onto the cold floor, I tried to shake off the haze that enveloped me. I flipped open my laptop and scrolled through my music library. I needed to hear something loud and energetic to get the remnants of the nightmare out of my head. I settled on Japanther, putting "Mornings" at the top of the playlist. At least the song title was appropriate. I waited for the music to work its customary magic, but it gave me little more than a tiny lift. Sighing, I flicked the laptop shut again and grabbed my toiletries bag.

After I finished showering and brushing my teeth, I went back to my room to get dressed. Headmaster Grimsby had contacted the househeads and teachers last night to tell them classes were canceled today. It felt weird to slip into jeans and a tank top with Monday on my calendar. Strange, how quickly I had become accustomed to putting on the black pencil skirt and crested blazer every weekday.

I grabbed my purse, then headed over to Adriana's next door. I didn't feel like going to lunch alone. I rapped twice on her door before she opened it.

"Persephone." She looked relieved. "Good, it's just you."

How every friend loves to be greeted. I sat down on Adriana's bed and watched her flip through the clothes hanging in her closet.

"So, how are you feeling this morning?" Adriana didn't wait for my answer. "I've barely slept at all the last two nights. I'm even having nightmares—which never happens to me."

If only we were all so lucky.

"I must look awful."

But of course she didn't. Adriana looked as elegant as always. Her pajamas were preppy perfection in signature Burberry plaid. After a few minutes she settled on a pair of cropped white pants and a purple boatneck top. On our way out of Kresky, I knocked on Toy's door, but no one answered.

"She's probably in the caf already," Adriana said as we headed down the gray slate walkway.

The brisk September air made me wish I had worn a jacket. Though the uniform had become habit, I still managed to forget how much cooler it was here than in L.A.

When we walked into the cafeteria, Toy was sitting at our

usual table, talking to Graham and Brody. I was a little surprised to see Brody there, given that Mr. Carr was his guardian. On the other hand, maybe he couldn't stand being cooped up in the house with people coming by to offer their condolences. Right after Athena died, all I had wanted to do was get away from the house and everybody in it.

"Hey." Brody's smile came out more like a grimace.

"You okay, Phe?" Graham looked at me with concern.

"Sort of. But I keep thinking about finding Mr. Carr."

Brody quickly looked down, concentrating on swirling a piece of pancake around in the ocean of syrup on his plate.

"I'm sorry, Brody." Clearly, my brain was still not functioning properly.

"It's cool. I don't want to sit here and pretend not to be thinking about what everybody's thinking about." He rubbed his temple. "I overheard the doctor talking to Pamela—Mrs. Carr," he clarified for us. "He said that Robert had a cerebral aneurysm, not a heart attack."

"That's a brain thing, right?" Adriana asked.

"It's the dilation of a blood vessel in the brain," Brody explained. "He died when it ruptured."

"Oh, my God," Toy gasped.

I swallowed and glanced around at the others. It sounded so awful, especially delivered in that flat monotone Brody's voice had taken on. Everyone was looking in opposite directions—down at the table or across the cafeteria—unsure what to do or say. Brody watched his own hand as he balled up his napkin into a tighter and tighter lump. Abruptly, he got up and strode to the door.

"What should we do?" Adriana stared after him. "I don't know what to say."

"Me neither. But maybe one of us should go talk to him." Toy looked anxious.

"I'll go make sure he's okay," I volunteered.

Brody stood a few feet outside the entrance to the cafeteria. His arms were crossed over his chest, and he held a lit cigarette in one hand. He was just letting it burn like he'd forgotten about it. "Hey." I clasped my hands in front of my waist, interlacing my fingers.

Brody gave me a head nod of acknowledgment.

"I just wanted to talk to you." *Though I have absolutely no idea what I can possibly say.*

"Zach send you on a cheer-up-Brody mission?" He narrowed his eyes.

"No. It's nothing like that." I scratched at the chipping polish on my thumbnail. "I just feel really bad about Mr. Carr."

"Why? You didn't kill him." Brody frowned and turned his face away from me to exhale a stream of smoke.

Yeah, but maybe I'm the reason he got killed. A picture of my bracelet lying next to his hand flashed in my mind. Had Brody seen the body? The red handprints?

"My sister died last year." I didn't know whether or not opening up to Brody would make him more open with me, but it seemed worth a shot. "And I'm still not okay. I don't think I'll ever get over it, but it hurts less with time."

"Yeah, well, I wasn't actually related to Mr. Carr or anything." Brody pulled out his pack of cigarettes, lighting a new one with the dying cherry of his first.

"I know. I'm sorry about your parents." I shook my head. "I can't imagine what that must have been like."

"I was young with my dad. And my mom . . ." Brody's jaw tightened, and his nostrils flared. "Well, you know. I'm sure Zach told you about our life span. She wanted it that way. She didn't want to end up a basket case." There was the slightest tremor in his chin, and his cheeks were blotchy and red.

"That's so awful." It was a terrible understatement, but even after everything with my sister, I still didn't know anything comforting to say.

"That's just the way it is." Brody sucked hard on his cigarette, as if he were trying to draw strength from it. "The way we are. But Mr. Carr—he was the only adult on this campus who gave two shits about me. The only one who paid any attention at all—and I didn't notice anything was going on with him."

I was about to open my mouth when Zach walked around the side of the building.

"Hey, I figured you guys would still be at lunch." He smiled at us, and I wondered if he could sense the heavy, suffocating tension in the air. "I came by to see how you were doing."

"I told you already. I'm fine, man."

"I know," Zach reassured Brody. "But I came in with my mom; she's talking to Pamela at the hospital. And I thought since I had the car, I would bring my skateboard, and we could drive to Springfield and hit the skate park."

Brody's face relaxed. "Yeah. That sounds good. I'm just gonna run back to the house and grab my board, and then we can go. Okay?"

Brody took off, looking several degrees happier.

I turned to Zach. "You skateboard?"

"Well, you could say that, but I suck at it. I'm basically comic relief for the other guys out there." His warm, throaty laugh lit me up inside. "But it's pretty much Brody's favorite thing to do, and I wanted to take his mind off stuff for a while."

"I know. He needs you." As Brody ran back across the courtyard, I gave Zach a tender kiss, keeping my mind blank.

I couldn't let Zach know what I was going to do. Brody's house was the logical place to look for evidence that Mr. Carr had been killed. Mrs. Carr was at the hospital talking to Zach's mom, which would probably take a while, and Brody was going to be gone for at least two hours. There was nothing to prevent me from sneaking into the Carrs' house and searching for proof.

Well, nothing except for good sense, and I was pretty sure I had given up on that a couple of weeks ago.

After Zach left with Brody, I headed to the teachers' cottages, a group of houses on campus where the faculty members with families lived.

I walked quickly, nervous that one of the teachers might see me. After all, even though it was Monday they, too, had the day off to deal with their grief. *As if the aftermath of death is like the twenty-four-hour flu and we'll all be over it by tomorrow.* I chewed on my thumbnail, wondering how I was going to figure out which house was the Carrs'. I couldn't very well go knocking on doors until I found it. Fortunately for me, there were mailboxes in front of each house with the teachers' names clearly marked on them. Even better, the Carrs' house was the last one in the row, so that on one side there was nothing but the woods and to the back there was only the hill going up to the hospital.

I went around to the side that was hidden from the rest of the campus.

I tried all the windows, but they were locked. There was a back entrance that opened onto the small stone patio. Without much hope of success, I tried the door handle. To my surprise, it turned.

Cautiously, I stepped into the kitchen and closed the door behind me. I walked over to the stairs on my right and peered up them, but I wasn't ready to explore the second story yet. After checking out a small coat closet, I decided to try the room at the end of the hall. The door was standing partway open. I peeked around it and froze, staring in disbelief.

This was the old-fashioned study I had seen in my vision at Rebekah Sampson's grave. There were the same heavy drapes pulled closed across the windows, the same dark wood bookshelves and imposing mahogany desk.

A chill ran down my spine, then I was hit with a flush of vindication. I was right. My dreams and visions had led me here—which meant Mr. Carr *had* been murdered and something in this office would help me find out why.

I stepped in, leaving the door open a crack like I had found it. It was weird actually being in this room, but at least I knew what I was looking for, and I wouldn't have to waste time searching. I went straight to the desk and pulled open the side drawer. The drawer was full of files, just as it had been in the dream, and I flipped through them until I saw one labeled BANISHMENT DOCUMENTS.

I pulled out the file and opened it. The first page was the list of people who had been banished from Shadow Hills in 1968, once again confirming my dream. I was grateful I had the advantage of a mind map to help me find what I wanted, but this was getting seriously creepy. I remembered the frightening face I had seen in the file in my dream, and I quickly closed the folder. I didn't want to look at that face again—not here, not now. Besides, it would be foolish to take the time to look at it. I'd just have to bring it back to the dorm.

I tucked it under my arm and glanced around the room, wondering if I should search for something else.

The sound of a key in the front door made me jump.

I slid the desk drawer back in as quietly as possible. The hinges creaked as the front door swung open. I froze, my heart pounding like crazy. The door to the study was almost shut, so as long as they stayed in the hall I would be fine. If they came in here, I was completely busted.

I breathed a little sigh of relief at the sound of footsteps on the stairs. Okay. Mrs. Carr had obviously gotten through at the hospital more quickly than I had expected. But I could slip out the front while she was upstairs.

I peered out. The foyer was empty. I strained, listening for the sound of footsteps above me. Not hearing anything, I cautiously edged out into the hall.

Just then the back door of the house opened. I jumped back inside the study, pulling the door almost shut again. How had Mrs. Carr gotten out there? I was sure I'd heard her go up the stairs.

"Pamela?" came the sound of a male voice, and I realized that somebody else had come in. Someone who knew Mrs. Carr well enough to call her by her first name. Who was this, coming in the back door so familiarly?

Whoever it was, his voice brought Mrs. Carr running down the stairs.

"I parked in the hospital lot like usual," I heard the man say.

"Good. It's even more important now that no one finds out about this."

I raised my eyebrows at that statement and leaned closer to the door.

"I have no intention of anyone ever finding out," the man told her. The footsteps started down the hall and abruptly stopped. Then there were some noises that definitely sounded like kissing. *Mousy Mrs. Carr is making out with some other guy already?* Her husband hadn't even been buried yet!

Unable to contain my curiosity, I opened the door a smidge more, putting my eye to the crack.

They were standing in the dimmest part of the hallway, beyond the light from any of the outside rooms, and the stairs obscured my view of them from the waist down. The guy was facing Mrs. Carr, his back to me, and he blocked the small woman entirely. His hair looked like it was probably light brown, but it was hard to be sure under the circumstances. He was definitely slim, though, medium height, and wearing a dark leather jacket. He could be anyone—well, anyone completely lacking in morals. Frustration built inside of me; I couldn't even grind my teeth or exhale too forcefully, for fear of being discovered.

I couldn't see anything from my viewpoint that would positively identify him. Then again, if I could see him better, he would probably be able to see me, too.

"I can't believe we have this place all to ourselves now. No more waiting. Sneaking around," the man murmured as he bent to kiss her neck.

They turned slightly, and I could see enough of the woman to confirm it was Mrs. Carr. Her hair was down in soft waves, framing her face instead of drawn back in its usual tight bun, but it was her.

Her eyes were closed, her head thrown back, as the man slowly unbuttoned her dull tan blouse, revealing a sexy maroon lace bra. Mrs. Carr was nothing like what she appeared to be. All of a sudden she snapped her head back up. I retreated a step. Had she heard me breathing or something? She *was* a BV like Zach.

"Did you lock the back door behind you?" she asked sharply.

"Why should I? No one else lives here anymore."

"Unfortunately, that isn't true. Brody still does." Mrs. Carr sighed. "My late husband never picked up the transfer petition forms so we could start the process. He always had a soft spot for that delinquent—who knows why. But if I do anything about it now, it will draw unwanted attention. I'll have to wait for at least a few months before transferring him."

Transferring him? The Carrs had been trying to get rid of Brody? Of course, it didn't sound like Mr. Carr had actually wanted to.

"So he could be here right now?" The man backed up a few steps, putting space between them. As if that would fool anyone—Mrs. Carr still had her bra exposed.

"He left for lunch about an hour ago. I think he's still there." She glanced around as if she was going to find Brody standing in the hall with them. I shrank back farther behind the door.

"God, Pam. Are you *trying* to get caught? I thought you agreed that we need to be careful."

"Oh, you mean I should be careful like you—dropping jewelry on the bedroom floor for Robert to find?" She snorted.

"That was an accident. It's not my fault you were too distracted to notice it before he did. Well, I guess the distraction might have been partially my fault." He looped his arm around her waist and pulled her close to him again.

"It's always your fault." Her remark was followed by a low giggle. Then they started down the hall—straight at me, it sounded like. I tensed, without a clue about what I would do or say if they came in here. But then the footsteps started up the stairs.

They took forever getting up the stairs, pausing several times, presumably to kiss some more. I was about ready to scream at them to get on with it when I heard a door closing on the second floor.

Now was my chance to make a run for it. I removed my shoes, then scampered across the hallway and out the front door, shutting it softly behind me. Mrs. Carr obviously hadn't locked it when she came in either, despite her scolding tone with the mystery man.

I ran back to Kresky Hall, too scared even to think about sticking around to see if Mrs. Carr's boyfriend ever came out of the house. Pamela's harsh comments kept playing in my head. She had been trying to get rid of Brody after everything he had already gone through. It was heartless. Mr. Carr had been Brody's only ally, and now Mr. Carr was dead.

Maybe he had stood up for Brody one too many times. Maybe he paid for it with his life.

Chapter Twenty

The next morning was Mr. Carr's memorial, and though it was uncharacteristically sunny outside the chapel, the mood inside was dark and unsettling. A lot of the day students sat in the back pews with their parents. Mr. Carr had grown up in Shadow Hills, so he'd had a lot of friends outside the teaching staff, and many of them had come to pay their respects here since his funeral was to be family only. I wondered if Brody would be allowed to attend. I turned my head slightly, trying to get a glimpse of him without full-on staring.

Brody was sitting with Zach's family, looking very normal in comparison to their collective attractiveness. Zach's mother was especially beautiful, with hair somewhere between pale gold and silver. Her beauty was icy, though, with precisely arched eyebrows and a perfectly defined jawline. Her rigid posture did nothing to soften her appearance, and I could tell from her body language toward Zach that she was still pissed at him.

When Zach called me last night, he told me that he couldn't come by to see me because his mom was mad at him and wouldn't let him have the car. Apparently, he and Brody had

skated for a lot longer than Zach—and certainly his mom—
had intended. I'd wanted to tell him about Mrs. Carr's affair and
everything I had found out, but I'd barely gotten to talk to him
on the phone. And now I'd have to wait until after school to
show him the folder. I couldn't exactly recount my trip to the
Carrs' house with Brody around.

The memorial was poignant. Even the speech Mrs. Carr gave
at the end of the service seemed heartfelt. If I hadn't seen her
making out with some other man about two minutes after her
husband had died, she might have had more credibility.

After my last class of the day let out, I headed back to my dorm
room, intent on studying the file I'd gotten from Mr. Carr's
office. But once I'd pulled it from the hiding spot under my mattress and placed it on my desk, I couldn't bring myself to open it.
Even though I wanted to know what my vision had been leading
me to, I was also really afraid of what I might find. And the idea
of seeing the picture of that man again . . . I shivered. I knew it
was irrational; it wasn't like the guy was going to reach out of a
photo and strangle me, but I couldn't deny that he terrified me
to my very core. That picture was the main reason I'd hidden the
file the moment I'd gotten home yesterday and hadn't looked at
it since. Until now.

I so don't want to do this by myself.

I reached into my purse to get my phone, and it started ringing. Zach.

"Hey, I was about to call you."

"Great minds think alike." I could hear the smile in his voice. "I was wondering if you wanted to hang out. Corinne's at one of her club meetings for the next hour."

"Yeah. Why don't you come over to my dorm? I have something I kind of wanted to run by you, anyway."

"Cool. I'll see you in a few."

As I waited for Zach, I tried to decide what it was that I was actually going to say to him. How was I going to explain having this file? Seeing Mrs. Carr and the mystery man?

I was almost certain now that Mr. Carr had been killed, but I was having trouble getting all the facts straight. I needed an outside opinion; I needed Zach. But if I wanted his help, I would have to tell him everything that had happened—my visions, the breaking and entering, all the stuff about the Banished. Everything.

It was a huge risk; Zach could easily decide that I was insane. Keeping quiet was the safest option, since most people would probably have me committed if I told them the things I'd been doing. But I wasn't dealing with most people. This was Zach.

As if on cue, I heard a knock on my door.

"Hey." I motioned for Zach to come in, then closed the door behind him.

Zach wrapped his arms around me, and I hugged him back even harder. I could feel his heartbeat reverberating through me, and I stood on my tiptoes to meet his soft lips. The kiss warmed my entire body, giving me strength.

"There's some stuff I have to tell you, but I don't want you to freak out." The words came out in a rush.

"That certainly sounds ominous." Zach tucked a lock of hair behind my ear.

"I know you think Mr. Carr's death was a natural one—"

"Not again." Zach sighed. "I spent five hours yesterday listening to Brody's reasons why *he* thinks Mr. Carr was killed."

"He agrees with me?" I felt slightly vindicated.

"Yes, and I have to admit you both have some good points, but . . ." Zach let his sentence hang there unfinished.

"But what? Why don't you believe us?"

"It's not that I don't believe you—I guess, I don't want to think that there's a BV out there killing people. Besides, there's no real proof that Mr. Carr was murdered—those handprints could have been his own."

"They could have, but will you at least hear me out?" I sat on my bed, and Zach sank into the desk chair across from me.

"Okay. Go for it." He leaned back, crossing his legs at the ankles.

"I think Mrs. Carr might have had something to do with her husband's death. I saw them fighting at the school dance not long before I found . . . him." I couldn't bring myself to say "the body" out loud.

"Lots of couples fight." Zach shrugged. "My parents fight at least once a week. It doesn't mean they're going to kill each other."

"But I saw Mrs. Carr kissing another man yesterday, at the very house where she and her husband had lived together. Does that sound like a grief-stricken widow to you?"

"Wait. What?" Zach sat up straighter. "Who was she kissing? And why would you be in the Carrs' house?"

"First: I don't know who she was kissing. Second . . ." I paused, unsure how to admit to breaking into his friend's home. I knew where that confession would lead.

"Go on." A note of unease was creeping into Zach's voice.

"I kind of let myself into the Carrs' house yesterday afternoon."

He stared at me. "Why on earth would you do that?"

"Okay." I took a deep breath. "I guess I should really begin at the beginning."

"Sounds like a good idea."

I told Zach everything, starting with getting the Devenish brochure that was mailed to Athena and ending with stealing the folder from Mr. Carr's office. I even showed him the green dream journal and the mark on my hip. Zach was shocked by many of the things I had done since I got here, and skeptical about the idea that my dreams were prophetic, but he didn't seem to be mad at me. In fact, the only thing that really seemed to piss him off was that Trent had stolen that letter and then tried to blackmail me about the library break-in.

"You certainly didn't learn anything from the 'curiosity killed the cat' fable," Zach teased when I had finished my confession.

I relaxed. "I may be a bit impulsive."

"You're a bit impulsive like Corinne is a bit controlling." Zach laughed. "Okay, hand over that folder."

He glanced at the first page, and the smile fell from his face.

Zach flipped to the next and his expression grew serious. There were pictures of the Banished on this one. Most of the photos were old, probably taken in the 1960s when the group was banned, but a few were more recent. *From the 1980s if clothing was any indication. The other BVs had obviously kept tabs on them for years.*

His picture was one of the older-looking ones. He was the hardest, coldest man I had ever seen. His face was as brutal and intense as it had been in my vision, his stare unrelenting. It was as if he were actually looking at me. He reminded me of Charles Manson.

"This isn't okay anymore, Phe." Zach was shaking his head slowly.

"Do you know who that is?" My chest was clenching tighter, even though I willed myself to take deep breaths.

"Damon Gates. He's a legend in the Shadow Hills community. The boogeyman meant to scare BV kids into staying on the straight and narrow." Zach grasped my hand harshly. I could feel his fear for me, traveling cold as ice through my veins. "If you were . . ." He dropped my hand and stood. "Corinne was right. I never should've let this happen." He began to pace around my little room. "I should have stayed away. I knew it at the time, but I couldn't—"

I was suddenly afraid Zach was about to leave me. I jumped up and grabbed his arm.

"This is about me, okay? Not you." The effort of keeping my volume low made my words tremble. "You didn't make me have visions; you don't have anything to do with this mark on my hip; you knew nothing about Sarah and the book and all that. *I* am connected to this town, and I have to figure out what that means." I paused. I was scared to say the words that ached inside of me. I was afraid of being vulnerable, weak. But if Zach left . . . "I need your help to do that. You can't just go." My voice cracked, and Zach's expression immediately softened.

He wrapped his arms around me. "Of course, I'll help you. I'd do anything for you." Zach took my chin, tilting my face up. "But you've got to promise to be more careful. You can't go off trying to track down the Banished. These people were kicked out of Shadow Hills because they were seriously dangerous. They had no regard for anything except themselves and what they wanted. I don't remember exactly what they each did, but I learned enough from my grandma to know they were evil."

"Can I see that for a second?" I took the papers from Zach and scanned the Brevis Vita Canon of Ethics. The government jargon was wordy, but it basically said that the BVs were prohibited from using their powers to cause harm and from revealing confidential information to those outside the BV community. Zach had told me they were serious about staying under the radar, but I hadn't realized until now *how* huge it was that Zach had trusted me with their secrets. I found the page that listed the crimes of the individuals banished. I held it out so we could both see it.

It had details about Damon Gates, his family and friends, and the crimes the Council suspected them of committing—*use of powers for illegal purposes or personal gain, memory tampering,*

impairment of free will, human magnetic field depletion, manipula-
tion of sensory perception.

"What do all these mean?" I asked.

"I guess if I don't tell you, you're just going to go break in somewhere else." It was a halfhearted attempt at a joke, but I figured Zach knew it was also probably true. "Back in the sixties the group was infiltrating large corporations and brokerage firms. Then they'd pool their information and exert their influence to get very rich."

"But what about the things Damon Gates was doing?" The list was extensive.

"He was into some very shady stuff. He liked to get into people's minds and control what they thought, felt—what they remembered."

"You mean BVs really can change people's memories?" Corinne's threat at the dance seemed even more menacing now.

"Yeah, but nobody does it. BVs can go before the Council and ask them to perform a deletion if they consent to it themselves. It can be useful for removing really awful memories, but the person has to fill out a ton of paperwork and convince the whole board that their case is severe enough to warrant it. Outside of that, it's strictly forbidden because it can be so harmful—BVs could commit crimes and then erase the victim's memory or implant an alternate version of what happened. That's why no one is allowed to manipulate memory except under the approval of the Council."

At least I didn't need to worry about Corinne doing that to

me. No matter how pissed she was, I couldn't see her defying one of the key principles the BVs lived by.

Zach went on, "Manipulation of sensory perception is kind of an offshoot of the memory thing. Apparently it was Damon Gates's specialty. It's extremely uncommon: you have to be in such complete control of another person's mind that you can maintain a moving, shifting image that isn't there. It takes tremendous concentration to implant thoughts moment to moment without any gaps in time."

"I don't understand how that's even possible." It was an insane thing to try to comprehend.

"I'm not positive of the mechanics of it, but obviously the brain can make you see things that aren't real, or else hallucinogens wouldn't work and no one would have schizophrenic visions. The thing is, it's almost impossible to keep the illusion going for an extended period of time without having physical contact with the person you're deceiving. People say Gates was born with the 'talent.' I wouldn't have believed it if my grandma hadn't sworn that Damon Gates once took her to a fancy restaurant in Boston and made the waiter believe he was Mick Jagger. And he sustained it the entire dinner, all nonchalant."

"So your grandmother dated him?"

"Only once. She said at first he was charming, but the more he talked, the more disturbing he got. Most of the Banished were in it for the money, but Damon's supporters went further. They wanted to improve their powers and life span by stealing energy from other people. The human-depletion thing."

"Wait." I hoped my assumption was wrong. "How could they steal a person's energy?"

"They'd put their hands on someone, pull his energy out, and absorb it. It made the BV stronger."

"And they wouldn't die as quickly?"

"Yeah."

"But what did it do to the people they stole it from?"

"The person was weakened, and I think if it was continual, it made them insane."

I thought about the senile BVs. When the Banished sucked energy from people, it was like they transferred their ill health to that person. It was awful but not inexplicable. Wouldn't many people give death away if they could? Self-defense was innately human. "What happened to Damon and the rest of them?"

"They went to London after they were banished, and I don't think they've been heard from in years."

"Somebody heard from them."

Zach frowned. "What do you mean?"

"The second day I was here, I went to the hospital to look at the museum, and I wandered down into that basement display area. While I was down there I overheard two guys talking about the Council and stuff. One of them was Mr. Carr, and he was arguing that the other guy needed to cut his ties to the Banished."

Zach stared at me. "Are you serious? That's a major offense."

"Well, Mr. Carr was threatening to tell the Council about it. So there's another person who might have killed him."

"Who was the guy?"

"I don't know; my vision was partially obscured by a supply shelf, and I didn't realize at the time that it was important." I stood for a moment, chewing on my thumbnail, then said, "I wonder if Mr. Carr ever actually went to the Council."

"I think I know how we can find out."

"How?" I prodded.

"My mother is on the Council."

"You're going to talk to your mom about this?" I squeaked. "I don't want your mom to think I'm crazy!"

"No, I can't tell her yet. She's a lawyer; she needs actual proof. But I can look in her files."

"She'll let you do that?" I asked skeptically.

"You're not the only one capable of breaking into an office." Zach gave me a mischievous grin.

"I don't want you to get into trouble with your mom, especially not over me."

"My parents do date nights every Saturday and Tuesday. I'll just look in her study after they leave tonight. If Mr. Carr told the Council about who was talking to the Banished, she'll have a report on it."

"Okay," I agreed reluctantly. It was one thing to put myself at risk, but now that Zach was going to be doing my dirty work for me, I was more apprehensive than ever. "Promise me you'll be really careful, okay?"

"I promise." Zach bent down and kissed me tenderly. "I've got to go; my mom's still pissed at me about being late yesterday."

"Call me as soon as you find anything."

"I will." Zach gave me one last kiss, then tapped me lightly on the chin. "And don't go breaking in anywhere while I'm gone."

"I won't." I sank down on my bed as he pulled the door shut behind him. *Great.* I was alone again with the file.

Trying to avoid looking at the photo of Damon Gates, I skimmed over the remaining pages. As I had thought, most of the information was biographical sketches of the people banished, and it wasn't all that interesting—that is, until I got to the very last page. Scrawled at the bottom in the kind of fast, practically illegible handwriting that teachers all seemed to have was a notation. It took a few seconds for me to make out what it said, but when I did, I dropped the file like it was on fire. Even without looking at it, the words were seared into my brain: *Banished present—possible interest? P. Archer?*

Chapter Twenty-one

I spent the rest of the day waiting to hear from Zach. And when I wasn't worrying about him, I was freaking out about the notation Mr. Carr had made. I tried to tell myself that what he'd written didn't mean the Banished were interested in me, but I couldn't make myself believe it.

It was the only plausible explanation for his phone call. Mr. Carr must have thought I was in danger. But I still didn't see why he'd had my bracelet.

Maybe it didn't mean anything. Maybe Mr. Carr had just found it and was going to give it back when he told me about the Banished. Of course, that was what made the least sense. Why would the Banished have any interest in me?

The evening seemed to crawl by more and more slowly as it wore on. I knew that nothing would happen until after Zach's parents went out, but it didn't calm my nerves any.

At eight fifteen my phone finally rang, and I nervously checked the number. It wasn't familiar, but I was pretty sure it was a Shadow Hills area code.

"Hello?"

"I think I may have found something." It was Zach.

"What is it?" I whispered, an involuntary reaction to the soft way he was speaking.

"I'll tell you when I get there. I'm in my mom's office at the hospital, and I don't want to risk anyone overhearing me."

"You went to the hospital? Why?"

"I'll tell you later. I'm coming back to your dorm now, but don't let anyone in except me, okay?"

"Not even Adriana or Toy?" My stomach churned. Zach was starting to scare me with his cryptic instructions.

"No one. Just wait for me, okay?"

"Okay."

"I'm serious, Phe. No crazy schemes, no breaking and entering, nothing. I want you safe. Promise me." Zach's voice was low, but insistent.

"I promise."

"I'll be there soon."

"But Za—" The dull sound of silence on my cell told me he'd already hung up.

I paced back and forth at the foot of my bed. Now that I wasn't supposed to leave, the room was getting smaller and smaller. I picked up an old issue of *Elle* and sat down on the bed, trying to ignore my increasing claustrophobia. But I couldn't concentrate. The fashion spreads didn't begin to hold my attention, and every time I tried to read an article, I felt like the words were dancing around on the page.

After thirty minutes had gone by, I jumped up and began pacing again. There was no use in pretending that I wasn't freaking out. I certainly wasn't going to fool myself. It was getting dark outside, and the dorm's curfew time was rapidly approaching. Why wasn't he here yet?

I wanted to call him, but since I didn't know where he was, I was afraid his ringing cell might get him in trouble. What if he was hiding from hospital security or something?

I looked down at my cell again. It had been over an hour. There was no way that he was just running late. I couldn't wait around like this any longer. I called Zach's phone and, with every unanswered ring, became more and more frantic. If something happened to him, I didn't know what I would do.

"Little Miss L.A., what a surprise. I knew you had to be involved somehow." Corinne's tone was unmistakable. *Why is she answering Zach's phone?*

"Where's Zach?"

"Not far from you, actually." Her voice was like barbed wire. "He's at Shadow Hills Memorial Hospital."

"At your mom's office?" Surely Zach hadn't confided in Corinne; the last thing she would want to do was help me. Maybe he'd just run into her there.

"Interesting you would know that, but I guess that doesn't really matter now. I found Zach in her office, unconscious and barely breathing. He's in the ICU, and he still hasn't woken up."

My breath caught in my throat, and I felt as if my heart had stopped altogether.

"Are you serious?" I managed to croak out.

"No, I just thought that would make a hilarious joke," Corinne snapped. "Of course I'm serious; this is my brother we're talking about here!"

"I'm coming over there." I tried to control it, but my voice was cracking around the edges.

"Don't be ridiculous. It's past curfew, and the nurses already kicked us, *his family*, out of the room. No one can see him again until tomorrow morning. They're still running tests trying to figure out what happened." Corinne paused. "I don't suppose you would know anything about that, would you?"

Silent sobs clogged my throat. I bit the inside of my cheek as I tried to regain my ability to speak.

"Is there anything I can do?" I finally asked. I didn't even care how pathetic or feeble I sounded.

"I think you've done enough already," Corinne told me. And then the line went dead.

Defeated, I sank onto my bed and dissolved into tears. Why had Zach gone to his mother's office at the hospital? What happened after he told me he was coming over? I was certain that Zach had been hurt because of me. Worse, now he was trapped, alone, and unconscious, in the very hospital where I'd heard Mr. Carr arguing with some guy about the Banished. The person who might have killed Mr. Carr could be in Zach's room right now, suffocating him with a pillow.

Don't even think that. I gave myself a shake.

Drawing a deep breath, I wiped the tears from my face. I wasn't going to let myself become a quivering puddle of fear. There was no point in sitting here worrying and not doing anything about it. I didn't care what Corinne said; I couldn't wait until tomorrow to see Zach. I was going over there tonight.

I pulled on my black hoodie and grabbed the pepper spray out of my purse—not that it was a lot of protection, but it was better than nothing. It was past curfew now, so I opened my window and flung my leg over, lowering myself softly to the ground. Then, keeping as low as I could, I took off toward the hospital.

At night the main doors to the hospital were closed, so I walked in through the emergency entrance. I half expected the security guard at the door to stop me, but he didn't even look up from his book. *His salary is well earned.* The ER's waiting room was deserted except for the security guard and a nurse who was behind a waist-high counter reading a magazine. She glanced my way as I walked in, and I made an immediate turn into the women's restroom. After a few long seconds I peered around the corner to the front desk. The nurse had returned to reading, so I slipped farther down the hall, looking for some sign of where I should go.

I noticed that there were four different colored lines running along the floor. I suspected they meant something, but I didn't know what. Fortunately, before I walked very far, I came upon a legend on the wall. The red line led to the ICU. I followed it until I came to a set of double glass doors with a metal plaque beside them that read INTENSIVE CARE UNIT.

The visiting hours were posted clearly on the door. I tried pulling on the handle anyway, but it was useless. There was a large button with a lock under it on the wall to my right. I pressed it, just in case. Nothing. I needed the key to make it work. I let out a sigh of frustration. I'd just have to wait for a nurse to come in or out. *But how can I follow her in without someone noticing?*

I thought about my escape from the creepy basement and how I'd hidden in an open supply room. Maybe I could find it or some other unlocked room down there. After a few minutes of searching, I located a set of stairs and went down to the basement. The corridors were empty and silent.

Wandering along the halls, I looked at the plaques beside the doors and there, across from me, was one marked HOSPITAL PERSONNEL ONLY. Crossing my fingers for luck, I turned the knob and pushed. It was open. Cautiously, I stepped inside and found myself in a sort of lounge area.

I wasn't sure what I was looking for. Then a sign on the wall caught my eye. To the left were the men's locker rooms; to the right, the women's. Locker rooms meant clothes, and surely that meant surgical scrubs.

A set of scrubs was hanging in the last locker on the row. I threw the large green uniform on over my clothes, wrapping the drawstring of the pants around my torso twice in an attempt to keep them from falling off. It wasn't the greatest disguise in the world, but hopefully it was good enough to keep anyone from looking too closely.

Within minutes I was back in the ICU wing, loitering near the double doors and watching the second hand inch around the clock on the wall. The squeak of wheels on linoleum preceded a gurney being wheeled down the hall. *Finally.* I turned and pressed the button on the water fountain, bending over to take a drink. The gurney whizzed past me, surrounded by nurses and doctors, and went through the previously locked doors. I followed close behind them and caught the door with one foot, slipping in after they disappeared.

The rooms of the ICU were glass walled, and I immediately spotted Zach. He looked so much smaller than usual, lying there with various tubes and wires connected to his body. I wanted to collapse into sobs, but there was no way a hysterical girl would go unnoticed, even in scrubs.

I took a deep breath and strode into his room like I belonged there.

I squeezed Zach's cold hand, and the lack of electricity I felt scared me more than all the medical equipment attached to him.

I closed my eyes and stood for a long moment, holding his hand, hoping that somehow our connection would transcend his unconsciousness.

I knew I didn't have much longer before some nurse came in to check on Zach, and it was clear I wasn't going to find any answers or do anything for him here. If I was going to help him, I would have to figure out how to on my own.

The problem was I didn't know where to start. I needed some guidance. I thought of what Sarah had told me. If I really did have some sort of link to Hekate—the goddess who supposedly led people through the darkness to the truth—now would be the time to take advantage of it.

What if I called on Hekate? Got help from her? After all, my visions and prophetic dreams must serve some purpose. They had arrived unexpectedly up until now, but maybe there was a way I could summon them.

If it would help Zach, I was willing to try anything. I wasn't sure how, but I was going to contact Hekate.

After ditching the scrubs and slipping out of the hospital, I ran back to the dorm, hauled myself through my window, and flipped on the computer. I did a Google search for "ritual Hekate guidance." But all the links I found were useless Greek mythology. I wanted to scream I was so frustrated. Closing my eyes to calm down, I concentrated on my breath going in and out like at the end of a yoga class.

If I could just figure out some way to connect with Hekate or Rebekah . . . *The book.* I reached under the mattress and pulled it out. I concentrated on the first page, squinting as if that might help, but there was no epiphany. I still had no clue as to how to break the code.

On the front cover was the symbol. I laid my hand over the carved leather Hekate's Wheel and tried my yogic breathing again. I concentrated on the word *vision*, trying to dam up the frustration building inside me, as I let the minutes tick slowly by. After almost half an hour I finally gave up.

"Useless piece of crap," I muttered, flipping through the pages. I wanted to tear them all out. Rip them to shreds. Take my anger out on something.

I stopped flipping in stunned amazement. *I can read this.*

A single page was suddenly comprehensible. Just a second before it had been indecipherable code, and now I could read it clearly. The wording was a little old-fashioned, the script curling like calligraphy, but it was English.

Something I had done had finally worked. I wanted to jump

for joy, but I contained myself, quickly reading over what was clearly a ritual. It called for several things I could get pretty easily—a bell, a white candle and a black one, a bowl of salt water, and an egg. *There's probably one in the dorm fridge.* There was a snag, though; the ritual had to be done in a sacred space that wasn't within the confines of a building. I had a feeling the party spot in the woods wouldn't count. When I saw the last item needed for the ritual, my breath caught in my throat. Graveyard dirt.

There's a perfect place for me to do this. The place where I had been when I had the prophetic vision of Mr. Carr's office. The place where I was closest to another "daughter" of Hekate. Rebekah Sampson's grave.

But first I needed to write down the incantations and a basic outline of what I was supposed to do. I reached across the desk to grab a notebook and pen. When I turned back to the book, I almost cried out. The words were gone. The curling script had become strange unknown letters again. *No!* I flipped through the book several times in a row. This couldn't be happening.

What if I couldn't remember the words or they had to be precisely correct? What if I accidentally called up an evil being, like in some horror movie? I'd just have to hope my memory was reliable. Hastily, I scribbled a few notes down.

I tiptoed quietly into the common room. There was a half carton of eggs in the fridge, already hardboiled. Perfect.

I moved over to the counter to look through the drawers. There had to be a pack of birthday candles somewhere . . . *Or not.*

But I found a box of Halloween-themed candles, complete with a jack-o'-lantern and a witch riding a broomstick. They were miniature and beyond silly looking, but there was a black bat and a white ghost—the two colors I needed. I took them out of the box and slipped them into my jeans pocket. Salt and a bowl for the water were in the cabinet, but I was stumped about where to get a bell. It wasn't like there was a concierge desk inside the dorms. I went back to my room to search through my boxes, even though it seemed pretty pointless. Why would I have a bell?

A memory hit me like the pop of an old flashbulb.

During a Mardi Gras—themed school dance back in L.A., Ariel had stolen one of the idiotic court jester hats all the chaperones were wearing. I was pretty sure she'd packed it for me when I moved. I pulled the shoe box labeled ARIEL STUFF from my closet shelf. There it was, that stupid purple-and-green hat with the little gold bells on it. I ripped one of the bells off and put it in my jeans pocket with the candles, then grabbed my key ring with the mini-compass from the top of my dresser.

I had everything I needed, but I still didn't want to go to a cemetery all by myself in the middle of the night. I thought of the way Zach had looked in the hospital. It didn't matter how freaked out I was; I had to do something to help him, and I had to do it now.

I pushed up the window and slipped over the sill, starting out into the dark night.

Chapter Twenty-two

I made it to Rebekah's grave without any problem—that is, if you didn't count jumping with fear at every gust of wind or creak of a tree branch—but I had no idea where to begin. I read over my little page of recollected instructions. *Might as well just jump in.*

I picked up a twig from the ground and, feeling extremely foolish, used it to draw a large circle around the grave and tree, leaving only a small space for me to walk back through before closing the circle. I picked up my bag of supplies and, consulting my mini-compass, set down the bell at the easternmost part of the circle and the bowl of salt water at the westernmost. Kneeling, I drove the small black bat candle into the earth at the southern spot. At the northern point of my site, I mounded up the graveyard dirt into a small hill. Directly in the center of the circle I placed the white ghost candle. Now I just had to recite an incantation I didn't really know.

I focused my mind on Zach's face and tried to push away all of my self-consciousness. The direction chants were the first ones and also the easiest to remember. I started at the east. "This sacred circle is cast by air." I rang the bell three times then set it back down. I shivered as the slight breeze began to blow a bit harder.

Moving to the south, I pulled out a box of matches. "This sacred circle is cast by fire." I lit one of the matches and held it to the wick of the bat candle until it caught.

Picking up the bowl of salt water, I dipped my fingers in it, then dripped water around the perimeter. "This sacred circle is cast by water."

I placed the bowl next to the ghost candle in the middle of the circle and moved on, only to be caught off guard by a loud crack of thunder in the distance and the distinct smell of forthcoming rain. *Okay, that's a strange coincidence.* Pulling in a calming breath, I took a handful of the graveyard dirt from the pile and sprinkled it over the line I had drawn earlier.

"This sacred circle is cast by earth. What is within this circle is between the worlds." The silence that met my ears seemed somehow too quiet, too still. I sat down on the ground, right behind the ghost candle, feeling more than a little nervous. The next part was the part that was the least clear in my memory.

"I have cast this sacred circle for the Goddess Hekate." As I lit the white candle, I realized I didn't even need the incantation from the book. A power was bubbling up inside of me. The words flowed from my mouth, not coming from my mind but from someplace much deeper. Buried within me.

"Come, Hekate, with your hound by your side, prowling the earth. Your howling fills my ears until I can hear nothing else." The wind whipped around me, lifting my heavy curtain of hair as if it were made of feathers.

"Come, Hekate, keeper of visions and prophecies and dreams. Lend me your sight and perception." A jagged streak of lightning shot across the sky, blindingly bright, but I wasn't frightened. Something had taken over, something strong and primal.

"Come, Hekate, with your long-dead whispers filling this space between the worlds!" My voice was loud and urgent; it sounded foreign to me. "Queen of spirits, ruler of the dark moon, bring me the answers I seek!"

I plunged my hands into the bowl of salt water. Another crack of thunder and lightning came, fracturing the heavens. Splitting open the clouds and releasing their cascade. As rain poured all around, my space under the tree was untouched—not a thing inside the circle was even damp. If anything, the candles seemed to burn brighter and brighter with every elapsed moment. With every word that passed my lips.

"Come, Hekate! Awaken insight through possession of my vessel!" My hands surged with power, and electricity sizzled across my skin. A force wrapped my body in weight, and I felt my back hit the earth.

The person I now knew to be Rebekah Sampson was standing before me at the foot of her own grave. Her form was pale and wispy, as if made of smoke.

"What is wrong with Zach?" I stood now, too, wanting to exert this newfound feeling of power. To make her answer me. She just stared mutely.

"Who did this to him? Who killed Mr. Carr?" I demanded.

Rebekah reached out and laid a hand on my brow. Images rushed into my mind. I saw a close-up of two hands clasped on either side of Mr. Carr's head. They were glowing red like someone was shining a light through them. On the middle finger of the right hand was a rectangular gold ring with a striped green stone in the center. As steam rose from the hands, the stone began to crack. The image flashed, and I saw Zach in an office, dropping a file folder in surprise.

Then I was looking at an image of myself standing in the graveyard, but I wasn't seeing myself as I was now. This was a vision of me from another time. There was fire in my eyes as I held out my left hand and drew a silver dagger across its palm. Blood welled up, and I turned my hand, letting the blood fall to the earth like raindrops.

I watched myself in the vision as I opened my arms wide and threw back my head, yelling into the black night, *"Phasmata repite ex sepulchris vestris, capite virum!"*

The ground began to shake, then abruptly stopped. Suddenly, the other me in my vision was gone, and I was standing before Rebekah.

"What does all that mean?" I asked.

Rebekah looked at me silently for a moment, then smiled.

"You will know when the time is right." She laid a finger to my lips, halting the sputtering words of dissatisfaction. "Hold out your hand."

I did as she instructed. There was no blood on my palm like there had been in my vision, no cut. Rebekah placed a large, uneven shard of glass in my hands, but it wasn't sharp. I peered down into it and saw the reflection of my sister. Not myself as I resembled her, but actually her. Athena. She was happy. I looked down at my chest. There was a large space gone, not bleeding or damaged, just a piece missing from a finished puzzle. A jagged, roughly triangular piece. After taking one more look at Athena, beautiful and at peace, I placed the shard into the space. It matched perfectly, instantly becoming one with my body.

"You are done now." Rebekah ran a hand down the side of my face, and I opened my eyes. I was lying in the same spot, but the candle in front of me was burned out and the rain had stopped. It felt like I had been there for hours.

Shakily, I sat up, feeling more or less like myself again. I was a little drained, though. Thankfully, all that was left was ending the ritual.

"This egg symbolizes new beginnings. It is both two halves and a whole." I peeled off the shell and dipped the bare egg into the bowl in front of me.

"I purify this with salt water as I purify my body." I ate half of the egg. "Tonight will bring about the start of my true self."

I laid the other half of the egg on top of Rebekah's gravestone. "I leave this as an offering to Hekate, to thank her for the power and the wisdom she has brought me."

Not that I can make much sense of that disjointed vision, I added silently.

"It is time for me to return to do the work that must be done. With these words, let this circle be open, yet unbroken."

I thanked each element as I gathered up their symbolic

objects. Then I smudged the line in the dirt with my foot before stepping out of the circle. I shivered as a gust of cool air blew past me. The circle had been like a protective bubble, but here I was again, back in the real world. I looked over at the hospital, the lights shining bright out of the second-floor windows, the intensive care unit.

With a sigh, I started my walk back to the dorms. Hopefully what I had done tonight would help. Maybe as I slept, my brain would untangle all the images and come up with some kind of amazing breakthrough. And I did have one new clue already. The cracked ring.

I woke up the next morning foggy and disoriented, partly because I had set my alarm extra early, but also because of a dream I couldn't quite remember. The half-formed ideas of what last night's vision had meant followed me as I showered and dressed. I couldn't get it out of my head even as I entered the hospital and headed toward the ICU wing.

"What the hell do you think you're doing here?" Corinne was charging down the hallway toward me, a manila folder in hand.

"I'm here to see Zach." I jutted my chin forward defiantly.

"Oh, so you're not here for this?" Corinne shook the folder in my face, and instinctively I grabbed for it, ripping it out of her hand.

"The only reason I'm here is to see Zach."

"That's funny, because I think the only reason Zach is *here* is because of you." Corinne's eyes flashed. "He never would've stolen files before you came along."

I looked down at my hand. *Had this been what Zach had called me about?* I flipped the folder open as Corinne tried to grab it. I jumped back and began to read, but a small picture stapled in the left-hand corner caught my eye. It was a photo of a copper bangle bracelet, but it bore an infinity symbol just like my ID bracelet. Seeing the stunned look on my face, Corinne leaped forward, wrenching the papers from my hands. But not before I read the caption under the photo. *The bracelets were ionized and used by Gates and his followers to help facilitate the transfer of energy, as well as identify their victims of energy consumption.*

My hands were shaking, and I felt cold as ice. It was clear now why Mr. Carr had thought the Banished might have an interest in me. He must have found my bracelet and recognized the symbol.

What Mr. Carr hadn't known, of course, was that it wasn't my bracelet originally. Was there any way Athena could have been involved with the Banished?

"What do you know about this? The ionization, the energy consumption?" I demanded.

"I don't know." Corinne shoved the folder into her bag. "And if I did, I wouldn't tell you."

Maybe she wouldn't normally, but Corinne always had to be the smartest, and I knew it.

"You don't understand ionization? I thought physics and chemistry were your thing."

"Fine." Her eyes narrowed. "Ionization is the means of converting an atom or molecule into an ion by adding or subtracting charged particles. Not that someone like you would get it,"

Corinne said. "So just stay the hell out of our business. This has nothing to do with you."

"Oh, yeah?" I dug the bracelet out of the pocket of my purse. "Then why does my bracelet have a symbol just like the one in the file?"

Corinne glanced at it, then rolled her eyes. "That doesn't prove anything. It's a totally different style, a different metal. Do you know how common jewelry with an infinity symbol is? And I seriously doubt the Banished moved to the Hollywood Hills." She took a step closer. To intimidate. "Listen, I don't know what you think you're doing. And I really don't care. But poking around where you don't belong is what got my brother hurt. And I won't allow you to put him in danger. If you care about him at all, you will leave him out of it."

"I care about Zach just as much as you do." My face was on fire. I blamed myself for Zach's state, but it was completely different to hear it come out of someone else's mouth.

"Then prove it." Corinne turned on her heel and headed down the hallway.

I stood there for a few moments, trying to decide what to do, before following Corinne. The hallway curved sharply to the right, and as I rounded the corner I heard the sound of someone crying. It was coming from an open doorway a few feet in front of me. The women's restroom. I stepped inside, the sound of wrenching sobs echoed in one of the metal stalls. All I could see was a pair of shoes, patent leather Mary Janes in a deep purple that was dark enough to pass for black. They were Corinne's school shoes.

Apparently, even Corinne couldn't be detached and

indifferent all the time. My anger drained away. Slowly, I backed out of the bathroom and made my way back to the ICU.

"I'm here to see Zach Redford," I told the nurse behind the front desk.

"Good timing." She stood up. "You caught him right before his next dose of meds. He's still awake." She smiled and led me over to the same room I'd been in last night.

He's awake. My lungs and heart and everything else in my chest loosened. Zach was awake. Corinne hadn't been crying because she'd been given horrible news. She was just stretched to the breaking point. Which I certainly understood.

"Phe." Zach smiled foggily at me as the nurse left.

"Hey, you." I bent down to kiss his forehead. "I was so worried. What happened?"

"I don't know." Zach's thinking frown was adorable. I scooted a chair closer to the bed so I could sit down. "I couldn't find anything in my mother's office at home. Then Corinne said she had to come to school for . . . something." Zach seemed confused. "I caught a ride with her. I figured I might find a file here."

"Didn't Corinne wonder why you wanted to come to the hospital?"

"I told her . . ." He frowned. "I'm not sure . . . My brain's not working very well. Oh, yeah. I told her I couldn't find my advanced calculus homework, and I thought I must have left it in Mom's office when I was with her this afternoon—I mean, yesterday afternoon. And then . . ." Zach was obviously having trouble remembering things. "Corinne let me off in front of the hospital and . . . it all sort of goes black." His frown deepened. "I can't remember what happened after that."

"You called me and said you'd found something," I prompted. "You were going to come over to tell me what. I was so worried when you didn't show up."

"I'm sorry."

I squeezed his hand. "Being hit on the head is an adequate excuse, I think."

"I wasn't hit on the head," he said. "The doctors say there's no sign of trauma, no lump or bruise."

Icy prickles of dread crept into my chest even though I had already half expected this to be the case. "So you were knocked out with what? Some kind of Vulcan mind meld?"

"I don't know. Corinne said she came down to the office when she got through and found me lying on the floor on top of a folder."

I couldn't suppress an even stronger shudder of fear. Had Zach's assailant knocked him out? Had he intended to do worse but been frightened off by the sound of Corinne's arrival? *If Corinne had been later in coming to check on Zach . . .* The images flashing through my mind made my breath feel like a knife in my lungs.

But Zach was going on, "Do you know about the folder?"

"Yeah, Corinne showed it to me," I fibbed. I wasn't about to embroil him in the ongoing emotional battle between his sister and me. He was obviously too tired to be discussing anything, much less such upsetting topics. "Let's talk about it later, okay?"

But Zach was not so easily diverted. "I'm really weirded out by all this. I think you should lie low for a while." He looked up into my eyes. "I don't want anything to happen to you."

"Same here." I pushed a stray lock of hair back from his forehead. "You just need to concentrate on getting better, okay?"

"Only if you promise to wait this out. Not to go off and do something rash."

I figured middle-of-the-night graveyard rituals might be misconstrued as rash, so I decided to keep last night's excursion to myself for the time being.

"I'll be careful if you are." *I can be careful while figuring out what's going on.*

"Deal." Zach stuck out his hand, and I shook it, feeling only a little guilty.

I had to figure this out—for Zach, for Brody, for Mr. Carr. I couldn't stand by and let someone else get hurt.

"Sorry, sweetie, but I'm going to have to kick you out now." The nurse was back, holding a small clear cup with several pills in it.

"I'll come by after school today." I bent down to kiss Zach on the forehead again, but he pulled me toward him, to meet his lips. I sank into his soft kiss until the throat clearing of the nurse behind me broke through my Zach-induced haze.

"Sorry." I couldn't keep from smiling as the nurse slid the door closed behind me. Zach was going to be fine. I would make sure of it.

Chapter Twenty-three

Breakfast was less quiet than it had been the last few days, but Brody still didn't say much. And I couldn't think about anything but Zach being in the hospital. I wondered if Brody had heard about Zach already, if that was part of the reason he looked so tired and drawn.

Before the first bell, a woman's voice came over the cafeteria's loudspeaker to announce that there would be an assembly in the chapel when the day students arrived. Several people cheered when she added that our first-period classes would be canceled again today. Brody and I were the only ones who seemed unexcited by the news.

"I wanted to talk to you, if that's cool," Brody told me as everyone dispersed.

"Sure." This came as a surprise, being that he was especially reticent today.

"Mr. Redford called me super early this morning to tell me about Zach. And when I went to visit, Zach said that you didn't believe Mr. Carr had an aneurysm either."

"Did he tell you about the handprints?" I had a million questions, but first I needed to find out what all Brody knew.

"Zach told me about that the day we went skating." Brody scraped his fork along his plate like a rake, eliciting a low metallic screech. "He also gave me his song and dance about it being self-inflicted." Brody dropped the fork, and it clattered loudly against the ceramic dish. "Mr. Carr had been acting strange ever since this school year started."

"What was he doing?" I leaned in closer.

"He was acting paranoid and suspicious all the time." Brody lowered his voice. "He even claimed that someone broke into the house."

"What did they steal?" I thought about the file back in my room. Maybe I wasn't the only person who wanted it.

"That was what was so weird: he said they'd left something in the house. Nothing was missing at all. No locks or windows were broken."

"So what did they leave?" I was pretty sure Mrs. Carr had bitched about Mystery Man dropping something upstairs.

"I think it was a necklace or a bracelet. I don't know; he found some woman's jewelry, and Mrs. Carr claimed it wasn't hers." Brody sounded like he trusted Mrs. Carr about as much as I did.

"But you don't believe that?" I supplied.

"Truth?"

I nodded yes.

"I think Mrs. Carr is having an affair," Brody clarified. "I think it was a present from some other guy."

I had to spill about my spying. I tried to think of an easy way to tell him, but there was no good lead-in for this. "I sort of broke into your house when you were at the skate park with Zach."

"Are you trying to say it was your jewelry? 'Cause that was a while ago." Brody was oddly unperturbed by my confession.

"No." I shook my head. Though I did wonder if it was somehow my bracelet. I couldn't imagine why Mystery Man would have had it, but Mr. Carr must have found it somewhere.

"Actually, Mr. Carr called my cell phone the night of the dance. He asked me to meet him outside—that's when I found him." The look on Brody's face made my chest hurt.

"Don't worry about me," he said, seeing my hesitation. "I have Zach for that."

"Okay." I agreed. "Anyway, I needed to figure out why he called me, and since I knew everyone was going to be out of the house that day, I went to see what I could find."

"I can't say I've never done any breaking and entering." Brody shrugged.

I would have to remember to ask about this some other time. "So I ended up in Mr. Carr's study, and there was a file in his desk about the Banished. And on one of the pages, Mr. Carr had scribbled my name down. Then yesterday when I showed Zach the file, it spooked him, and he volunteered to search his mom's office for more information about the Banished and Damon Gates."

"Good old Damon Gates." Brody smirked. "The BVs' version of Satan. He'll make your brain drip out of your ears if you're not careful. The Council's big on scare tactics."

"Since we're on the subject—" Maybe Brody could help me get this Council stuff straight. "Obviously the Council enforces the Code of Ethics and keeps an eye on the BVs." I thought of the spy-type pictures they'd had of the Banished. "But what happens if someone breaks a rule?"

"Let me give you a little background," Brody said. "The Council is a group of twelve BVs who run for election every ten years. They're judge and executioner. But in addition to them, the Council selects a board—which Mr. Carr was on—that takes care of misdemeanor charges and keeps track of BVs who are on probation. The Board also acts as a jury for people being brought up on grievous offenses. They hear the facts and can give input, but the Council is the final word."

It didn't sound totally fair, but keeping a secret governing body a secret was probably hard enough without attempting to have full-scale trials.

"So what kind of punishments do they give?" I pressed.

"Like I said, most of the stuff is misdemeanors, and you're put on probation for a while."

I didn't find it too surprising that he knew about the court system.

"Supposedly, if you do something really awful, they operate on your brain." Brody went on, "Like a lobotomy for our powers. But I doubt it's true. Just another horror story to keep the BVs in line."

"I saw something in the Council's files today that certainly scared me." I pulled the ID bracelet out of my purse for the second time this morning. "There was a picture of a bracelet in the folder, and even though it was a different style it had this same infinity symbol on it. The file said the bracelets were ionized and then the Banished used them on"—I thought back to exactly how it had been worded—"victims of energy consumption."

"Exclusive Donors." Brody frowned. "That's a major Damon Gates rumor. Back in the 1700s, it was accepted, like indentured servitude, but by the time the Council wrote the Canon of Ethics, it had been outlawed."

Now, that's something I wouldn't have expected Brody to know. "Anyway, these BVs in the sixties took it up again. They'd latch onto people and use them over and over, and they called them Exclusive Donors. I think the bracelets helped to keep them from poaching on one another's EDs. But ionized metal also makes it easier to transfer our energy to stuff, and I guess it probably works the other way, too, if you're trying to absorb energy."

I raised my eyebrows at him.

"You have to work hard to not learn things when you have a photographic memory," Brody said by way of explanation. He had his dumb stoner-act down pat—to the point that I sometimes forgot he came from a long line of mutant geniuses.

"Do you think the Banished had something to do with Mr. Carr?" he asked after a pause.

"I don't know what to think. I lost the bracelet about a week and a half after school started, and then I found it the night of the dance, lying in the grass right next to Mr. Carr's hand. I don't know how or where he got it."

"Maybe that was what he found that day." Brody leaned forward. "He did ask me once if I knew you, if you had ever been over to our house."

A shiver traveled up my spine.

"Which I guess means I'm wrong about Mrs. Carr and the whole affair thing." Brody looked faintly disappointed. He seemed to like Mrs. Carr about as well as she liked him. "Do you know how your bracelet could have gotten there? Did you break in before?"

"Monday was the first time I'd ever been in your house. But I did see something else that day." I chewed on my thumbnail. "Actually, I mostly overheard it—and I think it might partially explain the bracelet thing."

"Yeah?" His eyebrows quirked up inquiringly.

"You were right. About Mrs. Carr. She was there, kissing someone."

Brody was tapping his foot so hard the whole table rattled.

"You mean, after Mr. . . . ." He trailed off.

"Sorry."

"It's not your fault. You're not the slut cheating on your dead husband." Brody took a deep breath. "Sorry. I shouldn't be talking like that to you. I just . . . Mr. Carr was always nice to me, you know?" I could tell Brody was struggling to keep his voice steady. "Who was the guy with her?"

"I didn't see his face. All I could tell in the dim light was that he was slender and had light brown hair." I paused. "But Mrs. Carr did accuse him of dropping something on the floor that Mr. Carr found."

"Do you know why some guy would be carrying your bracelet around?"

"I really have no idea." My brain felt like a big mess of dead-end information. "Do you think Mrs. Carr might have killed . . ."

"No. I would, except I saw her that night. She was at the punch table the whole time. She didn't even leave to go to the bathroom." Brody snorted. "Keeping us children safe from the horrors of alcohol while outside her hus—"

The sound of the chapel bell cut through the stillness of the cafeteria. We were about to be late for the assembly.

"We'll talk about this after, okay?" Brody threw his backpack over his shoulder, and I grabbed my purse.

As soon as everyone was seated, Headmaster Grimsby told us all of our morning classes had been canceled for police interviews.

"To fill you in on how we will proceed, I have Police Chief Bradbury here." Grimsby motioned to the uniformed officer at the back of the stage.

The police chief stepped up to the podium. "We will be bringing you in twenty at a time to the in-school suspension room for semiprivate interviews." The cop cleared his throat, making the mic pop loudly. Several jittery students—including myself—jumped at the sound. "The Shadow Hills police force would like to thank you in advance for your patience and cooperation."

As much as the school was pushing their line that Mr. Carr's death was a natural one, I had a feeling the cops were leaning more toward my point of view. Why else would they waste time interviewing students? I wondered if Mrs. Carr had already been questioned. Brody said she hadn't left the dance, but she could have arranged for someone else to kill her husband. Maybe someone she was sleeping with.

"To make this as orderly as possible, we are going to call students by advisor. The first group will be Mr. Sherwood's advisees, Ms. Cardinal's advisees, Mr. Strobe's advisees, and Ms. Brooks's advisees."

As we filed out of the building, I saw that Brody was with Ms. Brooks's students.

Seeing me at the end of the line, Brody dropped back.

"Did Zach tell you about the cops?" he muttered out of the side of his mouth.

"What about the cops?" My chest started tightening up.

"They're BVs who are extremely skilled at getting into people's minds. They're taught techniques to help them decode your thoughts without even touching you."

"B-But they can't maintain that kind of thing for any length of time, right?" I spurted, clinging to what Zach had told me.

"The Council is in charge of hiring the cops in Shadow Hills, and they make sure only the ones with the best mind-control abilities and concentration get put through the training. And if they don't perform to the Council's liking, they assign them to desk jobs and traffic patrol."

"Really?" My voice came out squeaky.

"Yes." Brody assured me. "And the higher the emotions of the people they're talking to, the easier they are to read, so if there's stuff you don't want them to know . . ."

I thought of Zach and the trouble he could get into with the Council for telling me their secrets.

"How do you keep from being found out?" I had a feeling that with his pot habit, Brody was pretty skilled at hiding his thoughts.

"It's easier to do if you're a BV. More complicated neural pathways and all that."

I nodded like I understood.

"But just for insurance, I keep an image that is connected to a sound right at the forefront of my mind." Brody grinned mischievously. "I use the music video for Jane's Addiction's 'Been Caught Stealing.'"

"How does that help?"

"The noise and pictures generated in your mind cause a sort of feedback that makes everything else hard to get at. It's like a radio that's half on a station, half not; you can hear that a DJ is talking, but you can't make out the words." Brody sped up his lecture as we reached the entrance to the building. "Also, you want to keep your emotions as calm and level as you can, so try to relax and take some deep breaths." *Yeah, 'cause it's really easy to relax when you're lying to a cop.*

Getting the song running through my head was simple—I decided on "Skeleton Boy," a Friendly Fires song I knew all the words to, so I wouldn't get tripped up—but picturing the video was proving to be harder than I expected. My brain was obviously not wired in the same visual way Brody's BV mind was.

I concentrated on taking long slow gulps of air as I walked over to the desk that Chief Bradbury was sitting behind. I gave him a shaky smile and sank into the chair across from him.

"You're Persephone Archer, correct?" He wrote something down on a pad of paper in front of him.

"Yes." I did my best to pull up images from the "Skeleton Boy" video.

"And you are the one who found Mr. Carr?"

"Yes, sir."

"What were you doing outside while the dance was going on?"

"I was hot from dancing. I needed to get out in the cool air." I pictured the band dressed in black with the bright white snow falling all around them.

"Did you see anyone else while you were outside? Before or after you found Mr. Carr?"

"No. It was foggy. I couldn't see much at all." I thought of the fake snow forming stick figure skeletons on the guys.

"What about sounds? Did you hear anything?"

I shook my head. "No."

"Did you know Mr. Carr well?"

"Not really. He was my swim teacher, but I didn't have any contact with him outside of class." Silent singing and lying did *not* go hand in hand. It felt like I was trying to pat my head and rub my belly at the same time. Except a hundred times harder.

"Did you notice him acting strange in class? Did you see him get into arguments with anyone?"

"I thought the doctors decided he had an aneurysm. Do the police not believe that?"

Bradbury looked flustered; he clearly hadn't expected a student to question him. "It's not that—I was just wondering if you had seen him display any signs of head pain. Maybe the night of the dance?"

I started the song over again in my mind as I tried to decide whether or not to say anything about Mrs. Carr. Brody thought it was a waste of our time to look into her, but it wouldn't hurt to have the cops check it out just in case he was wrong.

"Well, I did notice Mr. and Mrs. Carr arguing at the dance at one point. Could that have caused an aneurysm?"

"That's not really my area of expertise. But I can certainly run it by someone from the medical staff."

Chief Bradbury scribbled something in the notebook, then handed me a business card. "This has the number for my direct line. Please call me if you remember anything more."

"Thanks." I dropped the card into my purse. Once I was out of the ISS room, I felt a million times better. I'd made it through the interview, and I was almost positive I hadn't been mind read. If he'd been able to pick up on my jumbled thoughts, he'd have kept me there a lot longer.

I was halfway to the SAC when I heard footsteps behind me in the courtyard. I turned around, expecting to see Brody. Instead, I came toe-to-toe with Trent.

"Hey, Goldilocks, where you going in such a hurry?" He brushed a piece of long hair out of his eyes, and something on his finger flashed in the sun. A large rectangular ring inlaid with a green striped stone.

Chapter Twenty-four

Trent was wearing a ring just like the one in my vision. I couldn't believe I hadn't thought of it earlier. That was the ring he'd been wearing the first time he cornered me, gripping my hand so hard I couldn't get away. Could Trent possibly be the one who had killed Mr. Carr?

It was hard to believe. Trent *was* incredibly creepy, but he didn't seem off-his-rocker psychotic. And he didn't strike me as the type to put himself in any kind of danger. I couldn't see Trent attacking Mr. Carr unless he had some self-serving reason for it. Or unless Mr. Carr was the one who initiated the confrontation . . . I looked at Trent with narrowed eyes. Was he the guy I'd seen with Mrs. Carr? Trent was small, but taller than me and slender, with dark blond hair that could easily be mistaken for light brown. I'd thought the guy was older than Trent, but how much of that was just a presumption that he was Mrs. Carr's age? Mystery Man had been wearing a leather jacket that might make someone Trent's size look bigger.

The whole idea seemed crazy, but I also wouldn't put it past Trent to have an affair with Mr. Carr's wife. On the other hand, there was the detail of his ring not being cracked. *Maybe my vision wasn't a revelation of a past event. Maybe it was a warning, a glimpse into the future.* What if that hadn't been Mr. Carr in my vision? What if it was going to be Zach?

"Cat got your tongue?" Trent raised an eyebrow, and I snapped my gaping mouth shut.

"I have to meet someone." I turned and started walking quickly back to the ISS room.

"The hospital is in the opposite direction!" Trent called after me.

I ignored him and kept going. I needed to find Brody to tell him about my new suspect. Luckily, I caught sight of him just as he was coming out of the building.

"Hey! How was your inter—"

I grabbed Brody tightly by the upper arm and pulled him behind one of the redbrick walls that hid the campus Dumpsters from view.

"Jesus! What's up with you?" He rubbed his biceps tenderly. "You've got quite a grip for a small person."

"I think it's Trent." I disregarded the "small" comment, which would've annoyed me at any other point in time.

"You think what is Trent?" Brody shook his head in confusion.

"I think Trent is the person sleeping with Mrs. Carr—and I also think he might have been the one who attacked Zach. His build and coloring are very similar to the guy I saw in your house, and he knows that Zach is in the hospital. I haven't said anything about it, have you?"

"No, but Trent could have found out some other way. They are related."

"But they hate each other, and their dads don't seem real fond of each other either."

"Yeah, but Trent was at the dance. I saw him. How could he have done it?"

"It would have been easy for him to leave the dance for a few minutes without being noticed."

"Do you have any other reason to suspect him?" Brody was still unconvinced. If I told him my graveyard vision story, he would just think I was crazier. I'd have to lie. Again.

"I recognized Trent's ring. I think maybe the guy with Mrs. Carr had the same one." I hadn't seen the guy's hands, so there was a chance he had been wearing it.

"You mean that flashy thing Trent always wears? The malachite ring?" Brody caught my look. "It's a green striped stone."

"Yeah." I nodded.

"Okay. I'll follow Trent around, see if he does anything suspicious. But you have to promise not to get yourself hurt in the meantime. I can just imagine what Zach would do to me if I got his new girlfriend killed."

I felt a fluttering in my heart at Brody's statement. Girlfriend. I was Zach's girlfriend. Of course, the "killed" part wasn't so great, but we would just have to make sure that didn't happen.

Letting Brody do all the Trent stalking should have freed me up to study in the library, but all I seemed to be capable of doing was staring blankly at my French book, lost in thoughts of the

Banished, Trent, and Brody. *My life keeps getting more and more confusing.*

Had Athena been involved in this stuff? It was pretty obvious that she'd been a daughter of Hekate and that she'd wanted to come to Devenish to find out more about Shadow Hills and Rebekah Sampson. But what did her bracelet have to do with anything? It didn't look like the one pictured in the file—it certainly wasn't copper. And I couldn't imagine that Athena would have met a scary energy-sucking guy like Damon Gates and not put something about him in her journal.

She probably never knew that BVs existed.

Still, it was strange that the guy Mrs. Carr was having an affair with had had Athena's bracelet in his possession at some point. With Mr. Carr, it made sense: I'd asked him to look for it, and if my interpretation of his note in the file was correct, he'd been concerned that the bracelet meant the Banished had an interest in me.

But why would the Mystery Man have had it? None of the BVs were poor. If he'd wanted to give Mrs. Carr a Tiffany's ID bracelet, he could've ordered it on the Internet. Then again, if you already had one, why pay for another? An infinity symbol could be a romantic thing, and it wasn't like the guy had any sort of scruples.

I let out an unconscious grunt of frustration, eliciting glares from two girls who apparently *were* having some luck with the whole reading-their-textbooks thing. At least, they were until I started making my animal-kingdom noises.

I stood up and shoved my books into my bag before heading over to the cafeteria. I was too antsy to be sitting in the library. Adriana was already at our table with her typical lunch of raw veggies and low-fat yogurt, which today sounded about as appealing to me as anything. My stomach was in knots, wondering what was going on with Brody and Trent. Sitting on the sidelines was harder than I'd imagined.

"Hey." I plopped my bag down, and the lunch table shuddered under the weight of it.

Adriana frowned at me. "Don't tell me that bag is filled with textbooks."

"I needed something to do. To take my mind off things for a while. I'm all grieved out right now."

"Tell me about it. I had my police meeting earlier, and I spent the last hour on the phone with my mom trying to convince her that I'm not in imminent danger of catching some kind of airborne aneurysm virus." Adriana crunched loudly on a slightly anemic carrot stick. "I mean, don't get me wrong, I'm upset about Mr. Carr, but it's not like we were best friends—I didn't even have a class with him. And now I'm supposed to be walking around crying like my grandparents just died. I can't imagine what it costs the administration to have that psychologist on call for a whole week."

I thought of what my parents had paid my shrink, and that had been for an hour.

"A ton of money," I said. "But their lawyers are probably telling them they need to do it so the parents don't get sue happy." I stole a piece of broccoli and took a bite. "It makes sense that they would want to have all their bases covered."

"Are you girls talking baseball again?" Brody sat next to Adriana, about as close as he could get without actually sitting in her lap.

"God, Brody. Ever heard of personal space?" Adriana scooted to the far edge of the bench seat.

"Shhh. We can't talk like that in front of Phe, sweetcakes." Brody winked.

"You are so gross." Adriana stood up. "I'm going to get something to drink. I need to wash the taste of bile from my mouth."

I cocked an eyebrow at Brody as Adriana headed off to join the rapidly expanding lunch line.

"Sweetcakes?"

"I had to get her out of here so I could tell you what happened," Brody explained. "Trent did some very strange stuff when I was following him."

"Like what?" My heart was already going a mile a minute.

"He set off the sirens on all the police cars parked in the teachers' lot, and when everyone went rushing out to see what had happened, he snuck into the ISS room."

"Really?" I leaned in closer. "What did he do?"

"Well, that's what I'm not sure of." Brody cracked his knuckles. "I couldn't exactly follow him. It was totally deserted in there, and he definitely would have noticed me. But I did tail him after he came back out, and he went straight to his locker and stashed his backpack. It was all very furtive."

"We've got to see what's in that backpack." I chewed on my

lips. "But how are we going to break into Trent's locker without him noticing?"

"Why are you breaking into Trent's locker?" Adriana set a can of Diet Coke on the table.

"He stole the answers to our comparative government test," Brody jumped in, answering for me. "If I don't get my hands on them, I am going to majorly flunk that class."

"I can probably help you with that." Adriana gave a little shrug.

"But you're not even in that class." *Not that I was either, but hopefully Adriana didn't pay enough attention to my classes to notice that.*

"No." She rolled her eyes. "But I can distract Trent so Brody can break into his locker."

"You'd really do that?" I asked. Adriana did have a rebellious streak, but she also seemed to have a bit of a crush on Trent. Or so I had thought, but maybe my radar was off these days, because she sure was eager to help Brody.

Or maybe she was just eager to flirt with Trent, I thought a little later as I stood guard in the courtyard, watching the two of them through the cafeteria window. Adriana had her head thrown back in what I could only guess was fake laughter since I had never heard a remotely funny comment pass Trent's lips. After she recovered from her fit of faux giggles, she laid a hand on his forearm and leaned in so close I half expected them to kiss.

"What could she possibly see in that tool?"

Brody's voice made me jump, and I spun around to find him standing right behind me.

"Maybe he doesn't sneak up on people." I glared.

"Yeah, well, some lookout you are, letting people sneak up on you."

"I'm supposed to be keeping an eye on Trent," I pointed out, but the sight of a bright red official police folder in his hands made me abandon my argument.

"I haven't opened it yet," Brody said, noticing my expression. "Mrs. Carr is making funeral arrangements right now, so we can go back to the house and look at it if you want."

"Yes." I started off without a second thought.

"Wait. Don't we need to get Adriana away from him?" Brody asked. "If we're right, Trent could be a killer."

Instantly, I felt guilty. I was in such a hurry to save my boyfriend that I was totally ready to overlook my friend's safety.

"We can offer to walk her to her next class on our way to the library," I said.

"Okay, but isn't that kind of a public place to be investigating sealed police files?" Brody said, then stuck the file into his backpack and zipped it closed.

"That's why we're going to take it to your house. We're just telling Adriana we're going to the library."

I went back into the cafeteria and headed over to the flirtatious couple. Brody followed me, a scowl on his face.

"Oh, hey! It's Brody and Phe!" Adriana said in mock surprise. "What are you doing here?"

"As far as I know the cafeteria is free reign at lunchtime." Brody crossed his arms over his chest. "Do you have a problem with that?" He glared at Trent.

"I don't think *I'm* the one with the problem." Trent tossed his long hair out of his eyes.

"Adriana, don't you have chemistry now?" I broke in. "'Cause Brody and I are walking that way, and I thought you might like to come with us." I gave her my best hint-hint, nudge-nudge look.

"I guess so." She shrugged.

"Good. Well, I want to get to the library before next period starts, so we better go." I avoided making eye contact with Trent. If he was already suspicious of me, this performance certainly wasn't helping matters.

"That must be my cue to exit." Trent's stare was burning through my skin. I could only hope he wasn't an advanced mind reader like the police. "I'll call you about Saturday," he told Adriana.

I took that as *my cue* to start walking quickly in the opposite direction. I couldn't get out from under his watchful gaze fast enough. Brody and Adriana trailed after me.

"What about Saturday?" Brody asked as soon as we were out of earshot. "You're not going out with that slime, are you?"

"Hey, you're the one who wanted me to flirt with him," Adriana shot back.

"No, I distinctly remember saying 'distract'—flirting was never mentioned."

"What are you, my dad?" She rolled her eyes.

"No. If I was, you might have learned some self-control."

I could already tell this was not the way for Brody to get what he wanted.

"Excuse me?" Adriana stopped in her tracks. "You're one

to talk about self-control, Mr. I'd-rather-get-stoned-than-be-a-productive-member-of-society."

"Oh, I'm sorry. I momentarily forgot that you're the Queen of Productivity. The Empress of Charitable Deeds." Brody smirked. "Bravo on all that shopping. Thank God you're around to keep those boutique owners fed and off the streets."

"I think I can get to class just fine on my own." Adriana's honey-brown eyes flashed gold in the midday sun as she turned and stormed off ahead of us.

"Great." I shook my head. "I'm so glad we made sure Adriana was okay."

"Oh, whatever. She's fine. That girl has Teflon-coated Kevlar feelings." Brody kicked a rock out of his path as we continued on to his house.

I had a feeling Adriana wasn't as impenetrable as Brody thought, but I decided to leave it alone. Relationship drama could wait. Right now we needed to find out what was so important that Trent would risk stealing it from the police.

Once Brody had checked the house and locked the doors, we sat down at his kitchen table to look at our findings.

"You want to do the honors?" Brody nodded at the red folder. I shook my head no. I had done a lot of not-so-legal things in the last two weeks, but this was the first time I really felt like I was involved in something that could land me in jail.

"Guess it's up to me then." Brody undid the brad closure at the top of the envelope and slid out four eight-by-ten glossy pictures.

"Oh, my God," I breathed.

Chapter Twenty-five

Each sharply detailed photo was shot at a different angle, but they all showed the same thing: the handprints seared into Mr. Carr's head. They were just as I remembered, except for one important detail my brain had left out—the thumb marks were right under his eyes. The only way Mr. Carr could have made those prints himself was if in the moment of pain he had crossed his arms in front of him, left hand to right cheek, right hand to left cheek. It was clear that someone else was facing Mr. Carr when they burned him.

"Looks like this lets the steam out of Zach's theory about self-inflicted wounds," Brody finally said. He exhaled slowly. "I know I was the one who suspected Mr. Carr had been killed—but I don't think I truly believed it until now."

I nodded. The conclusion was pretty inescapable. The marks looked even worse than they had in person. The bright wash of light from the flash had lit up every charred black smudge in the red viscous residue left by the hands that had murdered Mr. Carr.

"Does that look like the back of a ring to you?" I pointed out a spot on one of the hand imprints. At the bottom of the middle finger, there was a slightly deeper, very raw-looking wound.

"You mean that thing that's sort of like a crescent moon with the pointy ends cut off?"

"Yeah." It was on the right hand, the correct finger, but maybe I was just seeing what I wanted to see.

"It is a darker red." Brody's face contorted. "Like it got more burned or . . . something. And are those little charred lines in the middle?"

"They're sort of like hatch marks," I agreed. "Maybe it's some kind of pattern or engraving on the metal?"

"Did you notice anything on Trent's ring?" Brody was still staring at the pictures, his expression pained. It occurred to me this was the first time he had actually seen what Zach and I had told him about.

I stuck the pictures back in the envelope and closed it. I couldn't stand to look at them a moment longer, and I had no doubt that Brody felt the same. "The portion of the band that I could see was plain and smooth." I sat back, thinking. Was I absolutely positive it was the same ring? And how common might a ring like that be?

"Would it be unusual for a guy here to wear a large gold ring with a rectangular malachite stone in it?" I asked.

"I certainly wouldn't wear one." Brody snorted. "But BVs are pretty fond of malachite, since it's a copper carbonate. Copper's a great energy transmitter."

Like the Banished bracelet pictured in the file. If my bracelet had something to do with the Banished, surely it would be made of the same metal. As much as I hated to agree with Corinne, her assertion that the infinity symbol was just a coincidence seemed likely.

"But are you sure what you saw was gold?" Brody asked. "Because it heats up really quickly, and we can burn things if we're not careful."

"Maybe that's why he wears it." I thought of the bright red splotch he left on my hand after shaking it.

"If it's definitely gold, I would say that ring would be fairly uncommon."

"Well, at least we know one thing—if the police have these pictures, they realize it wasn't just an aneurysm that killed Mr. Carr," I said. "They may be keeping it quiet, but they've got to be investigating it as a murder."

"I guess." Brody tapped his fingers against the table. "The most important thing in Shadow Hills is always keeping everything a secret."

"But still . . . there's a killer running loose around here . . . a BV killer, at that. I mean, if they banish people for doing this energy-sucking thing, they wouldn't ignore murder."

"No. That's true." Brody didn't look as if that thought made him feel much better.

But it made me hopeful. I'd rather the police investigate a murder than Brody and me. Still, there were things they didn't know.

"They don't have any idea that Trent stole these pictures. And we can't exactly tell them," I pointed out.

Plus, the cops definitely wouldn't put much stock in my grave-yard vision.

"Or that Mrs. Carr is having an affair," Brody added, frowning. "I guess I could tell them I suspect her of it, but I don't have any proof. Are you absolutely positive it was Trent with Mrs. Carr? Because I can make that little pig squeal all by myself. In fact, I'd rather not hand him over to the police until I've had a chance to do my own interrogation."

This sounded like it would be as bad for Brody as it would be for Trent. I wished Zach was here; it wouldn't hurt for him to keep Brody in check. But right now that job was falling to me.

"I didn't get a good look at him. I don't *know* that it was Trent." I tried for a really unsure tone. "Maybe we ought to wait and talk to Zach."

"When's he getting out of the hospital?"

"I don't know. He seemed okay when I saw him this morning. He'll probably be out soon; why don't we tell him later and see what he thinks?" Brody didn't seem convinced, so I went on, "You know that the authorities will listen to what Zach says with a more open mind than they would either you or me."

"You're right," Brody agreed reluctantly. "Okay, I'll wait. But if nobody's done anything about it in a day or two, I'm taking matters into my own hands."

I'd have to talk to Zach soon, before Brody landed *himself* in jail.

"I'll snoop around the house a little, see if I can find anything about who Mrs. Carr is seeing." Brody looked down at the police envelope. "Speaking of Mrs. Carr, maybe I better not keep this here, where she might find it."

"Sure. I'll take it with me and show Zach." I stuck the envelope into my backpack and slung it over my shoulder. I wanted to get to the hospital before visiting hours were over.

Before I got halfway to the hospital, my cell rang. It was Zach.

"Hey." A smile spread across my face. "I was just coming to see you."

"I'd like that," he replied. "Only I'm not at the hospital anymore. They let me out about a half hour ago, and my dad brought me home."

"Oh." I stopped and turned around, disappointed. "Well, that's good—that you got out, I mean. But I'm sorry I didn't get to see you. Brody found out some stuff, and I thought you should know it, too." Not to mention the fact that I wanted to see Zach with my own eyes to make sure he was really okay.

"My parents have gone seriously overprotective. They're putting me on lockdown until the doctors figure out what happened. And who knows when that will be. Never, probably." Zach sounded uncharacteristically irritated. "Would it be cool if I came by tomorrow after school?"

"Are you feeling good enough to go to class?"

"Yeah, I'm fine. Even the headache's gone now. Mostly I'm just bored—and I miss you."

"I miss you, too." I managed to keep from adding how crazy I was about him and how far away tomorrow seemed.

"It's almost time for dinner." Zach sighed. "I've gotta go now, but I'll talk to you soon, okay?"

"Okay." I hung up the phone reluctantly.

By midnight I'd washed up and changed into a tank top and my ladybug boxer pj's, and the dorm was deathly silent. I was climbing under my covers when a soft tap at my window practically gave me a heart attack. I grabbed the pointed metal nail file on my bedside table as I got out of bed, then dropped to my hands and knees and crawled over to the window. Keeping my head as low as I could, I peered out into the darkness.

Zach was outside, wearing a black hoodie, looking nervous and totally cute. My whole body filled with light. He was here. I didn't know how or why, but he was here.

I unlocked the window and shoved it open in one quick movement. "What are you doing?"

"I snuck out." Zach grinned a huge grin. "I've never snuck out before. And I stole Corinne's car—just put it in neutral and rolled it out of the driveway." He looked adorably pleased at his criminal behavior.

"Why? I mean, don't get me wrong, I'm happy you're here." Ecstatic was more like it. "But what's going on?"

"I couldn't sleep. I couldn't stop thinking about you, wondering what you were doing. What incredibly dangerous stuff you were getting into." He laughed quietly. "Oh, and by the way, opening your window in the middle of the night to some strange guy, not the safest idea," he teased.

"I can take care of myself. See, I had a weapon." I held up the nail file before dropping it back on the bedside table.

"You're crazy, you know that?" Zach's laughter faded away. "You make me crazy." He leaned in the window, and I twined my arms around his neck. He kissed me intensely, as if we hadn't seen each other in weeks. I was overcome by the urge to hold on to him as tightly as possible. But with the windowsill cutting into me painfully, I released him.

Quickly, he slung his leg through the window and slipped inside, closing the window softly behind him.

"You're becoming a regular rebel without a cause," I joked, attempting to ease the sweltering tension between us.

"No. There's definitely a cause for it." Zach's eyes were darker than usual, a storm of desire and craving. He wrapped a warm hand around the back of my neck, making my body pulse with energy. Then he bent his head, and I reached up to meet him.

Zach pressed his lips tenderly to mine. I let my mouth part, and his teeth lightly grazed my bottom lip, kindling a fever inside me. Our kisses deepened, becoming more forceful. We stumbled back onto my bed. Without even thinking about it, I threw a leg over Zach and pressed my body against his as we kissed. I needed to be as close to him as possible. I didn't want us ever to be apart.

I ran my lips lightly over his neck, feeling the warm beat of his veins, and Zach's arms tightened around me. Holding me to him, Zach shifted us so that I was lying on the bed and he was hovering above me. I wrapped my arms around his neck and pulled him even closer. I could tell he was trying not to crush me, but I wanted to feel his weight covering me, protecting me. Like nothing else could ever touch me. Zach gave in a little, allowing his chest to rest against mine as I trailed kisses down his neck.

He drew in a sharp breath, and my whole body responded. He caught my earlobe gently with his teeth.

"Zach." His name came out a sigh. Immediately, he pushed himself up and away from me.

"What?" His expression was troubled. "Did I do something wrong?"

"No. I was just . . . caught up. I didn't know I was going to say anything until it was already out of my mouth." I sat up, too, suddenly feeling embarrassed.

"I don't want you to think I was trying to pressure you in any way. I mean, I don't expect to . . ." He shook his head. "I want us to take our time." Zach brushed my hair back from my face. "This is all I need right now, to be here with you."

"Me, too." I snuggled into him, laying my head on his shoulder. He wrapped his arm around me. Idly, he played with my hair, curling a strand around his finger, then letting it unspool. "When do you have to leave?" I didn't want him to, but I knew he would have to eventually.

"I wasn't sure. I guess that's up to you." Zach's voice was uncertain.

"Stay." It wasn't responsible—Mrs. Moore was right down the hall, Zach's parents could wake up at any moment and find him gone—but I wanted him next to me. *But what if Zach gets in trouble with his parents?* I had already landed him in the hospital this week.

"That was my choice, not yours," Zach responded to my unspoken doubts. "And if I get in trouble, *I'm* the one getting in trouble. I've been obedient my whole life." He rolled over so we were lying side by side, facing each other. "But I can't stay away from you, rules or no rules. I can't shut you out."

"You're the most important thing in my life." I wanted to say more, I wanted to tell him I was beyond in love with him. But my throat tensed up, and I wasn't sure I could get a word out. I was terrified by how much I needed him.

"Same here," he murmured into my ear.

Goose bumps covered my body at the soft touch of his breath against my neck. I kissed him hard, with all the emotions I couldn't express in words.

Abruptly he pulled back. "Did you hear that?" Zach's lips were red, and his hair was disheveled; I knew without checking that I was in the same state of disarray.

"No," I answered, "but then again, I don't have your BV hearing."

"Does Ms. Moore make rounds this late?"

"Not usually. It was probably just the plumbing or something. This building makes weird sounds at night." I got up, and Zach propped himself up on one elbow, watching me walk to my door. "That's probably why Ms. Moore never notices us sneaking out."

I opened my door a tiny sliver. A girl came out of the bathroom, then was gone from my slim window of vision. I listened to the padding of her slippers and didn't close my door until I heard hers shut. I locked the door—better to get in trouble for that than to get caught with a boy in my room—and turned back to Zach. He was standing next to my computer, studying something.

"It was nothing, just a girl from our floor," I explained, but Zach didn't seem to care about that anymore. He was holding the red file from my desk.

"Confidential—Property of Shadow Hills Police Department?" Zach read. "What are you doing with this?"

"Brody and I got it. It's pictures of Mr. Carr's body." I went back to the bed and sat down. I had a feeling this might turn into a very long conversation.

Zach sat beside me and pulled the photos out. I didn't need to say anything; he understood immediately. "Somebody did murder Mr. Carr."

"I don't see any other way it could have happened."

"And a BV did it. But who?"

"Well . . ." I shifted a little.

"Phe . . . what is it? You're making me nervous here."

"Okay. The thing is—I had another vision last night. Well, I didn't just have it. I asked for it."

He stared at me. "What? What do you mean?"

"I was so worried when you got hurt." I took a deep breath. "So I tried to induce a vision."

"Seriously?"

I nodded. "I couldn't think what else to do."

Zach raised an eyebrow—he was waiting for the other shoe to drop. Like it always did with me.

"I decided the best place to do it was on Rebekah's grave."

This brought Zach to his feet.

"Why would you decide that? What, there were no creepy dark alleys available?"

"Shh." I waved my hand, motioning for him to keep it down. "Don't wake up Ms. Moore."

"Phe . . . you've got to stop this." He sat back on the bed. "You're going to get hurt."

"By ghosts?" I asked skeptically. "I'll admit it was spooky, but, I mean, really—who is going to be out in a graveyard in the middle of the night?"

"Apparently you."

I ignored this and continued my story. "The point is, I had a vision of an intensely hot pair of hands on somebody's head. The killer had on a distinctive ring—and it cracked from the heat. Then this morning, I ran into Trent, and he was wearing a ring just like the one in my vision."

"And Trent's ring is cracked?"

"No," I admitted. "But maybe my vision was a warning—Mr. Carr might not be his only victim."

"Wait." Zach put up a silencing hand. "Why would Trent kill Mr. Carr? He barely knew him."

"Maybe not, but I think Trent knew Mrs. Carr. Very well."

"Okay, let's say you're right. Trent *is* a bottom feeder—I can even see him having an affair with Mr. Carr's wife. But killing him? He doesn't care enough about anything to kill someone."

"There's more. Trent's the one who took the police photographs." I repeated the story Brody had told me. "Why would he do that unless he's trying to hide something?"

"I don't know. *You've* got them," Zach pointed out. "How'd you get them anyway?"

"Brody snatched them from Trent's locker."

"I hate to think what you and Brody would've done if I'd been in the hospital for longer than a day. Seriously, Phe." Zach let out a loud exhale of frustration.

"Hey, *we* weren't the ones who stole the pictures," I pointed out.

"Yes, you did; you just stole them from a thief."

I rolled my eyes.

"And what about the thing with the Banished? The guy at the hospital that you overheard talking to Mr. Carr? That couldn't have been Trent," Zach challenged. "And there was the phone call that night at the dance. Mr. Carr wouldn't have called to tell you about Trent's affair with his wife."

"I know. I wish my visions were clearer."

"That's another thing. You admitted you didn't know if your vision was of the past or future. The person who killed Mr. Carr might not have been wearing a ring."

I pointed to the photographs. To the spot on the handprints where you could make out the shape of the back of a ring.

"Are those roman numerals?" Zach leaned in closer to look at the hatch marks Brody had noticed earlier.

"Maybe—does Trent's ring have roman numerals on the band?"

"Yeah. A four, for Trent Redford IV."

"But there are only three marks here and no IV," I held one of the photos right under the lamp, squinting to see every detail.

"Trent isn't the only guy with a ring like that." Zach sat back, shaking his head slowly. "His dad has an identical one. Except he's Trent III."

I stared at Zach, feeling cold all through. "Your Uncle Tripp?"

"Yeah." Zach stood up and started pacing back and forth across my small room. "My great grandfather had the original ring—with one roman numeral. And my granddad had a replica—with two roman numerals."

I got to my feet, too. "What does Tripp do? Didn't you say he worked at the hospital?"

"He's the assistant director of gene research. He tests us, every single Brevis Vita, once a month to chart how the disease progresses."

"That's what you and Corinne were doing at the hospital the first day I met you?" Everything was coming together now, crashing into me, wave after wave.

"Yeah." Zach's jaw tightened. "He's quite possibly the most dangerous person to us. He could tell the Banished stuff that the Council hasn't even learned yet."

For a moment we just stared at each other. Finally, I asked, "And if he was the person I heard talking to Mr. Carr?"

"He's powerful, and when it comes to his self-interests, well, he's proved to be pretty ruthless in the past. I'd say he'd be more likely to fry somebody's brain than Trent would. Trent's slick—really skillful but not so much with the power." Zach stopped pacing. "You know, Tripp might have been the one with Mrs. Carr. Dad's always thought Tripp cheats on his wife. It's one of the main reasons my dad dislikes him so much."

"Why would your dad care?"

"Lillian, Tripp's wife, was my dad's high-school girlfriend. Then my dad left for college, got together with my mom, and Tripp got Lillian. But my dad's still protective of her. Mom hates it."

"Can't say I blame her." I wouldn't want Zach watching over one of his exes.

"Yeah, but that's not really the point right now." Zach started pacing again. "Do you think Tripp could have been the guy with Mrs. Carr?"

"Possibly." I tried to picture him in my mind's eye. "He had on a leather jacket that made it hard to tell what size he was, and I never saw his face. But his hair was similar."

"Tripp does have a leather jacket. Of course, so do tons of other guys." Zach let out a sigh. "We can't just accuse him of murder. We don't have any proof."

"How can we get proof?"

"I parked in the hospital lot instead of on campus. I'm not sure if it'll still be there, but I saw Tripp's car." Zach paused. He looked like he was formulating a plan. "We can search his car for anything that connects him to the Banished. Maybe we can even find the ring."

"So, what are we waiting for?"

Zach eyed my boxer pajamas with the little ladybugs printed all over them.

"Oh, yeah. I guess I might want to change." I'd been so caught up in everything tonight that I had completely forgotten what I was wearing. "Um . . . can you . . . ?" Just the thought of undressing with Zach in the room made my pulse race.

"Yeah, sure. I'll be outside." Zach crawled out the window.

I threw on some jeans, pulled a T-shirt over my thin tank, and grabbed a hoodie, then climbed out after him.

"I just talked to Brody." Zach closed his cell phone as I dropped down next to him. "Apparently, the police picked up Mrs. Carr earlier tonight. They wouldn't let Brody stay in the house by himself, so he's been sitting in the waiting room at the station for over three hours. He was only able to call me because the officer keeping an eye on him finally went to the bathroom."

"Did they say why they were taking her in? Is Tripp there, too?"

"Brody said they won't tell him anything, but he saw one of the most powerful elders from the Council go into the interrogation room. And that's not a good sign. At least not for Mrs. Carr."

"Yeah, I kinda figured that." I chewed on my bottom lip. "Should we still go look for Tripp's car?"

"Well, if they've taken him in, this would be a good chance to search it without worrying about getting caught. And if they didn't arrest him, then they're not on the right track and we still need to find something to prove our theory."

"Okay then." I started walking. "Let's go."

I felt strangely exhilarated as we got closer to the hospital. This could all end tonight. The fear, the uncertainty—I might soon have answers that would put them both to rest.

"It's still here." Zach pointed to the black Maserati I'd seen Trent roar off in that day at the SAC.

"Does Trent drive it, too?"

"Yeah. Trent worships Tripp, and ass kissing will get you everywhere with my uncle." Zach slowed his pace and glanced around cautiously as we emerged from the side of the hospital building. "Trent always borrows the Maserati when he's after a girl; he thinks it makes him an irresistible bad ass."

I let out a little snort of laughter. "I can tell you it certainly didn't work in my case. I mostly thought he was a tool."

"And that's why I like you." Zach gave me a sexy smile.

"How are you going to do this without anyone hearing the alarm or seeing us?" I looked back over my shoulder at the front door to the hospital. We were totally exposed now, standing in the brightly lit parking lot next to the sleek car.

Zach looked up at the offending streetlamp hovering above us.

"It's just like Tripp to park his car under a spotlight," Zach muttered. He walked around the car and laid his hand against the steel base of the light. He furrowed his brow in concentration, and a moment later the bulb flashed and went out with a loud pop. I jumped, startled by the sound.

"Sorry, I can usually do that quieter." Zach came back to the driver's side, where I was standing. "I feel like my abilities have been sort of out of whack today. Hopefully I'll still be able to disarm the alarm." He gave me a grin to let me know he was joking, but I didn't feel all that reassured. I squeezed my eyes closed as he reached for the door handle.

"Phe, it's fine." Zach laughed. "I've got it taken care of—no alarm."

Hesitantly, I opened one eye and then the other.

"We better hurry, though." He sat down in the bucket seat and reached over to open the middle console.

I walked around the front of the car and slid into the passenger's side. The strong scent of the Maserati's interior washed over me, and my stomach lurched with recognition. That syrupy, vanilla scent with the musty undertones . . . it smelled like the person who had tried to trap me in the hall outside the darkrooms.

"What is that smell? Is it Tripp's cologne?" I asked.

"Uh, no. It's his tobacco. Black Cavendish, I think." Zach sniffed the air. "It is pretty saturated in here; he smokes his pipe in the car."

"That's what I smelled on the guy who chased me, the one who knocked over the soda machine."

Zach looked at me, gripping the side of the console so hard his knuckles were white. "Tripp better pray he's in jail."

His words left an implied *or else*. I didn't want to find out what the other option was.

"We need to find some evidence fast," I said. "I'll get the glove box."

The small compartment was filled with papers, and I knew anything as heavy as a ring would have fallen to the bottom. Pulling out the insurance certificate and owner's manual, I shone the light from my cell phone into the compartment so I could see better. But there was no glint of metal, not even from a tire pressure gauge. As I put the papers back in, I noticed a bank slip. *Transferred funds?*

"Look at this." I handed it to Zach.

"Damn, he's transferring hundreds of thousands to a bank account in the Cayman Islands."

"He's about to run?" I guessed.

"Looks like it." Zach ground his teeth. "Keep searching; he can't leave without his car."

I felt around under the seat. "Nothing here. You got anything?"

"Not yet. He could have put it anywhere. It could be at home in a jewelry box, for all we know." Zach hit the steering wheel. "Shit."

"We could check his office. Or maybe he's still wearing it," I suggested.

"Not Tripp. He's a total perfectionist and as anal as the day is long. He wouldn't sport anything that was broken or banged up. And it's evidence. He probably hid it somewhere."

I thought back to the time when Ariel and I had been in her brother's car on the way to a huge party and he'd gotten pulled over by the LAPD. He'd had to stash a bag of pills.

"There's one place we haven't looked." I pulled open the ashtray; it was full of change. I guess it was too small for dumping your pipe tobacco.

"Already looked through that. It's just coins."

"But I bet you didn't look here." I pressed down on the

release lever for the ashtray and slid it all the way out. Then I reached my hand into the space left behind. I felt my fingers make contact with cold metal. I knew before I even pulled it out that it was the ring.

Zach looked at the cracked green stone in a mix of horror and triumph. "Now we know for sure. Tripp killed Mr. Carr."

Chapter Twenty-six

"I'm going to find him." Zach reached for the door handle.

"No, wait!" I grabbed his arm. I'd never seen Zach look like this, and it scared me. "Shouldn't we call the cops? I mean, this is enough to convince them, right? There's probably DNA on this ring from Mr. Carr."

Zach stopped, frowning, and I could feel the tension in his arm ease a little. "You're right." He pulled out his cell phone and punched in a number. "I have to call my dad first. I need to tell him what's going on."

He put the phone up to his ear, and I could hear the faint sound of ringing.

"Dad?"

I could barely make out mumbling on the other end of the phone.

"Well, actually, I'm *not* home. I'm outside the hospital."

Slightly louder mumbling.

"I snuck out, okay? But that's not important. I just found out something huge . . ." Zach took a deep breath. "Tripp killed Mr. Carr."

Complete silence.

"Dad?"

Another low rumble escaped from the cell.

"I'm not jumping to conclusions. Brody called me from the police station; they took Mrs. Carr in earlier." Zach explained all the things we had found out. When he'd finished, he waited, listening to his father.

"Mom's over there?" Zach asked, then said, "Okay. You call her so she can tell the Council. I'll make sure Tripp doesn't leave."

That brought an agitated spike of noise from the other end. Zach clenched his jaw, his eyes bright and hard, and I felt sure he didn't like what his dad was saying—no doubt because Mr. Redford was telling Zach not to confront his uncle, an order I very much agreed with.

"But, Dad—" There was another rumble of noise, and Zach sighed. "Okay. You're right. I won't leave Phe alone."

"What did he say?" I asked as soon as the phone clicked closed.

"My mom was already called away to some emergency Council meeting. Which means they must have gotten Mrs. Carr to talk."

I had no interest in finding out what had gone on in that interrogation room tonight.

"My dad's going to call the Council's office and tell them they need to speed things up because Tripp is now a flight risk. Then he's going to have Chief Bradbury meet him here. He also told me to stay in the hospital lobby until then, and under no circumstances are we to go after Tripp ourselves." Zach didn't look terribly pleased about this request, but it certainly seemed like a good idea to me. "For now, though, we need to get away from this car."

I slid the ring into my pocket, replaced the ashtray, and we got out. Zach was resetting the alarm when I felt a strange tingling on the back of my neck.

"Well, kids . . . admiring my Maserati?" We turned. Tripp Redford's tone was relaxed, but his expression was alert. "You're out a little late, aren't you, Zach? Didn't you just get out of the hospital?"

"You should know the answer to that—you're the one who put me there," Zach retorted, his eyes flashing.

My stomach turned to ice. Tripp wasn't just Zach's uncle anymore, we now knew that he was also a killer.

"Don't be ridiculous; I didn't touch you. Clearly, you hit your head harder than anyone realized," Tripp told him, his voice contemptuous. The charming demeanor he had displayed at Oakhaven was gone completely.

"You're bluffing," Zach told him flatly. "I didn't remember at first, but now it's coming back to me. I saw you on the way down to Mom's office."

I wondered if Zach really was recovering his memory or if he was the one bluffing now.

"You're lying." His uncle's eyes flashed, and he took a step forward. "And who do you think everyone will believe? Me or my poor confused nephew who just got out of the hospital?"

"I know who Dad will believe. He's on his way here with

Chief Bradbury," Zach went on. "I've already told him everything about you and the Banished. About your affair with Mrs. Carr. Your girlfriend's being interrogated, by the way, so you might want to explain killing Mr. Carr before she does it for you."

I knew that Zach was hoping Tripp would give himself away, so I watched Tripp's face intently, looking for any change in his expression. Something that meant Zach's words had hit home.

A look of shock passed over Tripp's visage at the mention of Mrs. Carr, and there was a flash of something else—like for a split second it had been Trent rather than Tripp standing there in front of us.

I stared at him, unable to believe my eyes. I glanced over at Zach. He was also gazing at Tripp in amazement. I opened my mouth to say something, but an overwhelmingly loud sound drowned out everything else. I turned and saw a helicopter descending onto the hospital's emergency landing pad. But this was no white EMT helicopter with a red cross on its side. No, this one was sleek and black, free of any distinctive marks.

"I know it's you, Trent!" Zach shouted over the roar of the helicopter.

"You're delusional!" the man yelled back.

I turned back to Tripp. My eyes were having trouble focusing. It was like I was watching a quick-cut CGI action sequence where you can't see what's really happening because it's jumping around too fast. Tripp wasn't moving, yet he was still . . . blurry.

I grabbed Zach's hand so even if he couldn't hear me, he would still be able to figure out what I was thinking. "It *is* Trent! He's doing that perception manipulation thing!"

"You're crazy! That's not possible!" Tripp/Trent yelled, but the more frantic he got, the harder it was to hold on to whatever kind of mind trick he was pulling. He looked like a morphing image paused in the middle of its transformation. "We're not wasting any more time on you." Zach started to step around him. Tripp/Trent pulled back his arm and punched Zach square on the jaw. Zach barely flinched and responded with a powerful blow to the diaphragm. Trent lost all control of his illusion as he doubled over in pain. He tried to regain his balance, but Zach slammed his fist into his cheek and Trent crumpled to the ground, out cold.

"Come on! If we wait any longer, Tripp'll be gone!" Zach pulled on my arm.

"What about what your dad said?" I shouted back.

"Screw that! We don't have time to wait around!" And with that, Zach took off at a neck-breaking pace. I held on to his hand tightly, struggling not to fall over my own feet as I tried to keep up with Zach's long strides.

"It'll be easier this way. No guard!" Zach let go of my hand to wrench the back door open. As he took off down the maze of hallways, I slowed a little so I could breathe while still staying close enough to keep sight of him. Finally, mercifully, he made a turn into an open office, and I was able to come to a stop, bent over and panting. When I finally straightened up, ignoring the stitch in my side, I saw Zach standing behind a desk covered in boxes of files.

"The cabinets have been totally emptied," he informed me, as if I couldn't tell that by the vacant drawers standing half open. "He's taking all the test results, the gene research . . ." Zach shook his head in disbelief. "God knows what he's already told them."

I walked around the desk to stand by Zach.

"It'll be okay. We'll catch him before he leaves." I hoped my voice sounded reassuring because I had no idea if what I was saying was even true.

"He could be gone already for all we know." Zach kicked a box on the floor, sending it slamming into the wall.

"He wouldn't have left his stuff here." I pointed at the briefcase on the desk in front of us.

"Very good observation, Ms. Archer."

We whirled around. Tripp, the real Tripp, was standing in the doorway.

"Hello, Zach." He sauntered in slowly, obviously not worried that we posed any sort of threat to his escape plans. Zach took an intimidating step toward him, but Tripp simply smiled. "Don't tell me you're going to try to stop me."

"What do you think? And it's not only me, Tripp. My father's on his way here right now. Along with the police."

"Oh, Christ!" The older man scowled. "I might have known you and Grant would do something like this. I had hopes for you, Zach. Your mother's a strong woman, and so's Corinne. But clearly you take after my spineless brother."

"It's not spineless to be loyal. Dad would never do anything like this. Dad would never deal with the Banished. Or sell us out for money or power or whatever the hell made you do it."

"I did it for my father!" Tripp thundered. The air crackled with electricity. "You think I did this for me? I did it to save your grandfather. You've seen him, the way he is—a mindless invalid. The man who once was the finest medical mind in this community. In this country. Now he's lucky if he can remember his name."

"How the hell does that justify your trading secrets to our enemies?"

"They taught me how to help him. They showed me how to give him back his energy, his power."

That was probably what Tripp was doing the day we saw him at Oakhaven. The day Zach told me how well his grandfather was doing. It was easier to hate Tripp when I thought he was purely evil. But in his own twisted way, he had been trying to help. To take care of his family.

"You've been sucking energy from people." Zach shook his head. "You've been stealing their life force and transferring it to Granddad." He looked like he was trying to wrap his mind around the idea.

"Give the boy a cigar," Tripp proclaimed sarcastically.

Zach's rage seemed to lessen a little. "Tripp . . . you don't have to run. Tell the Council why you were dealing with the Banished. They'll understand about your trying to help Granddad."

"You think they'll understand about murder?" Tripp retorted sarcastically. "They won't give me a slap on the wrist for Carr."

"Why did you kill him?" I burst out, unable to hold back any longer. "Because of Mrs. Carr?"

He glanced at me, startled. "How the hell did you—" He shook his head, dismissing the question. "Doesn't matter. No, I did not get rid of him because of Pamela. Pamela is . . . a side issue."

I bet she'd love to hear that.

"Then what *was* the issue?" I pressed. "What was worth murdering your friend? And what did it have to do with me? Why did you steal my bracelet?"

"I didn't steal your stupid bracelet—you dropped it in the gravel that day I met you in the parking lot. You were fidgeting annoyingly with some zipper on your purse. All that wonderful energy you possess was radiating off you. The more nervous you were, the stronger the energy got. Of course, you're still clueless." Tripp snorted.

"Why did Mr. Carr have my bracelet in his hand when I found his body?"

"I was carrying it when I was with Pam; it fell out of my pocket in their bedroom. But that bracelet means nothing. It's merely a piece of jewelry until it's ionized."

"That's it, isn't it?" Trapping me, taking my bracelet—it finally made sense. "You were going to ionize my bracelet and hand me over to the Banished. That's why you attacked me in the photo lab that night."

"You're not quite as clever as you think." He gave me a condescending smile. "Why in the world would I give you to them when I could use you myself?" Tripp turned back to his nephew. "Your little girlfriend could have been very useful. Your grandfather could have fed off her for weeks. Is a piece of ass really worth losing him?"

Zach punched Tripp hard in the face. A punch that would've easily knocked out his son. But Tripp recovered quickly, shaking his head at Zach like he was a foolish child.

"This isn't about you. Now, get out of my way." Tripp started toward the box on his desk.

Zach stepped in front of him. "Are you just going to skip out on Lillian and Trent?"

"Trent knows why I have to leave."

"Yeah, well, he didn't know about the part where you cheated on his mother."

"But I bet you were happy to inform him. You're exactly like your dad. So self-righteous." Tripp's mouth twisted. "I can't stay here. You think I'm going to allow the Council to stand in judgment of me? So they can try out their new 'reprogramming regimen'? That's just a fancy name for what boils down to a shock-treatment lobotomy."

The rumors Brody heard were true. An image of Trent's medical genius father drooling onto a straitjacket filled my mind. It was understandable why they had to do it—prisons weren't equipped to detain someone with mind-control powers—but I wouldn't wish a high-risk, traumatic medical procedure like shock treatment on anyone.

"If you believe I'm going to stand by and let them strip me of *my* abilities, you're even more delusional than Grant." Tripp stepped around Zach to grasp his briefcase.

"There's no way I'm letting you leave with that."

"I don't really see how you're going to stop me." Tripp picked it up, the gleam of challenge in his eyes.

Zach took another swing at Tripp, but the older man dropped the briefcase and caught Zach's fist all in the split second before it made contact. I could hear the popping of Zach's knuckles as Tripp squeezed his hand. Zach gritted his teeth, and I could tell he was trying not to cry out in pain. Then, almost so fast I didn't see it happen, Tripp kicked Zach's legs out from under him, and he fell to the side, landing with a crunch on his left knee. Tripp lunged toward his fallen nephew, but Zach shot up, slamming his shoulders into Tripp's mid-section and propelling him back into the row of file cabinets behind him.

They crashed into the cabinets, and I heard Tripp's head bang against the metal. Then, with a roar of rage, he flung Zach away from him. Zach landed hard on the desk and slid across it, sending files and books and a lamp skidding off onto the floor. Though Zach was larger than his uncle, it was clear that Tripp was far more powerful and using an energy that was greater than physical strength.

I felt helpless, useless. I hated doing nothing, but I was afraid if I did anything Zach might get hurt trying to protect me.

Tripp rushed at Zach again, slamming his foot into Zach's injured knee so that he crumpled to the floor in agony. Zach tried to stand up, but with a horrible guttural sound of pain, he fell back into the side of the desk. Tripp had a strange disconnected look in his eyes as he reached his hands out toward

Zach. Fear seized my heart. I had seen the burns on Mr. Carr. There was no way I was going to let that happen to Zach.

I grabbed the first heavy thing I could find, the briefcase that had fallen off the desk when Zach landed on it. Swinging with every ounce of strength in my body, I slammed the case into Tripp. He stumbled and looked over at me in surprise. When he caught sight of the briefcase in my hand, surprise changed quickly to anger. Lightning fast, he lunged at the briefcase, but I sidestepped and he missed it by an inch.

This is what he wants. This is what's important.

Something resembling a plan flew into my mind. If I could get Tripp out of this office, maybe I could stall him long enough for Zach's dad and the cops to get here. Tripp was definitely strong, but I was small and determined—and maybe even fast enough to keep him one step behind me. I darted out of the office and ran back the way Zach and I had come in, bursting through the outer doors and barreling on toward the school—and away from the black helicopter waiting for Tripp.

The campus lay before me, pristine and untouched by the terror I was experiencing tonight. The school had dorms filled with people who would hear me scream, which made it my best option. The quickest path was through the graveyard, so, already gasping for breath, I took off at a sprint, bearing down on the old cemetery.

There was no way I was going to be able to hold Tripp off for long, and I was terrified of what he would do when he finally caught up to me. I made myself push through, trying to ignore the burning in my thighs and lungs. I had to keep going. The farther I got, the farther away Tripp was from Zach.

I ran faster than I had ever moved before in my life, but I could still feel him gaining on me. So close now that I could feel his hot, ragged breath on my neck. Then suddenly his weight crashed into me. The ground rushed up to meet my face, my cheek smacking against the hard-packed dirt of a burial plot. Tripp flipped me over onto my back and the briefcase went flying into the gravestone next to us. As it made contact, the case popped open, spilling folders, papers, and vials of what was most certainly blood. But something else had fallen out, too—the metal glinted in the moonlight. A letter opener.

I scrambled across the grave to get it. The weight of the stone grip felt reassuringly heavy in my hand. As Tripp lunged at me again, I stabbed blindly. With a sickening sound, the opener went in, but then I felt the hard obstruction of bone vibrate through it. I yanked the blade out. It had made contact with his shoulder, but the cut didn't look deep enough to cause any real damage.

In fact, it didn't seem to faze him at all. Before I could stab him again, Tripp locked down on the metal end of the letter opener and pulled. I clung to it as tightly as possible, my fingers turning white with the effort. Letting out a grunt of frustration, Tripp grabbed my wrist, wrenching it painfully. I wanted to cry out, but I didn't want Tripp to know how close I was to being beaten. I gritted my teeth and held on to the handle even tighter than before; I was gripping it so hard that the dull edges were cutting into my skin. When I still didn't let go, Tripp pulled my hand straight back until it touched my forearm. I heard something snap before my brain registered the agony.

A howl of pain that didn't even sound human escaped from my body, and I let go of the letter opener and rolled onto my side in the fetal position.

Tears sprang into my eyes as white-hot pokers shot from my wrist into my hand and arm. *Get up, get up, get up!* I didn't have time to lie here nursing my wounds. I pushed myself to a sitting position with my good arm, then up to kneeling, cradling my other, battered wrist. It was red and swollen, but there were no bones poking up, straining against my skin. While I was struggling to stand, Tripp had gathered everything up and was locking the briefcase.

I stumbled forward as he took off back through the cemetery toward the waiting helicopter. My whole body was screaming for me to give up, admit defeat, but I kept on. Suddenly, Tripp stopped moving. I could see his knees straining to lift his legs, but they wouldn't budge. It was like he had walked into quicksand. Which was impossible.

Then I saw Zach. He was limping as fast as he could toward us, grimacing every time he stepped on his left leg. His expression was curled up, twisted in concentration. His stare was focused on Tripp's feet the same way it had been when he had moved the soda machine. But instead of flying backward, Tripp was locked in place. Zach was now only four or five feet away from us. I moved closer, my wrist piercing at every jostling movement.

"Phe, stay where you are!" Zach was dead serious, but it didn't matter. I needed to be next to him. I kept going.

"I guess you're more powerful than I thought, Zach." Tripp tried to bring his foot up again. It hovered a half inch from the ground then slammed back like a shoe stuck in taffy on an old cartoon. "I mean, moving an inanimate object is one thing, but restraining me—that takes talent."

Sirens were wailing in the distance. The fact that we could hear them over the helicopter noise assured me the police weren't far away.

"You have no idea what I can do." Zach's eyes flashed as he stepped closer to his uncle. In my peripheral vision, I saw Tripp pull his arm back. Apparently, his upper body was still mobile. Then I saw the glint of a blade. Tripp was going to stab Zach with the letter opener. Zach would be within arm's reach with one more step.

In that split second I made a decision. I had lost too much already. To have Zach taken from me was more than I would be able to live with.

I jumped between them, shielding Zach with my body.

I felt the cold metal plunge deep into my stomach. Tripp pulled the letter opener back out and blood spilled down the front of my tank top in a red waterfall. I turned to Zach, trying to hide the fear in my eyes.

"Phe! No." Zach was shaking, staring at me in shock. "No. You can't." He pushed his hand against the hole in my stomach, attempting to dam up the river of blood. It gushed out around his fingers.

"I'm sorry," I managed to choke out before falling to all fours. The crimson liquid poured out onto the dirt.

"Phe! Hold on. I'll get you to the hospital." Zach knelt next to me, wrapping his arm around my chest to pull me up. I coughed. That tangy metallic taste was familiar. There was blood in my mouth.

Tripp had regained control of his legs. He hit Zach in the face with his briefcase, just as I had done to him. Zach lost his grip, and I fell back to the ground.

"Phe!" Zach was flung backward as if he had been hit by a freight train. I saw Zach's face, filled with rage. But he was pinned to a tree, unable to move.

"You think you have power? This is power." The skin on Zach's neck was twisting like he was being choked, but his uncle was nowhere near him.

A puddle of my blood spread like an ink stain across one of the ancient cemetery plots. I felt dizzy and sick. The pain in my side took over my whole body. I couldn't concentrate. My vision was growing dark around the edges.

"Phe! Look at me! You can't die! You can't!" Zach's yells were muffled. Strangled.

Zach looked away from me, concentrating on his uncle. Zach was getting stronger; I could see it in his eyes. There was a fire raging there. Zach sent his uncle flying with his teleki- netic energy. Tripp tried to stand, but Zach barreled into him, hitting him square in the chest with his shoulder. They both fell to the ground, with Zach on top of Tripp now, pinning him down. As I watched, Tripp slammed both his fists hard into Zach's lower back. Zach let out a grunt of pain, and his hold loosened. Tripp seized the opportunity to shove Zach off him, and Zach rolled. His head cracked sharply against a tombstone, and he went limp, a rose halo bleeding out of his head onto the grave marker.

For an instant, Tripp froze, staring at Zach, stunned. Then he staggered to his feet and slowly began to stumble back toward the hospital. Tears rolled freely down my cheek as I crawled over to Zach, trailing my blood all the way. It couldn't end like this. If Zach died, I had given my life for nothing. I pulled him into my lap, cradling his head. He was still breathing. I looked around. Tripp was limping through the graveyard, clutching his briefcase like a prize. *How could the cops not be here yet?* It seemed like it had been hours, when in reality it probably hadn't been much more than a few minutes. As my tears fell onto Zach's face, mingling with the blood, I remembered the vision I had had at Rebekah Sampson's grave—the dagger slicing my hand, the blood on the graveyard dirt, myself transformed and shouting out an incantation. I had known then that it was a vision of me at another time.

I placed my injured hand on my hip. I could feel the mark burning with power, healing the pain in my wrist instantly. A wave of knowledge hit me with the force of a solid object—the time in my vision was now. I had to do this; I wasn't sure I would be alive much longer. Tripp was almost out of the graveyard.

I pushed myself up to my feet, using a strength that was beyond adrenaline. It didn't even feel as if it were coming from inside me. I was pulling the energy up from the earth, from the ground that my blood had just fed. I let my head fall back, and the words flew from my throat. The voice rising out of me didn't sound like my own. It was ancient and deep, timeless and dark.

"Phasmata repite ex sepulchris vestris, capite virum!"

Figures formed over their graves, whisper thin at first, like smoke. Melding together into grayish-white shadows of their former selves. And at the head of the group was the woman from my dreams, the one who had been leading me to this destiny. Her form was sharper, clearer than the rest. It shone with an unearthly blue light.

The other spirits looked to her, and with one motion from her hand, they descended upon Tripp. His face contorted with his screams, but I couldn't hear them over the howling wind swirling around the cemetery. The wind lifted the dirt from the ground, forming a circular barrier; we were in the eye of the tornado. The phantoms were holding Tripp, pinning him down. Their hands and arms stuck through his body and into the ground like metal tent pegs. I saw actual scratches appear on his face, small pools of blood rising from where the spirits had impaled him.

Rebekah glided over to me, her shimmering mirage just inches away. She placed a weightless hand over the split in my side. I could feel her force mending everything in me. Like invisible stitches, she pulled the gap closed. Soon all that was left was a nasty scratch and some dried blood.

"What about Zach?" Another tear escaped me, falling softly down onto his face.

He will be fine. Though she didn't speak, Rebekah's voice resounded through my head. Below me, still lying on the blood-soaked ground, Zach was slowly coming to, blinking groggily. Finally, the lights of the police cars were visible coming up the drive to the hospital.

"It's okay now," I told Rebekah. She held up her hands, and slowly the other figures backed away from the half-dead body of Trent's father.

"How are you controlling them?"

I'm not. You are. Rebekah smoothed back my blonde hair, so much like her own. Her touch was a feather-light breeze.

"Phe?" Zach was staring up at me in confusion. "I thought you were . . ." His eyes shone wetly.

"So did I." I turned back to Rebekah, hoping maybe Zach had seen her, too, but she was gone. They all were.

I glanced over at Tripp, shivering and shaking on the ground. There were blood splatters on his clothes, but the wounds had closed up. The scratches on his face and hands were healing. His eyes, however, were staring blankly into space. He obviously wasn't getting up anytime soon.

"Phe—what happened?" Zach looked to Tripp, then back to me again.

"I don't know . . ." I breathed. I dropped down beside him. "I remembered this stuff I said in Latin during my vision at the graveyard." I shook my head. "The words just came out of me, and these spirits started appearing . . . they listened to me; they stopped Tripp. And Rebekah—she laid her hand on my side and healed me. I don't know how, but she did."

"It doesn't matter." Zach groaned as he pulled himself up to sitting. "The only thing that matters is that you're okay." And he kissed me like he had thought he was never going to be able to do it again.

Chapter Twenty-seven

Movement at the hospital caught my attention, and Zach and I broke apart to see what was going on. The helicopter was leaving. Leaving Tripp behind. The police cars' red and blue lights washed over it with alternating flashes of color as it ascended into the sky.

As the cops parked in the lot, an ambulance pulled away from the hospital and drove over the curb and onto the grass, rolling to a stop right in front of us. One paramedic pulled out a stretcher and helped Zach and me onto it. The other grabbed his bag full of medical supplies and ran over to Tripp. By the time the police made it to where we were, the black helicopter was long gone.

The paramedic examined us and declared me "fit as a fiddle." And while I wouldn't have put it quite that way, my wrist barely hurt anymore, and there was absolutely no pain in my stomach. I wasn't even dizzy from the blood loss. But there also wasn't any way to explain my spontaneous regeneration, so I kept quiet about my earlier knife wound, pretending that the blood on my clothes must have come from Zach's head.

After he finished checking me over, the paramedic cleaned Zach's head wound, which turned out to be only a shallow slice half an inch long. "Nothing too serious," he assured Zach. "Scalp wounds always bleed profusely. You might want to come down to the hospital and get it stitched up, though."

From the look on Zach's face, I figured that wasn't too likely. After the paramedic wrapped up Zach's left knee and ankle with Ace bandages, he left to join the other paramedic working on Tripp, but not before warning us to stay where we were.

Noticing that we were now available, the police chief came over to question Zach and me. Chief Bradbury listened intently to our whole story, conveniently overlooking how we had come to find Tripp's ring and interrupting only twice to ask for clarification. When we were done, Bradbury placed Tripp's ring in a small bag to be taken to the Shadow Hills Police Department's forensics lab for DNA testing. After giving us strict instructions not to leave yet, he headed toward the deputy, who was reading a now-conscious Tripp his rights.

"Hey!" Grant Redford was running up to us. "Are you two okay?" He wrapped his arms around Zach in a tight hug.

"Yeah, Dad, we're fine," Zach assured him. "The paramedic gave us the green light."

"Thank God." Grant sighed and let Zach go, taking a step back. "Listen, I'm going to go talk with Chief Bradbury real quick. Don't move, okay?"

"We're already on top of it." Zach smiled.

I laid my head on his shoulder and looked out across the

campus below. In the nearby teachers' cottages, I could see that some lights were on. No doubt they had been disturbed by the sirens. But farther out, the dorms were still dark. Now that things were calming down, I felt drained, like I was recovering from the flu. I let out a little sigh as Zach smoothed my hair back and lightly kissed my temple.

I couldn't wait for this to be over so I could go back to Devenish and Kresky Hall. Back home.

A deputy was coming toward us, leading a handcuffed Tripp over to the parking lot full of police cars. Tripp stared at me, the hate in his eyes burning my skin like lye. My stomach recoiled inside my body, making me feel as if I might throw up.

"If you think you got the bad guy, you're wrong," Tripp hissed as he approached me. "You just made things worse for yourself. Not a good time to show your hand. Not at all."

"Come on. Move it." The deputy pushed Tripp forward and past us, but he couldn't keep Tripp from turning around to flash me a smile. A smile that froze me to the very core.

"Don't pay attention to him." Zach took hold of my chin and turned it so I was gazing into his soft blue-green eyes. "He's completely crazed right now. Nothing he's saying means anything."

I nodded silently and glanced over at Chief Bradbury, who was embroiled in an intense conversation with Zach's dad. I wanted to get out of there. I wanted it to be over. After a few minutes, Grant shook Bradbury's hand and came back to where we waited.

"Looks like you're done, at least for now," he informed us.

"They're going to put some extra security on you kids for a while, but besides that, things should be relatively normal."

It seemed almost anticlimactic.

"But what about Brody?" Apparently, Zach didn't feel this was sufficient either. "What are they going to do with him now?"

I laced my fingers through Zach's. His concern and fierce loyalty made him even more incredible. I'd always had that kind of support from Athena, and I had felt its absence when she was gone. But now there was at least one person who understood and accepted all the strange and varied facets of me, even if I never told another living soul about my newfound powers.

"That was one of the things the Council discussed tonight. They're going to put Brody with a family where he'll be safe." Mr. Redford placed a calming hand on his son's shoulder.

"Great, more guardians. That'll really help him with his trust issues."

"Actually, I think it will. He's with your mother and Corinne over at the Council office right now, finalizing his future living arrangements." Grant smiled. "He'll be moving in with us immediately."

"What? Really? He is?" Zach sputtered.

"I hope you don't mind." Grant laughed.

"Of course not." Zach grinned, but in the next moment his smile fell away. "Does that mean Mrs. Carr—"

"She's resigning from her teaching job at Devenish, but as for the legal stuff, I'm not sure if they're bringing charges against her. She owned up to the affair with Tripp." Grant rubbed the back of his neck the same way Zach did whenever he was embarrassed. "But she still claims that she knew nothing about her husband's murder."

"Maybe she didn't." Zach shook his head. "I still can't believe Tripp would do that. Murder his friend. Betray us."

Grant massaged his temples.

"Look, I'm not saying your uncle had the right to do what he did, because there are no excuses for his actions." He took a deep breath. "But, that being said, he did it for your grandfather. He always thought I gave up on Dad too easily. Now the Council is going to sentence Tripp to have a procedure . . ." Zach's dad stared down at his feet. "They'll both be like that, stuck in Oakhaven. Tripp will be locked up the rest of his life." Grant's expression was pained. It wasn't identical to my situation, but his sibling was being taken away from him, too, and I knew what that felt like.

I shifted uncomfortably. It was weird watching such an intimate exchange, but I didn't want to make things more awkward by getting up and leaving.

"Tripp told me that he was going to try an experimental treatment on Dad. I said I didn't want any part of it and just let it go at that." Grant shook his head. "I was the oldest. Tripp was my responsibility. I knew something was wrong when he sent Trent to warn me away, but I thought he was using an untested drug or classified research information. I should have made sure. If I had been there for him, maybe he wouldn't have been so easily swayed by the offer the Banished made him." For the first time I could see the resemblance between Corinne and Grant. The intense, sometimes misguided, family obligation.

"Dad, come on, you know that's not true. Tripp may be younger, but he's an adult. He's the only one responsible for his actions." Zach paused. "And you know Granddad would never have wanted to get better by hurting other people."

"Yeah." Grant nodded slowly, like he didn't quite believe it. "Listen, I thought maybe tomorrow you could take the morning off from school, and we could go visit your grandfather—while he's still doing better." Mr. Redford's voice was hollow, and I realized he had lost more than a sibling tonight. He had lost the last shred of hope for his father.

"Is he going to start . . . reversing?" I could feel Zach's energy pulling into him like a tide. There was coldness against my thigh where a minute ago his own had warmed it. I pressed my palm tighter into his.

"Hopefully not too quickly, but yeah, eventually he will go back to the way he was before." *And then he will get worse.* The unspoken words hung in the air in front of Grant, as palpable as if they had been written there. "Why don't you walk Phe back to her dorm, and then you can meet me at the car."

Zach wrapped his arm protectively around my shoulders, and we made our way back to the campus. We were both quiet as we walked. I was exhausted, but still somehow electrified. Not in the way I was when I touched Zach; this was coming from inside myself. I had controlled a primal force tonight. I had awakened the dead, jolting them with words like jumper cables. Words that I wasn't even sure of their meaning.

Whatever they meant, those words had changed everything. My life was never going to be the same after what had happened here tonight. As much as I wanted to try to go back to being normal—whatever that was—I knew it was impossible.

It wasn't even about the things that had gone on—Mr. Carr's death, the book from Sarah, the ritual. It was me—who I was fundamentally at my core. I had a power. A power I could feel strumming through my nerves and muscles and skin. A power as real as that possessed by any of the Brevis Vitas, though mine probably wasn't as scientifically explainable. Hell, I didn't know if it was explainable at all.

I felt more strongly than ever that I was supposed to be at Devenish. My sister had been called, and I had fulfilled her last wish by coming here. Now I belonged to Shadow Hills. I was needed here. I didn't know what for, but for the first time since Athena's death, I felt focused, like I had a purpose. There was a reason I was still alive.

I had a destiny: that I was sure of. Now I just needed to figure out what exactly my destiny was.

Though maybe I'd hold off until tomorrow. It was way past curfew, and I still had a beautiful boy to see to before I could go to sleep.

Acknowledgments

A HUGE thank-you goes out to Meredith Kaffel, my talented and consistently amazing agent, for loving *Shadow Hills* and for never tiring during the search to find a perfect home for it. This book would not be a reality without you and your impressive commitment to it. I owe you so much that I don't know how I will ever manage to repay you.

To the wonderful group I have had the pleasure of working with at Egmont—especially Super Editor Greg Ferguson, Regina Griffin, Elizabeth Law, Alison Weiss, Robert Guzman, Nico Medina, and my copyeditor Nora Reichard—your advice, editing, and general wisdom has been immeasurably helpful. This is the best publishing house in the world and I'm so glad you decided to publish *Shadow Hills*. Go Team Egmont!

I also want to thank Russ Galen—who, whether he intended to or not, became an invaluable mentor—for taking me out for coffee. You gave me the encouragement I needed when I was at my most discouraged. That three-hour talk is the reason this manuscript didn't end up in my recycling bin. I also want to thank you for the most critical critique I'd gotten thus far in my publishing journey. It was what helped me whip *Shadow Hills* into shape, and I truly believe I would not have landed a wonderful agent like Meredith Kaffel without your straightforward (and some might say, blunt) words. I will be forever grateful.

I'm only here because of my parents, Candace Camp and Pete Hopcus, who let me follow my own path. I know it must have been scary when I decided to go to L.A. instead of college, but I don't think I could have written this story if I hadn't had those experiences. There were many points in my life when other parents would have been disappointed, but you always believed in me, even when I wasn't so sure that you should. Thank you for all your support. And, Dad, I will always be overjoyed that you read and loved *Shadow Hills* despite the fact that you are about as far away as you can get from its target audience. Your faith in me means more than you will ever know.

To my love, Brent Barker, who inspired the romance that winds through this book: I never had any interest in writing a love story until you became a part of my life. I felt a connection the very first time I saw you walk by as I sat on the steps outside Griffin. That connection has lasted through the years and continues to grow stronger every day. You are my Nick Charles, and I hope to forever be your Nora.

And these acknowledgments wouldn't be complete without a thank-you to Jessica Wooldridge and Brittani Beitman-Nearing. You are the best friends a writer could have. Jessica has been unflaggingly excited to read every story I've handed her, and she was the first person (well, other than myself) to fall in love with

Zach and Phe. She read close to every version of *Shadow Hills*, and Brittani filled in to read the others. They were the first fans of this book and they supported me all through the stressful selling process. You two should get awards for gracefully putting up with my publishing-induced mood swings.

And, finally, I'd like to acknowledge the many great teachers I've had through the years, even the ones who were not technically teachers. Particularly Kat Candler, Terri Weiss, and Marco and Diane Perrella: you may not have taught me writing in the traditional sense, but in your own ways you taught me how to craft a story. I also want to say thank you to Adam Wilson for trying to awaken my (still dormant) love for math and for bringing me to The Griffin School, where I got to work with the spirited Elizabeth Miller, who taught all of her students to think for themselves, and the sweet Pam Arthur, who practically let me design my own reading curriculum. It was during this time that I discovered the still-inspiring books *Rats Saw God* by Rob Thomas and *Foxfire* by Joyce Carol Oates.

There are so many more people that I owe great thanks to, but if I included them all here, Egmont would be forced to publish another novel just for my acknowledgments. Please know that even though you might not be on this page, you are in my heart.

ANASTASIA HOPCUS
wrote her first book in the second grade. It was titled *Frederick the Friendly French Ferret* and was seven pages long. During high school she wrote numerous short stories and started (but never finished) three screenplays, all as an alternative to doing actual schoolwork. At the very wise age of twelve her career ambition was to drive a Mack truck, but when that didn't pan out, she tried acting, bartending, and being a receptionist in a dojo before finally returning to writing. Anastasia loves horror movies, Joss Whedon, obsessing over music, and British accents. She lives in Austin, Texas, and *Shadow Hills* is her debut novel. You can visit Anastasia online at www.anastasiahopcus.com.

12/15   12   8/15